The Doppelganger

A Tale from the Realm of the Blind

William Wilkin

Bell Street Publishing, LLC

Bell Street Publishing, LLC

Published by Bell Street Publishing, LLC,
7360 Middlebrook Cir
Nashville, TN 37221-6545

Copyright © 2020 by Bell Street Publishing, LLC

ISBN: 978-0-9600387-4-9

First Published in the United States, 2020

Cover Art:
Digital Painting: James W. Wilkin
Graphic Design: Matthew A. Stone

Contents

Acknowledgments

I owe an immense debt of gratitude to several people who have contributed substantially to this book's artistic integrity.

There are my two sons, James and Matthew Stone.

James contributed the digital painting on the cover which captures as I never could my vision of the sense of the book. He also made a number of graphic design suggestions that are incorporated in the cover design and interior of the book.

Matthew Stone made manTy suggestions for the layout and design of the interior as well as completing the cover layout.

My wife, Lou, contributed in both obvious and subtle ways to the completion of the book. She is a Spanish teacher and has extensive experience editing and correcting texts—both student and professional. Any remaining grammatical and spelling errors must not be accounted to her. They proceed from my eccentric ideas about the value of deviating from standards occasionally to accurately portray a state of mind or emotional content. A subtle way that she supported the completion of this book was her endless patience with those eccentric ideas.

In addition, she was willing to endure the many, many times that I worked into the early morning hours pursued by my characters who insisted on telling their stories at the most inconvenient hours.

She has always been emotionally constant in the shifting winds of our lives throughout the long thankless years of the struggle to bring these stories to print. Bravo Lou!

Prelude

For those of you who have not read any of the preceding books, I will warn you that this preface contains spoilers. If you want to learn about the story line to the point where this book begins, you could read the stories in sequence—*In the Realm of the Blind, The Chessmaster, The Spare Wizard, The Ministry Witch and other Tales of Perfidy, Wandering with Wizards, The Boy Genius,* and so on. However, reading the first book by itself would give you a good grounding in the Realm of the Blind.

This story takes place in the universe of the Realm of the Blind where Hogwarts School for Witchcraft and Wizardry exists. It is a residential finishing school for magical youth. It is located in northern Scotland.

The main character, James Wendt, is an English literature Professor and Muggle (non-magical). He has been hired by the Headmaster Albus Dumbledore to bring diversity to the school and the slightest touch of liberal arts education to an institution that is basically a vocational school.

Other staff at Hogwarts include Rubeus Haggrid (Professor of Magical Creatures), and Professor Flitwick (Professor of Charms), the Librarian, Ms. Pinz; and the Nurse, Madame Pomfrey.

It would be to carry coals to Newcastle to attempt a more detailed review of the story line up to this point. Instead, I will provide you with a quick glossary of the characters who are referred to in the book by more than one name. Thus forewarned, you will be forearmed against the use of multiple names or nicknames for each character:

- Nicholas Brahms aka The BG, The Boy Genius, Nicky is a computer security guru and all-round genius.
- Wainwright is the executive officer of the USS Ohio, a Trident nuclear submarine. He is frequently referred to as the XO.
- Phillip Minns aka The Lieutenant was a Lieutenant in the US Army stationed in Iraq fighting ISIS.
- Ginevra Weasley aka Ginny is an Auror who was the sometime lover of Professor Wendt.
- Cecily Brewster aka Sissy (only to family) is the step-daughter of Jaimie Brewster nee Sinistra. Jaimie's relationship to Professor Wendt is so complex that readers are referred to *The Revenge of the PAK* for more details.

You should also be warned that there are a number of aliens whose names (unpronounceable by humans) are replaced by the names of well-known fictional characters so that the humans in the story can identify their role and have a pronounceable name.

Boys Night Out

As Ginny disappeared, I realized that I was in the first stage of grief—denial. I had just held Ginny in my arms, kissed her, listened to her story, and seen her take the floo network away from me. It was forever. But I just couldn't believe it.

I couldn't keep myself from thinking about all my relationships, examining them for points of failure. It seemed like I'd never faced a break-up like this before. I considered my relationships one at a time and was shocked.

I poured a drink to help me face the awful truths of my life. The longer I thought, the easier it was to drink. I lost track of time. I ran through my stock of whiskey slowly. I guess I'd been working on it for a couple of days.

I'd mixed it with my stock of sodas to make it last longer. I suppose toward the end, I was just in pain and grief without making any attempt to rise out of it.

□

The next day nothing happened. I drank and slept, got up, and drank some more all day long. I could not think of anything that it made any sense to do.

The next day, I had run out of whiskey and sodas. It seemed just right. My life had run out of meaning. Why should this day be any different?

I must have passed out. I heard a sound and found that my head was lying on my desk. I struggled to rise. I half-way was up, but fell again. Then there was a hand under my arm, and I magically rose from the desk

3

and found myself sitting in my desk chair. A voice asked, "What in the world has happened to you?"

I tried to focus my eyes on the sound, but they were pretty blurry. I managed to ask, "Do you have anything to drink?"

The voice said, "You look awful. Have you been here ever since Jaimie revived you?"

I croaked (my throat was pretty sore, and I really was thirsty), "Sure."

"I'm getting you some water." The voice then said, "*Aguamente.*" Then, there was a glass of water at my mouth and the water was slowly trickling into my parched throat. I tried to force more down, but the hand that was holding the glass wouldn't let me.

□□

After a while, my throat wasn't so parched, and I could talk a little without croaking. The voice, which I could now focus on and turned out to be Jaimie's husband, Ed Brewster, asked, "What happened to you? I had ex-pected to hear from you before this."

I said, "Oh, just leave me alone."

Brewster persisted. "Not until you tell me what's happened to you."

He had kept letting me sip water. I now felt like I could give him an answer that would either get rid of him or get rid of me—one of the two. "You're right. I'm in a bad way. You can help. And both you and Cecily will be happy about it too."

He was anxious to give me assistance. He said, "Whatever! Just tell me what I can do."

I answered, "Good. I've got a gift for the two of you that you'll really appreciate. I'm going to give you Jaimie back for good. You must have a sample of her hair for the next time that she's to return."

He nodded silently. I went on. "Just get it, put it in the polyjuice po-tion, and I'll drink it. Right now. You can have her back forever."

"What are you talking about?"

I chuckled mirthlessly. "It's what you both want. You want her back forever. I'm ready to give her to you. Forever. No strings attached."

Brewster was silent for a while. I couldn't see what the problem was. They both were in love with Jaimie. They must hate me. It was their big chance. I said so. "You aren't going to get a golden opportunity like this more than once. Go get her. Go get Sissy. She'll want to see her mom just as soon as Jaimie's here."

4

Brewster sat in the red leather chair. He stared at me for a while and finally said, "No. I'm not doing it. Certainly not before you've told me what's going on."

"Do I have to get Slughorn or Dursley myself? They have the potion, and I'll bet that damn Dursley has some of her hair as well. If you're not anxious to have Jaimie back, I'll bet Dursley will be."

Brewster still just stared at me. Then he rose slowly and said, "You're right. They will want to see you. I'm going to get them right now."

"Damn right you will." He backed out of the office and closed the door behind him.

I continued to sip water as I waited for the dynamic duo to arrive. Eventually, they did. Brewster opened the door and was the last to enter. Slughorn walked hesitantly toward me, his eyes widening as he got closer. He asked, "Wendt? Is that really you?"

I swept an arm at the guest chairs. "I seem to be getting a lot of that lately. Take a seat." Slughorn took the red leather, and two yellows went to Dursley and Brewster.

Brewster started the conversation, "Professor Wendt wants for you two to brew some of the polyjuice potion, put some of Jaimie's hair in it, and send him to oblivion – permanently."

Slughorn shook his head slowly and asked, "Is that really true, Wendt?"

I nodded forlornly. Slughorn stared in apparent disbelief. He finally said, "Merlin's Beard! Wendt, why in the world would you want to do that!"

Dursley awakened from stunned silence. He said, "It's one of your tricks, isn't it, Professor? There's some reason that you want to do this crazy thing. You're trying to prevent something awful happening. I don't know what it is, but I know there's something important going on."

I took a swallow of water from my glass and gagged. I guess I thought I still had whiskey in it. "You're bloody right. There's something important happening. I'm sick of being here. His wife. . . " I almost couldn't finish the sentence, but I did, "deserves to live the rest of her life without my taking big chunks out of it."

Slughorn jumped in. "Well, my boy, that's not strictly true. Your body is restored to the state it was when your last hair sample was taken. So, at worst, you return to age when you last turned your body over to Jaimie. If we had a large enough supply your hair or finger nails from earlier, you

5

could actually be younger than when you turned things over to Jaimie. So, you see, you are actually at least four years younger than the number of years since your birth right now. That would make you about . . . oh. . . thirty. . ."

I'd been listening to Slughorn in growing resentment to his smug assurance that I would want to be even younger than I was. That is, have more years of life than I thought I had left. I broke into his lecture and said, "No, you old fool, I don't want to live longer. I want to be finished NOW!" That shut the mouth of that blowhard.

Dursley, who had been mostly silent so far, said, "Sure. Sure. We'll brew your potion, and return Jaimie. But that's a tricky potion. You don't want to get it wrong. Who knows what would happen if we got it wrong? You don't want to screw Jaimie, do you?"

I shook my head truculently, but didn't say anything.

Dursley went on. "Exactly. It will take some time. We'll let you know just as soon as it's ready." All the time that Dursley was speaking, Slughorn was shaking his head. Dursley didn't pay any attention. "Why don't we go out to Hoggsmeade, find someplace quiet to have a drink or two and you can tell us all about your problem. It can be a last minute meeting of the Old Boy's Club."

The idea of a drink appealed to me. So, I got unsteadily to my feet, shook off attempts to help me out, and headed for the door. Brewster said, "Why don't we take the floo to the. . . oh, let say, the Hogshead."

I nodded, and Dursley took my hand as we entered the floo connection.

I almost lost it when we landed in the soot of the floo of the Hogshead. I guess that I was lucky to not have any food in me and precious little liquid either. Dursley helped me to a table in a quiet corner. Of course, all corner's of the Hogshead are quiet all the time.

Aberforth approached us to ask for orders. Dursley took the lead immediately, "A decent whiskey for the Headmaster, Brewster, and me. Professor Wendt will have. . ." He hesitated enough that I was ready to suggest something. Dursley beat me to it, though. "Professor Wendt will have a good whiskey, too, but first, let's have a bowl of soup with some bread. What is the soup *de jour*?"

Aberforth scratched his chin and said, "Well, we've always got bean soup, but we've also got a nice salmon chowder today." Brewster shook his head at that, so Dursley took his advice and took the bean soup for me.

I was slowly becoming accustomed to the idea that I was not going to be sent back to oblivion right away. That and the fact that I was actually kind of hungry forced me to decide to accept having some soup and bread before any more whiskey.

As we waited for our food (me) and drink (everyone else), I was becoming more willing to talk about my tragedy. Brewster approached the subject obliquely. "I deeply appreciate your willingness to give yourself up for Cecily and me. Let me assure you that I wouldn't do that for you."

I scoffed. "Thanks."

He forged on, "It's because I wouldn't do that for you, that I want to understand why you would do it for me." There were muffled sounds of agreement. I wasn't ready to just start talking about my grief, so I waited for my soup to arrive.

Aberforth must have had it simmering on the stove all day. It arrived quickly and was hot. The end of a loaf of bread that came with it was cool, but it must have been baked that day. It was some variety of rye. I had begun eating ravenously both the soup and bread that seemed made for each other.

Dursley put a hand on my arm and said, "Not so fast. You may end up leaving a lot of that in the loo." I slowed my pace. That gave me an opportunity to talk.

I began. "I know you're going to think that I'm crazy to be taking it so hard, but I had hardly come back to life when I was rejected by my. . ." I searched for the right word. Was she my girl friend? She was my girl friend, but so much more than that. Was she my lover? Of course! She was more than that. She and I had sparred over the years. I thought she was a hard-nosed Auror first, second, a rival in our struggles against threats to wizards and Muggles, and finally a friend.

Then, completely out of the blue, she had become my true love. She was independent. She could argue with me without ever affecting our love. She was smart. The only woman who had ever matched her in being a perfect person and mate was Minerva. I then thought about her aspect that I'd almost forgotten. She wasn't the most beautiful woman that I'd ever seen or even the most beautiful person that I'd ever met. She was the most beautiful complete person I'd ever known. I thought about Haley when I thought about beauty personified. Haley was a stunning beauty, but she couldn't do half the things that THE woman could. She couldn't drive me crazy with desire while we tried to best each other at ideas. She couldn't do magic, of course. She couldn't outrun me up the hills around Hogwarts. She couldn't make me laugh like a loon at her terrible puns. She wouldn't fight me with everything she had to keep me out of danger or join me in the danger from which she couldn't keep me.

7

I'd almost finished the bowl of soup while I was thinking. My companions didn't try to get me to talk or reveal what I'd been thinking about. Instead they sipped on their drinks. Finally, Aberforth brought me my drink. Rather than downing it at one or two gulps, I sipped. Then I said, "You've been patient. I'll tell you what has happened. I was gone for three years— more or less. When I left, I had a relationship with a woman whom I thought would be with me forever. It's funny about this polyjuice potion that you brew. You take it, and you disappear completely. A different person emerges. So, you wake up one day, and you wonder if you've been gone at all. The love of your life, whom you light up with joy every time you're together, walks in the door. She tells you that you're finished. She says that her old boy friend has come back and spent months in her company. It's the ultimate break-up from left field.

"Life leaves no crumbs under the table for me. I've done everything that anyone could wish to do. There's nothing left for me. Jaimie has a family and all her life ahead of her. She should get to live it."

Dursley scoffed. "You've had break-ups before. Haven't you learned anything from them."

I answered, "Nothing like this."

He went on. "Come on, I know about Jennifer." Everyone else turned their attention to him and asked, "Jennifer?"

I was flummoxed. "You don't know about Jennifer."

Dursley shook his head and said, "Didn't I tell you about meeting her?"

I wasn't sure, but I said, "OK. Let's talk about Jennifer. I met her and started seeing her months before I came to Hogwarts. I liked her a lot. Maybe I even loved her. Then I met Minerva. I slowly came to realize that I was in love with her. Before that happened, Jennifer knew that I didn't love her. Technically she broke up with me, but before that happened, I'd really broken up with her without quite knowing it. It wasn't a gut-wrenching break-up for me. For Jennifer, it was."

Slughorn nodded almost imperceptibly as though he'd been through that, too. Brewster insisted, "OK. Maybe your Jennifer wasn't that for you, but you surely have been through this before, haven't you?"

I almost laughed. "Oh, I've dated and even had other lovers than Minerva, but they were all different."

Dursley asked, "How?"

I thought back over the decades. "OK. The first summer after I started with Hogwarts I went back to the States for the summer. On that flight I met a young woman whom I took on a road trip. It lasted about a week. We drove around the Midwest and spent every night together. It was a tempestuous relationship. It lasted that one week. When we came back to England, we lost track of each other. You might have thought that was a terrible break-up. It wasn't. I was coming back to Minerva. That re-union in Heathrow convinced me that I was in love with her."

Dursley actually laughed, "What about Aurora? You've had more dates with her than anyone other than Minerva, surely. There must have been a break-up with her."

I shook my head sadly. "No, you're wrong on both counts. I've had more dates with other people. Also, how can you break up with someone with whom you've never been in a relationship? Of course, maybe you consider a string of practical jokes to be a relationship."

Slughorn said one word, "Haley."

I sighed. "Haley and I were only ever on one real date. You see, we were together on four occasions.

"I met her because she was the Maid of Honor for Sally's wedding. We met when the ladies went wedding dress shopping. They wanted me to instruct her about magic, witches, wizards, and so on. They finished shopping before lunch. The cowards all thought that I would do just fine giving Haley the low-down on magic over lunch.

"Well, there was a lot more to do than just bring her up-to-date on witches. I ended up listening to a fair chunk of her life story. It took most of the day and well into the night. I couldn't help telling her a fair amount of my story. The two had more in common than I would have guessed.

"Anyway, by the end, she confessed that she was in love with me."

At this point, Brewster interrupted me. He said, "Come on. You don't really believe in love at first sight, do you?"

I said, "I know. That's only for teenagers, right?" Brewster nodded vigorously. I went on. "Well, there's been research done that shows that if a couple who have never met before, answer twenty questions about themselves and stare into each other's eyes for four minutes without talking, they will fall in love."

Brewster was about to interrupt again, but I beat him to his question. "Sure, I didn't know what the questions were, but the point is revealing honestly deep truths about yourselves. Believe me, we got a whole lot deeper than any questions made up by psychologists do. We probably talked a lot longer than the study subjects would. By the end, we were gazing into each other's eyes pretty intently. I don't know how long, but I'm pretty sure more than four minutes."

Brewster still seemed to be skeptical. He asked, "Did you fall in love with her/"

I said, "You know, we've missed an opportunity here. This is a club

9

meeting, right?"

Dursley and Slughorn agreed. I went on. "Then we ought to offer Ed a membership in the club, don't you think?"

Dursley and Slughorn agreed vigorously. Brewster asked what went on at club meetings. I said, "Exactly what you see today. The club consists of Hogwarts male staff who get together about once a week for lunch to discuss topics of mutual interest." Dursley laughed at that.

Brewster looked between Dursley and me. He asked, "OK. What's the catch?"

I said, "Well, the catch is that all members have to give their oath that what is said here stays here." I quickly added, "Exceptions to that rule being illegal, immoral, or fattening things."

Brewster scoffed. "Unbreakable Oath, I suppose."

Slughorn answered, "Oh, no. We are strictly on personal oath. If you would make your personal oath, we'd be happy to include you as an honorary member of the club—your not being on the staff."

Brewster nodded slowly and said, "Sure, I probably won't be able to attend many meetings. I think I can see why you want to get me to take this oath. You're going to reveal something that you'd rather not got around generally. I get it. Just understand that if what you're about to reveal is immoral, I won't be bound to silence."

I agreed. "Good enough. Then, I'll go on. The answer to your question is that by the end of the evening, I did feel quite a lot of affection for her. Honestly, she was staying at the hotel where we met for lunch. As we stood to leave, I'm pretty sure that she wanted me to join her in her room. I might have done as well. We were interrupted by the waitress who had our bill. That interruption was the only thing that kept us from. . . well, you know.

"That was not the most intense of our meetings. The next meeting was with most of the rest of the wedding party. There was nothing particular that happened at that meeting. I was determined that it wouldn't. The next time that we met was the day before the wedding rehearsal when everyone was together at Hogwarts. I don't entirely know how she did it, but she managed to get hold of Dursley's love potion. She spiked both our teas with it. We spent the night together. Fortunately, there was no sex. There might easily have been but we both felt that we had all the rest of our lives to pursue our love.

"If you really want to know how the we took the antidote to the love potion, you'll have to get Mr. Dursley or the Headmaster to fill you in. The antidote was administered before the rehearsal. I had no part of the wedding, so I sat at the back of the Great Hall for the wedding and lay as low as I could. I couldn't completely avoid dancing with her during the wedding reception, but I came away without anything like a break-up." I paused.

Dursley picked up on that immediately and asked, "That wasn't the last time that you and Haley were together, right?"

I had to admit it. "Right. After the death of Minerva, I resigned from Hogwarts and went to the States to grieve in my home town. Haley learned where I had gone and followed me there so that she could try to coax me back to England and Hogwarts and, she hoped, her arms.

"In one way, it worked better than her wildest dreams."

Slughorn broke in, "Is that why you returned?"

I agreed. "Mostly, but it wasn't the only reason. She caught me on the rebound, emotionally vulnerable. She and I spent a few days together living the dream that she'd had at Sally's wedding. We spent those few days together in a sort of whirlwind romance. We flew back to England together, but she was not the only reason that I returned."

Everyone stared at me. I went on, "The other reason was that there was another woman who wanted me back at Hogwarts. She met us at the airport and disapparated us to our homes. We dropped Haley at her place first. Then she took me to her home—not to Hogwarts."

Dursley nodded wisely. "That's why your 'break-up' with Haley wasn't a real break-up. You were already in a relationship with someone else. You always seem to luck out with your loves."

I frowned at that. "You need to listen to Socrates. You don't know whether a life has been good or not until the very end."

Dursley laughed. "You don't need to tell me about Karma."

Brewster asked, "So this mystery woman was the one who just broke up with you?"

Dursley asked, "You don't have another love on the side?"

Slughorn wanted to know who she was. I said, "It's funny. I don't think that we set out to keep it a secret, but it just seemed to work out that way. When I got back to England, she took me to where she lived. That happened to be with her parents. We started off perfectly honestly with them. They were both magical. I don't know that they were very happy to have me as the fancy man of their daughter, but they were good about it. They let me stay with them for a few days.

"Later, of course, I returned to Hogwarts and resumed my position. You all know about that. What you don't know is that my love and I spent most evenings together. She usually came to my office through the floo connection. Most of the time, she'd bring parchments to work on from her job. She'd sit on the floor in front of the sofa in my office and use my coffee table as a desk. I'd work on lesson plans, grading, etc. while she did her

11

work. A lot of the time, I'd just look up when she came through. We'd just smile at each other. Almost always, though, we'd talk over a drink at some-time during the evening.

"Of course, there would be times that we'd go out to dinner. Most of the time, though, she'd pick up something from the Ministry of Magic cafeteria or a chip shop on the way to my office. She'd eat while working. I usually had dinner in the Great Hall, of course.

"We certainly would make love some nights. Mostly, though, we would spoon in bed and then go to sleep. We fell into that routine so natu-rally that I thought there was nothing strange about it. Now, I see that it was both beyond the normal and something that we never appreciated fully.

"You all know that I had to turn my life over to Jaimie. You know the deal that I made to receive my life back from Jaimie after three years. My lover and I understood that she would be waiting for me when I returned. She was waiting for me when awoke a couple of days ago. She completely shocked me by admitting that she'd met and fallen in love with someone else. They were to be married soon. That was the only real break-up that I ever experienced. Even Minerva's death didn't hit me as hard.

"I was present with Minerva when she died. We were all fighting for our lives. Her death was a terrible shock, but I knew that I'd done every-thing I could to save her.

"When this break-up happened, I wasn't around. I couldn't defend my-self. It was all long over when I learned of it. It was hopeless. I am hope-less."

I looked directly at Brewster and said, "Now, you know why I want to give Jaimie her chance at a good life."

We were all silent for several timeless minutes. Then Dursley asked, "Who was she. . ." He then answered his own question, "Ooo, I know. She came from the Ministry. It was the Minister of Magic, wasn't it? She al-ways had a soft spot for you. AND, she had no scruples about catching you on the rebound after Minerva's death."

I laughed. It was the first time since I'd come back from the Void. "That's an amazingly good guess. If I didn't know better, I'd be convinced. No, it wasn't Pamela. In a way, I'm surprised that she didn't try something like that."

Slughorn guessed next. "How about that blonde. You know, the dirty blonde who was in Potter's year. She was always kind of. . . oh, strange. She wouldn't have been troubled by your being a Muggle. I always thought she was pretty smart. Your brains would have appealed to her. She always said exactly what she was thinking. I think that would have appealed to you."

12

Again, I had to laugh. "Isn't it Luna Lovegood that you're thinking of?" He nodded. "Right. No, she was attractive in a lot of ways, but I think she sort of fancied Longbottom from her year."

Brewster said, "I know who it was. She visited me shortly after Jaimie returned the last time. She made it clear that Jaimie and I had better stick to our agreement. She didn't hesitate to threaten. It was Ginny Weasley, wasn't it?"

I agreed. "Yes. She explained to me a number of times why she loved me. I don't think that I ever really understood, but there was no doubt of the genuineness of her feelings for me. I never deserved being with even one woman like either Minerva or Ginny. It's proof that people never get what they deserve."

Slughorn reflected, "You and Ginny? I would never have thought. You must be nearly twenty years older than she is." At that he took on a thoughtful look as he gazed upward and toward his left. After a moment, he said, "Maybe not. As I was saying before, you may be several years younger than your chronological years. When were you born?"

"Nineteen sixty-five."

He seemed to be doing some deep thought. Then he said, "I think your real age might be only about a dozen years older than she is—not an awful difference. I once knew a couple. The wizard was about . .."

That did not help my attitude. I said, "I might as well be one hundred twelve years older than she is. We're not together any more."

That brought Slughorn back to the present. "Well, what I really want to know is this. Will you teach English literature this year?"

With some food in my stomach and a little good whiskey, the world looked a lot better than it had before. "Maybe. Give me a couple of days to think about it. School doesn't start for at least. . ."

Dursley said, "Five days."

That sunk me into the depths of despond again. "I don't have my lesson plans. That's so, so, much work that. . ."

Brewster smiled once and said, "Jaimie told me that she had prepared for you by planning the first term—all classes."

I didn't think I could come up with a retort, so I said, "I'll give the term a try and see how things go, Headmaster."

That was the end of the meeting of the Old Boys' Club.

First Classes

After the beginning of term meeting banquet, Slughorn summoned the teachers and staff to the Teachers' Lounge. It was the first time that I'd attended a meeting in the Teachers' Lounge with Slughorn in charge. The first full year that he was Headmaster, I'd taught, but he was still getting into the swing of being the regular Headmaster—not just a substitute. He'd missed a few of the usual formalities such as a beginning of term teacher's meeting in the Teachers' Lounge.

I sat in the last row of chairs that had been set up for the meeting. First Filch and then Dursley came to sit next to me. Filch hadn't seen me since I'd returned. I'd spent the few days that I had in my office with occasional visits to the Great Hall for some meals. Filch greeted me as though I'd returned from the dead, which I had, in a way. He said, "Merlin's Beard! Look what Mrs. Norris dragged in. I hope you're hear to stay."

"I hope so, too."

Filch wanted to know what had happened to me. I said, "Why don't you and Dursley get together. He can give you the full story. I'm sorry to say that a couple of days ago, we had a quick Old Boys' Club meeting. We didn't have time to include you and Hagrid. I'm truly sorry, but it was a very difficult moment for me. Mr. Dursley and Slughorn intervened to help me get through it."

Filch was fit to be tied. However, Slughorn was just calling the meeting to order and he had no choice other than holding his peace for later.

Slughorn began with the obvious. He said, "I'm sure that you've all aware of the fact that after a lengthy absence, Professor Wendt has returned to teach English literature. Of course, I only announced the bare fact at the banquet. We almost never comment on instructors' personal lives before students. However, I want to expand on what I told you when three years ago, Professor Wendt took an extended leave of absence from Hogwarts.

14

He was replaced, of course, by Professor Brewster.

"You should harbor no suspicions that Professor Brewster's performance was such as to cause me to sack her. I was very pleased with her teaching and would have been happy to renew her contract indefinitely. However, personal commitments have forced her to request a leave of absence which will likely last three or more years. I'm not at liberty to reveal the cause of that leave of absence, but I can assure you that it only redounds to her credit."

Filch rose and asked trunculently, "What happened to Wendt the last three years?"

Slughorn shook his head and mumbled, "Why is it always me?" Then he raised his head and said, "I'm sure that Professor Wendt would enjoy filling you in—after this meeting. Now, for more serious topics. Let's review the school year serious dates.

"The first Hogsmeade weekend is October 13. We need sign-ups for chaperones for that weekend. I've posted a sign-up sheet on the bulletin board over there. Unfilled slots will be assigned by me to the people whom I don't like very much. So, let's all sign-up and avoid finding out whom I really don't like.

"Halloween is on a Wednesday. We will celebrate it on Saturday, October 27. I just want to remind all staff who have joined us the last couple of years that there is a history of Professor Wendt somehow managing to involuntarily entertain the Great Hall with his impressions of famous wizards and witches. There's always something to look forward to when Professor Wendt is here for Halloween.

"Christmas this year is on Tuesday. The week before Christmas will be term finals week. The Christmas Party will be the previous Thursday. All exams must be completed by Thursday noon." With that there was a collective groan of dismay.

Aurora stood and asked, "That's impossible! We've always had four full days of final exams. Don't forget that we have to work around Owl and Newt exams too!"

Someone else shouted out, "Don't forget that last year, we started exams on the Friday before the final week."

Slughorn looked up to the heavens and said, "We'll just have to work through it. The Board raised hell last year for starting finals a day early."

It turned out that there were no new teachers this year, unless you counted me as one.

After the meeting, Filch seized Hagrid and Slughorn. He declared, "It's high time for an Old Boys' Club meeting. I'm calling an emergency executational meeting right now! Let's go to the Three Broomsticks and get a few things straight-like."

Slughorn plead, "Really, it's not that far from the closing time for the Broomsticks. By the time we get there, they'll be calling last drink."

Filch was persistent, "You know perpetually well that we can take the floo right here in the Teachers' Lounge direct-like to the Broomsticks. We can get two, maybe three good stiff ones in that way."

Everyone was grumbling, but since Filch and Hagrid had been left off the last meeting, the rest of us felt indebted to them to give them a "make-up" meeting. When Filch saw that he had gotten his way, he said, "Uhm. I think it might be a good idea for Slughorn to take Wendt here, his being a squib. Uh. . . I think Dursley and I will just take up the rear to make sure that no one gets waylaid."

So, the five of us landed in the Three Broomsticks. There was one pair of gaffers at the bar sipping at ales. We took a table in a corner. I was about to sit when Filch asked me, "Uh. . . Wendt. Seeing as you're the junior in senioritance here and this being your first meeting in a while, why don't you just pick up the first round?"

I was recovered enough from my grief that I could laugh with the old scoundrel and said, "I hardly see how that is just." Filch started to splutter something, but I hurried on. "Given all the fine reasons that you just gave, I think that I ought to stand all the rounds tonight."

Filch's startled look turned to one of pure delight. He said, "You don't hardly need to go that far. I was thinking of picking up the next round."

I pretended to consider the proposition briefly in which Filch's expression turned back to one of fear mixed with consternation. I quickly added, "Generous though your offer is, I just can't permit you to do it. I stand by my decision to stand all the rounds tonight. What does everyone want?"

Dursley and I had Jameson whiskey, since the Broomsticks didn't carry Dewars. Hagrid had the house ale in a tankard the size of a kitchen sink. Slughorn had a dry white wine, and Filch opted for a fire whiskey at first, but changed his order to Jameson. I went to the bar with the order. Rosmerta asked me how late we'd be there.

"Oh, probably until you kick us out. Please just repeat drinks for our party as necessary and charge them all to me. This is the last night before the term starts."

She shook her head at us, but didn't object. I returned to our table with the first couple of drinks followed by Rosmuerta with everything except Hagrid's ale. He got that himself.

Filch started the business part of the meeting off, "Well, at the top of the agenda tonight is the minutia from the last meeting that not all of the members were able to attend because of the oversight of the organizers to invite the most important members."

Hagrid said, "Oh, Mr. Filch, I don't think we're the most important members, right." He nudged Filch gently with a massive elbow that grazed the top of Filch's head.

I took the floor to say, "Look, mine is the fault. So should mine be the remedy. Here's what happened."

Filch turned his attention from Hagrid to me. I went on. "The meeting was to condole with me over my recent grief. I just returned from exile. I was gone because I was helping the Muggle government deal with a possible invasion of the Earth. I had to be gone for three years. The mission was successful, but when I returned only a couple of days ago, I discovered that the woman that I'd been seeing and loved as dearly as my life had broken up with me."

When he heard those words, Filch jumped up and exclaimed, "Who is the faithless wrenched, misguided miss who could do that to you? Why, I'll. . . put such a hex on her that she won't be able to walk straight for a month!"

I shook my head sadly, "You'll do no such thing. I was the one who abandoned her. She had every right to dump me. However, if you promise not to curse her, I will reveal to you who the young lady is."

Filch seemed to be weighing the matter in his head. He finally, drawled, "Well, as a special favor to you, Professor, I'll not do anything dramatical to her even though she deserves all the hexing that this evil eye can yield up." With that he squinted at me in demonstration of his evil eye.

I replied, "Since you've promised not to harm her, I'll tell you who it is. Just remember that I still have deep-felt sentiments of love for her."

Filch urged me on. "Of course, I'll honor those sentimentalities, Professor."

I then revealed her name. "It was Ginny Weasley."

Filch's dropped jaw could have done credit to Hagrid. He asked, "Surely not! Ginny is a bonnie lass. A bonnie lass with a temper, but I can't believe that she'd have dropped you."

"I'm afraid it's true, and I can't really blame her. After all, I was gone for three years with not a word sent to her."

Hagrid agreed and added, "If you say so, it must be true, but she's missed out on what a wiser woman took advantage of. I'm sorry for her loss."

No one chose to add anything, so I declared that we needed to move on to new business—having another round of Rosmuerta's finest. Filch was completely onboard with that, so we had one more round and left before Ross-Muerte called for the last round.

□

The next day I started my first class with my usual introduction. I was forced to endure multiple questions about what had happened to Mrs. Brewster.

After the first class I began each class with a standard FAQ:

"I know that you all wonder about what happened to Mrs. Brewster. You should+know that there was nothing wrong with Hogwarts, nothing wrong with any class that she taught, nothing wrong with the Headmaster, and most especially nothing wrong with any of you that caused her to take a leave of absence.

"I am not here as a punishment to anyone, possibly excepting me. Now if anyone has a sensible question that isn't covered by what I just said, I'll answer the first three. Then personal questions will be strictly forbidden for the rest of the school year. Now, take a minute to think. Then if anyone has a question, lift your hand and we'll see what happens."

There were three minutes of absolute silence then a fourth year student near the back of the class stood timidly and asked, "Is Mrs. Brewster pregnant?"

There was a lot of laughter, which I permitted. Then I declared the end of questions. I said, "Five points to Huffelpuff for a sensible question not covered by my statement. Now we are back to our work."

The first week or two I was very busy adjusting lesson plans from Jaimie's to my style. Every time that I thought about her while I was doing that, I wondered what had happened during the three years that I was gone. She'd left a brief note that informed me about her becoming a mother, and, of course, Ginny gave me far more detail than I wanted to know about her and Potter. However, she also told me about some of the projects that I'd worked on before I had to leave the scene.

Of course, I could inspect Jaimie's memories. I just couldn't bring myself to do that. It seemed unethical. It seemed nosy. The biggest thing was that I was afraid to look at those memories.

□□

The next day I was grading some papers when there was a knock at my door. I said, "Come."

I didn't recognize the young woman who enter my office hesitantly. She seemed familiar, but I couldn't place her face. When I didn't recognize her she came hesitantly to my desk. She stood behind my old red leather

18

guest chair. She asked, "Don't you recognize me, Professor?"

"I'm afraid not. . . Wait." I then had a glimmer of recognition. "You're Sissy Brewster!"

The beginnings of worry lines in her face cleared, and she sat confidently in the red leather chair. "Yes, Professor."

I shook my head with regret and said, "Oh, Sissy, I'm sorry that I couldn't come to your graduation. Of course, you know why it was unavoidable, but I'm still sorry."

She nodded and said, "I know. That's OK. I mean no offense, but I'd rather have my mum with me than you be able to attend my graduation."

I chuckled. "None taken. How did you do on. . ." I couldn't finish the question because she interrupted me.

"Oh! I almost forgot. I have a little something for you." She opened her handbag. Out of it came a photo. She handed it to me. "This was taken on my graduation day. What do you think?" She beamed as she asked.

I looked at it carefully. It was about 4 by 6 inches. It showed five people: Sissy, her dad who was holding a baby who must have been around a year old, and Jaimie, holding a toddler who was probably a girl. My mouth dropped open as I looked at Jaimie. Like all wizard photos, there was movement in the picture. Jaimie and Ed Brewster were facing each other. They were apparently talking. Sissy was staring at the camera with a bored expression. Then, they all turned toward the camera and smiled. It was just as though the photographer had said, "Look here, smile big, and say cheese." Then, Jaimie winked at the camera. The sight of her took me completely by surprise. I guess my mouth dropped open.

Sissy asked, "What is it? Did I make a funny face?"

"Oh, no. It's just that I never saw Jaimie before—especially in a photo with motion. I was just surprised."

Sissy scoffed. "Never saw her before. You saw her every day that she looked in the mirror, didn't you?"

I made a face of frustration. It took me a couple of minutes to work through my answer. Sissy was patient as I did. "Here's the thing. Close your eyes."

"What??"

"Nothing awful is going to happen. Just close your eyes." She did—somewhat reluctantly. Then I said, "Now, remember what I look like. Try to picture me in your mind."

She said, "Ok. I've got it."

"Are you sure?"

"Yes."

"Remember what my nose looks like?"

"Yes."

"Got my ears in mind?"

"Yes."

"How about my mouth?"

She was beginning to be a bit testy. She answered, "Yes! I've got all of you in mind."

I got up, walked around behind her, waited a minute, and told her to open her eyes. She was a little startled to not see me in front of her. She got up and swung around enough to see me again. I then asked, "How does your memory compare with reality?"

She sat again. I walked around back to my chair across the desk from her. She thought about it and said, "You are pretty much the way I remember you, but there are noticeable differences. Your nose is a little wider than I remember." With that realization, she laughed. "Sorry. I guess I just had an idealized picture of you in my head."

"Right. That's what happens with memory. It's always different from the reality. Lawyers know that no matter how striking an incident was, no two witnesses remember it the same way, and nobody remembers it exactly as it happens. That became ridiculously obvious when traffic cameras and body cameras began being used in court hearings."

She stared at me. "What is a body camera? Do people have cameras pointed at their own bodies all the time?"

I chuckled. "No. Police have started wearing video cameras that show what they saw. There are tons of cases where the videos from those cameras differ tremendously from what police remember. Of course, some of that difference is probably the police having selective memory that favors their side of the story. However, a good bit of it is just that people don't have good memories for what they see.

"You probably had a good memory of what I look like because you just saw me just before you closed your eyes. If you hadn't seen me in a few months, the differences would be bigger."

Sissy asked, "So, you're saying that your memory of what mum looks like is old. She's changed and you might not have had that good a memory to start with?"

"That's right, but that's not all. I only saw her through a mirror—usually when she was looking carefully at her face to make sure her makeup was on right."

Sissy smiled. "You mean your makeup was on right, but, she also looked at herself in a full length mirror to check her outfit."

"That's true, but in both cases, she was mostly not looking at herself as a whole—just trying to look for things out of place. That overlooks the

20

other thing about looking at yourself in the mirror. It's not really the image that other see of you. It's the mirror image. That is always different."

Sissy thought a minute. "OK. I get it."

"There's one other important thing. Her memory of herself was always colored by how she 'saw' herself—forgive the pun—that is, the attitude she had toward herself. Most people have a rather negative opinion of themselves."

Sissy shrugged. "OK. So, she looked a lot different than her memory of herself. Hey, she looked at herself just before she took the polyjuice potion. That memory wasn't years old."

I nodded. "True, but I haven't looked at her memories from the last three years."

Sissy seemed puzzled. "Why not?"

"It's common ethics. That would be far worse than reading someone else's diary without permission. I admit that at first long ago, I did look into her memory some. I didn't really understand how this thing works back then. Now, I would only do that in an emergency."

Her mouth formed a big "O." Then she asked, "So what difference struck you? Does she look like an old woman to you?"

I didn't want to answer that completely honestly, but I decided that I had to at least hint at how I felt. "Well, actually, I was struck by how attractive your mom is. I never got that sense from her memories of herself. Oh, she knew that she was fairly good looking, but she never realized how striking she is. I hope I haven't offended you."

Sissy was silent and then said, "No. no. I guess I never thought about that myself. I was mad at her when she first started dating dad, so I thought she was just a sort of tart. Sorry."

"No problem. I understand that."

"Then later, when we got to be friends, I thought she was great, but not necessarily. . . amazing looking. But now I see it. She picked up the photo that I'd laid on the desk." She gazed at it and said, "Yes. I definitely see it now. You know, she's still pretty—even though she's older."

All I could say was "Right." Then I changed the subject. "I see in the photo that you're wearing some honor stoles. What were they?"

She sort of shrugged as though they were of no importance. "You know, I almost didn't wear them. It seems to me that those sort of honors aren't all that wonderful. They always just separated me from others."

I chuckled. "Still, what were they?"

"Oh, I got the McGonagall prize for transfiguration and the Arithmancy prize."

I asked, "Were you ever a Prefect?"

She laughed at that, "Are you kidding? That's the most worthless thing that you can be at Hogwarts. I'd rather sit in my room and eat leftovers than be a Prefect."

"OK. Then what about Owls and Newts?"

She finally smiled at that. "I got an Owl in every test I took. I'm afraid I missed two Newts though."

I laughed. "It must have been senioritis."

She stared at me. "Did you say arthritis?"

"No, senioritis. It's named after what we in the States call 7th years. Seniors get so anxious to be done with school that they get lazy. Somehow, though, I can't see you as lazy."

She turned a little red. "I wasn't lazy. I just got tired of potions and the history of magic. That and chess were the reasons I sort of fell down in those subjects." She smiled, turned red, and added, "You know, I became an International Master at the end of the school year."

I practically jumped across the desk, I rose that quickly. "Congratulations! This calls for something special." I looked at her carefully and asked, "Are you seventeen yet?"

"Yes, I had my birthday last month."

I pursed my lips. Then I added, "You're not a student now."

She squinted at me and asked, "What in the world are you thinking of?"

"Well, I'd like to celebrate all that—graduation, getting all those Newts, becoming an International Master." I hesitated again.

"Come on, out with it."

I crossed the Rubicon. "Perhaps we could celebrate with a little drink?"

She smiled broadly. "You mean like fire whiskey?"

I shuddered. "I most certainly don't mean fire whiskey. I mean something good. I mean this." I reached into my lower left drawer to find my bottle of Johnny Walker Blue Label. I set it on the table. Then I said, "You have to swear not to tell your parents." I choked on that.

Sissy said, "Don't worry. I know what you mean. Sure. Do you want the Unbreakable Oath."

I laughed. "That thing is way overused. No, your personal honor would be just fine."

She nodded. I got out two glasses and asked her to provide two ice cubes each. She said, "Uh, sorry. I don't know that spell yet."

"Doesn't matter. It's better without ice the first time." I poured two fingers in each glass and lifted mine to the air for a toast. "To a great student and chess master."

She lifted hers uncertainly and said, "To a great teacher." We touched glasses. I took a good sip as did she. She suppressed the gag reflex and said, "Strong." We then sat. I asked her, "So, what are you planning on doing now?"

She took another sip and handled it fairly well. She said, "I was recruited by AA."

I gagged at that.

She asked, "Are you OK?"

"Yes, yes. The AA?"

"You know, the Auror Academy."

"I understand that that's quite an honor. You have to be a really accomplished witch to qualify for the Academy. Do you want to be an auror?"

She smiled. "No, I want to play chess."

I smiled at that. "Then I think that is what you should do—especially if you can support yourself that way. Can you?"

She nodded. "I think so. You know, it's fairly inexpensive to live a simple life as a witch, provided that you travel by disapparation most of the time and by port key only when absolutely necessary. I can live at home, except when at tournaments. Now that mum's gone, I do all the housework, cooking, and so forth. Dad's happy to have me around always, but he's especially happy now that mum's on. . . leave. I have started winning money at tournaments. That's enough to finance trips to other tournaments."

I said, "That's good. Have you thought about corporate sponsorships?"

She stared at me and just said, "Whut?"

"Corporations frequently sponsor athletes as a form of advertising of their brand."

She shook her head as though she were dizzy. Then she asked, "You're going to have to explain that to me. Let's start with corporations. Then do sponsor. Then, how do athletes fit in, especially with me. Then what are brands?"

"Well, it doesn't happen much in the wizarding world, but in the Muggle world, corporations frequently sponsor athletes. First, let's talk about corporations. They're like companies only usually bigger. For example, you know about businesses like Madame Malkins."

She looked suspicious but asked, "Is she a company?"

"She isn't, but she owns a business—her clothes store. An example of a larger business that is like a corporation would be Gringotts."

She seemed to get that. She then asked, "OK. What about sponsorships?"

"Well, a sponsorship is really just another way of advertising. Sometimes, companies advertise by putting an advert in the newspaper—like the *Prophet.*"

She nodded. "Sure, I know about that."

"OK. Sometimes, companies advertise by having an athlete use their product—and reminding everyone that the athlete uses it."

Sissy almost jumped out of the red leather chair. "You mean like Quidditch teams that use Nimbus brooms?"

"Exactly. I think I've seen adverts in the *Prophet* by Nimbus about their being the official broom of the 2002 Quidditch World Cup."

She smiled. "You bet you have." She added, "Is that what you mean by 'brand'? Nimbus is a brand, right?"

"Yes."

"I see. But I also see a problem."

I smiled. She was a smart one. "Just why would any company want to sponsor a chess player?"

"You're right that companies usually pick very popular sports when they are looking for an athlete to sponsor."

She interrupted me. "Where do I fit in as an athlete? Surely chess isn't a sport?"

I laughed. "You'd be surprised at the 'sports' that get sponsors. Auto racing, for example, is a sport that gets tons of 'sports' sponsorships."

She stared at me. "You mean cars, right?"

"Yep."

Then she shook her head and said, "Maybe chess **IS** a sport."

She finished the last of her drink and asked, "A little more?"

I shook my head. "No, ma'am. This was a once-in-a-long-while offer. If you win the world championship, then yes."

She grumbled, "Stingy."

"Maybe, but when you're older still, we can revisit. For now, you're in training."

"OK—for now. So, how do I get a sponsorship?"

I finished my drink and set the glass on the edge of my desk. "Well, people get sponsorships by being good in their sport."

Sissy almost whined, "But, I'm good."

I frowned. "I guess I need to be more specific. If you're in a very popular sport, you just need to be good at your sport. . ."

She interrupted,."You mean like Quidditch?"

"In wizarding, yes. For Muggles, that would be football. If you're in a less popular sport, such as cricket, you need to be better than good. If you're in a sport that's not very popular, then. . ."

Sissy said, "You'd better be great."

"Right."

"So, that's me?"

"Not quite, your sport is less popular still. You have to be world champion or at least be in serious competition for it."

She leaned back and said, "Do you have something else to drink?"

I smiled. "How about some tea? I have a pot. Could you warm it for me?"

She went over to my bookshelf where Jaimie kept a teapot on a trivet. Jaimie liked hot tea. I still kept water in it. I used sterno to heat my tea water when I really wanted it. Sissy had the water boiling in a few seconds. Jaimie had a nice tea set that she stored under the bookshelf. I brought out two cups. Sissy glanced at them and said, "How lovely. I wouldn't have guessed you had such good taste in china."

All I could do was grimace as I poured hot water and gave Sissy a teabag. I commented, "I have sugar, but no cream."

She replied, "I don't use either." Then she began. "The way that you get to be chess champion is that in odd number years, you play in continental championship tournaments to qualify for the Candidates Tournament. That tournament, to be played next year, has sixteen players who play in a two-round knockout tournament. They are best of six games with tie-breaking rules. Then the best eight players out of that tournament will play in the Championship Tournament. That tournament is also a two-round knockout tournament."

"Not an easy path." I commented.

She said, "Actually, it's not as simple as it sounds. I've left out some important details. For example, additionally there are spots for really strong players who don't qualify by being continental champions."

"OK. So, are you playing a continental tournament?"

"Sure."

"Then, if you win that, you can start looking for sponsors. But, there are other things that we can do right away."

She smiled broadly and asked, "We?"

I had slipped into thinking about Sissy the way I had thought about Cedric. I reflected on that and then said, "Well, that assumes that you AND your dad are willing for me to help with your career more than just sitting in my office and talking."

She took a sip of tea and said, "Why does my dad have to be involved in this decision?"

I stood and paced for a moment as I thought. "Look. You are an adult by wizarding law, but you're still pretty young. As a matter of fact, in Muggle law you would still be considered a minor."

She said defiantly, "Well, I'm not a Muggle am I?"

I was still standing. "That may be, but I won't work with you without your father's permission."

"Since when do you need my dad's permission to do anything?"

I shook my head in frustration. "Some people might think that I was trying to take advantage of a very young woman. Having your father's permission protects me from that—at least some."

She laughed. "How anyone could think that you could take advantage of me IS a laugh."

"I don't care. If you don't agree to that, we can end our discussion right now."

She seemed surprised by my forceful statement. "Ok. You don't have to shout. I'll talk to my dad tonight."

I went on. "Here's another thing we can do. . . Let me ask you if you ever read the *Prophet* sports pages."

She shrugged. "No. Why?"

"Well, I do sometimes. I've never seen a chess article there. It would help to make the sport more popular. That would help with sponsorships, especially if you were mentioned in some of them."

Sissy scoffed. "Well, that would be really easy."

I smiled. "Well, I just happen to have a contact or two in the *Prophet*. I think we might just pay a visit to one of them to introduce you and encourage her to write some good articles about you. Of course, you've got to be winning for that to work."

Sissy smiled. "Her, eh? Do we have a little romantic interest here?"

I frowned. "Believe me, there's no love lost between us."

She scoffed. "Sure," dragging it out.

I added, "Once you've got some notoriety, you can approach businesses for sponsorship. For example, it's not unusual for clothing makers to sponsor sports figures for wearing their clothes while playing the sport."

"What? I don't wear anything special while playing chess."

"You might wear outfits provided by Madame Malkins, hmmmm?"

She looked upward to the left and said, "You mean that she really might give me outfits to wear?"

I nodded and added, "Maybe not much more, but it's a start and will give you more exposure. You'd be sure to see adds that reminded people that the World Chess Champion contender always wears outfits from Madame Malkins when she plays."

Sissy smiled broadly at that. "What about other sponsors?"

"Oh, I expect that you can get better sponsors that Ms. Malkin as you win more tournaments. As a matter of fact, I have a contact or two in a fairly large company that I might be able to turn into a sponsorship."

"Cool. Who is it?"

26

I smiled. "Sorry. I'm not going to reveal that until you are contending for a championship."

"Oh, Pooh. You are no fun."

"Look at it as incentive to win."

"I'll talk to dad tonight. I'll send you an owl right away if I've got permission."

I agreed and said, "I'll be back in touch as soon as I can to set up a meeting."

Then she walked over to the hearth and asked, "May I use your floo connection?"

"Of course." She stepped in and disappeared.

The next day I received an owl. It was from Ted Brewster. It confirmed his permission for Cecily to work with me in obtaining sponsorships for her chess career. It came, as owl post frequently seemed to, at breakfast in the Great Hall. It was delivered into my plate of sunny-side up egg by an owl that seemed to have been trained by every other owl who had delivered mail to me.

After I separated the note from my eggs, I got a fresh plate with fresh egg from the platter on the head table. I had just broken into the yolk when I heard a screech over my head. I closed my eyes and waited for the inevitable plop as a package hit my plate and squashed the egg. That one was a large, heavy envelope. I decided to take my third plate of breakfast up to my office where owls can't dive bomb you.

In my office, I opened Brewster's letter first. I was sure I knew what was in it and was not worried about it. The other worried me. His letter was just fine. I'd get to work on it shortly.

The other letter, which was as thick as a manuscript was from Gringotts. It was announcing the next quarterly board meeting that was to be held on October 24, a Wednesday, at 7 PM. The agenda consisted of:

- Meeting minutes from the last meeting (attached)
- Review of operating results
- Report on the adoption of the new paper galleon
- Discussion of whether to license printing of paper currency to a subcontractor (white paper attached).
- New business

I decided that things could have been worse. Nothing world-shaking had happened while I was gone. As I went through the attachments, I discovered an additional note that had not been mentioned. It was a note to me from the CEO, Glazblatt. I was to do the report on the adoption of paper galleons!

I began thinking about the various things that I had to do—communicate with the Brewsters, the *Prophet*, the various people at Gringotts. It was beginning to look like I'd have to have a part-time wizard assistant. It had been so much easier, of course, with Minerva and even with Ginny. Now what would I do?

I could mooch off my friends. I would have to start here at Hogwarts. Maybe, I could put an ad in the *Prophet* for a personal assistant. In the mean time, I'd start drafting letters, pretending that I had a reliable way of getting them delivered. I started that immediately.

The next day I dropped a note off that didn't require magic for its delivery. It went into a pigeonhole in the Teachers' Lounge. I did that in the morning. At lunch, the recipient stopped by my seat at the head table, leaned over my shoulder and whispered, "I'll be at your office this evening at eight as requested."

I didn't have time to reply before we both had to be off to classes. After dinner, I was in my office lost in grading when a knock sounded on my door. I'd lost track of time and didn't realize that it was already 8 PM. "Come in."

She opened the door, walked to the red leather chair and sat. "What can I do for you?"

"Well, Aurora, I have a big favor to request. Before I tell you what it is, would you like something to drink?"

She asked, "Blue Label?"

"Sure." I brought out my bottle and a pair of glasses. She cleaned them with the scurgio spell and put two ice cubes in hers. She inclined her head toward me to ask if I wanted ice. I nodded. Then I poured a generous amount into each.

She rubbed her hands together in anticipation. I was afraid of what might be the cost of this favor, but I hadn't a lot of choices. "Here's the deal. I need some letters posted. It would be a big help if you could do it."

"Interesting. You know, I think this is the first time that you've invited me to your office. And it's to ask a favor."

I sighed. "Yes. I'm willing to provide something of value in return. I wouldn't insult you by offering money." I hoped that she wouldn't offer services for free. Hoped.

She closed her eyes and pursed her lips. That went on for several minutes. I was about to check to see if she'd fallen asleep when her eyes
snapped open and she said, "Well, well, well. Professor Wendt caught without a plan."

I said, "Just stop gloating and ask for your pound of flesh."

"Oh, nothing so drastic. I'd be happy to do it for a small favor in return."

I dreaded saying the words, but I decided to get it over quickly. "You
want to do something for Halloween, right?"

She drawled, "Well, I didn't say it. . ." She hesitated but when I was
about to speak, she quickly added, "but yes!"

I had decided that I'd agree to that, especially if I could get as much
help as I needed until something better could be arranged. "That's OK, but
I need more than just a letter or two sent."

That caused her to pause. She asked, "You're looking for a secretary to
do your magic stuff, aren't you?"

This was awful. "Yes. I don't know how long this will go on."

She closed her eyes again and her lips pursed and loosened repeatedly.
Finally, she opened her eyes again and asked, "Look. I don't mind doing
the occasional favor for you. As a matter of fact, I'd have done it for nothing."

I shook my head. "Give me a break! Talk about kicking a man when
he's down."

"You don't have to do anything for me at Halloween."

I shook my head again. "No, I'll go through with it. How could it be
any worse than what's happened before?"

She took a deep breath. I guess she was preparing for giving me the
bad news that was about to come. "Can't you get someone else to help
you? What about someone in the Old Boys Club?" I was openly surprised
that she knew about it. She added, "Don't be surprised. It's not as secret as
you fellows seem to think it is."

I started to tick off the members of the OBC. If she knew about it, she
probably knew the likely members as well. "OK. Obviously, Filch can't
help me." I ticked one finger. "Slughorn is my boss. Asking him to be my
secretary would be the ultimate example of 'managing up.'"

She said, "Never heard of that."

"It's what it sounds like. Anyway, then there's Hagrid. He could do
some things, but I think he's still overawed by being a professor. I don't
want to ask him to help me with menial tasks."

She interrupted. "But it's OK to ask me to do those menial tasks?"

I opened my mouth to say something. I didn't know what, but Aurora saved me having to come up with something. "Oh, I'm just kidding you."

I went on. "Dursley is a possibility. I just don't want to pull seniority on him."

Aurora said, "Well, I guess you are out of options. But I'll send a couple of owls for you, no problem."

I smiled. "Well, it just happens that I've got one for you right now." I opened a drawer of my desk and took out an envelope that was already addressed, sealed, and contained my letter. I handed it to Aurora.

She glanced at the address and laughed. "I'll wager that this doesn't contain a deposit for your vault."

"It's none of your business." Then I added, "I'd really appreciate it if you'd get it off ASAP.'

She smiled and asked, "Would you like to come up to the owlery with me to see it off?"

I smiled, too. "Based on the last time you posted something for me to Gringotts, I'll just pass on that good idea."

She finished her drink, turned, and casually strolled off holding the envelope up. She said, "As you wish."

I then turned to the other letters that I needed to write and post.

The next day was a difficult one. The problem of long term magical help was weighing on my mind. It was so bad that I let a third year boy get away with a little prank. He set the wastebasket in my classroom on fire. If I'd only had more presence of mind, I could have caught him red-handed with his wand in his hand by looking in my very reflective photo of Professor Dumbledore. I had considered changing it with each change of Headmaster, but somehow, I could never bring myself to dethrone him from his place of honor.

By the time that I reached the end of the day I was exhausted and didn't have an idea about how to deal with my muggleness. I was sitting on my sofa with a drink in hand when someone knocked on my door. I bid whoever it was to enter.

It was Aurora. She walked up to the sofa and said, "Looks like a good place to sit."

I was so discouraged that I just motioned beside me. She promptly sat. I offered her something to drink.

"Oh, you will be so thankful that I came that you'll want to make it some of that scrumptious Blue Label."

I just shrugged and rose to get the bottle and a glass. She materialized a cube of ice in it—and mine. I poured, sat, and asked, "OK. I'm listening."

She raised her glass to her lips and took a sip. "You really have been off your game lately."

I scoffed. "Don't I know it?"

"Why don't you hire a student to help you with all the little magic chores that you can't do for yourself?"

I considered the idea and said, "Well, it would have to be an upperclasman, surely. It wouldn't happen often, but I'd like someone who could disapparate. That would make it a sixth or seventh year. Yes. Probably a seventh year at least seventeen years old "

Aurora enthused, "Perfect. There have to be some who would like to make some galleons." She noticed the frown on my face. "What's wrong with that?"

"Well, it couldn't be anyone in one of my classes. That would be improper in quite a lot of ways. It couldn't be a young woman, even if she were an adult, it would be just too dangerous. I'm not sure that leaves anyone."

Aurora said, "You're such a gloomy Gus. You should take a look through your class rolls."

Gloomy Gus went on. "There's the additional problem that anyone who qualifies might not be interested in working for me."

It was at that very point that someone walked out of the floo connection. Aurora exclaimed, "What the bloody. . ."

Unfortunately, I recognized who it was. I just said, "Javeen, what are you doing here?"

She said, "Well, you seem to be having a party. I suppose that I shouldn't interrupt. . "

Aurora instantly said, "This is strictly a school conference."

Javeen scoffed.

I said, "We were just trying to figure out a way for me to have magical services available to me by hiring an assistant."

Aurora said, "I think I'd better leave. She looks like business."

I said, "Oh, she is."

Aurora said, "Bye. If you don't mind, I'm going to take my glass of this wonderful liquid. Don't worry. I'll return it tomorrow."

I just nodded. Then I turned to Javeen. "Well, what ill wind blew you through the floo?"

She took Aurora's place on the sofa. I was standing. I walked to my desk as I said, "You came here for business. I do business at my desk." I added to myself, "normally."

"Fine. Since you were having a drink with your 'business' associate, I'd like one too." She took the red leather chair. I scrounged around for another glass. She did something that cleaned the interior and provided one spherical ice cube. I poured some of my precious Blue Label for her.

She asked, "Aren't you going to freshen yours up?"

I just frowned.

She said, "Well, since you're going to be that way, I came to answer your letter."

I said, "It was addressed to the CEO."

She smiled a beatific smile and said, "You know that executives trust their executive secretaries to handle most issues. I knew that I could handle you. . . er. . . your problem."

"Well, let's hear what you have to say. How can I figure out how widely used the new paper galleons are?"

She drawled, "Well, I don't exactly have an answer for that, but I can help you with your other problem."

"Which is?"

Javeen said, "Don't be tedious. You apparently no longer have the services of that red-headed bit. . . Auror. Just what happened?"

"None of your business. Now, if you actually have business and it seems like you don't, let's get to it."

Her smile was a mile wide. "Actually, I do. The other problem you have is that you don't have someone to help you with magic."

I laughed. "I suppose you have someone in mind who could help me." The words were hardly out of my mouth when I realized that she probably did. "You are not, absolutely not thinking of. . ." I couldn't bring myself to say it. So, she did.

"Right. I'm the obvious person to be your Personal Assistant. I've got oodles of magic. I know you pretty darn well." She leered suggestively at that. "AND, most importantly, I'm very willing to help."

I thought a moment. Maybe she didn't realize just how much help I'd need. So, I said, "Well, from past history, I probably need to post several letters a week. I occasionally need to travel by floo. On rare occasions, I need to disapparate. But here's the thing. I don't know when I'll need to do those things. I might go several days without needing anything, but then suddenly, I might need to do all of them. The times would be very irregular. You've got a day job. How could you be available at a moment's notice? I can't send you an owl or anything."

She was unmoved. She leaned in toward the desk, which was kind of comical. given that her feet didn't reach the floor and her arms barely reached the arms of the deep red leather chair. She said, "I thought you were sensible. Now you know that my boss would be very happy for me to make you my number one priority. Besides that, you know that would make me very happy, too."

"How could that possibly work?"

She smiled an incandescent smile, placed an index finger on her chin, and said, "You know. I didn't think of it till now, but I could stay here when I'm not working."

My mouth dropped and I exclaimed, "Whut!"

"Sure. It would be easy. I could sleep on your sofa. I'd take the floo to my apartment to change and shower before work. I could eat at the employee cafeteria in Gringotts. Maybe we could go out to dinner once in a while."

Again, I exclaimed, "Eek." I took a minute to consider my answer. "OK. First, I am not ever, ever, taking you out to dinner."

"Oh, I wasn't thinking of you taking me out. I would take you out."

"That's not happening either."

"Well, a girl had to try, didn't she?" She hurried on. "But there's nothing wrong with my staying here. You'd have your bedroom. I'd have mine."

"OK. I sometimes have students come in for office hours. You can't be here while I'm meeting students."

She frowned. "But I wouldn't be here until after the close of business. Surely you don't have evening office hours?"

"You're right. But, I do sometimes have fellow teachers drop by after hours."

"They're all adults aren't they?"

I grimaced. "What if I need to send an owl or something while you're at work."

Her easy smile told me that she'd thought about that. She said, "I have a little gift for you." She opened her purse. She took out what looked like a normal galleon. She held it up so that I could see it clearly and said, "Here's the thing. If you hold this galleon between your thumb and forefinger and squeeze, this ring." She held up her right hand. There was a ring with an emerald stone on her ring finger. "This ring will flash until I stop it. Go ahead. Try it."

I sighed. Then I took the galleon and squeezed it gently between my right thumb and forefinger. The emerald jewel flashed dully. "OK. You have proved your point. How does that work anyway? I'm not magical at all. How can I activate that thing?"

She smiled. "I can't claim credit for it. It was actually invented by the American Aurors. It uses an anti-muggle spell. It's very weak. When you, a

33

muggle, squeeze it, you create a magical force of. . . uh. . . reduction, reagent. . ."

I supplied the word from physics. "It's reaction. That activates the signal to my ring. OK. But this deal only lasts until I can find a different assistant."

She nodded and said, "Understood."

"Well, since you are here to help. I'm going to use you. I have a couple of letters that I want you to send. I don't have them written yet, but I'll do that right now."

She just nodded happily. I started composing my letters. One was to Rita Skeeter and the other was to Sissy. I wanted her to know that I'd not forgotten her. I didn't have much to tell her. I just didn't want her sitting around all day waiting for a letter that never came. It took me a while to write a draft of each and then the final version. All through it, Javeen was patient and quiet. After a while, she got up and perused my bookshelf. She finally pulled something off the bookshelf and returned to the sofa. After a while I couldn't resist the temptation to learn what she was reading. I asked, "What did you take off the shelf?"

She smiled shyly and said, "Come over here and I'll show you." Then she patted the spot on the sofa next to her.

This time, I smiled. "Not this time."

She just pouted a little pout. I finished the letters, addressed the envelopes, and sealed them. "Would you please send these off?"

She took them and said, "Nothing would give me more pleasure."

I watched her out the floo connection.

I thought that I'd seen the last of her for the night. I was wrong.

There was a commotion in the floo. I looked just in time to see Javeen walk into the room carrying what looked like an overnight bag.

The first thing that she said was, "Where can I put a couple of emergency outfits that I brought?"

I was terribly afraid to ask, but I screwed up my courage anyway to ask, "What is an emergency outfit?"

She stared at me as though I were a troll fresh from the hinterlands. Then she said, "Well, of course, I don't intend to keep my regular clothes here. I'll leave early in the morning to go to my apartment where I can wash, change, and get ready for work. BUT, you know, sometimes emergencies come up, and your outfit is unpresentable. Then, you have to have a backup. And, of course, you have to have more than one because you never know what color shoes you'll be wearing when emergencies arise."

It seemed almost sensible the way she said it. So, I said, "All right, but just two outfits, and you have to hang them on the back of the door into the loo from the office." She accepted that. Then I said that I'd get sheets and blankets so she could sleep on the sofa. I turned to get them from my apartment when another thought occurred to me. I gritted my teeth as I made the offer. "I think I'd rather that you not keep them in the loo. Sometimes, guests, including students, use it. I suppose that I have to offer you a corner of my closet."

Her face lit up. She tried to suppress the smile that had appeared on her face, but I couldn't help noticing. The awful thing was that I couldn't think of an alternative. I invited her to bring her outfits into my apartment. She entered and slowly turned, taking in the entire room. Now, she couldn't suppress the smile. She said, "You know, I've never been here before." I tried to encourage her to bring her outfits to the closet, but she ignored me. She walked slowly around, examining my dresser, the small writing table that I kept in a corner, and especially, the tall mirror that I'd hung near the closet. She glanced at a notebook on the writing table that was left open.

She asked, "What are you writing? And, why not do your writing at you desk in your office?"

I said, "Not that it's any of your business, but I do some recreational writing—little accounts of things that happen to me. I like to use the office purely for school business."

She asked, "What about Gringotts business? Where do you work on that?"

"In the office. It's all business there."

She turned her head a little away from me and shyly asked, "Do you ever write about me?"

I had had enough of this snooping. I answered curtly, "If I ever publish any of it, you're welcome to buy a book and read for yourself."

She walked back to the writing table and looked at the page of the notebook that exposed. Fortunately, I'd just started the page. I didn't think she'd have the temerity to pick it up. I was wrong. I rushed over and closed my hand over the notebook. I said, "I never allow anyone to see my unfinished works." I couldn't avoid covering one of her hands with mine. She smiled the little, shy smile again. Then she released the notebook and continued her tour of the room.

She commented, "Oooh. I really like this. It would be ideal when I have to change here." Then her attention turned to the bed. "That's a queen size, isn't it? What tales could it tell if it could speak?"

I took that as a rhetorical question and tried to ignore it. You'd think she were viewing an apartment that she was considering renting. I closed my eyes, trying to pretend that she wasn't there, but she interrupted me by asking, "Aren't you going to show me where I can hang my outfits?"

All I could do was to open the door to the walk-in closet. I moved some of my clothes aside to make room for hers. She said, "You have lots of room that you don't use. Couldn't I bring a couple of more outfits?"

I said, "No. Let's go. I've still got grading to do."

She asked, "How will we regulate use of the loo?"

At last, I had a question that I could answer! "Here's the way it will work. The loo has two doors both with locks on the inside. Whoever is using it will lock both doors. When finished, she will unlock both doors. Easy-peasy."

She suggested that we needed a schedule in the morning for use of the loo. "I have to get up very early for work. I suggest that I get to use it first in the morning. I should be finished by 6:30. You can use it then. Does that interfere with the breakfast schedule in the Great Hall?"

I said grudgingly, "No. I suppose not." The truth was that I frequently wasn't even awake before seven. I then got the bed linen out of the closet and walked us into my office. I dropped them on the sofa and asked her to wait until I'd retired for the night to make her bed. I added, "I expect you to unmake your bed every morning before you leave for work."

She smiled that little smile that was becoming ever more irritating to me and asked, "Do I take the bed linen back to your closet before I leave?"

"No. Just put it behind my desk."

Again, that smile showed up, "Aren't you afraid that visitors will wonder what it's for?"

I almost snapped. "Visitors must surmise what they will surmise. That's my worry."

She went back to the sofa and sat. She had brought a copy of the *Prophet* with her. She started reading it. I said, "In case you get bored with the *Prophet* you can always read the current issue of *The Times* which I keep on the bookshelf or the *Scientific American*.

She replied, "I will when I'm interested in fantasy."

That was the end of our conversation for the evening, except for exchanges of "Good Night" when I went to bed.

The next morning, I could have thought the whole incident with Javeen was part of a bad dream except for one thing. That was the pile of neatly folded bed linen and blankets behind my desk. Everything else was as neat as a pin.

At breakfast, I was interrupted by an owl. The strange thing was that I had a cup of yogurt on my plate, but the owl missed it. Instead the letter landed on the table beside my plate. I was about to open it but decided instead to finish breakfast. I'd open it in my office. When I arrived, I immediately opened the envelope and discovered a letter from Rita Skeeter. It simply said,

Professor Wendt,

Let's meet for lunch next Thursday at noon. I suggest the Three Broomsticks. If the time/place is acceptable, you needn't respond. That should make it easy for you. I must admit that I have a certain amount of anxiety concerning what you might ask.

Yours, RS

I immediately wrote a note to Sissy, asking her if the time/place was acceptable for a meeting with Rita Skeeter. I addressed an envelope and felt that I might not have a made a huge mistake in accepting Javeen's offer. There would be a lot of letters going out, not to mention travel.

I wrote a note to Slughorn, asking if I could have a meeting with him in the next day or two. I left it with Sally, his personal assistant. She greeted me as though she'd not seen me in years. I guess that was not so far off the mark. She said, "I wish he were here right now, but he's filling in for the potions professor who has a case of the spatter goit. He should be back later this morning if you'd like to wait."

"No, that's all right. Later is fine."

She asked, "How are you doing? I know you were pretty depressed when you returned from wherever you were."

I shrugged and said, "It was tough being back after such a long break. It was a break with lots of changes including a break-up with my girl friend."

She shook her head sadly and asked, "Who was your girl friend?"

I shook my head too.

Later that evening after dinner, Javeen popped into the hearth in my office. I smiled despite myself. I could send her off on a mission. I handed her the envelope. It made her happy to be doing me a favor. It made me happy that she'd be away even though I knew she would be back later. By the time she got back I'd already gone to bed. I left a note on the sofa for her, saying that I'd already gone to bed.

The next morning, Sally dropped by my first class with a note. I was about to call the class to order, so I just stuffed it into an inside pocket of my robes. After the class was over, a student came up to ask a question about the next test. I had forgotten about the note almost until my next class started. When I did remember, I hurriedly pulled it out of my robes and opened it quickly. I swore to myself when I saw that it was from Slughorn. He wanted me to meet him during the free period that I had at 11 AM.

Just before eleven, I entered Slughorn's office. Sally greeted me but asked me to wait in the outer office until Slughorn arrived from his substitute class. He bustled in, not noticing me. He walked directly to Sally. He asked her, "For goodness sake, find me someone to substitute for me in at least a few classes. Isn't there someone?"

She shrugged. "I'm trying hard to find someone." She hesitated, glancing down at her desk. She looked didn't look up and almost whispered as she said, "There is someone."

Slughorn just continued his harangue. "There's got to be someone. Say, can't we try to steal the potions instructor from Beaux Batons?"

Sally just sighed. "I've tried. I've even sent an owl to a couple of the American schools. Nobody is willing to give up anyone. Sorry. But there might be someone here."

Slughorn seemed to hear that for the first time. "Here! How's that possible? I thought you checked with everyone here in England."

Sally looked him directly in the eye and said in a dangerous, determined voice, "I'd didn't mean in England. I meant here in Hogwarts."

Slughorn finally seemed to hear. He took a step back and asked, "What? How can there be someone here?"

She shook her head in confusion and said, "How can you have forgotten about your co-author?"

His mouth dropped open. His eyes moved about the room as though there were someone else who could help him. In the process he noticed me. He asked me, "Would you hire Dursley as an instructor?"

I shrugged. "I don't know anything about his qualification as a teacher. But surely he is as knowledgeable about potions as anyone with the possible exception of you yourself."

He looked around the room, I suppose looking for someone who would have a minority report to offer. Of course, there was no one. He raised his eyeballs and said, "I suppose that I don't have that many options. I can either spend all my time teaching potions and give up being the Headmaster. . ." With that, he turned to me and asked, "What about you? Would you be interested in being Headmaster?"

It was a measure of his desperation that he would even suggest that jokingly. After all, I was a Muggle, but this didn't seem to be a joke. I could only chuckle and compliment him on his sense of humor in such dire straits that he would make such an offer.

He nodded in resignation and turned back to Sally. "Go ahead and make an appointment with Dursley for an interview. The way my luck is going, he'll turn me down. Then what will I do? Offer the post to Filch?" With that thought he shuddered and turned back to me. "I suppose you still want to meet with me even though I have scrolls to grade coming out of my ears not to mention experiments to set up for both my afternoon double classes."

I smiled shyly. "I'm afraid so."

Then come in my office. Once we were in and seated around his desk, he asked, "What is it that you want from me?"

I said, "I've got a favor I want. Do you still have good contacts at the *Prophet?*"

Slughorn grimaced. "Yes, I do—the Chief Editor. I can always get a letter to the editor published whenever I want."

I smiled. "Good. I'd like to get a change in the editorial policy of the paper."

Slughorn shook his head. "You don't want much. I guess I owe you a good-sized favor. I can only try. What is it that you want?"

I tried to sound casual. "Oh, nothing big. I'd like the *Prophet* to add a small column to the sports page."

Slughorn scoffed. "Oh, nothing big. Just a new column. Do you have any idea what's the most popular section of *the Prophet?*" He didn't hesitate to let me give the obvious answer. "It's the Sports Section."

I shrugged. "I'm not asking you to guarantee there will be a new column. Just get me an introduction and a recommendation."

Slughorn growled. "OK. I can do that. Just what kind of column do you want them to add? Backalley Bridge?"

"No. Nothing like that. Just a Chess column."

Slughorn just shook his head. "No problem. I'll send Ponsonby an owl of introduction. He'll be happy to see you. Just one thing—I'm not telling him what you want. You're on your own there."

"Sure. I can't ask for more. That's all that I wanted. I really am thankful to you."

Slughorn said, "Just why do you want to have a chess column in the *Prophet?* That doesn't have anything to do with your protégé Diggory?"

I wished that I could ask for something hard to drink, but I had classes left in the afternoon and sure didn't want to go into them with alcohol on my breath. Slughorn seemed to sense that I might want a drink. He opened his mouth and asked, "Was there something that I could offer you to. . . uh. . . drink." He quickly added, "You know—tea, water, butter beer?"

I shook my head. "No. It isn't really about Cedric. You probably don't realize it, but there's another Hogwarts student that IS a really good chess player. That is, she was until this year. She was graduated in the spring."

Slughorn wrinkled his brow trying to deduce about whom I was talking. I saved him the effort by telling him. "Cecily Brewster is the student that I'm talking about. She's developed over the last couple of years into a very strong player. As a matter of fact, she just reached the International Master level. That makes her a legitimate contender for the world championship. I want to help her continue her drive for that goal."

Slughorn asked, "How in the world would having a chess column help her develop her chess?"

"You're used to sports like Quidditch. The good players earn lots of galleons by playing well. They also get sponsorship from companies that use their names for advertising. Chess is not in that class. Even if you win tournaments, you can't afford to just study chess and play. Popularizing chess would make it easier for her to get some sponsors."

Slughorn nodded and seemed satisfied. I got up to go. I'd reached the door when Slughorn hesitantly said, "Uh, one last thing. Have a seat."

I did. He sat for a moment with his eyes closed and pursed his lips. That motionless state continued for several minutes. Then he opened his eyes with a satisfied look on his face. "Yes." He closed his eyes for a mo-ment again and then continued, "You know, there's a little favor that you could do for me. The more I think about the idea of having Dursley as a long-term substitute for the potions class, the more I begin to think that it's not that bad an idea."

I simply said, "I agree."

"Then you wouldn't mind sitting in on an interview with him?"

I tried to evaluate if there were any problem with the idea. I didn't see one, so I said, "Oh, as a favor to you, I wouldn't mind sitting in. I don't know what good that would do you, but. . ."

He quickly supplied something. "You know that we always have two interviewers present when we meet with a job candidate."

"Of course, but I thought it was usually the Headmaster and either the Assistant Headmaster or a subject matter expert teacher."

Slughorn agreed but added, "There's a problem with the Assistant Headmaster sitting in on the interview. I hired him recently and don't have a good feel for his sense of judgment of teaching skills. Besides that, there isn't a subject matter expert available on potions. In that case, I choose an experienced teacher who can help judge the teaching skills of the candidate."

I was dumbfounded. "Look. I have a fair amount of experience teaching, but I'm sure not a wizard and I don't have any knowledge of potions."

Slughorn chuckled. "Potions is almost a Muggle subject. You use a cookbook and very little magic in brewing potions." He paused and laughed, "You could teach potions, you know. As a matter of fact, I'd ask you to do it if it weren't even harder to find an English lit substitute than a potions substitute."

"Well, I'm glad I'm not a candidate for that position. Oh, I suppose that I could sit in on the interview. Just remember that I'm prejudiced in favor of Dursley."

Slughorn shook a finger at me with a good-natured smile. "You know that I'm perhaps even more prejudiced toward him than you are. You know our book sales have been trending up, and we're making a pretty penny now. As a matter of fact, if I'd be very tempted to retire if it weren't that I feel a certain duty to Hogwarts. I don't know why Dursley doesn't leave off being an apprentice janitor for something better. Heck, even for nothing. He could live quite comfortably from the sales of our book."

I was ready to head for lunch. I got up to go, half expecting to be interrupted again. I wasn't. "Do you want to go down for lunch?"

"Oh, no. I've go to do some real Headmastering. I'm doing a working lunch." He went out with me to the outer office where he asked Sally to get him something to eat and bring it up to the office. So, Sally accompanied me down.

The Prophet

Slughorn had more influence than I expected. The next day I found an owl waiting for me in my office when I arrived there for office hours. It was perched outside my office. I opened the door and invited the owl in. It flapped up onto the red leather chair. I sat on the edge of my table facing the owl. It extended it's talon forward and let me untie the message. It was simple. It was from Ponsonby. He wanted to know if I'd meet with him, the next day for lunch at the *Prophet* offices at noon. I rapidly wrote a letter to Ponsonby accepting the invitation. I then wrote a swift note to Sissy, asking her if she could come to lunch. If so, she should come to my office by 11:30 AM.

I addressed envelopes and decided that I'd wait for the faithful Javeen to put them in the mail. I wasn't easy about waiting that long, but I felt pretty confident that she'd show up.

She did. I had the two letters in her hand almost before she'd gotten out of the hearth. I plead, "Would you please get these in the mail as quickly as you can?"

She nodded slowly and asked, "Would you mind telling me what this is all about? The editor of the *Prophet* and Cecily Brewster seem an unlikely pair of people to be getting letters. Hmmm." You know it might make a difference to how quickly I get this mail off if I thought I would know why?"

I wasn't really surprised at the request. It wasn't really confidential information even though I wasn't anxious to let it become known generally. So, I replied, "Sure. There's no reason you shouldn't know. "

She smiled radiantly, "Wonderful. You always seem to be involved with interesting things. I'm glad that you're going to share with me." With that, she winked at me and immediately turned to leave via the floo connection. She was back amazingly quickly. Her first question was, "How about a drink?"

"Sure." It gave me a couple of minutes to think through what I'd say. I definitely was not going to give her any of my great Blue Label. I got the Jameson out, which Jaimie apparently liked. I had to admit that it was pretty good. Javeen hurried the process along by cleaning out the glasses and loading them with ice. All I had to do was pour. She took a sip and smiled in appreciation.

Then she said, "Now, give!" She was sitting on the sofa and said, "And join me while you're at it."

I dragged one of my yellow guest chairs over next to the sofa and sat. She frowned. She asked, "Afraid I'm going to bite?"

"Yes. On to your question. It's really straight-forward. One of my former students has become a rather good chess player. As a matter of fact, she's in the top tier of players in the world."

Javeen asked, "So?"

"Well, some publicity would be useful for her. I'm trying to get the *Prophet* to give her and chess in general some coverage. Right now, I think that most people think that chess is just a game for children."

Javeen nodded slowly and asked, "She's a former student. So, she's graduated?"

"Sure."

"Then, she's an adult?"

I didn't like where this was going, but I kept on with it. "Yes," I said with gritted teeth.

She smiled. "I thought so. Is she a romantic interest? Is that why you are helping her career?"

I controlled my emotions and said as calmly as I could manage, "No. I hardly know her. I met her about four years ago. She was never in one of my classes. The last three years I've been away—as you know very well. She just reminds me of Cedric. She had a lot of chess talent when I met her. She's apparently developed it well—on her own. I kind of think of her as the person that Cedric would have become had he lived. So, I want to help her when I can."

Javeen took a sip and chewed on that idea for a minute. Then she said, "So, what are you doing with the *Prophet*?"

"I was invited to lunch tomorrow by the editor. I'm going to try to get him to run a chess column in the paper."

She smiled broadly. "And, of course, you need someone to get you to the meeting. That would be just perfect for me—to help you."

"Well, I'm counting on Cecily to give me a lift there."

Javeen nodded knowingly. "How convenient." Apparently, she wasn't buying that I was just being a mentor.

I went on. "Besides that, you've got to work, don't you? You can't be running off to take me places."

Her eyes glistened. "I'd like to take you places that you've not been, and I've got permission to take some time off to help you."

I grimaced. Of course, she did. Her boss, her father, was still hoping for some sort of liaison that would help him keep me as a consultant and board member for Gringotts.

She asked, "When is your meeting?"

I decided that I'd not hear from Cecily before sometime tomorrow morning at best. I probably did need backup transportation. "Tomorrow at noon for lunch. It would be nice if you could drop by around 11:45 in case Cecily can't make it, but you are not going if she's here to take me."

Javeen shook her head negatively and clucked her tongue. I got up and said, "I've got some lesson planning to do." She opened her traveling bag and took out a copy of *Witch Weekly*. I asked, "Do you actually read that thing?"

She shrugged. "Sure. I like keeping up with fashion."

□

The next morning, I had too many classes to worry about the upcoming meeting, but at eleven, I finished my last class of the morning. I went to my office to do some last minute planning of the upcoming meeting. For that kind of serious thinking, I kept a yellow legal pad in my desk.

As I was making notes, there was a flapping sound from the direction of the window. I looked up to find an owl at my window. I opened it. The owl seemed to be in a hurry. It was holding a small scrap of parchment in its beak. I took it. It hardly had released the message before it flew off. "OK. No treat for it you," I thought. The note was from Sissy. She couldn't come with me. She was very sorry. I went back to my desk to await the inevitable. It came quickly. There was a whoosh from the hearth. Javeen stepped out.

She read my face perfectly. "I see that your Cecily can't help you. Very well. I suggest that we disapparate right away."

"Sure. Let me put my jacket on." I usually wore jeans and a dress shirt under my robes when I was teaching. I had a sports jacket that I added to the ensemble while taking off the robes for more formal occasions. I walked over to the floo connection where Javeen took my outstretched hand in both her hands. We stood there motionless for a moment. I started to say something, but she anticipated me. "Sorry. I was thinking dissapparation." She then dropped one of her hands to the pot of floo powder. She casually threw it down, saying, "*The Prophet* publishing office Reception Area." She then took my hand in that hand again as we materialized in the *Prophet* building. I'd been there several years before, but I hardly remembered it.

We went inside to find that the editor was waiting for us. He said, "Let's go out to my favorite restaurant for lunch." No one complained. It turned out that his favorite restaurant was a diner in a suburb. He gave us the name. Javeen had some trouble disapparating us there. As a matter of fact, we took two wrong disapparations before she got it right. She took my hand with both hers all three times.

We finally arrived. Ponsonby asked how we'd taken so long. I just shook my head in resignation. Amazingly the place didn't have a hearth, but it was a wizarding restaurant. There were a variety of witches, wizards, and even a few goblins eating there. It was a seat yourself establishment. We took a booth. After we'd ordered,. Ponsoby came to the point. "I have two questions. First, Slughorn says that you want a big favor from me. What is it? Second, why is the yard gnome along?"

I could feel Javeen's anger, and I couldn't blame her. I said, "First, her name is Javeen. She's the personal assistant to the CEO of Gringotts."

Ponsonby quickly said, "Sorry. I didn't realize that you represented one of our advertisers."

Javeen's reply was icy. "No offense taken."

Ponsonby didn't seem to notice the irony. I said, "Well, the answer to the first question is that I want you to add a sport to your coverage."

He asked, "What in the world do you want? We already cover the main wizard sports—Quidditch, of course, broom racing, carpet racing." He quickly noted that carpet racing didn't happen in England but that overseas where it was legal it was quite popular." He laughed and added, "We even cover major Muggle sports like football, cricket, and even rugby. What's left?"

I said, "Well, there's. . ."

I didn't get to elaborate because our food arrived. Ponsonby's expression turned to one of joy and he said, "Ahhhh!" We couldn't go on until he'd sampled his banger. When he was finally ready, he took over the conversation again, asking, "You're surely not thinking of a Muggle sport like contract bridge?"

I was about to object that contract bridge was not a professional sport when he corrected himself. "Oh, yes. I meant. . . what is it. . . replicant bridge?"

I muttered to myself, "Duplicate.." Then I went on. "I want chess."

Ponsonby stared in puzzlement, "You don't mean the children's game, wizard chess?"

"No, I mean the professional sport, chess."

He considered a minute as he continued absentmindedly on the bangers and spuds. "All right. As a favor to Slughorn and the little lady. . ." He interrupted himself with laughter and said, "No pun intended." He continued laughing.

I noticed Javeen start to raise a hand. I immediately smothered it with my hand and gave my head a slight negative shake. I whispered, "Talk later." Her hand relaxed and slipped around to caress my palm briefly. Ponsonby was still laughing at his joke.

Javeen said, "None taken."

By that time Ponsonby appeared to have forgotten his comment. He just said, "Whut?"

I just smiled at him and hoped that Javeen was as well. Ponsonby said, "How many column inches do you want?"

I said, "One column for the height of the page."

He whistled and said, "One column for half page height."

I grumbled but agreed. He went on. "We'll run a column whenever there's solid chess news—whatever that is."

I countered, "OK, but we get an article in the Sunday supplement. I'd suggest a profile of first tier chess players, starting with major wizard chess players. Also, the columnist gets to decide what is major chess news."

Ponsonby shook his head. "You expect me to give up editorial decisions to a columnist? Who would I have that could be chess columnist anyway?"

I'm sure it was a rhetorical question, but I took it as a real question. I said, "I have someone in mind."

"So, now you're assigning reporters, too?"

I tried to be modest when I said, "I have someone who owes me a little favor."

"You are crazy. Who is it?"

"Rita Skeeter."

He chuckled. "I suppose it would serve her right. She thinks she's the best thing since wands. Still, there's only so much that I can stand. What do you expect?"

I smiled. "I expect you to be fair." Javeen smiled and patted my hand.

Ponsonby asked, "You're picking up the tab?"

I laughed. "I always was."

He said, "Then, done and done. I've got to get back to the office. I'll let you handle things here with your little friend."

I gritted my teeth but managed to keep from screwing up our deal. The waiter came with the tab. Both Javeen and I reached for it, and we both seized it. I said, "I told Ponsonby that I had it."

Javeen smiled. "I don't care. I've got lots of money."

"So, do I."

Javeen said, "I've got a credit card."

"So, do I."

She put her other hand over mine and said, "Wouldn't you really prefer to let me pick it up."

It was a temptation, but I said, "No. AND, I've got to get back to school for my next class." I paid for lunch. We went outside and disapparated to the Three Broomsticks and then took the floo to my office.

□□

I didn't even mention to Javeen that I had lunch the next day with Skeeter. I had to have Sissy along for the meeting, so she might as well take me there.

I was back in my office about a half hour before noon. This time, I didn't have to plan quite so carefully. Skeeter owed me or at least ought to. Sissy arrived shortly after. She materialized in the floo connection and strode up to me with her right hand extended. We shook. She asked, "Ready to go?"

"We should wait a bit. I don't want us to seem too anxious. Actually, I'd like to arrive just at noon."

Sissy smiled. "OOOkay. This should be interesting. It reminds me a bit of some chess players that I know. They push you right to the edge with constant pressure."

I chuckled. "Believe me, she is cool as an iceberg."

By this time, I was ready. "OK. It's time to go. Take us to the Cauldron." I held out to my hand. She took it firmly, threw some floo powder down, and sent us tumbling through the ether to land in the hearth of the Cauldron. I glanced around and saw Rita sitting at a table in the corner. We went over and joined her.

She smiled a wan smile and stood. "Well, this must be your Ms. Brewster. Congratulations on your recent victory."

I was pleasantly surprised that Rita had done her research. "Well, it's good to see you as well."

She laughed. "It has been a while since I last saw you. What have you been up to?"

I smiled, "Doing nothing useful. But right now, I am doing something useful. I have a favor to ask."

47

Just then, a waitress dropped by our table and took our orders. Rita and I had eaten lunch here so often that we gave her our orders immediately. Sissy pondered over the menu. She half-way placed an order and then finally decided on fish and chips.

After the waitress left, I answered Rita's question. "The reason that we're meeting has to do with Sissy's occupation. She plays chess."

Rita, who was always quick on the uptake, said, "You want me to write articles about her career."

I nodded.

"There's just one problem. I don't assign stories to myself. You'd have to talk to my boss."

I smiled. She said, "You did, didn't you? What did old Ponderous Ponsonby have to say?"

"He said that you were going to write a regular column in the sports pages on chess."

She laughed. "I don't know anything about chess."

Sissy said, "When have you ever let that stand in your way?"

Rita's mouth dropped open. "Where did you get that? Have you been channeling Wendt?"

Sissy said, "My dad never liked you much. When you took Riddle's side after the death of Dumbledore, he could have wrung your neck."

Rita's mouth fell. She mumbled, "Yeh, There were a lot of people like that." Then she said, "OK. I owe you guys. I guess I owe both of you."

I said, "You have the greatest reference in the world to help you write stories. She'll provide great analysis of games." Then I added, "Oh, yes. Besides writing daily columns, you're to write pieces for the Sunday supplement. They're to be profiles of great chess players."

Rita nodded resignedly. "I suppose the first will be a profile of Cecily."

I shook my head. "No, the first will be one of Cedric Diggory."

"Oh, yes. He was one of your students. Died in the maze of the '95 Tri-Wizard Tournament."

Our food arrived. We ate in silence. There was nothing much more to say. As we finished, Sissy and Rita were setting up a schedule for getting together to consult on ideas for articles. I picked up the tab. Sissy took me back to my office.

The meeting had been very draining. I steeled myself to face my afternoon classes. I could really see why Slughorn was anxious to get out of teaching as soon as possible.

Potions

Sally left a note in my pigeonhole on Friday. I was to meet Slughorn in the potions classroom at 1 PM Saturday afternoon. Friday evening, when Javeen arrived after work, she had her arms crossed. She walked over to the red leather chair, sat, and glared at me. Then she said, "Are you ever going to do anything about the report you owe us for the next board meeting?"

I answered, "You know that I've been up to here with work this week. I haven't forgotten it." I didn't say what I was thinking—that I hadn't had any ideas yet.

She was determined to force me to think about it. She said, "OK. But you surely have been thinking about it. What have you got?"

I buried my face in my hands. What did I have? How do you track money. It's easy—sort of—when you're dealing with electronic transfers. How did you track cash whether specie or paper? Finally, I said, "I just don't have anything right now. Give me some time over the weekend and I'll come up with something." I hoped.

Javeen's expression softened. She said, "Sure. It's all right." She stood and walked around my desk. She laid a hand on my shoulder and said, "Why don't we have a drink and you can relax." I sighed and agreed. She had glasses out and ice cubes in them before I'd gotten a bottle of Jameson out. Javeen took the bottle from me and poured a couple of very stiff shots. We both raised them to our lips and drank.

Javeen said, "Why don't you just sit down over here," as she took one of my arms and guided me over to the sofa. I sat and took another sip. She walked around to the other side of the sofa and massaged the back of my neck. "You just need to close your eyes and let me loosen up those tight muscles back here.

I did. The rhythmic kneading of my neck did work a sort of magic. I let my eyelids droop. Javeen said, "Just let me take this drink. I think you've probably had enough tonight." I heard the clink of ice against glass as she set the glass on the coffee table. My eyes were closed, and I felt her slip into my lap and sort of snuggle down with a hand on my shoulder and her cheek, warm against my chest. She said, "Now isn't this just so snuggly that you just want to lay down and share this warm blanket with me? I fuzzily realized that somehow she'd gotten the blanket and spread it over us. I sort of drifted off to sleep.

Later I woke and found that Javeen was awake, resting on my arm, gazing at my face. She said, "You look so rested here, sleeping in my arms."

"Perhaps. I have to get to my bed. I never sleep well out of my bed."

She stretched, got up, and said, "I suppose you're right. Off you go."

I dragged off to bed wishing that I'd not let her coax me onto the sofa. Nothing had happened—exactly.

□

I slept in late. That is, I would have except that there was a knock on my door at 7:45 AM. I shouted out, "Go back to bed!"

It was too late. I struggled out of bed and fumbled my way to the loo. The door was locked! Of course, it was locked. What else could it be. After an endless interval, Javeen's voice trilled, "The loo's all yours." I went in and took a quick shower that was cool. She'd taken all the hot water. I dressed and entered my office.

Javeen looked like a cat I'd once had. Every now and then it caught a chipmunk or bird and carried it to the back door of our house. It was as proud as punch. Javeen smiled radiantly and said, "I wanted to make sure that you didn't miss breakfast. A good breakfast is the start of a good day."

I squinted at her and wished I had the "evil eye." She was totally oblivious to the "eye". In the Great Hall, there was the usual scattering of students and teachers for breakfast on weekends. However, Professor Slughorn was there. He had apparently finished breakfast and was waiting for me. He came to a seat next to me and asked how I'd slept. I answered, "So-so."

"Well, I wanted to talk to you about our meeting this afternoon. It's the job interview for Dursley. How do you see your role?"

I shrugged. "You'll lead. Introduce the duties of the position, the salary, the perks, and so on. We'll give him a chance to explain why he wants the job—if he wants it. He should describe the positives that he brings to the job. I'll ask relevant questions that might have been missed as

50

we go along."

Slughorn asked, "Don't you think we should ask him about his weaknesses?"

"No."

Slughorn stared at me in amazement. "Why not?"

"He'll reveal those as he talks about his positives. They'll tell us what he thinks are important and thus we'll find what he thinks is less important. Those are where his weaknesses lie. Now I don't say that we shouldn't ask him about the important things that he didn't cover. His answers will reveal his weaknesses. For example, suppose he doesn't say anything about how he handles discipline. We ask him how he intends to handle discipline. That will tell us a lot about that potential weakness."

"Slughorn just said "Oh. Then he added, "I wish I'd had you in interviews before. Let's meet in the potions Classroom about fifteen minutes before he's due to show up."

I agreed and we parted.

After lunch Dursley came up to my office. He knocked and entered before I'd invited him in. That didn't surprise me. We'd lived together for the better part of a term. He noticed the bed linen behind the sofa and noted it, "Well, Professor, it looks like you are always ready for a roomie—like when we were rooming together."

I had long ago honed the skill of answer questions without answering them. I said, "It looks that way doesn't it?"

He shook his head while staring at the floor. "I see you've not given up on the Socratic method or is it Platonic?"

I just smiled. Then he went on. "But I've not come to discuss your roommates. What is this meeting about this afternoon?"

Now was my turn to stare incredulously. "You don't know?"

He smiled and said, "You're not the only person who can use your techniques. Apparently not."

I frowned. "I guess Slughorn must use some of Dumbledore's ideas. He once recruited Slughorn to come back to teaching by showing up unannounced at Slughorn's. . . uh. . . vacation home to invite him to teach."

Dursley laughed. "I never really knew Dumbledore, but I hear that he could do the darnedest things. OK. That still doesn't explain what he wants from this meeting."

I hung my head sadly. I guessed that I'd have to spell it out. "Well, Slughorn is in a bind. His potions teacher is sick and likely won't be back to school before the next term. He wants help with the potions classes."

Dursley stared for a minute. Then he said, "I get it. He wants a lab assistant—somebody to help set up the lab for experiments. Maybe help with grading potions. I'm sure that Mr. Filch wouldn't mind my splitting my duties between potions and grounds maintenance."

I sighed. "That's a very reasonable idea, but that's not what he wants."

Dursley was stumped. "Well, what in the world does he want?"

"He wants you to teach the potions classes."

Dursley's mouth dropped open. Then he realized that had happened and he quickly snapped it shut. "Why would he want me to teach!"

"Oh, it's a series of unfortunate events. His potions teacher is sick."

"Why not just hire a potions instructor from some other school?"

I scoffed. "You have no idea how hard it is to find qualified potions teachers. None of the other magic schools of Europe or even the States wants to give up their instructor."

"What about potions masters working for companies?"

I shrugged, "I don't know. Why wouldn't potions masters in commerce jump at the chance of teaching squirmy 1st years? Or mischievous fifth years?"

Dursley grumbled a bit and said, "OK. You've answered my question." He thought a moment and asked, "What if I don't want to teach the squirmy 1st years either."

I smiled at the thought. "Just tell him 'NO.'"

"But he might fire me."

I actually laughed. "Oh, sorry. It's just too rich—the idea of his firing you. But, if you're worried, listen politely to whatever he has to say and then politely say, 'no.'"

He was still grumbling, "I wish you were going to be there."

I was genuinely surprised. "Didn't Slughorn tell you that I will be there?"

"No."

"Well, I am." I got up, walked to the door, opened it, and said, "See you in the potions Classroom." Dursley took the hint and left my office.

□□

I waited for the last minute to show up in the potions Classroom. Slughorn was there, apparently setting up an experiment at each of the workstations. He looked up and said, "Cutting it kind of close, aren't we?"

I shrugged. "I've done a lot of thinking about this. Are you ready?"

Just then, Dursley knocked on the door and entered upon invitation. He spoke with the innocence of a newborn. "What can I do for you, Professors?"

Slughorn invited him to sit. We all pulled lab stools up around the teacher's desk. Slughorn opened the conversation. "Let me tell you why I've asked you two here."

Dursley was attentive but showed no sign of anxiety. He said, "Yes, sir."

Slughorn went on. "You may not be aware of the fact that the usual potions professor is ill, and we really don't have a good idea of when he will return. I've been unable to find a substitute teacher for him. So, I've been filling in for all his classes. It's a deuced nuisance at best. It's keeping me from doing my duty as Headmaster."

Dursley smiled and asked, "How can I help?"

Slughorn stared down at the floor as though he'd just noticed a fifty galleon coin there. Then he took a deep breath and said, "I need you to. . . that is, I'd like you to. . ." He was stuck. He looked over at me and mouthed a word that I couldn't make out. I guessed that he wanted me to make the ask.

I did. "It's a little embarrassing for all of us, I think. Professor Slughorn would like you to take over the teaching duties of the potions classes until the regular professor returns."

Dursley could have been an actor in a different life. The surprise appeared as real as any that I'd seen. He appeared to have been struck speechless. I kept going through the routine since Slughorn seemed stuck for the moment. "Of course, you would have to be willing to teach and we'd have to do an interview to be sure that you meet our requirements as a teacher. This is the interview if you are interested."

Dursley drawled his answer out. "Well, I don't know. I'd certainly like to help you, but I've never done any teaching. I might just stand up in front of the class and freeze."

I thought to myself, 'If anyone knew you half as well as I did, they'd not believe for a moment that you'd freeze up in front of a class of fifth years."

Slughorn said, "We've had a lot of history together. You clearly know as much about potions as any teacher other than me. I'd like you to be our substitute teacher. You'd receive the same salary as I did when I was a rookey potions professor. That's about twice your current salary. Also, you'd get to use the potion professor's office and apartment. Why don't you tell us what strengths you have for teaching."

Dursley said, "Well, truthfully, I can't think of any that I have."

I asked, "What do you think about discipline?"

Dursley turned a little red and said, "Well, actually I was more of a discipline problem than having any solutions for discipline."

I asked, "Would you say that you really know your typical troublemaker?"

Dursley actually laughed. "You know, I once was a janitor at an inner-city school where there was a youth gang. They did all kinds of vandalism at the school. I did sort of shut them down."

I was surprised. "I had no idea that you had that sort of experience."

He turned a brighter shade of red and just nodded. He went on, "I have to tell you that I don't know anything about planning lessons or running a classroom."

Slughorn said, "Well, I could help you there. Maybe for a week or two, the two of us could team teach. You could watch me do lesson plans and start to do them yourself. Maybe I could learn something from you."

Dursley showed the first real excitement of the interview. He asked, "Would you really do that for me?"

"Of course, I would. Listen you don't have to make a final decision right now. We could do a trial period. If you wanted to continue on your own at the end of it—with plenty of advice and assistance from me, I think it could work out fine." He turned to me and asked, "You'd be willing to answer questions and help out, wouldn't you, Wendt?"

I guess I didn't have that much choice. I just smiled wanly and nodded.

Slughorn exclaimed, "Capital! We'll start on Monday. . . with your permission Mr. Dursley."

He agreed, but asked, "What about Mr. Filch? It seems like I'd be leaving him without help."

I frowned. "I'll help you break the news to him. He's clever. I'm sure he'll get along for a while without you."

As we left the classroom, Dursley asked me, "What do you say you, me, and Filch go out to do some serious drinking tonight and kind of sneak up on him with the news?"

I had to agree. "Sure. Invite him. Let's go to his favorite."

Dursley said, "That'd be the Leaky Cauldron."

"I thought so. Good. Bring him up to my office whenever you and he are ready. We'll take the floo connection from my office."

⊡
⊡⊡

I arrived back at my office. I found Javeen there. I said, "I thought you'd only be staying here school nights."

She smiled sweetly. "Why no. You might need my services any time. "

"Not tonight. I'm going out with the 'boys' tonight. Some are wizards. So, vamoose the ranch."

She frowned. "I'm not sure that's really a good idea."

"Good or not, you need to be gone before they start showing up here."

She was clearly unhappy about it, but she really didn't have much choice. She fired a parting shot though. "Well, if I'm not here, you've got to promise me to come up with an idea that we can implement for doing the money study. I'll expect that by the time I return Sunday night."

I thought, "Yeh. Sunday night—a school night." I said, "OK. I'll see what I can come up with, but I'm not making any promises."

Her frown turned to a smile, and she said, "That's all I ask." She stepped into the hearth and blew a kiss at me as she disappeared in a cloud of floo powder.

I thanked goodness. I had a couple of hours of uninterrupted time to catch up on sleep. I closed the drapes and tried to shut down all the conflicting thoughts in my head.

Suddenly, there was a pounding in my head. Or was it a pounding on a door somewhere? Yes. It was a door. I struggled up and made my way into the office just in time to see Dursley followed by Filch enter. Filch said, "How can you be sleeping when there's serious drinking to be happening!"

I said, "If you had to. . . oh, never mind. Let's just get on our way."

It was a tight squeeze getting all three of us in the floo at the same time, but where there's a will, there's a way. Filch had enough will for the three of us.

We bounced out of the Cauldron floo into a room that packed with Saturday night revelers. Filch rubbed his hands together and said, "Now this is something like the good old days."

In theory we were there for a meal accompanied by drinks. In reality, Filch was more than happy when Tom, the barman, informed us that there would be about a half hour wait for a table. We'd have to wait at the bar. Fortunately, there were more than three empty stools together where we could sit. I suggested that Filch order for all of us. That was dangerous, but it was also a sure way to get on Filch's good side.

Filch asked for separate tabs. I interrupted and insisted that there be only one tab—mine. That pleased Filch, of course, but I think he was fully expecting it. I did suggest that we rotate through different whiskeys. We ended up doing a variety including Jameson, Dewars, Johnnie Walker, and a few others that escaped my memory. By the time we were seated and our orders were delivered, I thought that Filch was sufficiently softened up so that we could bring up Dursley's new position.

Dursley had been furtively signaling me for a few minutes. I took the hint and broached THE topic. "Mr. Filch, don't you think that Mr. Dursley is a fine fellow?"

Filch assented. I then took the next baby step. "You know that he's a great potion-master."

Filch agreed. "Here's a toast to Dursley, the great. . . uh, potionerizer."

I nodded and we drank. Then I said, "You know, he's so good that he could teach the potions class. "

Filch said, "Sure! He could teach potions. He could teach any class!"

I went on. "As a matter of fact, he just might get to do that—at Hogwarts."

"Sure he might!" Filch enthused.

I said, "As a matter of fact, he's going to start this Monday."

"Sure he could start Monday!"

Then Dursley said softly, "I am going to start this Monday."

The table became deathly silent. Filch said, "You know, I thought you might just have said that you were going to start teaching on Monday, but that's not possible. . . . is it?"

I said, "Mr. Filch, he is starting on Monday."

Filch gave half a laugh and asked, "How can you do that and help me?"

Dursley said, "I don't think I can do both."

Filch didn't say anything. Then he sniffed and asked, "Do I have to call you professor?"

Dursley laughed. "You call me whatever you like."

Filch sat for several minutes in silence. Then he asked, "Am I still you loco parent?"

I couldn't tell whether Dursley was about to laugh or cry when he replied, "You are the most loco parent I've ever had."

Filch nodded and said, "Bloody right I am." Then he took a deep drink and said, "We need another round here if we're going to toast Dursley for his lateral promotion."

We'd passed the point of greatest dynamic stress. The rest of the evening was good. I don't know what time we got home, but I know we went via another wizard bar. Whether it was an accident or intended I couldn't say."

Cash is Not Fungible

I found myself in the Board Room of Gringotts Monday night because on Sunday evening, Javeen carried out her threat to return for the next school night. I knew we'd have to talk about my research project. The moment that she stepped into my office, her mouth was open to remind me of my promise.

I beat her to it. "I know you want me to tell you how I'm going to do the report for the Board Meeting. I've got an idea."

Her face lit up as though I'd just told her that I could increase the profit of Gringots by twenty percent.

I gave her the bad news. "Now, it's just an idea. I need some help on it."

Her smile deflated. "I guess I should have known it would not be easy. OK. What do you need?"

I invited her to sit on the red leather chair, but she tried to talk me into sitting with her on the sofa. I wasn't having any of it, but I did offer her a peace offering. "Let's have a Blue Label." She agreed graciously.

When we'd both gotten glasses with ice and Blue Label, I started. "OK. We're gong to have to exchange information. First, I'll give you some information. Then you reciprocate."

She happily agreed, and I began. "Muggles have dealt with this situation for thousands of years. The first reference that I'm aware of is in the Greek playwright Aristophanes' comedy, *The Frogs*. It has a name—Gresham's Law. Gresham lived in the 1500's."

She interrupted gently. "The history is interesting, but what does the law say?"

Basically, it says that bad money drives out good."

She cooed, "Really. It sounds like a war over money."

It occurred to me that she would think that kind of war fascinating. I was almost sad to disappoint her, but I did. "Well, what it really means is that if you have two kinds of coins of the same nominal value, people will hoard the ones that are made of the more valuable material. In the nineteenth century, silver coins came to dominate in the US and gold coins were hoarded."

Javeen said, "But that doesn't happen with silver sickles and gold galleons."

"You're right. It only works when the two different kinds of coins have the same denomination. That isn't the case with sickles and galleons."

She nodded and gazed up into my eyes as though I knew the secrets of the universe. I continued. "Now with gold galleons and paper galleons, you would think that gold galleons would disappear in the vaults of your clients and everyone would use paper."

She nodded and complained, "But we don't know if that's happening."

"Right. The thing is that it's hard to tell because nearly everyone uses vaults. They move money in and out without you goblins knowing whether they move gold or paper or a mixture in and out."

She frowned. "You're telling me that you Muggles know that?"

"Sure. Our banks keep complete track of what kind of money goes into and out of our banks."

She seemed frustrated. She asked, "You don't mean to tell me that Muggles put up with that kind of intrusion in their private business?"

I shrugged. "I'm afraid so. There are advantages to it."

She squeezed out of her mouth, "I can't believe. . . Oh well." Then she asked, "What's your idea?"

I shook my head. "First, I need some information from you."

She smiled again and said, "Anything YOU want."

"Right. Well, first explain to me the details of how your credit cards work."

She stared at me. "What in the world does credit have to do with coins and paper money? And I thought you invented credit cards—at least for Gringotts."

I answered, "Just humor me and an answer will appear. I hope."

She shrugged and said some gobbledy-gook word. Most of the time I'm happy that I don't speak gobbledy-gook. Anyway, she continued in English, "It's pretty simple. A witch buys something and pays for it with a credit card. The seller makes out a receipt and an impression is made of the credit card. The seller periodically takes those to Gringotts and we give her the money in exchange for the receipt. Big deal. So what?"

"All right. Where does the money that you give her come from?"

That puzzled her momentarily. Then she slapped her forehead. "Of course, we have a fund that we use. We started out with a little seed money, but it quickly got paid back from fees that retailers pay for the privilege of using our service.

"On a monthly basis we bill customers for the charges they made. Most of the money in the fund comes from those charges."

I asked her, "What happens when wizards buy from other wizards?"

"What do you mean?"

I answered, "I mean do wizard merchants charge in galleons?"

She scoffed. "Of course, they do."

"What about when wizards purchase from Muggle merchants with credit?"

She shrugged. "They get charged in whatever currency the merchant uses—pounds, US Dollars, French Francs, and so on. In practice, Barclay's converts the Muggle currency to galleons, sickles, etc. They pass that along to us, and we collect from the wizards. Then we pay Barclay's in pounds and sometimes in galleons."

This was becoming interesting. "Why would you ever have to pay Barclay's in galleons?"

That stumped her for a while. Then she waved her hand like a student who has the answer to a particularly difficult question. "OOOh! I know. Sometimes Muggles buy from wizard retailers."

I nodded. "I knew that happened. I just wasn't sure. Thanks."

She smiled a radiant smile and told me that she was always happy to be helpful to me. She went on. "Now, what's your idea?"

"Please give me a few minutes to think through this. Also, would you like some more Blue Label?"

She nodded enthusiastically. I added to her glass and some to mine. Then I began. "There's a phrase that is used some in accounting circles—fungible. Money is not normally fungible. That is, you can't trace its use. Once money is deposited in an account, you can't say that money was used for any particular purpose if the account is used for several purposes. That's your problem with the tracing the use of coins and paper money."

Javeen grumbled, "So, we're SOL?"

"I don't think so. Your settlement account. . ."

She asked, "What?"

"The account from which you pay merchants and your customers pay you is a real vault, right?"

"Yes. So"

"It has whatever cash that your customers use to pay you, right?"

The light bulb seemed to go off in her head. She spoke slowly, working through the implications of that. "Then, we could just count up the coins

59

and paper money in that and get an idea, right?"

"Yes, since there's no reason to think that customers would pay you differently than they pay businesses directly, that should be a pretty good measure of how money is used."

She seemed deep in concentration for a bit and then said, "Of course, some of the time our customers just ask us to take money directly from their vaults, rather than coming in to pay themselves." She smiled craftily, "You always trusted us."

I smiled too. "You—that is Gringotts—are trustworthy."

She went on. "Most people, especially wizards, don't trust us completely. They pay those monthly bills themselves."

As she was thinking, other possibilities occurred to me. "There are other accounts like that."

Javeen said, "Well, I can think of at least one. Barclay's has an account like our settlement account. It has coins and paper money in it."

I said, "Good. We need to get them to report on the ratio of coin and paper in their account."

Javeen looked toward her left and seemed deep in thought. After a while she said, "I've got to do some research on that. I'll do it tomorrow at work. Have you got anything on tomorrow night?"

I shrugged. "No. Just the usual."

"Good. Be prepared to go to Gringotts tomorrow night for a meeting to explain what you just told me."

I wasn't happy about that, but what could I do? "Sure, I'll try to organize my thoughts more for a presentation."

She tried to coax me onto the sofa, but I demurred. After all, I had to do some lesson planning tonight that I would have done tomorrow night. Of course, maybe I'd really luck out and not have to go to Gringotts tomorrow night.

□

I couldn't really enjoy dinner Monday night. I was just sure to the bottom of my being that I would be traveling to Gringotts shortly after I finished my meal.

I was not disappointed. That is, if you mean by disappointment not getting what you expect even if it's not really what you want. Javeen showed up about an hour after I arrived at my office. It was just long enough that I'd begun to hope that I'd have a night off.

She whooshed into the office from the floo. She held out her hand toward me even before she'd completely cleared the hearth. "Hurry, we've not got a lot of time." That didn't encourage me, but I'd signed on for it, so I got up from my desk chair briskly and joined her at the floo. She seized my hand and dragged me into the floo.

We landed in a room that I recognized, the outer office of the CEO of Gringotts. Still holding my hand firmly, she dragged me into the inner office. Glazblatt stood, and we shook hands. He invited me to sit. Once I was seated, he signaled to Javeen who immediately asked, "What would you like to drink?"

I decided that I needed to keep my wits about me here as I rarely needed. "Hot tea would be wonderful."

Javeen asked, "Sugar, cream, artificial? Black, Earl Grey, Green, Lapsang Souchong?"

"Straight Earl Grey, please."

She pointed at a teapot that had floated in from another room. It quickly started whistling. Meanwhile two cups flew to the three of us. They had teabags. The teapot filled our cups starting with mine and ending with Javeen's.

Glazblatt opened the discussion. "I'd like for you to explain your research program and what you need from us."

I nodded quickly and began. "I need three things from you."

Glazblatt stared at me in surprise and asked, "I thought Javeen said you needed two things."

"She was right when she spoke with you, but a third item occurred to me today." I proceeded to go through my first two requests. Then I explained my third. "As I explained about the other two, it's necessary to examine accounts that you actually have access to. There is a third kind of settlement account that you have access to of that sort."

Gorblatt seemed deep in thought. Javeen was gazing at me in apparent admiration. I went on. "In all your branches that have virtual vaults. . ."

Glorblatt interrupted me to say, "That's all of them."

I went on. "Anyway, your virtual vaults all are real vaults but the money in them could belong to anyone. It's just another sort of settlement account that you keep cash in to satisfy requests from vaults in different branches. . ."

Javeen corrected. "Or the home office here."

"Right. Anyway, those settlement accounts all give you a read on the extent to which paper money is used."

Glorblatt asked, "So, you want us to lump them all together and give you an average."

I rocked my head right and left, "Not exactly. I'd like you to give me the raw numbers from each branch along with its location—continent and city."

Glorblatt agreed to do that and then said, "I don't know what the ratio is in Barclay's. We'll have to make a request to them. I'd like you to deliver it personally and perform the count."

I was puzzled. "Why me? Don't you trust Barclay's to do the count accurately?"

Gorblatt growled softly and said, "I always prefer for an employee to do Gringotts business whenever feasible."

I shrugged. "I understand that, but why not send a different employee?"

"I try to always send a wizard employee on these errands that require dealing with humans."

I was still confused. "I'm not a wizard. and I'm not the only human employee you have."

Gorblatt frowned. "I only have a handful throughout the organization. It's true that I have William Weasley here, but for something so delicate as checking the Barclay's account I'd want a Muggle. You are the only one."

I capitulated. Javeen said, "We'll set something up. It'll probably be next weekend. All banks are open on weekends, and you won't have classes to teach."

I thanked her for her consideration. I rose in preparation to go, since we seemed to be finished. Glorblatt rose as well but suggested, "Won't you stay a bit for something wee to drink?"

I pulled out my go-to defense in such situations. "It's a school night. I've got to get to bed early."

He chuckled. "Well, I don't want to keep you out of a warm, snug bed."

"Right."

Javeen took my hand at the earliest possible moment to lead me back to the floo connection. After we left the inner office, she added a hand on my forearm as though I were infirm—or her boyfriend.

Halloween Comes Only Once A Year

I was in my office grading parchments while Javeen was sitting at my desk reading a copy of *Scientific American*. I couldn't imagine why she wanted to read it, but she was. Every now and then, she would interrupt me with a question.

For example, at one point she asked me, "What are strings?"

I was dumbfounded. I started to answer the question as though it were really serious. "Well. Strings are cylinders that have a radius hundreds of times sorter than their length. Typically, they are no more than. . ."

She interrupted me again. "No. I mean, I know what that kind of string is, I think. I'm talking about the kind of string in this article about String Theory. I can't make out from the article what those strings are made of."

I sighed. This had the making of a long conversation. "OK. They're not made of anything."

She stared. It was going to be long, but maybe I could short-circuit it, "The thing is that nobody knows what anything is made of. Think about water. What's it made of." I didn't give her much time to admit that she didn't know. I just plowed on. "Water's made of hydrogen gas and oxygen gas. What's hydrogen made of? It's made of a proton and an electron. What are protons made of? Quarks—two ups and a down quark. I think. What are quarks made of? Either nothing or quark." I finished as though I'd won the debate.

She asked hesitantly, "Maybe strings?"

"Right. Maybe."

She clapped her hands and smiled as though she'd solved the mysteries of the universe.

Just then there was a knock on the door followed, after an imperceptible pause, by the sound of the door opening. Then there was a voice that said, "Sorry, I didn't know you were entertaining, Wendt."

I looked up from Javeen to see Aurora standing in the doorway, still grasping the door handle. I replied, "I'm not entertaining. Javeen is entertaining herself." I added, "I suppose I should introduce you two."

Aurora walked over to my desk. I said, "This is Mrs. Aurora Brahms. She's the astronomy professor here. Aurora, this is Javeen, an employee of Gringotts." I turned to Javeen and said, "Would you please give us a little privacy to discuss what I'm sure will be a professional question?"

Javeen asked, "Would you like me to go into your apartment?"

"No. If you want to be useful, you could go try to find me a can of Dr. Pepper, which is an American soft. . ."

She said, "Oh, I know what Dr. Pepper is." She stepped to the floo connection.

As she left, I said, "Don't be in a hurry."

Aurora took a Kleenex from her purse and dusted the seat of the red leather chair before sitting.

I said, "I'm pretty sure I know why you're here, but why don't you tell me anyway?"

Aurora shook her finger at me as she said, "Now, it's not what you think—exactly."

"What is it—exactly?"

"Well, it's October. Halloween is approaching. I thought that you might want to continue our tradition, BUT." I had begun to object, but she continued. "I suggest that you choose whom you go disguised as. Also, you could even suggest my disguise."

That was an unusual approach that she'd never tried before. I asked a few questions. "We're talking about the old polyjuice potion, right?"

"Absolutely."

"You wouldn't change up things on me at the last minute, such as changing whom you would impersonate?"

"Never."

I closed my eyes and steepled my hands as I thought through the implications. Then I asked, "Do you have any suggestions about whom I might impersonate?"

She thought a moment, too, and then said, "None."

I nodded slowly and said, "I'll consider it. I'll consider it seriously. I don't have a choice yet on whom to impersonate, but I'll let you know within a week or so if I will take you up on your offer and whom I want to be."

She rose and said, "I can't ask for more than that. Thanks." With that she turned and exited my office without looking back. I'd risen as she left and remained standing in amazement. This behavior was completely uncharacteristic of her. What had happened? Of course, there had been four years elapse since we'd last had a Halloween together. Maybe she'd changed.

About a half hour later, Javeen appeared in the hearth. She stepped out with two cans of Dr. Pepper in her hands. She handed one to me. We opened them and took a sip. I asked where she'd found the Dr. Pepper.

"Tom at the Leady Cauldron has never stopped stocking Dr. Pepper since you first requested it."

Barclay's Cooperates

Thursday night Javeen brought news. She came out of the floo beaming with joy. She announced, "It's set. We've got the count at Barclay's set up for this Saturday. Do you have any problems with that?"

I shrugged because I didn't have any commitments. I did ask, "What time are we leaving?"

She took the red leather chair and suggested that we have a drink. I agreed. "Blue Label?"

"Of course." she agreed happily.

We sat and had a sip. She then answered my question. "We're to arrive at the home office at 9 AM. Would you like to have breakfast before we arrive? My treat."

I resisted the temptation to roll my eyes. Instead, I said, "I really should be present at all meals in the Great Hall if possible. I'll have breakfast here on Saturday."

She pouted. "Surely you could skip this one time?"

I was straight-forward. "I could, but I'm not going to."

She was not happy, but that wasn't my lookout.

Saturday morning, I set my alarm because on Saturdays I'd normally only get up early enough to catch the end of breakfast at 9 AM. If I'd only thought, I'd have realized that I'd not need to. I was awakened at 7 AM sharp by a sharp rapping on my door. I groaned. "It's way too early in the morning to get up. Is there a fire?"

Javeen said, "No, silly. It's already seven in the morning. I've been up, washed, and dressed. You've got to get moving!"

I groaned and did the same. When I was finished, I entered my office on the way to the Great Hall. Javeen was still in the office. I suggested that she might want to get some breakfast.

She agreed and said, "Are you sure that you won't have breakfast with me?"

"Yes, I'm sure. I should be back here shortly after eight. See you then."

When I arrived in the Great Hall, breakfast was lightly attended. Slughorn appeared to be well into the meal. There were a couple of other professors at the head table. Slughorn signaled me to join him. I did. He asked, "This is an unusual pleasure. You usually don't show up until nine —if at all."

"Sure. I set my alarm for the wrong time. Since I was up, I decided to come down to breakfast."

Slughorn looked around quickly. He looked furtive. Maybe he wanted to make sure that no one heard what he was about to say. "It's actually sort of lucky. I've been meaning to talk with you."

I shuddered internally. "What's the topic?"

"Dursley's teaching. I think he's doing an acceptable job. I sat in on a couple of classes."

I thought that was good. Then Slughorn went on. "As a matter of fact, I think that I might want to keep Dursley on permanently. Honestly, I can't say that I'm a much better potionier than he is. He seems to have an intuitive feel for the class's mood. He seems to know who the trouble-makers are instinctively. What do you think?"

I didn't need this just as I was getting ready to go with Javeen to Barclay's. I finished chewing thoroughly a bite of bagel and responded. "I like Dursley. I'm glad to hear that he's doing OK in potions. Here's the thing. Don't you have a contract with the current potions professor?"

Slughorn made a non-committal nod and said, "Well, splatter goit is tough to cure. Ronald may not be back in time to start the next semester. If he isn't, I'd like to have Dursley finish the year. Even if Ronald's ready to come back before the end of term, I think I'll ask Dursley to finish the term out. If Dursley finishes the year as potions professor, I'd almost certainly offer him a contract for the next school year."

I was stuck having to comment. I said, "It seems to me that you've got a couple of problems if it shakes out that way."

Slughorn said, "You mean what to do about Ronald's salary if he doesn't finish the year. I've already decided that. I'll buy out his contract. With all the trouble that I've had finding a sub he shouldn't have any trouble finding a new position. I'll give him a good reference. What else did you have in mind?"

Then his mouth made a big "O". "You mean Filch."

"Yes. There's Filch. Can he really handle the workload of being sole janitor?"

"Besides that Filch has been complaining about Dursley being tied up with teaching. I think he really misses Dursley."

I said, "I'm sure you're right, but that isn't the only thing I had in mind."

"What else?"

I took a deep breath. Why did it have to be me! And now, of all times. I had to say it. "What about the parents? I'm sure they're very understanding about a professor whose illness forced you to find an undistinguished substitute. Among Muggle schools, it's not unusual to have substitute teachers for lengthy periods of time that are not particularly skilled in the subject they teach.

"However, to finish the school year with such a teacher would anger many parents, I think."

Slughorn stood suddenly and then sat again. "But Dursley is a wonderful potion-master. He is already a decent teacher. That would be crazy!"

"Crazy or not. I think that you will face that."

Slughorn's face fell. "I suppose you're right. There's also worse. I suppose that the Board will be angry as well."

I nodded. Then I glanced at my wrist. It was already half past eight! I had to get back to the office. I bid Slughorn a good morning and rushed up to my office.

I opened the door and entered. Javen stamped her foot. "What have you been doing! We have to leave immediately. There's some details that I have to tell you." Then she held out her hand. "Hurry."

I had no choice. I took her hand. We walked into the hearth, and we spun into another hearth. I didn't recognize it at first, but when we went to the bar and I bought a couple of butter beers. We went to a table. Javeen quickly said, "I won't be accompanying you into the bank. This will be your calling card that will prove to the officials there that you are our representative." She held out a hand that contained a purse much like mine.

She said, "Only the person who will meet you can open it. The contents is a document naming you as our representative."

I laughed. "You've gone to great lengths. This is very strange."

She shook her head. "Not so much. We've always dealt with Barclay's through intermediaries. Bill Weasley did the detailed negotiations with them. He proved to them that there were really wizards and magic. He negotiated the details of how we create credit cards and our dealings. They never have seen a goblin. We intend that they never do."

I nodded. "Right. I've got it. It's getting to be time. Let's go."

We walked out of the restaurant and walked into an alley. Javeen took my hand. We appeared in another alley. Javeen held my hand. "Around the corner is the main entrance. There will be someone to meet you in the lobby. Do you still have the coin to recall me?"

"Yes."

"Good. Now go!"

She let my hand go. I walked around the corner and saw the main entrance. Inside there was a reception desk. Someone sat behind it. Beside it stood a figure whom I knew. I didn't recall the name at first, but by the time we shook hands, I was able to say, "Well, it's been quite a long time since we last met, Quinn."

"It has been. I think you have something for me."

I agreed. I handed her the magical purse. She handed it to the reception desk attendant and said, "Try to open this."

The attendant was surprised, but gave it a decent try. After trying a wicked looking pair of scissors, she just handed it back to Quinn. Quinn took it and opened it effortlessly. She took out a scrap of parchment. I never knew what was written on it, but she smiled and said, "Let's go. It's going to be a busy day."

I said, "I'm curious about one thing."

She asked, "Go ahead."

"Why were you the one to meet me? This can't be your area of expertise?"

She chuckled. "It isn't. However, I was the only bank officer who knew you well enough to be sure to recognize you."

I had to admit that it made sense. Of course, she didn't know about polyjuice potion, but after all, I knew I was the genuine article.

The attendant had me sign in and gave me a visitor badge that was good for only that day.

We reached a bank of elevators. One of them took us down a couple of levels to the vault area. A uniformed guard inspected our badges and allowed us to pass. We reached a gate that looked more serious than ceremonial. Quinn had a key that unlocked it. We passed into a corridor that had a number of doors opening off it. Quinn used her badge to unlock its electronic lock. We went in, and the lights came on automatically. There were several metal boxes about the size of "banker's boxes". She opened them one at a time. Half of them contained bills banded together in thick wads. Half of them contained rolls of coins.

Quinn explained the procedure. She picked up a clipboard that had a few sheets of paper. "We'll record our count on these. There will be three copies—one for the bank, one for my personal file, and one for Gringotts. Of course, normally, we'd count independently and compare results. The amount of cash is so great that we can't do that. We've got bill countering machines that will count and bind in bundles of one hundred bills. We've got a coin sorter that will sort, count, and wrap coins in groups of fifties."

I knew it was a vain hope, but I asked anyway, "Can't we just count the bundles and wrapped coins?"

Quinn said, "God, if only we could. It wouldn't be a minor task just to do that, but Gringotts insists on a recount of what's already wrapped. So, here's the low-down. We'll start with the hundred galleon notes, breaking the bands. Then we'll feed them into the counter, which will re-bind them. We'll count the bundles independently. While we do that, we'll randomly select a dozen or so each to open and manually re-count as a quality check. If we agree, we record the results and move to the next denomination. We do that until we're finished."

I looked at the boxes of bills and coins and wished that there were some magical way to do it. Quinn had already started. She had seated herself at a metal table, She said, "Get a move on. We'll be here all day as it is."

I picked up a bundle and started tearing. We finished the first denomination through the whole process shortly after eleven. We had hand-counted a few bundles and sent them through the sorter a second time. Then we agreed on the total count and wrote it on the tally sheets. I asked, "Don't you think we might take a break for lunch."

She just frowned at me and said, "Let's break for lunch after we finish the tens." We did that. It took us until 1 PM. I was bushed by then. Quinn had brought some cold-cut sandwiches, cut-up vegetables, and a couple of cookies for lunch for us. It was good and was over way too soon. We spun through the ones by 3 PM. The coins were formidable. They were heavy. The counting machine almost shook the floor with the load of coins we sent through it. However, we had our procedure down pat from the bills, and we had finished the hundred galleon coins and the ten's by 5:30.

Quinn suggested just soldiering on. I agreed and added, "I will buy you the best dinner you've ever had when we're finished." Then I remembered that I'd made that promise about four years earlier and kept it. I didn't think we could fit Paris in tonight. She was about to object when I corrected. "Actually, you've already had it, but I'll treat you to a great dinner."

She laughed. "You're a joker, but I'll take you up on that offer just to prove how funny you are."

We actually finished the coins before 7 PM, but of course, that wasn't the entire story. We checked and double-checked each other's numbers and signed them. She wouldn't leave me alone, so we both had to go up to her office and her boss's office to drop off the tally sheets. It was nearly eight before we left the bank. She called a cab. When we got in, I said, "Your call on restaurant. Don't spare the galleons. What will it be?"

She called for a cab. We boarded, and she named a restaurant unknown to me. I sat back and let the cabbie drive. If I were Sherlock Holmes, I could have figured out where we went. I wasn't, and I didn't. It was a fairly small place, but it had valet parking. The maitre d' placed us at a small table in a corner. I said, "I'm surprised that we could get in this late on a Saturday night."

She smiled. "Not a lot of people know about this place. It's rarely crowded, which is fortunate because they don't take reservations."

"What do you recommend?"

"Everything. You can't possibly go wrong on any dish that you like and most that you don't like."

"Great." I looked at the menu. It was full of fascinating dishes. I closed my eyes and dropped my forefinger onto the menu. It was pointing at something that I didn't recognize and might not even be able to pronounce correctly. When the waiter arrived to take our orders, I pointed at the item.

Quinn laughed. "That was bold."

"This is probably going to be the only time I will ever eat her. Why not be bold?"

As we waited for our entrees, Quinn opened her purse, reached in, and brought out a galleon bill. I asked, "Where did you get that? Don't tell me that our count is off?"

"No it isn't. I went to the foreign currency window and traded some coin of the realm for this." She held it up in front of my face. I could see that it was a one galleon bill.

I asked, "OK. So what?"

"Why don't you tell me everything you know about it?"

I thought about what I knew about it. Some of what I knew, I knew because I'd suggested the possibility to Gringotts. Part of what I knew would come from Jaimie by my rifling through her memories. Part of what I knew was covered by the confidentiality agreement that I'd made with Gringotts. It would take a little time to disentangle all of that. I temporized with honesty. I said, "Well, some of what I know about that is covered by an NDA. Part of it comes form a private communication from a woman. You have to give me a few minutes to decide what I can ethically tell you."

She smiled and shook her head dismissively. "Just tell me what you feel comfortable about."

I started with information that was not proprietary to Gringotts. "It all started about five years ago when the world was still recovering from the invasion of the Souls. The Souls' management of the world's economy had led to its growing rapidly. That was OK when the grease of the world economy wasn't money. After we phased back into using money, it was discov-

71

ered that there wasn't enough money to perform this service efficiently."

Quinn chuckled, "That realization was one of the outcomes of our seminar back then. It started people thinking seriously about this. That realization resulted in the fairly rapid expansion of the money supply via low interest rates and actually printing a lot of money. That happened gradually over the last several years." She slowed as she said that, adding, "That's what happened with the wizarding world, isn't it?"

I answered, "Not exactly, but close enough. What actually happened was that the situation had gotten rather bad. The supply of gold limited the amount of expansion of the wizard money supply that was possible. The answer, which seems obvious in retrospect, was to expand the money supply with paper money, which could be created relatively easily."

"You mean that there wasn't any wizard paper money before the Ghost invasion?"

I snickered. "I'm afraid not. It was only a couple of years later when the monetary crisis was becoming unavoidable that Gringotts, which is the sole mint and print shop for money, decided that it would be important to do desperate things to deal with the problem." I paused for a little thought about how to proceed.

Quinn said, "Well, don't keep me in suspense. What happened next and what did you have to do with it?"

"I suggested two revolutionary ideas. One was buying gold from Muggles."

She immediately asked, "What are Muggles?"

I smiled broadly, "We are Muggles—a wizarding word for non-magical people"

Quinn seemed amazed. "You mean that wizards didn't buy gold from Muggles before?"

"Not in any quantities. Think about that time. There was some trade between Muggles and wizards, but it was mostly things like restaurants and raw foodstuffs, not raw materials for industry. Without much trade, it would be hard to trade in large quantities of valuable things like gold."

"OK. What was the second thing?"

"The invention of paper galleons, of course."

Quinn said, "Revolutionary, of course, but was there anything particularly hard about it?"

I nodded. "Actually there was. Since you haven't dealt with wizards much, you don't know the limitations that they work under.

"First, wizards, with a few exceptions, can duplicate almost anything."

Quinn scoffed. "That 'almost' doesn't seem like much of a limitation. It seems like all wizards must live in the lap of luxury."

I smiled, "You'd think so, but let me tell you about the limitations—first, food. They can do exact duplicates of any food item."

Quinn smiled. "I could live with that—especially if I could duplicate this prime rib roast."

"Think about it—exact copy."

She thought a minute and said, "Don't get it."

I replied, "A week old carrot duplicated gives you a second week old carrot."

Her mouth formed a big "O". Then I went on. "Second, they can't. . ."

She interrupted. "If they could duplicate coins, the value of any money would be. . ."

"Right, zero."

She summed up. "Then they can't duplicate metals at all?"

"Just precious metals. They can duplicate lead and iron."

Her face showed puzzlement. I said, "Doesn't make sense does it?"

She just said, "Right." Then she added, "But that allows the existence of money. Otherwise, you'd have to have something like cryptocurrencies to have money."

I nodded. "That's another limitation, electronics work not at all in the presence of much magic. Even simple electricity doesn't work much."

She laughed. "No electric lights."

I nodded. Then she went on. "So, can printed paper be duplicated?"

"For the most part."

"Then how does this. . ." She held the one galleon note that she had up in front of my face, "work?"

"Sorry. I can't tell you. That's something that I can't tell you because of an NDA."

Her face fell. Then she examined it closely. She went back to it every now and then as we ate our meals. One time she stopped to say, "I understand why this bill is called a galleon. There's an image of a wooden sailing ship on one side of the bill." She gazed at it a minute and then asked, "Did I see it rock a little in the waves?"

I shrugged and said, "Yes."

"Bloody. . ." Then she looked at the other side and said, "This portrait is almost as ugly as the one on the fifty dollar bill of you Yanks. Who is it?"

"Oh, I think you're being too generous to it. It's the CEO of Gringotts."

She laughed loud enough to attract attention from other tables. "You mean it's not some great wizard hero or prime minister or something?"

"He got the contract to print money. I guess he's got some say over it."

We continued the meal. Despite the maitre d's suggestion of wines, we both chose to have Johnnie Walker Blue Label. He stopped just short of sneering, but that was his problem—not ours. Off and on, Quinn lifted the galleon to the light and stared at it. We chose to split a single order of chocolate mousse tart. While we waited for it to arrive, Quinn came to a realization.

"I've been looking at the watermark and colored threads in the bill. There are yellow threads in the bill! They can't be duplicated can they?"

I was forced to share common wizarding knowledge, "No. They can't."

She laughed again. "That's it! Gold threads that can't be duplicated. I suppose they turn to lead if you try to duplicate them. Is that it?"

I smiled. "Something like that."

She smirked. "I knew it. I just knew it would be something like that."

Just then our desert arrived with two spoons. She took one taste of the heavenly mousse and said, "Leave it to the wizards to figure out how to turn gold to lead."

"Yup."

As we finished, she said, "Oh, I wish that you were a wizard. I'd dearly love to see you duplicate that bill. I'd like to see what the duplicate looks like."

I laughed. "I don't think that I've ever wished that I were a wizard."

The waiter had delivered a cup of coffee for her and one of tea for me. We were sipping our hot beverage of choice and whiling the evening away without conversation when she held the galleon up to the light one more time. She gazed at it for a while. Then her eyes widened and her mouth dropped open. She exclaimed, "I see it now! The golden threads form an image. It's you!"

I shrugged. "I can't say."

She stared at me hard and said, "It sure is. You invented the anti-counterfeiting scheme, didn't you! Of course, you did. That's why you're on the Board of Gringotts."

All I would say was, "NDA."

"NDA my foot. You are a pill—stringing me along the whole time, coaxing me into figuring it out for myself."

I said, "It must be time for me to pick up the check."

She scoffed. "It sure is. You must be able to eat at restaurants like this every day morning, noon, and night."

I lifted my hand. That was all that was required to summon the waiter. He stood silently by our table. I opened my purse and pulled out my Gringotts-Barkley's credit card. He took it and left. He was back quickly with the check. It was not itemized. It just had an amount—a four figure amount. I thought to myself, "If you have to ask, you can't afford it." I just signed the check, leaving a substantial tip for the wait staff.

We left the restaurant. Quinn made a phone call for a cab. She asked me if she could drop me off somewhere. "Or, you could come up for a drink."

I took a deep breath. Quinn was smart, hard-headed, lovely in a way that defied age. I had no idea how old she was.

She interrupted my thoughts. "Well, come along. When we reach my flat, you can decide what you want to do."

It seemed like a risk-free offer, so I accepted. At that time of night—after 11 PM—the streets were relatively quiet. We both rode with our thoughts. I couldn't think of a reason not to take up her offer. The trouble was that I couldn't think of a reason to accept it. I know that lots of guys would jump at the chance to sleep with her for the reasons that I'd just thought through. The trouble was that I didn't have any real desire for her. I was still pretty much in the thrall of Ginny. It wasn't that I didn't enjoy an evening with a lovely woman—young or older. It was that I needed to really want to go to bed with her. If Ginny disapparated into the cab at that moment, I'd have jumped at the chance for a one-nighter with her. I sure didn't feel the same about Quinn, though. Oddly, I kind of wished that I did.

We reached her flat. She repeated her offer. I tried to be really honest and not hurt her. I said, "Look. I'm trying to get over a lady I was in a relationship with. I still have it pretty bad for her."

She sniffed, "Too bad. I'm pretty bad myself. Oh well, you can take the cab wherever you want."

I said, "Not necessarily. I already have a ride arranged. Thanks." I paid the cabbie and Quinn entered her building. I returned my credit card to my purse and rummaged around for the magic coin. I found it and activated it. It seemed like a quarter hour, but it was probably only four or five minutes before Javeen materialized next to me,

The tightness in her voice belied her unhappiness. "I suppose it took you that long to count the money?"

"Oh, it was a long count—well after eight, but I took the Barclay's person who helped to dinner. I just dropped her off at home."

She couldn't find anything to complain about, but she clearly wasn't happy. She finally said, "Since you got me out so late, the least that you could do would be to take me out for a drink. . ." She added under her breath, "Or two."

I decided I owed her, so I agreed. She held out her hand. We ended up at the Cauldron. Tom just nodded when we came out of the floo connection. I went over to him and said, "Two Blue Labels please." We then went to a small table near the fire. Tom dropped off the drinks. He winked at me and asked, "Are you wanting a room for the night, it being so late and all?"

That was all I needed. Javeen looked over at me with big hopeful eyes. I said, "I think not tonight. It's been an extremely long day."

That idiot Tom snapped out, "All the more reason to spend a restful evening here."

I sighed. "I'll tell you what. Javeen can stay the night on my knut, but she'll have to drop me off at school."

Tom turned to Javeen. She said, "That's all right. I'll just drop Wendt off and go on to my place after." We finished our drinks and left via the floo for my office. When we arrived, I said, "Javeen, let's just call it a night. I suppose that you want to do a postmortem of the count today. I'm totally shot. Let's sleep in tomorrow, and by the way, I mean sleep in. Then we can work tomorrow."

□

The next day didn't turn out to be a working day. However, I did sleep in late, skipping breakfast altogether. I don't know what Javeen did. She was not around when I strolled leisurely down to an early lunch. I took my time with lunch. Since weekend meals—except for Sunday dinner—are casual, I was not surprised to find people choosing a seat that wasn't assigned to them at the head table. Dursley drifted in and sat next me even though technically he should have sat at the very end of the table.

He greeted me. "Professor Wendt, how are you this weekend. I've not seen you in so far."

I smiled. "I'm fine, and how are you, Professor Dursley?"

"All right, I suppose. I'm still uneasy being called 'professor'. I've not been teaching very long and I sure don't feel old and musty." He quickly added, "No offense meant."

"None taken. How's Mr. Filch doing?"

"Oh, he's OK—I guess. I don't see him a lot lately, but I do make it a point to go out with him one night a week. Oh, yes. Don't forget that we've got an Old Boys Club meeting coming up on Thursday."

I grinned widely. "I wouldn't miss it for the world." We talked about nothing in particular and parted after a leisurely lunch.

That afternoon, I worked on lesson plans for the week—something that I would normally do on Saturday. The afternoon was well gone when there was a knock on the door of my office. I growled, "Come in." I was sure it must be Aurora wanting to know whom I wanted to impersonate. I'd not had a moment to think about it. Now, I'd have to admit that I'd not given it any thought.

I was pleasantly surprised to see that it was Sissy. I rose instantly to greet her. With downcast eyes, she said, "I hope I'm not interrupting something, Professor."

"Not in the least. I really could use a break from lesson planning. Thanks for coming. What can I do for you?"

Her countenance brightened, and she said, "It's something I want to show you, but I suppose that you've already seen it."

I shook my head. What could it be that I might have seen? She had been holding a newspaper under her arms. She brought it out and laid it open to page one on my desk. She triumphantly said, "There!"

It was just that miserable *Prophet*. I said, "Yeh. The Sunday *Prophet*."

She stared at me and said, "You've not seen it then."

"No. I usually read the *Times* on Sunday." I pointed over to the bookshelf where the untouched Sunday *Times* lay. "Is there actually something interesting in this edition?"

She laughed. "Take a careful look."

I looked at the page, which had all the usual articles of questionable value. Then I noticed the index to sections of the paper. The Sunday supplement magazine caught my attention. It featured an article by Rita Skeeter. I quickly shuffled through the various sections to find the *Sunday Magazine*.

I pulled it out and could hardly restrain a tear. The cover photo was of Cedric Diggory. He was shown bent over a chess board, apparently studying a position. The view was from a position that an opponent standing over the board might have. Like all wizard photos, this one had motion. Cedric raised his head to look up at the unseen opponent with a friendly smile on his face. That did bring some tears. The headline was "Retrospective on a Wizard Chess Great – Cedric Diggory". The byline was Rita Skeeter. So, she'd fulfilled her promise. I quickly turned to the start of the article on page four. It started:

> "More than ten years have passed since the Chess Master Cedric Diggory won an international chess tournament in Paris, France. He was barely sixteen at the time. Most masters have been playing for most of their lives at that age. Cedric had been playing for barely a year. He had been compared with a young Bobby Fischer, the first American World Champion of Chess.
>
> He began his career with a chance game against Ronald

Weasley.

. . .

This article begins a series of Sunday supplement articles about famous chess players. Also, this reporter will be writing chess columns for the sports page on a daily basis. I hope to find a loyal readership for these articles among my fans and sports fans

. . .

The article had a photo of Cedric posing with his parents. He was holding a large champion's cup. I recognized it as a trophy that he'd won at a British youth tournament. Open tournaments don't usually award trophies.

I scanned through the article but would read it carefully later. I asked Cecily, "Could I keep this copy of the *Prophet*?"

"Sure. My dad has bought about a dozen copies. He wants to give one to all my relatives."

I was puzzled and showed it. "I know that your dad is a fan of Cedric, but surely not that big a fan."

She shook her head jauntily. "Rita interviewed me extensively for the article. There are a number of verbatim quotes in the article."

I smiled. "Good. She's doing her job then."

Sissy asked me, "What do you think about attending my next tournament?"

"When?"

"Three weeks from now in Barcelona, Spain."

"I'll have to see. It's really busy here. On the other hand, I'd really like to go. Get me a schedule of you games. I'll try to arrange transportation for a day or two."

Sissy said, "You bet. I'll have one for you in a day or two. AND, I'm sure that I can arrange transportation for you."

As we were talking, there was a whooshing in the floo. Javeen would have to show up now. We both turned just in time to see her step out of the hearth. Everyone's faces showed surprise. Both Javeen and Sissy asked, "Who are you?"

It was inevitable that they would meet. At least we were all in the room at the same time with an opportunity to talk things through. I did. I said simply, "Javeen, this is Cecily Brewster, who just was graduated from Hogwarts. Cecily, this is Javeen who works for Gringotts. I work as a consultant for Gringotts. She is occasionally here to help with issues involved with my employment."

Neither of the ladies seemed any too satisfied with the other's presence. We all stood there for a moment in silence wondering where to go from here. Javeen broke the silence. "Professor Wendt and I have some confidential Gringotts business to discuss." She nodded her head toward the door.

Sissy frowned and said, "I guess I should be going, Professor Wendt. Just get in touch when you know what days you want to see me play." With that she walked out the office door. Fortunately, they didn't have to pass any too close to each other as Sissy left.

Javeen sneered and asked, "What does little miss graduate play that you want to see—football?"

I said, "She plays chess."

She looked like she had some choice comments about chess, but there was something that interrupted her. There was a whoosh from the hearth and someone walked out—Rita Skeeter. They were both shocked into silence. Then Javeen asked, "I'm here on Gringotts business. What are you doing here?"

Rita answered, "I'm here on business of *The Prophet*. Why are you here—to foreclose on a mortgage? Who are you anyway?"

Javeen said, "Well, I work for Gringotts in the Boardroom. I know who you are. Eveyone would recognize you from your photo in your column. You really look good in your photo."

Rita said cautiously, "Thanks."

Javeen said, "You're welcome. What is it—a dozen or so years old?" She looked meaningfully at the paper under Rita's hand and added. "I see that you've had a promotion to paper delivery girl." That was followed by a profound silence that I didn't want to interrupt. I was curious to see how long it could continue. They both stood with their hands on their hips in a definitely threatening pose. After a couple of deep breaths, Javeen shook her head in resignation and said, "This is getting to be a bad habit. When will you two be finished with your *tete-a-tete*?"

I finally spoke. "I have a hard stop at six when I'm required to be in the Great Hall for dinner." I turned to Javeen and said, "Any time after that."

She nodded and mumbled something like, "There had better not be any more unexpected visitors." Then she stepped into the floo and was gone.

Rita opened the paper that was under her arm and beamed like a schoolgirl who had just gotten ten points for Ravenclaw. She laid it on my desk and asked, "Have you seen the *Magazine* section?"

I nodded. "Yes, I did. I haven't had a chance to read it in detail, but I thought that what I'd seen was good." I hesitated and added, "I'm just curious why you didn't interview me for the article."

Rita beamed again. "Oh, there are several reasons. First, I wanted it to be a surprise for you. Second, I wanted to feature Ms. Brewster in interviews." We had sat around my desk as we talked. She leaned across the desk and said, "I've got better plans for you."

I said hesitantly, "Oh?"

"I'm going to do an article on you. I'm thinking of titling it, 'Master of Masters. You know, the man behind the Grand Masters of Hogwarts."

I laughed. "You know, I probably know less about playing chess than anyone in this school. I wouldn't last twelve moves against either of them ever—from the beginning. You've got to look somewhere else for the reason that they've done so well."

Rita laughed, too. "Methinks you protest too much. The great teams aren't coached by great players. They're coached by people who understand how to get the most out of their players."

"Since when have you been an expert on sports?"

Rita was silent. So, I asked, "When do you want to do this interview."

"Right now. If we run out of time before your hard stop, I can always come back for more."

"Then let's get going."

Rita asked, "Let's lubricate the vocal chords with a little of the famous Blue Label, hmmm?"

I acquiesced by digging deep into the lower left drawer of my desk while I asked, "How do you know about my Blue Label?"

Rita just shrugged. "We journalists don't reveal our sources."

Meanwhile, I'd found a couple of glasses. Rita used the *scourgio* spell to clean them. I asked, "Ice?"

Rita stared in surprise. "And ruin them? By the way, don't be stingy either."

I wasn't. She took a good sip and said, "Well, to start, why don't you just tell me about how you met Cedric and got him on his way to being the chess-master that he became?"

So, I started.

□□

The first time I notice Cedric was on the Hogwarts Express. I was patrolling the rail cars. I was going through a car where Ronald Weasley was playing Cedric. I stopped because Weasley was considered one of the best chess players at Hogwarts. He was only a second year, but I think that he'd not been beaten once through his first year at Hogwarts—even playing much older students. What had attracted my attention was that Weasley was clearly on the ropes in his game. In the few minutes that I watched the game, Cedric finished him off.

I didn't think much of it at the time, but by the Christmas vacation, Cedric was asking for help with playing chess seriously. I helped him get into a big tournament held annually at Christmas in London. It was his first serious tournament. He was competing in the lower division of the tournament, but he made it to the second round and won a couple of games. It was an amazing result for a rookie. Through the rest of the school year, I arranged tournaments—mostly youth tournaments.

The next school year, Cedric really took off. He won the British youth tournament. He competed in the Trafalgar Tradewise Tournament in the upper division. He got into the second round. He didn't win the tournament, but he picked up lots of points. Later in the year we were entered in a tournament in Paris. It was an amazing performance. Most of the games were beautiful. The final was probably the best game he ever played. It was also the last tournament game that he played.

The rest of the school year, we didn't go to another tournament. Then the next semester, Hogwarts was consumed with the Tri-Wizard Tournament and visitors from other schools.

Cedric received an historic invitation to participate in a youth tournament. The winner would get to play a series with the world champion. I tried my hardest to convince him to play the chess tournament. His father wanted him to play in the Tri-Wizard. I didn't have a chance. Cedric thought he could always go back to chess after the Tri-Wizard. You know the outcome of that.

To sum up, I thought he had a chance to be world champion if he stuck with his chess after graduation, took part in serious tournaments regularly, and of course, had some good luck.

Rita's Quick Quotes Quill had been writing wildly. She was following it as it caught up with my statement. When it was finished, she said, "Well, I'll just ask a couple of quick follow up questions now and let you get to dinner. First, when you started working with Cedric, what year was it?"

That made me think carefully. I thought out loud, "Let me see I started at Hogwarts in '90. It was my third year, so that would make it '92—the fall."

She noted that and said, "That's been quite a while—fifteen years. You're becoming a fixture here, right?"

I frowned at that. "Well, Mr. Filch is a fixture. I've been here a while, but not continuously. I just came off a three-year sabbatical. Before that I had a year or two when I was only part-time." I thought a moment.

Rita said, "Don't forget the year that Riddle took over the Ministry. You were sacked that year." She became quiet and added, "That was the year that I was in exile." I didn't blame her for wanting to pass over that.

I thought some more. "Well, there was also the spring term when I took a leave of absence with the Headmistress to. . ." I stopped short, realizing that I was about to go into an area covered by a Non-Disclosure Agreement.

Rita picked up on it instantly. "What was that year again?"

I tried to dodge the question. "Does it really matter? I wasn't working with anyone on chess that year and I didn't think I would again."

She shrugged. "I guess not. . . Oh! Don't forget the year that the Souls took over the world. Hogwarts was closed then, at least as an educational institute."

I chuckled. "Maybe I've not taught as much here as I've been absent."

She clucked her tongue and said, "This is just a bare outline. I'll be back again to flesh it out more and ask some more probing questions."

"Yeh, Maybe you're too good a reporter." I thought. I said, "Well, I'm on my way to dinner so that I won't be tardy." She walked to the hearth and flooed away somewhere.

Dinner was as it always was at Hogwarts, scrumptious, varied, and plentiful. It was good to have a break from the lengthy day of interruptions. I got back to my office and finally turned back to lesson planning. I had just got a good start when the now very familiar whoosh of someone coming through the floo sounded. I didn't even look up. Why would I? It was sure to be someone wanting something.

I heard Javeen's voice say. "What! No one here already?" She sat in the red leather chair and said, "Here's the thing."

Just then, there was a knock at the door. The door immediately opened. There was only one person who would do that. I said, "What can I do for you Aurora?"

She walked directly to take the red leather chair but discovered that Javeen was firmly ensconced in it. Aurora said, "Oh, sorry. Are you still doing Gringotts business?"

Javeen ground her teeth and said, "I can't catch a bloody break!" She got up and walked resignedly to the hearth.

Aurora said, "You can go ahead. I'll come again later."

However, Javeen had already whooshed out of the floo. I said, "Would you like something to drink?"

She shook her head. "No." She sat and said, "Have you decided on someone?"

I was briefly confused, but recovered. I opened my mouth but realized that I really hadn't made a decision. I said, "Give me a minute. I've got a couple of people that I'm considering. I'll pick one right now." Of course, I'd not really given any thought to it. If a hundred or so people could be considered a couple, I was considering a couple. I decided that I couldn't put it off any further. The problem was choosing someone who wouldn't get me in trouble. Then it occurred to me. "I want to impersonate Filch." Then an inspiration struck me. "And I want you to be Dursley."

Aurora was completely surprised. She sat with her mouth open. I confirmed my choice. "Yes. That will be good. It will be easy to get hair samples from both."

She was still stunned. I got up and was about to usher her out when she said, "I think I'll take that drink after all."

I thought, "Surprising, but why not?" I got out my Blue Label and glasses. She didn't even offer to clean the glass or provide ice. That was all right. I handed her her glass and took a sip from mine. She said, "Sorry. I just have always chosen whom we would impersonate. This is a tough one. Oh, it's easy to get the hairs. The problem is trying to put yourself into the head of the person that you're impersonating. Either one of those two would be tough for me."

I could hardly feel sorry for her considering all the people she'd forced on me at the very last instant. She finished off the drink in a single swallow. That was an awful use for Blue Label, but it was her choice. She left, and I returned to lesson planning. It was getting late enough that I had to be satisfied with planning less than a full week tonight.

I'd hardly gotten started when the whoosh of Javeen returning sounded. She looked around the room, apparently looking for someone else there to interrupt her. She walked to the red leather chair and said, "Whom do you think will walk in now?"

I laughed. "Oh, there are so many professors here at Hogwarts who haven't been through this office—not to mention the rest of the wizards of the world."

She frowned. "That isn't funny."

"Well, the only way we'll find out is for you to start off on whatever you want to talk about."

"OK. The branches of Gringotts have been working on the counts of currency that we want them to do. Most are finished by now. The rest should be finished by Tuesday morning. I can bring them by that night."

I expressed my pleasure. Then, I thought about the data analysis that I wanted to do. I said, "What I wouldn't give to have a computer laptop to do some calculations."

She said, "I want to do a little research. I'll be back before the evening's over."

She left, and I thought that I might be done with her for the evening. I wasn't. She was back within the hour. She walked with a spring to her step. She must have something good to report—for her. She said, "I think I can arrange for a laptop for you to use."

I said, "Sure, all you have to do is drop me off at a Fedex. They all have computers that you can hire."

She shook her head and smiled. "We won't allow such proprietary data onto a computer that we don't control. You'll have to use one in one of our facilities."

I remembered that they had a rented office with a high capacity copy machine and who knew what other office equipment.

She said, "We'll go Tuesday night if the rest of the data is available then."

"No can do. I've hardly done any lesson planning this weekend. I'll have to do it almost day by day. We'd better do it on Saturday."

She was so frustrated that she stood and paced behind the red leather chair. She finally said, "OK. But if you get time before the weekend, we're going to go do your data analysis right away!"

"Sure."

I worked for the rest of the night and got to bed at a decent hour.

⊞

The week was pretty quiet. Late on Monday night Javeen announced that the last of the data had been collected. She wanted me to go with her right away to do my data analysis. Of course, I couldn't. I still hadn't finished planning for Tuesday.

On Thursday, Rita showed up wanting to do some follow-up questions. Javeen was furious. "You've got time for Rita, but not for. . ." She couldn't say what it was for with a journalist in the room. She fumed as she strode up and down.

Rita replied reasonably, "I've got a deadline to make. I don't have a lot of questions. I should be done quickly. You don't even have to leave, Javeen."

"I won't."

Rita took the red leather chair and said, "OK. First, you haven't told me much about the character of Cedric. How would you describe him?"

I took a deep breath and thought. "Well, he was probably the most kindhearted person I ever knew. For an example, when he won the British Youth Champion, during the awards ceremony, he joined the runner-up at his table. He was very kind. We had a good visit. As a matter of fact, he was always gracious in both victory and defeat."

"I covered the Tri-Wizard. He seemed just too goody-goody to be real. Are you saying that he was really that way?"

"Oh, absolutely. There were lots of incidents in the Tri-Wizard that you never knew about. They showed his true character."

"Would you care to share one or two of them?"

I decided that I couldn't give up such information. "No. There are confidential things that I won't share."

She was clearly disappointed but went on. "You said that you thought that Cedric's dad influenced his decision to compete in the Tri-Wizard rather than chess. Would you expand on that? Did you ever confront him about that before or after the tournament?"

Here was another touchy point. I had to consider the feelings of Cedric's family. I said, "We did speak. Obviously we had differences of opinion. It was always respectful."

Clearly the old instinct to find something titillating hadn't left her, but she had to be satisfied with what she had. "Well, you're busy. I'd like to come back on Saturday to hear about Ms. Brewster. Can we set a time?"

"I have another commitment in the morning. Let's make it mid-afternoon. Say three?"

She agreed and left.

Saturday came without incident. I was awakened by Javeen bright and early at 7 AM. Oh, I longed for the time that I'd no longer need her. She must be as impatient as I was. Maybe, she'd cut back after the board meeting on Wednesday. For now I was stuck getting up, getting ready for the day, and having breakfast. At least I didn't have to do that with Javeen. She was a real pain urging me on to hurry.

I decided to have a quick breakfast and finish the tough part of the day —work on my report with Javeen. There was literally no one in the Great Hall. Technically, the breakfast on weekends starts at 7:30. I arrived at 7:40. No one was in the hall at all. I wondered if there were anyone to take complaints. I didn't have to. When I took my seat, the Head Table suddenly filled with the normal breakfast items. I had a quick breakfast and was back up to my office. At least, Javeen didn't complain about how long it took to return.

What she did however was different from usual. She ran a finger around the edge of the hearth and said something under her breath. Then she used floo powder as usual. We stepped out in the ante-room to the Board Room. She turned to me and answered my unasked question. "We have to go through this floo connection to get to the one with the computers. Sorry about the extra steps." She then went to her desk and picked up a normal file folder and asked me to hold it. She then took my other hand, led me to the floo and repeated the finger action on the hearth. Then we took the floo as normal.

We landed in what seemed to be the strangest computer room that I'd ever seen. There were the usual things—large format printers, copy machines, desktop machines, drop ceiling, raised floor, fluorescent lighting, even some sort of rack mounted server. Then, there were the unusual things—the hearth we had used, a cauldron and Bunsen burner on a table, a large cage with several owls, bags of owl treats, etc.

I had been staring at the bizarre room that seemed to take up at least half of the floor of the building where we were. Javeen hadn't let go my hand. She dragged me over to a corner of the room where there were several office-style cubicles. She said, "Come on. Don't gawk all day. Haven't you ever seen a back room before."

"I have. I just have never seen anything like this."

"Well, get over it. We've got work to do." She sat down in front of a laptop. She lifted the lid and said, "Pull up a chair. You're going to be in the driver's seat in a minute."

I carefully avoided seeing the password that Javeen entered. After it booted up, she opened an icon on the desktop, Excel. She handed me the folder and said, "There are about 280 Gringotts branches around the world, including the home office. The file folder was indeed thick with parchments. The results had been transcribed so that there were ten on each sheet. The folder was still pretty thick. I opened the folder and started on the first. Javeen sat as close to me as she could, looking around my body to see what I would do.

What I did was pretty simple. I labeled columns for branch number, name, city, country, continent, amount in coin, amount in paper, and percent paper, I then started filling in the slots. It took all the morning to transfer the data. When I finished it had just gone noon. Javeen asked if we could have some lunch.

I said, "You understand that I have a hard stop at 2:45. That only leaves you fifteen minutes to get me back to my office. I don't know how long it will take me to do the data analysis that I want to do, but I don't think it could be less than an hour or so. We have to be back here by one. Right?"

She said, "I know a bar that specializes in quick lunches. Come on, let's go."

It might specialize in quick lunches, but we still had to go through two floos to get there and two to get back. We arrived in a bar that I'd not been in before. They seemed to recognize Javeen there. We were seated immediately, and a waitress took our order. I glanced at the menu and decided on bean soup and a green salad. Javeen ordered a dish that I'd never heard of. I did my best to avoid getting a very good look at it. She was right about the service being fast. I let her pay for the meal. We got back to the back office before one.

I did my data analysis, which was pretty easy with Excel. I wrote quick notes and printed off multiple copies of the notes, spreadsheet and graphs that I developed. I had to admit that with the office tools they had in the back office, it was pretty easy and quick. We got back to my office a little after 2:30.

I sat and cleared my mind of finance and tried to re-orient it to the history of Sissy. Rita walked through the floo spot-on at three. Javeen had retreated to the sofa. I had to compliment her on her patience and helpfulness. The beam of her smile was not as bright as it had been, but she clearly appreciated the compliment. She asked Rita if she minded her staying in the office.

Rita said, "Not at all." She turned to me and said, "OK. Let's get going. We're burning sunlight."

I took a deep breath to center myself and remind myself of the important points that I wanted to make. "First, I want to say that I've not got a tremendous amount of personal information about Ms. Brewster. She was never in one of my classes. I met her as an advanced second year. She was like Hermione Granger who could have graduated after six years. Hermione technically never graduated, but like the Weasley twins, she had learned far more than the typical Hogwarts graduate.

"Anyway, she approached me to recruit me as a chess coach. She had fallen in love with chess while playing with her father whom she eclipsed by her first year at Hogwarts. She continued playing him for a while because he was the best opponent she could find. Finally, their games had become so one-sided that she came to me. Her father was a fan of Cedric's despite his brief career. She learned that I had been Cedric's coach and tried to get me to coach her."

Here Rita interrupted me. "You sound like you never coached her."

"Not to any great extent. I played a game with her to assess her skill level. I could tell that she was very good from that game. I promised that I'd seriously consider coaching her if she had her father's permission. I also warned her that my entire experience with Cedric had been exhausting and came to a tragic end. I couldn't promise that I was up for another chess coaching experience.

"I did give her the few pieces of advice that seemed useful to me, and I gave her a gift. I'd bought Cedric a copy of the book, *Modern Chess Openings*. He used it extensively. When he died, his parents gave it to me as a souvenir of Cedric. It had extensive notes. I couldn't think of a better gift for a rising chess star than an annotated copy of that book."

I paused because I was on the verge of tears at that memory. Rita just stared at me and asked, "I'm surprised that you could give that memento up."

I regained my composure and said, "It seemed to me that if I couldn't help by coaching her, the least I could do was give her that gift. I had a number of mementos from Cedric. I had copies in his hand of his record of moves for games that he'd played—including the greatest game that he'd ever played. His parents gave me photos, too. That reminds me. Where did you get that photo that was the cover of the *Sunday Magazine* last weekend? I'd never seen it before."

She smiled. "You'd never seen it?"

"No."

"Well, his parents had a family portrait made every year. The year that he won that big Paris tournament, they had that photo made at the same time. They framed it and kept it in his room as a sort of memorial. They let me make a copy of it for the magazine cover."

I felt a catch in my throat. "I'm really glad that you uncovered it. I framed it myself. I keep it in the bookshelf over there."

She glanced over her shoulder and nodded when she saw it. "I'll get a better copy for you."

She asked a question, "Why didn't you decide to take Ms. Brewster on to coach?"

"Well, the decision was taken out of my hands."

She tilted her head to invite further comment. I went on, "Well, I had to take an involuntary sabbatical of the spring term shortly after Ms. Brewster requested me to be her coach. She did obtain a coach in the form of the substitute that replaced me. I think that it was lucky that Ms. Brewster had my substitute, Ms. Sinistra, as a coach. In these coaching relationships, having a coach of the same sex makes life much easier for everyone."

Rita ogled me. "You probably are right. There are enough cases of abuse in those sort of situations that I suppose it's good that you weren't faced with that temptation. However, what in the world happened to you that you had to take a sabbatical? Health?"

I chuckled to myself. "Well, you might call it health-related. However, I'm not going to tell you."

She frowned at me. "Now, you should know me well enough to realize that I can dig up almost anything that people want to hide." She hesitated and added soberly, "Just think of the job I did on Dumbledore."

I growled and said, "I'd think that you'd want to leave that sleeping dog lying."

She quickly said, "Yes." She added, "Surely there are people who know what happened to you."

"My wife knew of course. The Headmaster's personal assistant knows, but I'm pretty sure you'd never get a peep out of her. That's about it."

She asked, "What about your substitute, Ms. Sinistra. And who is she anyway, a relative of Mrs. Brahms?"

I was surprised that she remembered that Mrs. Brahms had been Ms. Sinistra before her marriage. I said truthfully, "She's a distant relative of Aurora. I'm really sure that you won't get anything out of her."

Rita just stared at the motionless Quick Quotes Quill and said, "What can you tell me about Ms. Brewster's career even if you didn't coach her?"

"Really not much. It's certainly been meteoric. I was out of the country and not following chess the last couple of years. You'd get much better information from the chess magazines."

She gaped at me. "I can't believe that you didn't follow her at all. She must have had a coach. Who was it?"

I laughed. "I can't believe that you haven't learned that at least. It's her mom. . . actually step-mom, the current Mrs. Brewster. I'll save you a few minutes research by telling you that she was also my substitute both times that I was away."

Rita gazed at me speculatively. "You must be pretty close if she subbed for you both times you were gone."

"You could say that."

"I'm going to look her up. In the mean time, do you have anything to add?"

I thought a moment and said, "I'll say this. If you're going to win big in chess or any sport, you have to have something of the killer instinct. You have to hound your opponent to the ground. That was something that Cedric, though a fierce competitor, as Dumbledore would say, never really had. I don't know if he'd have made that final step from contender to world champion without that characteristic.

"On the other hand, Cecily does have that trait. I'll tell you something I have from Mrs. Brewster. Ms. Brewster could be relentless and even ruthless in the pursuit of something she wanted. I wasn't around enough to directly observe that characteristic."

Rita pressed on. "Anything else at all?"

"No."

She took out a business card from her purse and handed it to me. "If you think of anything else that you'd like to share, please get in touch." She chuckled. "Literally, just squeeze the card between thumb and forefinger. I'll be messaged and will get back to you."

I rose to escort her to the floo connection. As we went, she glanced at her wrist and said, "It's about dinner time. Would you have dinner with me tonight?"

I shrugged. "Sure."

Javeen, whom I'd almost forgotten was there, jumped up and exclaimed, "You're going to dinner with HER?"

"Yes."

Javeen opened her mouth. All that came out was, "But, but. . ."

I said, "Bye." Then Rita and I stepped into the floo and out into the Cauldron. It was a little early for the dinner trade. It had only just gone a quarter to five. Tom gave us our choice of tables. He took our drink order and was off.

Rita said, "I have a question for you that's strictly off the record."

"Good."

"What do you do for fun?"

I chuckled. "Well, lately I don't have much time for fun. However, when I do have time, I go to the occasional football or Quidditch game. I also read. I try to keep up with *The Scientific American*."

She immediately asked, "Which is a lady devoted to science?"

I chuckled. "Which is a magazine published in America. It has in-depth articles about all sorts of scientific research."

"Sorry I asked. Anything else?"

"I sometimes go to films."

She nodded slowly. "I've been to a couple of films. Would you like to go to one tonight?"

The question completely surprised me. "Maybe. Let's see what is available." When Tom came with our drinks I asked him if he still kept a copy of *The Times* at the bar.

"Sure. I'll bring it over right after I get your order."

He did. I turned to the entertainment section and scanned the movie adverts. I saw one that attracted my attention. "Have you ever seen a western?"

"I don't think so. What is 'a western'?"

"It's a story set in the desert southwest of the United States, usually in the second half of the 19th century. They usually have a lot of action and some amount of violence."

She thought a minute and said, "I'm game. What do you have in mind?"

"3:10 to Yuma."

She smiled. "Let me guess. Yuma is a town and 3:10 refers to a train that leaves at 3:10 in the afternoon for Yuma."

"Right. It's more of a suspense thriller than an action movie, but I've not seen it, so I can't be sure."

She smiled and said, "I'm game."

"Good. It starts at 7:30, so we've got time to have a leisurely dinner."

"Sounds great."

We had a good meal. Not Hogwarts good but quite decent. We stepped outside, and she disapparated us to the theater. She had insisted on paying for the meal. I insisted on paying for the movie tickets. Despite all the time-wasting that we could think of to do, we arrived at the theatre an hour early. I bought tickets, but insisted that we do something other than wait around for the movie to start.

She agreed, but at first we couldn't pick some good way to waste the time. Then a thought occurred to me. "Why we don't go to a Starbucks for a cup o'?"

She shrugged. "Sure."

Then I gave her an address. She asked me, "You don't memorize the addresses of Starbucks do you?"

I said, "I used to work at that Starbucks."

She smiled. "Every take girls on a date there?"

"Yes."

"I thought so."

The Starbucks was still there. We wasted an hour and returned to the theatre. We arrived just before the scheduled time of the movie. Of course, we had to sit through commercials and previews. When the theatre finally darkened completely and the movie started, she took my hand. After a while, the hand dragged mine to her thigh. A little later, she turned to face me and we kissed. She did that at the most suspenseful parts of the movie.

After it was over, we left the theatre hand in hand. That was not just because we needed to disapparate. We stopped in front of an alley. She faced me and said, "I won't invite you to come up to my apartment. I don't sleep with people that I write about. Some reporters think that can give them special insight into their prey. I don't." There was a moment or two of silence that followed. Then she said, "You know that business card that I gave you?"

"Yes."

"You can use it for more than business—especially after I've published

91

my article."

"Noted."

Then we returned to my office via the Cauldron. When we arrived in my office, we stood in front of the hearth looking at each other not sure what to do. I looked at her carefully for the first time. I reflected that she'd changed a lot since I first met her more than fifteen years before. She had been hard-edged and caustic. Her hair had been tightly curled. You felt like you could cut yourself on it as though it were made of tightly coiled springs. In the old days I'd not have trusted her if she told me, as she had today, that something was completely off the record.

Now, she was very different. I believed that what I'd said was truly off the record. Her appearance reflected the change in her character. Her hair was still blond, but with strands of gray. It was a little longer, hanging loose, soft almost to her shoulders.

I tried to deduce her age. I knew that she had as a young reporter covered the first war against Riddle. That would have been in the late 70's. She must have been in her early twenties then. That would make her birth date in the mid to late 50's. So, she would be in her late forties now, maybe 50. Out of my mouth came the soft words, "Yes. I think I will use your business card."

She smiled and touched a forefinger to her lips and then to mine. She backed into the hearth and whooshed away. I stood there staring into the hearth until Javeen's words awoke me. She said, "Now that your hussy is gone, do you think we can come back to Earth?"

I said nothing and simply went into my apartment for the night.

Wednesday came, and I began to wonder what to expect. After all, I'd not been in a board meeting in almost four years. I had so many papers that I dusted off my briefcase to carry all the papers. Javeen was anxious to get on the way early. I think she was anxious to see my report. I'd not let her see what I'd written. That was difficult when she wanted to sit next me the whole time that I'd been using the Gringotts' laptop.

I held her off as long as I could, but we entered the floo an hour before meeting time. Her argument had been, "I have to be there at least this early to set up the meeting room and make sure I can greet board members as they arrive."

I agreed. We arrived. I went into the Board Room and watched Javeen set up. She was very efficient. She had already made the name tents. She distributed the agenda. I looked at it and found nothing unexpected. I was the main event for this meeting. I read my report a couple of times until I couldn't stand to see the words any more. Until the words were only individual meaningless sounds.

Eventually other board members arrived. They sat and exchanged a few words with me. There were new members whom I didn't recognized. I started to introduce myself. I didn't finish. The person would immediately say, "I know you. You're our only Muggle member, James Wendt."

One said, "I really liked your personal assistant."

I said, "Yeh. I like her, too."

Finally, Glorblatt arrived and called the meeting to order. He began, "Well, it's with great pleasure that we welcome back Professor Wendt to a board meeting. As a matter of fact, we want to celebrate his return and his marvelous invention of paper money with a little party."

With that signal Javeen wheeled in a cart that had a cake. It was iced to look like a paper galleon bill—with the Glorblatt side up. There was butter beer and tea as well. We took a break as Javeen sliced up the galleon cake and distributed them along with beverages. When we all had our cake in front of us, Glorblatt said, "Well, enough of frivolity. We have a report on the success of the paper galleon from none other than its inventor, Professor James Wendt."

There was some polite applause, and then it became deathly silent in the Board Room. I handed out the packets that I'd brought in my briefcase. I then said, "The packets that you have include an analysis of the question about the acceptance and use of paper galleons among the wizarding public.

"Briefly, there are significant technical problems in actually measuring data that shed light on that question. I finally decided that using the balance between specie and paper money in bank settlement accounts was the best that we could do. The overall result is that throughout the world somewhere around 60% of currency in circulation is paper and 40% is specie. Here in England, the split is 78% paper and 22% specie.

"That substantial difference led me to investigate how much variation there was and what caused it. A useful measure of variation is standard deviation. The standard deviation in this distribution is 21%. That is really high. Exhibit 1 shows the distribution plotted as the number of occurrences of a particular percentage paper vs. the percentage itself. You can see that the distribution is roughly Gaussian.

"Exhibit 2 shows the distribution by continent. Each continent has an average percent and a very narrow standard deviation. This shows that the acceptance of paper currency depends critically on the continent. Please notice that the continents with the lowest acceptance rate are also the ones furthest from England.

"These results show pretty conclusively that Gresham's law applies to wizard money as well as Muggle money. Please see appendix A for a brief review of Gresham's law and its history.

"I believe that the future of wizard money is the fairly rapid replacement of specie with paper currency. I don't think that the smaller denomination coins will be replaced, but certainly the large denomination ones will. You see this stratification in almost all Muggle money.

"Consequently, I think that Gringotts should prepare to issue more paper money, possibly doubling the supply of paper money in the next couple of years.

"Are there questions?"

One of the board members wanted to know how much paper money had been issued so far. I didn't know, but I offered to find out and add that to the minutes of the meeting. There were no other questions. The meeting then turned to more mundane issues like the financial report and vault occupancy projections.

When the meeting closed, Glorblatt invited me to join him for drinks. I insisted that I couldn't stay out late because it was a "school night." He assured me that we wouldn't be out later than 10 PM. I reluctantly accepted. Of course, Javeen took my hand and we whooshed through the floo network to their favorite goblin bar.

After we'd ordered, and received drinks Gorblatt said, "We're really happy to have you back, of course. Your personal assistant did a creditable job in your absence. Mrs. Brewster was actually rather clever in the way that she managed the program to print paper money. But, I can't tell you how happy I am that you are back."

Javeen nodded enthusiastically. She asked, "You were gone for over three years. Is an absence like that going to happen again?"

I said, "I'm not going to guarantee anything."

Glorblatt nodded knowingly. "Well, there is some information that you maybe aren't aware of. In the first place, when the first batch of paper currency came off the printer and was accepted by the Ministry, we granted you a generous six digit bonus."

"Thank you."

Glorblatt went on, "There's another bonus each year on the table for you—provided that you attend every board meeting of the year. The bonus would be ten percent of the profit that we make on minting coins and printing currency."

I said, "Very generous. No one can predict the future, but I can assure you that it is my solid intention to be present for all board meetings and whatever else my position requires for the next three years."

Gorblatt asked, "What is it with three years? Three on. Three off?"

I smiled, "I'm not going to tell you."

Glorblatt was obviously disappointed, but didn't say anything.

We finished our drinks. Javeen put her hand on my thigh and said, "We are glad to have you back."

I smiled. "I am, too." I was stuck about what to do with the hand on my thigh. Javeen had me over a barrel. As long as her father were with us I couldn't say or do what I normally would if we were in my office—remove it from my thigh dramatically and give her an ultimatum about the use of hands. I pointed out that it was a school night, and I needed to get back to school.

Gorblatt agreed but mumbled, "Why you keep working there when you could retire and live off your other income I don't understand."

Javeen and I went to the hearth. I took her hand, and we arrived in my office.

Filch Redux

Thursday was the day for the Old Boy's Club meeting at lunch. It had been so crazy that I'd completely forgotten. While I was having breakfast, Hagrid came over as the meal was ending to remind me of the meeting at noon.

I asked, "Meeting?"

"Sure, professor. You know, the OBC."

I nodded.

That noon Filch showed up at my office just before noon. He entered without knocking. He was almost the only person who felt free to do that. Even Aurora made a perfunctory knock Anyway, Filch demanded, "Come on, Professor, we're burning daylight. Let's get moving."

He escorted me all the way to the Three Broomsticks. The other members were either there already or shortly would be. When we all had arrived and ordered, Slughorn introduced the topic of the day. "Gentlemen. This is a red letter day. Professor Wendt is back after a three year absence. This is our last meeting before Halloween. That raises the question of the year—who is Professor Wendt going to go to the party as. . ." He paused, apparently thinking that I'd just pick up the hint and run with it.

I said, "You're just going to have to show up and see what happens."

No one was particularly surprised. That didn't mean that they were done giving me a hard time. Hagrid said, "I think we ought to try to guess who?"

Slughorn said, "Let's see. Who has Wendt not impersonated? He's not impersonated me. Maybe it's me. Has he ever impersonated you, Hagrid?"

Hagrid chuckled. "That would be a laugh."

Dursley said, "I don't remember ever being impersonated."

Filch said, "It absoviosly me—who's known him the longest here at Hogwarts and was his drinking buddy the longest. It's a no brainless."

I myself laughed. "I think you must have it."

Filch's face fell. I guess he thought that if I admitted it, I must be try-ing to trick him. I almost wished that I could assure him that this was "his" year. "Well," I thought, "He'll enjoy it all the more when he discovers the truth."

We had a decent lunch. It was a good break from the last couple of weeks. The next few days I wasn't even bothered that Javeen was always around in the evening and the weekend.

□

The next Wednesday morning at breakfast, Slughorn made an announce-ment after the traditional break for a moment of silence. He turned away from the podium and took two steps. Then he turned back to the podium. "Oh, yes. One more thing that I almost forgot. Today is Halloween and to-morrow is a school day. The year has been going so well that I think we should have a holiday tomorrow so we can all enjoy Halloween tonight."

A shout of joy from the students along with a round of heart-felt ap-plause from the Professors greeted that announcement. I felt really happy. I was running the show tonight with Aurora. I was impersonating someone who should be perfectly safe. What could happen? The obvious answer was nothing. The answer of my emotions was nothing. Still. . . Still.

The dinner that night was even more exceptional than usual. The only item on the menu that I didn't really like was the pumpkin juice that was *de rigueur* for all to drink as a sort of toast for the evening. I could never un-derstand what anyone saw in that drink.

For once, I was anxious to get up to my office to meet Aurora. I even considered going directly to her office. I finally decided that I didn't want to scare her off. I arrived at my office. I went into my apartment where I'd rummaged around to find a garment that would not be out of place if he were wearing it. While I was doing that, there was a knock on the door. I took my outfit into the office just in time to hear Aurora mutter, "Where are you, you coward?"

I stepped up to her and said, "Good to see you."

She stared at me and asked, "Who are you and what have you done with Wendt?"

"I swear I have not yet taken polyjuice potion, and I am indeed Profes-sor James Wendt of Hogwarts."

Aurora smiled in relief and said, "Come on! We're burning moon-light." She pulled two vials out of her purse. One was labeled "D". The other was labeled "F". "Could we do this with some Blue Label?"

I chuckled. "I don't know whether it's a waste of good whiskey or not, but I'd sure prefer to take it in Blue Label than straight." I got my bottle out of the lower left drawer and poured a generous portion into a pair of glasses. Aurora handed me the vial labeled "F". I added the vial to my glass.

I was about to drink the bilious concoction when Aurora interrupted me. "Oh, wait. I brought a set of dress robes for you."

I objected, "But I have something that I'll wear that I think is right up Filch's alley." I lifted the set of robes from behind my desk.

Aurora glanced at them and said, "No. No. Filch actually does on rare occasions wear real dress robes. She reached into her purse and pulled out a set of dress robes which were obviously of an ancient design but not wear-worn. She said, "Even Filch himself wouldn't doubt you in this."

I shrugged. Whether or not that was right, it was only a party. So I accepted them. I tossed off the polyjuice potion, which was rendered tolerable by the Blue Label and retreated to my apartment to change into Filch togs. When I had changed and came out, Aurora had become the very image of Dursley. I asked, "You ready to go?"

"Sure."

We went down to the Great Hall. The band was still warming up. We went to the refreshment table where the house elves had just set up a wonderful spread. I put a few appetizers on a paper plate and tasted. While we were standing there, Slughorn sidled up. He took a plate as well and asked me, "Do you have any idea who Wendt is coming as."

I shrugged. Slughorn said, "You'd know if anyone would. Are you sure you don't have a hint?"

I shook my head, and Slughorn wandered off. Just then, the band struck up a hard rock tune that made me glad that I didn't have to dance to it. There were a couple of similar songs. Then, they switched to something slow. About that time, Ms. Pinz came up to the table. She said, "Well, Mr. Filch, you look especially good this evening."

"As do you," I said. The strange thing was that she did look especially good. Her hair was done differently than normal. It was always drawn up into some sort of bun, but today was different. It actually reminded me a lot of Minerva's hairdos. I took a much closer look at her and realized that she wore a very flattering set of dress robes—very different from her usual.

She noticed my attention. She started to ask something, but I broke in. I asked, "Ms. Pinz, the band is playing something that even I can dance to. Would you like to dance?"

She flushed a nice shade of pink and said, "Why Mr. Filch, I think that would be. . . would be. . . quite lovely."

I took her hand and led her out onto the dance floor. The faux Dursley tried to get my attention, but I was only paying attention to Pinz's face, her eyes, her hair. We started in a standard pose with one arm on her shoulder and the other holder her opposite hand up. It was pleasant, and we exchanged pleasantries about the quality of the refreshments, the size of the crowd, the unusually warm weather, and so on.

Sometime during the second dance, my arm slipped down to hold her waist and we were suddenly dancing cheek to cheek. As we danced, she was humming in time with the music. It seemed the most beautiful tune that I'd ever heard. I said, "Do you know, Ms. Pinz, I do think that you look exceptionally lovely this evening." She started to protest, but I broke in. "No, really. I mean, you always look lovely, but there's something about you tonight that I can't put a finger on. You really might be the most enchanting woman at the ball."

I could feel on my cheek the expression of her face change. I imagined that it had become a dreamy smile. She said, "You know, I've always liked you Mr. F. I don't know why I never really had the courage to tell you."

I replied, "Oh, you have always held a special place in my heart." She chuckled at that, and she pulled me even closer. I brushed her cheek with my lips and wished that I had the daring to turn that into a full kiss.

Just then, out of the corner of my eye, I saw the real Filch coming toward us. I straightened and said, "That joker, Professor Wendt, is headed this way. I need to tell him something."

Just before he arrived into talking range, I turned toward him and said, "You, Professor Wendt, have quite a nerviousnous coming disguised as myself." I looked over at Ms. Pinz and said, "I don't blame him wanting to be mistook for me, but you don't get to cut in between me and the loverly Ms. Pinz."

Filch was beside himself. He opened his mouth once or twice to say something but didn't. Then, as we started to dance away, he said, "You can't do this. I didn't mean you to. . . to. . ."

I said to Ms. Pinz, "He does do a good job of impersonifying me, doesn't he? You'd almost think he was channelizing me." I don't know if she actually heard what I said. She had laid her head on my chest and was humming again."

After the next song, the band took a break. Ms. Pinz looked up from my shoulder in some surprise and said, "I just got a shipment of books in and haven't cataloged them yet. Wouldn't you like to come up to the Library and help me with that."

"Cataloging with you? It sounds charming."

She then took my hand and led me out of the Great Hall and up to her library. After she unlocked the door and led me in to the Librarian's Desk where the unopened box of books rested, she asked me if I'd ever had a tour of the Library.

"No, ma'am."

"Then, I will show you around." We didn't actually finish the tour of the Library. As a matter of fact, we hardly had gotten started. She led me over to a study carrel. She pointed out that the bench inside was large enough for two to sit. She said, "Let me demonstrate." She sat and drew me down to sit beside her.

Once there, I asked, "Do students ever come into one of these to canoodle?"

"What is canoodling?"

I demonstrated. I encircled her waist with my arms, gazed into her eyes for a long moment, and then kissed her. She responded pleasantly. Then, she said, "That was really nice."

I repeated. This time, I opened my mouth slightly and ran my tongue around her lips. She offered not the slightest resistance and actually opened her mouth some. From that point all thought of touring the Library or cataloging books disappeared from both our minds. The main focus of our attention for quite a while was satisfying our partner.

I didn't let my hands go idle. I caressed her back and then sent a hand up her back and into her hairdo, searching for hairpins to remove. I actually found a couple when she pulled away from me and said, "Silly man. What are you doing?"

I smiled a silly smile and said, "I want to let your hair down."

She smiled shyly and said, "Why didn't you say so, let me help you." She took my hand in hers and guided it up to her bun, where we efficiently removed the rest of the hairpins. With that finished, I drew her hair down over her shoulders and back. We returned to the lip action and I ran a hand gently through her hair.

Then an idea struck me. "Let's make a bed of books on the floor."

She looked at me as though I were crazy, and then her eyes lit up. "Yes, we could lie on them." We went to the nearby stacks and brought handfuls into the carrel and spread them about. I sat on them and drew her down next to me. We then lay on them. I kissed ever part of her face that I could reach.

After a while, I drew back a little and gazed at her lying on her side on the bed of books. "You are the queen of books."

She laughed at that. Then she drawled languorously, "So, do you know what I wish?"

Incapable of speech, I just shook my head.

She took both my hands in hers and said, "I wish that I could just put you on a bookshelf—a bookshelf in the restricted section. I wouldn't let anyone touch you, let alone take you out. When I closed the Library for the night, I'd lock the door and take you down from the bookshelf lovingly. I would take you into my bedroom and remove all my clothes. I'd get into bed and caress your spine." She pantomimed each action as she spoke it. "I'd open your cover, lick my finger, and turn your pages one at a time. I'd stop now and then and kiss one of your pages. I'd sleep with you beside me in bed. When I got up in the morning, I'd dress in front of you and then take you back to the restricted section. I would put you in your place on the bookshelf and never let anyone touch you—ever!"

All through this discussion, her breath came ever more rapidly. She looked down and said, "Yes. Rise for your queen." After a pause, she took a deep breath and said, "I'm going to slip into something more comfortable. Just you don't move an inch." With that she made a motion with her hand as though she were putting a book back on the shelf. Then she got up and walked off toward the entrance to her apartment.

I was up indeed. However, just then, I felt that dislocation of all the bones in your body that you feel when the polyjuice potion begins to wear off. "Bloody. . ." I thought, "I can't let her see me change into Professor Wendt." I got up, ran out of the Library and down to my office. There were still sounds coming from the party, so it was still going. I took off Filch's robes while I was transforming. I kept thinking, "Hurry! Hurry!" Then when it was almost complete, I put something of my own on. I ran out of my office, down the hall, and up to the Library.

I reached the door, which I thought that I'd left open. Not only was it closed, but it was locked! I banged on the door, heedless of the noise. After two or three minutes, I heard Pinz's voice on the other side of the door saying, "Go away. Anything you need will wait for the morning!" In the background I heard Filch's voice say, "Get rid of the sod and get back here on the triple!"

The sound of Filch's voice kept me from saying anything. I turned and headed back toward my office. On the way, another wave of desire swept over me. A vision of us spending the night in her bed came to me. I imagined waking late in the morning. We'd talk languidly in each other's arms. We'd gaze into the other's eyes. We'd have lunch and go for a walk arm in arm around the lake-shore. I stopped and started back for the Library slowly. I thought about what I'd do. "I'll bang on the door until she comes. I'll ask her to open the door and see me. I'll fall to my knees and kiss her feet. I'll beg her to let me stay the night." I stopped before I reached the Library. That dream was nothing more than that—a dream, the hangover

101

from too much polyjuice potion. I returned to my office.

□□

The office door was ajar when I entered. I thought that it must be Aurora transforming back, maybe in the loo. She'd just left the office door open. Then I heard rather than saw the door to my apartment start to open. I had a sort of premonition. I jumped behind the sofa. I dug in my pocket for my purse. It was lucky that I changed back into my normal clothes. They had my purse with my Glock. I managed to get it out about the time that the intruder said, "Who's there?" The voice was a woman's voice that was vaguely familiar, but I couldn't identify it.

I said, "Who are you?" I stuck my head above the sofa just enough to get a glimpse. I was greeted by some spell whizzing near my head. I had the slightest glimpse of a brunette. I stuck my hand around the sofa and fired a shot in the general direction of my desk. There was the satisfying sound of a bullet hitting the desk. Then I said, "What are you doing here?" I heard an almost instant echo of those words in a woman's voice that was tantalizingly familiar, but I still couldn't identify it.

I decided that maybe I should identify myself. "I'm Professor James Wendt of Hogwarts."

The voice replied. "I'm Professor Jaimie Sinistra of Hogwarts."

The import of those words must have struck us both at the same moment. We both said, "That's impossible!"

I said, "If that's true, tell me something that only I would know."

She replied, "You first."

I said, "All right." Just then she stuck her head around the desk and shot a spell at me. It missed. I said, "One more of those and we're done parlaying. I'll be trying to maim or kill."

She answered, "I'll accept that. No more attempts to kill or maim."

Of course, I didn't trust her, but if she was honest, we might be able to figure out what was going on. I picked something that only she would know. I said, "You know that only a few people know of our double existence. I'll name two. You name the rest. There's Slughorn and Dursley. Now you."

She snapped back, "It's a no-brainer that those two would be involved with potions, but the other two are Sally Pearson and Aurora Brahms."

I didn't answer right away. She was right about the ones who knew, but there was another. Why didn't she know about him? She said, "Right?"

I said, "Partial credit. You missed someone. Why? I'm not totally satisfied."

102

She shot back, "There isn't anyone else. I'll tell you something that only you knew. When you finished working with the NSF, you went for a river cruise in America."

I shot back, "A lot of people knew that."

"I'm not finished. After the river cruise you spent a couple of days in New York City. Again, I know, other people knew that. The night you stayed there Minerva went to visit a friend." I started to open my mouth, but I decided to let her proceed. "While she was gone, you went down to the coffee shop in the hotel to have a drink and read the New York *Times*. You ran into an old girl friend who worked for a cruise line. You ended up spending the night with her."

I said cautiously, "Still, I wasn't the only one besides her to know that."

The ersatz Sinistra replied, "Yes. She knew. As a matter of fact, she encouraged the two of you by saying, 'Someone's going to have a good time tonight.'"

I was forced to say, "That's right."

Just then, there was a whoosh from the floo connection, and Javeen stepped out into my office. Sinistra said with cold fury in her voice, "Get out. Now." She accompanied it with a warning spell that hit the mantle of the hearth and broke my framed photo of an ersatz Albert Einstein at a blackboard explaining relational databases. Javeen said, "I didn't know you had company. I'm gone for the night."

Sinistra asked, "What does she mean, for the night?"

I was still hiding behind the sofa, but I'm sure she understood when I said, "I've got a feeling you're going to know more about her than you want to before we're done. However, I'm still not satisfied that you are re-allly, 'you'."

Sinistra agreed and asked for a detail that only I would know. I had one that would satisfy anyone. I said, "Think back to when Minerva insisted that I leave the country. I went to my rooming house from when I first came to England. I lived in a garret for a while on the top floor. It only had one window—a dormer window. The casement was an old-fashioned one with a window that used a counter-weight on a pulley to make it easy to raise and lower the window. The counter-weight was accessible through a little door held in- place by a small screw. I opened that door and put my money into it for safe keeping. The police never found it."

She was silent for a while. Then she said, "That is truly something that no one else knew about and that you had no reason to reveal to anyone."

I said, "Now, you tell me one that is completely unambiguous."

Her voice was taut as she said, "I've got one that absolutely no one but

103

I know. It was on Christmas day of my first year. I had gone to a bar. I was alone there except for the bartender and one other customer. He came to sit beside me and offered to buy me a drink. I refused the offer. He stayed and talked for a few minutes. Then the world became tipsy. I know, it's not much of a word, but that's the way I felt. I don't remember much for a while. I have little snatches of memory as he helped me to an elevator and up to HIS room."

Here she stopped. I wasn't sure whether it was because she was holding back tears or because she didn't want to say what I was becoming increasingly sure that she would say. The tears did come. Then she said, "God I don't want to say any of this. It shows how hideous a person I am." Again there was a pause and an examination of the floor. I knew that I only needed to give her time to press through.

She gave a little nod and looked up directly into my eyes. "I'm not going to tell you the whole story even though I'm convinced you know it already. I'm only going to tell enough to convince anyone that only I knew it and that it is true." She took a deep breath and then the plunge. "I woke up on the bed in his room. I still had all my clothes on. I tried to summon my wand from my purse that was closed. I lost consciousness again. When I awakened, the wand was in my hand, he was petrified, and I had enough presence of mind to. . ." She slowly said the next words, "Force him to take the Unbreakable Oath." There was a pause and she said, "I won't tell you what the oath was. You undoubtedly know it. He died within a few hours at most. I'm sure that he couldn't have told anyone this story before he died."

I was satisfied. I said so. "OK. I trust you. You could no more harm me than you could hurt yourself. As a matter of fact, harming me would be hurting yourself. I'm going to stand and lay my Glock down on the sofa pointing into the sofa. I hope you'll do the same with your wand." Then I stood and walked around the sofa. I took a seat in the red leather chair—perhaps the first time that I had ever done that. She stood from behind the desk, laid her wand down on the desktop on the furthest corner.

She said, "Where do we go from here?"

"First, maybe we should try to figure out how we are both siting here in the flesh together." I held out my hand to shake hers—just to be sure that we were both standing together in the flesh. She shook my hands. She sat behind the desk as though it were the most natural thing in the world to her.

I had a suggestion. "When did you first notice that the world was somehow. . . uh, strange?"

She didn't have to think for more than a couple of seconds. "Just when you opened the door, and I heard someone enter my office." It was jarring hearing her use that phrase, "my office."

"OK. Then what had you done just before that?"

Again, there was no hesitation although the answer was lengthy. "Let's see. I have to give you some background. As you probably know Aurora can be a pain in the 'arse'. She is as bad as the God of Mischief, Loki, or Puck. It doesn't matter whether you turn her down flat on her little Halloween pranks, she just goes ahead and does them.

"So, I was determined to avoid that one more year. My solution was to disappear on Halloween."

I asked, "You mean by going to Paris or Dublin or somewhere?"

"No, by going to the Room of Requirement."

I nodded, "Good idea."

"But I wasn't satisfied with that. I also stepped into the vanishing cabinet that's located there. I stayed in there until I was sure that the party must be over. Then I left the Room of Requirement and checked for party noises coming from the Great Hall. Nothing. Then I walked down here and found that my office was a mess. Even worse, my apartment was awful and full of men's clothes. I don't get it. What happened?"

"I think there's only one explanation. It has something to do with using the vanishing cabinet, and I have the beginnings of an idea about an explanation."

Her jaw set in a scowl, "Well what are you waiting for? What's your idea?"

I said, "You know about string theory?"

"Yes. Some. I know that it explains the existence of elementary particles by saying that they are strings. The mass and other properties are explained by modes of vibration of the strings, like the different notes that a violin can make are determined by the vibration modes of the violin strings."

"Good. That's the basics, but there's more, much more, to it. What you described was the beginning of the theory about thirty or so years ago. It would have been an intellectual curiosity if it weren't for one fact that was discovered as people worked hard to improve the predictive power of the theory. They tried expanding the theory to more dimensions than three. They made an amazing discovery. At eleven dimensions, General Relativity appeared in the solutions."

I hesitated for effect. Jaimie seemed deep in thought. Then it was as if a light bulb had gone off in her head. Her mouth opened wide as did her eyes. She said, "Wait a minute. String theory is a quantum mechanics theory, right?" I nodded. Her eyes popped wider. "General Relativity and Quantum Mechanics together in the same theory!"

"Right."

She actually laughed. "Einstein searched for that for the rest of his life after he published General Relativity. He never found it! And it came right out of String Theory!"

"Right."

She sobered a bit and said, "But it requires eleven dimensions, right?"

"I'm afraid so."

She laughed again. "Where are you going to get eleven dimensions? There are obviously only three dimensions. This is a festral that won't fly."

I chuckled. "Well, it will bear that interpretation, but the attraction of a theory that unites GR & QM is so great that most people aren't willing to give it up without a real fight."

"I get that. So there must be some ideas that could save String Theory. What are they?"

"Basically the favorites break down into two classes. Either some sort of force restricts us to three dimensions, or, the extra eight dimensions or whatever are actually there but sort of rolled up very tightly so that we don't observe them."

She stared at me and said, "Pretty desperate, aren't you?"

"Well, considering that you only get one Einstein a century, people are pretty desperate."

"What has this got to do with why we are here together?"

I started improvising. "Well, would you like something to drink first?"

She smiled. "Sure. Do you really keep Blue Label in your desk?"

"Take a look and see."

She opened a couple of drawers, and her eyes grew like pie plates. "Yes, you do." She flicked her wand and two glasses flew from the cabinet in the bookshelf. They were clean and contained ice. She poured us a couple of stiff shots. She proposed a toast. "Here's to String Theory."

I took a sip and started in earnest. "Here's what I think happened. Since there are eight extra dimensions, there's plenty of room for lots of three dimensional universes. I think that somehow when you stepped into your vanishing cabinet in your universe, you stepped out in my universe."

She thought about it and asked, "But lots of people used vanishing cabinets. As far as I know, no one ever disappeared or appeared, apparently from nowhere."

"Look. I barely understand the physics of String Theory and the mathematics of it not at all. I'm not a wizard. How do you expect me to explain what happened to you in your vanishing cabinet?"

She contemplated the floor and then said, "All right. Let's go to talk with someone who is a great witch. Let's go see Minerva."

I opened my mouth but couldn't force anything out. Jaimie asked,

"There's something wrong, isn't there!"

"Minerva died several years ago."

Jaimie exclaimed, "How is that possible?" She shook her head, "Dumbledore gone, Snape gone, and now Minerva gone. Who's left?"

"Our Headmaster is Slughorn. We can go to talk to him, but it's late. I want us to figure out what the differences are between our universes before we approach them. Also, it's pretty late right now. We'd only wake him up and make him angry at us."

She was clearly frustrated. She rose and stamped back and forth behind her desk. "Well, we're going to do something. Let's find out how different your universe and mine are."

I agreed. "Fine. There are some obvious differences that we already know about. Here Minerva is gone. She's not in your universe." I was afraid to ask for details. For example, did she consider herself to be a widow? How did she feel about me?

Jaimie asked, "How did she die?"

That brought us to the outskirts of a difficult question—how did I survive and supplant Jaimie? I held that question at bay and proceeded on the original question. "You had the Souls in your universe, right?"

"Sure. We were lucky to get rid of them. Did they kill her?"

"Not exactly. It's a story. We did defeat them. Minerva and nearly all wizards and witches survived, but that wasn't the end of the story."

"You don't mean to say that they came back after you gave them such a terrible ultimatum?"

I sighed sadly, "Yes. They were stuck between a rock and a hard place. They were being attacked by a race that is far smarter than either us or the Souls. They were so smart that the Souls didn't even realize that they were under attack. They came to us in desperation."

"I suppose you didn't turn them down like they richly deserved." She leaned in to hear more.

"No, we didn't realize they were being attacked either. We accepted their belief that they were victims of a plague that killed everyone that contracted it—100 percent mortality. We were almost as scared as they were."

"Who was this mystery race? Where did they come from?"

"We never learned what they called themselves. We decided to call them the PAK."

She interrupted me. "The PAK. That was science fiction. Larry. . . oh, what is his name?" I was about to continue when she said, "Of course! Larry Niven. The super race from the center of the galaxy."

I shrugged. "We needed a name. It seemed appropriate."

Excitedly she said, "It seemed appropriate to YOU. You named them, didn't you?"

"Sure. Anyway, we didn't know that at the time. The Ghosts—that's the name I prefer for the Souls—asked for help politely. There was a serious debate about what to do with them. We ended up sending a small party to help them figure out what was going on. Minerva and I were with them. It turned out that the PAK were poisoning their food supply."

"That was just a trick to get the Souls to reveal the location of their home world."

She said, "It worked. What were these PAK going to do?"

"Oh, they had a weapon that they could turn the Ghosts' home star into a nova."

She gasped. "That's impossible!"

"Oh, I'm afraid it was possible. They had a faster-than-light drive. They were going to use it to turn a good fraction of the star into a fusion bomb."

She was still doubtful.

"Oh, believe me, it was possible. In this universe, there's a new big crater on Mars that the PAK blasted as a demo."

Jaimie sunk back in her seat and put her head in her hands. "How did you stop them? You did stop them, didn't you?"

"Sure. It was a suicide mission for the PAK. They were going to fly their ship into the star. Minerva staged a mutiny. We won. She died." She was silent for a while. Then she said, "Wait! You said that the PAK tricked you into helping them. Blasting that crater doesn't seem like too much of a secret plot."

"You're right. The PAK came back. Then it wasn't subterfuge. It was outright blackmail. They said, 'You know where the Ghost star is. Lead us to it or we'll destroy your planet instead'."

She twirled my swivel desk chair around a couple of times. I guess that's what she does when she wants to think hard. When she stopped, she asked, "Did they kill the Ghost star that time? I'm guessing they didn't, right?"

"No, they didn't. Let's just say that we convinced them to negotiate. Or really, it would be more accurate to say that when we left the Ghost solar system, they were negotiating. We don't know what the outcome was."

"How in the world did you get them to do that?"

I sighed. "It's far too long a story to even start tonight. Let's just say that you can be very convincing when you want to."

Her head popped up, and she stared at me, "Me? What do you mean?"

"Are you really surprised? You know that I have your memories—or at least this universe's version of your memories. I've been very respectful of them lately, but it's hard to keep out all recollection of your dealing with the PAK."

She asked, "Just how did you manage to come back and send me . . . er this universe's version of me to oblivion? Did I just commit suicide to give you back your life?"

"No. You didn't. We cut a deal. It was good deal. You would go off and save the Souls. In return, you'd get three years to start a family and see Cecily graduate."

Her mouth dropped open. She noticed and closed it. Then she asked, "Who in the world is Cecily? AND what's this about a family?"

I was the one to be surprised. I hadn't expected this big a difference in our universes. "Uhmm. Cecily is your step-daughter. You and Ted Brewster are married. You've had two kids."

She deepened the mystery by asking, "Who is Ted Brewster?"

I dropped back into my armchair. I thought and sipped the Blue Label. I empty my glass and absently held it up for more. Jaimie provided. Then I said, "OK. This is going to require a lot of explaining. It's got to be done now. Before long Ted is going to get wind that you are 'back'. He's going to demand to know what's gone on. Both of us need to be prepared for that."

She scoffed. "Right-o. Let's start with Ted."

I said, "No. We're starting with Cecily. Do you mean that you don't remember Cecily Brewster at all?"

She had added some Blue Label to her glass and said, "Let me think. There is something about that name." She sipped and thought. Then she said, "Yes. I do remember her—sort of. She was a war orphan. Both her parents died in the second war against Riddle. She was raised by an aunt and uncle. I remember her as intelligent, hard working when she was motivated, and a decent kid."

It was my turn to scoff. "Huh! At least we can agree that there was a great war against Riddle. In this universe, her dad didn't die. She was raised as a sort of tomboy. Her dad was interested in chess, and she taught herself to become Master level. She wanted help to become another Cedric Diggory. She approached me to tutor her. I wasn't up to it after Cedric.

"Then you came along. She approached you, and the two of you sort of struggled to find the right relationship. Eventually, you gave her some help and got her going."

She just stared and said, "Amazing."

"Right. Anyway, She also helped you."

Jaimie scoffed, "How could she do that?"

"She introduced you to the love of your life."

She just stared, so I answered her unasked question. "She introduced you to her dad. The two of you really hit it off. Before the term was over, the two of you married."

She still had no comment. I asked a question. "You've learned an awful lot about what has been happening in this universe. What has been happening in yours?"

She filled her glass, glanced at mine, which was still pretty full, and began.

"As you know, I came into being when Aurora gave you the 'new improved polyjuice potion'. I took your place on the Gringotts board pretending to be your agent. Of course, I continued your general program on the Board and won the rest of the Board over to accepting me. However, the secretary to the Board, that Javeen, never really trusted me. I think she rather fancied you. She always was suspicions of my motives."

She stopped a moment in apparent surprise. "What's going on between you and Javeen right now? You don't mean to tell me that it was mutual?"

Would I never rid myself of that Javeen? I shook my head and said, "No. She wishes. She's been staying in the office most night—NOT my room because without Minerva I don't have any of the little services that magic provides you that you probably don't notice—owl mail, disapparation, the floo network, and so on. She's been doing that supposedly because it's in Gringotts interest for Board members to have those little niceties. Of course, you're right, it doesn't hurt that she's got a 'thing' for me."

Jaimie's stare became even more wide-eyed. "Surely, you don't mean she's been staying with you as a sort of house elf for years and years!"

"No. You forget that I've been—let us say—uh 'gone' for almost four years off and on. Then too, Javeen is not the only young lady who fancied me since Minerva died."

She made a face and said, "So, you prey off of impressionable young things to get 'services'?"

"No, no. In the first place you can hardly call Javeen 'impressionable'. The other young lady is even less 'impressionable' than Javeen if you can imagine that. As a matter of fact, you could even make the case that she has been taking advantage of me."

Jaimie went on. "There were not a lot of big developments on the Gringotts Board. There was one significant development. The wizard world had what I think is called a 'liquidity crisis' in the Muggle world. It's never before developed in the wizard world. The goblins were quite confused by what was happening."

I nodded. Of course, I'd been through that myself several years ago.

She went on. "The problem was recognized. There were no magical sources of gold adequate to make enough galleons fast enough to correct the problem. I provided a way to get adequate gold. We bought from Muggle sources and depended on loans from Muggle governments to buy the gold. We've been paying them off for years in a variety of ways—magical favors, the trade surplus from magically produced goods."

I asked the leading question, "Do you think they'd have come up with that solution without you?"

She waffled. "Well, I suppose they might have."

I shook my head in the negative."Don't you believe it." Then I smirked and said, "I want to show you something."

Jaimie cautiously asked, "Just what do you want to show me?"

I laughed. "It's nothing bad. Just close your eyes and hold out your hand."

Still cautious, she asked, "Which one?"

"Doesn't matter." She held out her left hand. I opened my purse and pulled something out, that I placed in her hand.

"Am I supposed to guess what it is?"

"No, just open your eyes and examine it."

She did. Her eyes bulged as she drew it close to her eyes. She turned it over and over in her hand, examining it closely. Then she asked, "Where did you get this?"

"I took it out of my vault at Gringotts."

She held it up to the light. Eventually, she said, "Did you have this made as a demonstration of what might be done?"

'No, it's real legal tender for settling 'wizard debts public or private.' See. It says so right on the bill."

She scoffed. "Come on. Be serious. It's impossible to make paper currency that can't be duplicated."

I said, "Take a look at it carefully. Note the watermark."

She looked at me and then at the bill again holding it up to the light. She said, "OK. So what?"

"Now duplicate it. I know it's a simple spell. Most witches can do it."

She smiled. "You bet I can. I can do it silently." She laid the bill down on the desk, flourished her wand, and there was a second bill beside it. She picked it up, examined it carefully, including the watermark. "It looks duplicate to me."

I shrugged. "Well, let's go on to other topics. Did you never have any love interests in your life?"

She shook her head. I asked, "What about Mr. Dursley?"

"Mr. Dursley? Why he married that Pamela woman before I'd even met him. Why would you think that he might be interested in me or I in

111

him?"

"Well, in this universe, he hasn't married her yet. I don't know whether or not he will, but I do know that he had a thing for you. He was sad when you let me come back the first time."

Her eyes shone for a moment and she asked, "Really? I had no idea."

I scoffed. "Just like you have no idea that you're a stunning beauty."

"Oh, come on. I'm pretty—maybe. But stunning?"

"No matter. He wasn't available, but what about the rest of the world of available men?"

"I love my job. I rarely left the castle on holidays. I never met another Brewster—a widower who had a child in school. It's not so strange."

"What about you? Minerva died five years ago. You never married again?"

I shook my head. "I thought I'd found another Minerva. She and I were happy. Then I gave you back your life and got your husband to promise to get you to give me my life back after three years.. When I returned, she'd reconnected with a former love, and that was it."

She listened carefully and reached out to touch my forearm. I shook my head. "I'm still struggling with the loss. It's. . ." I couldn't look her in the face because I was ashamed to admit that I still felt grief at times.

She glanced down when I did. She twisted her head, reached down, and picked one of the bills up from the desk. She looked at it closely and held it up to the light. Then she picked up the other bill and held them both up to the light. She asked, "What happened to this bill?"

I forced my eyes up and squeezed them tight shut so that no tear would escape. Then I asked her, "Tell me what you see."

She looked up at the bill with the light flowing through it. She said, "What's happened to the watermark? Part of it was yellow. Now it's grey." Then she gasped and said, "The yellow is actually gold isn't it. You can't duplicate gold! That was your idea! The Goblins used it! You must be as rich as Croesus."

I realized that I didn't know just how well off I was. "I don't know. You must know that I've been rather well off for quite some time."

"Yes, but I never looked into it. I had the Goblins give me an accounting of my earnings from being on the Board from the moment I took your place. It was good. I opened a separate vault for my earnings from Hogwarts and had the amounts of my earnings from the Board transferred to my account. Once I started getting a share of the earnings from minting coins from Muggle gold, I began to be well-to-do, but nothing like you must be!"

"You know, I'm happy to hear that I'm rich—probably, but I'd be a lot happier if I'd not lost my lover."

A sly look came over her face as she asked, "Who was she anyway?"

"No can tell. What about the rest of your life? Did anything interesting happen?"

She smiled. "You know all the interesting things. Teaching English literature to students of all ages who have hardly read a page of great works. I kept your subscription to *The Times*. I watched the entertainment news. I occasionally went to concerts—Pink Floyd, string quartets, the Twisted Sisters. Ditto for plays. I dropped your subscription to the *Scientific American*."

It's strange what will trigger a memory. That reference to the *Scientific American* brought memories flooding back of Minerva and me sitting in her office. She would read *Transfiguration Today*. I read *Scientific American*. I remembered how she used to call it the Scienterific American when she wanted to tease me.

Jaimie said, "I'm sorry. I didn't mean to criticize the *Scientific American*."

"It's not that. I just thought about. . ." Something caught in my throat and I could not pronounce Minerva's name.

Jaimie patted my hand and said, "I know." Then she asked, "What do we do next?"

I glanced at my wrist and said, "Well, it's still pretty early to go camp out in Slughorn's office. It's even a little early to show up for breakfast. I guess I'll go down to the kitchen's and beg a sampling of breakfast for the two of us. I'll just. . . "

She jumped up and said, "Great idea. Let's go!"

I stood and said, "It is not a good idea. I'm going alone. We don't want to reveal your presence until we've got a better handle on next steps and explanations about what's happened."

She was disappointed. "I don't like it, but I have to admit that you were always better at thinking things through. All right. If they've got any crisp bacon, I would kill for it."

I assured her that I'd find what I could. I left before she could change her mind. The castle was utterly quiet. Not even Filch and Mrs. Norris were out on the prowl. Of course, he had a good reason not to leave the comforts of bed—whoever owned the bed. On the way down I couldn't help remembering the many trips that I'd made down and up these very stairs in the midst of turmoil.

In the kitchen, there was the chef and the sous-chef overseeing the beginnings of breakfast. When they noticed me, Kretur hurried over and asked, "Who is you being? I knows Professor Wendt. He would never to be coming into the kitchen before breakfast. Who is you really?"

I shrugged. "There is always a first time for everything. I've not been to bed tonight."

He asked, "Is the Filch beating your brains in for impersonalizing him? Is you hurting so much that you be not able to sleeping? If he is, he will have to answer to Kretur!"

"No. No. Kretur. It's a long story. I hoped that there might be something for breakfast that would be available early. I didn't each much for dinner last night because I was waiting for all the good things at the party. Then I spent so much time dancing that I didn't eat at the party. I'm famished enough for two."

"I wants you not to have hungering. We is making a start to work on breakfast. Want you eggs and bacon and toast? We's sorry that we is not able doing more quick."

I smiled. "That would be wonderful. If you could do two eggs sunny-side up, two over easy, and two scrambled, it would be great. Throw in lots of crisp bacon and half a loaf of bread toasted. I don't know how to thank you"

"You is not thanking Kretur. We is only wishing there was more to do. Sitting at the table to wait."

I did. When you have three house elves working on breakfast for you, you count on it being scrumptious, plentiful, and fast. They brought two platters. One had the eggs. Another, the toast piled high and already buttered beside a stack of bacon. They expected me to sit there and eat it all.

I said, "I'd really like to stay and eat it here in the kitchen like the old days, but I've really got to take it up to my office."

Kretur's eyes fell. Then he brightened. "We is taking it up for you."

It almost broke my heart to say. "Sorry. I'd really like to take it up myself."

They finally gave in. I almost ran up the flights of stairs. When I reached my office, the door was open. Jaimie took one of the plates and I the other. We redistributed the food among the two plates. I always keep some plastic-ware in a desk drawer. Jaimie complained about using it, but hunger overcame silver protocol. We polished off the provender in short order.

When we were satisfied, I said, "It's still before anyone but the hungriest is up. We've had a long night. How about trying to catch a few hours of sleep and then tackle Slughorn in his lair."

She said, "OK. I guess I can sleep out here in the office. Anything that Javeen can do I can do better."

"Are you sure you don't want my room?"

"It's bad enough having to sleep in this pigsty of an office. I can't imagine and don't want to see what your apartment is like."

"OK. Don't forget that you had the opportunity to sleep in the comfy bed while I took the comfy sofa. You'll find the bedding behind. . ."

She finished the words for me, "I saw the bedding behind the sofa. Did Javeen use it?"

"She cleaned it after every use."

She almost growled, "I hope so. I'm going to use the *scourgio* spell myself."

As usual the occupant of the sofa awoke before I did. We were up about 10:30 AM. She was banging on my door announcing that she'd already finished with the loo, and why wasn't I up already? I grumbled to myself and rolled out of bed. Aloud, I said, "I'm coming. I'm coming." I was only half awake. When I was fully awake, I realized how serious what we were about to do really was. No one had ever come from another universe.

I wasn't in a hurry in the shower. I dressed and entered my office. Jaimie said, "Well, finally! Let's go." We walked down to Slughorn's office briskly. At least, she did. When we were approaching it, she realized that it was the Headmaster's Office. She declared, "You didn't tell me Slughorn was the Headmaster."

"Oh, I suppose I make all sorts of assumptions about what you know and don't know. Yes. He succeeded Minerva—first temporarily and then permanently."

She nodded, taking in the surprise pretty well. We arrived and ascended to the outer office. Sally greeted us and then gasped when she realized who we were. She gaped at us and quickly adjusted. "Please wait here a minute. Slughorn is in. I'm sure he'll see you quickly."

She practically sprinted to the door to the inner office. She entered, closed the door behind her, and spent less than a minute before returning. She said, "Please come it." We entered.

Slughorn invited us to sit on the sofa. Then he pulled his wand and used the *petrificus totalis* spell on both Jaimie and then me. She almost got her wand out in time to do something. What she would have done, I never found out. Since we'd both been stunned before, I didn't feel too guilty about not being able to assure her that it was only temporary.

Slughorn turned to Sally. He said, "Go get Aurora as quickly as possible. Have her come up here prepared for trouble. Then go get Dursley and bring him up as well."

I wasn't completely surprised, but I had hoped that we'd at least get to explain what happened before any drastic actions were taken. Where I was sitting, I could see Slughorn's desk and part of the chairs that are normally used by guests. I had no view of the door to the outer office.

Aurora entered first. She walked over to Slughorn's desk, looked at us, and said, "Oh, shit. Who are these two?"

"That's why you're here. I'm going to the Auror Office to get somebody here to work on that question. I want you to watch them carefully. I petrified them. They should be safe until I return, but don't take any chances. If either shows any signs of the spell wearing off, you stun their ass. Got it?"

She was clearly surprised. "Uh. . . sure. I agree, I guess. They can't both be the real McCoy. I'll not take any chances." Then he walked into the hearth and left by the floo connection. Aurora walked around the desk and sat, seeming to want to keep something between her and us. Shortly after, Dursley arrived.

He said, "What's up?" That was before he noticed us. Then he exclaimed, "Bloody hell! Who are they?"

She nodded. "That's the question, isn't it? Slughorn has gone for Aurors to help us settle that question."

He walked up close to us. He stared at each of us intently. Then he said, "I would swear that they're both the real deal. I suppose neither is. But, why?"

Just then there was a whoosh, and someone exited the floo connection. I didn't have a view of the floo, so I couldn't tell whom. I heard a familiar voice say, "Well, well, well, Professor Wendt caught unawares. And who else do we have here? A Jaimie Brewster. OK. Headmaster. Would you like to explain why I'm here?"

Slughorn said, "I'm sorry. I didn't want to explain at your office. It's kind of a secret that I'm about to tell you."

I couldn't see her face, but I'd heard the tone before when she was disgusted with someone. "You're on the verge of filing a false complaint if you don't explain how this is a problem."

He sighed and said, "Would you mind doing that Professor Dursley?"

Ginny scoffed, "Since when are you a professor, Dursley?"

Slughorn explained. "He's a substitute teacher, so he gets the provisional title.

I could tell that Ginny was on the point of making a sarcastic comment, but held it. What she did say was, "Hurry up."

Dursley said, "This is strictly a secret. This doesn't have to get out, does it?"

Ginny said, "It all depends. Get going."

Dursley muttered something and then said, "He's what happened. Aurora used an experimental polyjuice potion on Wendt for a Halloween prank."

Ginny said, "I should have known. Go on."

"Well, it does something like make you the twin of the person whose hair was used to make the potion. And it's permanent."

Ginny began to get the idea. She said, "Ahhh. Then Wendt became somebody's twin. So, why is he still around, and who was it?" Then she began to really get it. "I see. So, he became the twin of Mrs. Brewster here. Then Aurora reversed the potion. So, what's the problem?"

Slughorn said, "Have you ever seen Wendt and Brewster together at the same time?"

She said slowly, "No. And I kind of wondered about that. What's the big deal? They're here together now."

Aurora said, "Wendt didn't become Brewster's twin. He became my twin."

Ginny stared and her head slowly twisted so that her right ear almost reached her shoulder as she stared at me. "I see. So, at least one of these two is a fake." She thought a bit more. "Probably both." Then she sat on one of the guest chairs and put her chin in her hands that were supported by her vertical forearms resting on her knees. Everyone's attention was focused on her.

She eventually stood and said, "There seems to be only two ways to handle this. We can assume that they are using normal polyjuice potion and wait for them to change back. How long have they been like this?"

Slughorn said, "They walked into my office a little over an hour ago." Then he looked over at Sally and asked, "Isn't that right?"

She shook her head and said, "I'd say closer to one and a half hours."

Ginny nodded and looked over at Slughorn. "What's the longest that that ordinary polyjuice potion could last before the subject began to change back."

Slughorn thought a moment and said hesitantly, "Well. . . Using the maximum safe dosage, I'd say, oh, four to five hours. If you only tried to avoid serious side effects, maybe five to six hours. That's absolute tops."

"Thanks. So, I'd say, let's let these two sit until 5 PM. If they've still not changed, then we unfreeze them and take the second route. We interrogate them with questions that only they would know. So, all four of you, try to come up with questions that only they and you would know the answer to."

Dursley asked, "What about you?"

"Oh, I'll be thinking, too. We need to set a guard here—just in case. You and Slughorn are elected." She was looking at Aurora.

Aurora asked, "Why me?"

Ginny scowled. "You got us into this. Only just."

Aurora walked out of my line of sight and said, "What are Aurors for anyway?"

Ginny laughed, "Pulling people's bacon out of the fire. You just have to watch the bacon." She then walked into the floo connection and was gone with a whoosh. Slughorn and Aurora debated a schedule for standing guard. Aurora thought that since we were in his office, he should watch the whole time except for a biology break. He insisted that the duties be shared fifty-fifty. Since he was the Headmaster, he won that debate.

The wait was boring, but at least, it wasn't one where I was afraid of what might happen at the end. The worst that could happen was ending up in Azkaban for a while. The worst right now was not being able to communicate with anyone including my partner in this fine mess.

There was a change of guard at about 3 PM. Slughorn left his chair behind his desk and went somewhere out of the office. Aurora took over but didn't sit behind the Headmaster's desk. She sat on the red leather chair. She brought a bottle of water and a stack of parchments. Apparently, she was grading.

I was getting hungry but that wasn't my greatest worry. The next two hours was just as boring as the first two. Eventually, I heard a whoosh next and prayed that it was Ginny returning to set about the interrogation. It was. The first thing that she said was addressed to Aurora. "Where's Slughorn and Dursley?"

Aurora said, "I don't know. I'll check with Filch about Dursley. Maybe I'll run into Slughorn on the way." She apparently left then.

Aurora was back with Dursley after Slughorn arrived on his own. When they were all assembled, Ginny gave them their orders. "All of you be ready to stun them when I release the spells. I don't want you in the same line of sight from them. Spread out. Slughorn, you can sit behind your desk. The rest of you remain standing." She then pulled up a chair in front of me, but not very close. She raised her wand. She apparently used the spell silently because I didn't hear anything, but I regained control of my muscles. She then said, "We're going to interview them separately. The one not being interviewed will wait in the outer office for our interview. Don't think I won't stun you again if you do anything funny."

I just could not resist the temptation to make a joke. "If you think that anything I've done so far is funny, you've got a strange sense of humor."

She tried to maintain a straight face, but a her lips curled up slightly. She then said, "Aurora, levitate this Brewster person into the outer office while we're interrogating Wendt. Dursley, you keep watch on him out there."

He protested, "Why do I have to do that?"

Ginny simply said, "You didn't have to watch him in the afternoon." The way she said it left no doubt that Dursley only had the option to ask, "How long?" rather than argue.

When Aurora had returned, Ginny asked, "Who's got a unique question that only Wendt and you would know how to answer?"

Aurora answered, "I do. I'm going to ask him about something that only four people know about. Two of them, Professor Dumbledore and Professor McGonagall, are dead."

Ginny nodded to her. She asked me, "In your fifth year here, you used polyjuice potion to appear like someone. . ."

I quickly answered, "The false Professor Moody."

Aurora came back, "That's not the question. As it started to wear off, you then began to appear like someone else. Who?"

"I looked like Barty Crouch Jr. whom everyone thought was dead. That was why no one recognized him. . . er. . . me at first."

Ginny stared at Aurora in surprise and asked, "Right?"

Aurora nodded. Ginny turned to me in surprise and simply asked, "How?"

"Ask the real expert—Slughorn. I've no idea. All I know was that the Moody whose hair Aurora got for the polyjuice potion was actually Barty Crouch Jr. using polyjuice potion to impersonate 'Madeye' Moody."

She turned to Slughorn and repeated the question, "How?"

He just shrugged and said, "I've not the slightest. I've never heard of anyone using polyjuice potion made from hair of someone already using polyjuice potion. I suppose I could have written up a paper on the case if I'd known about it, but we had bigger fish to fry at the time. The Ministry really didn't want anyone to know that Barty Crouch Jr. had been on the loose for nearly a year without the Ministry knowing."

Ginny looked around the room and asked if anyone else had any unique knowledge shared with me. Slughorn said, "I've not got one. I don't think that I ever had a memorable one-on-one incident with Wendt."

Ginny thought a while and then asked me, "I'm sure you remember the day before you left England for America after the death of Minerva. Tell me how you boarded your ship."

I worked to prevent laughing at her question. Then, I spoke as carefully as I could to prevent embarrassment for everyone. "I disapparated on-board."

She persisted. "Precisely where did you land?"

I growled in frustration. "Would you let me write it on a piece of parchment?"

She actually laughed and said, "I suppose so." Then she materialized a piece of parchment from her purse along with a quill.

I wrote, "Landed in bed of my ship cabin."

She glanced at it and then used her wand to burn it to vapor. She said, "Ohh-Kay." Then she said, "Bring Brewster in."

Aurora did. Jaimie, as I preferred to think of her, was set down on the sofa. I got up and moved to a guest chair. No one objected. Ginny took the same chair she had with me, lifted her wand, and Jaimie relaxed from her somewhat unnatural pose.

Ginny, who always is courteous toward those who are under her super-vision, gave Jaimie a couple of minutes to adjust to being unfrozen. Then she asked, "Aurora, please ask her the question that you asked Wendt."

Aurora did. The answer was essentially the same. Ginny then asked Jaimie, "I'm sure you remember the day before you left England for America. . ."

I interrupted her. "Ginny, do you accept unreservedly that I'm Wendt?"

She looked at me in disbelief. She said, "Are you serious? Why does it matter?"

"Just go with me for a minute. Do you believe me?"

She grabbed my arm and whispered, "Come with me." She led me into the outer office. No one was there because Sally had come into the inner office with Aurora and Jaimie. Ginny asked me, "What are you playing at?"

I almost snarled. "You know me. You know I'm not going to lead you wrong. I've got a reason for what I want to do."

"Do me a favor and tell me that reason."

I grimaced because I had to convince her of something that I wasn't completely sure of myself. I began, "If you believe that I'm Wendt then I have a ton of memories that are in common and only the two of us know."

Ginny was clearly conflicted. She nodded slowly to herself and said, "I'm going with you. Don't let me down."

I didn't say anything. We went back to the inner office. I walked around to the chair that Ginny had been using. I sat, looked Jaimie in the eye, and realized that I'd looked her reflection in the eye a lot but only through a mirror. Now it was face to face. Then I asked the question. "I went to a chamber orchestra concert with someone. I much later realized that that person might have had designs on me. Who was it?"

Her answer was, "It was. . ." She was poised to say the name. Then she asked for a piece of parchment and quill.

Ginny scoffed. "Doesn't anyone just say things out loud." However, she did provide the quill and parchment. Jaimie wrote something on the parchment and handed it to me. I glanced at it and put it in my mouth, chewed it thoroughly and swallowed.

Ginny asked, "I suppose that was the true answer."

"Yes."

Ginny frowned. "So, where does that leave us? The two of you can't exist together, and yet, here you both are."

Jaimie winked at me and said, "Professor Wendt has an explanation. I don't know that I entirely understand it, but it seems to explain a lot."

Everyone turned toward me. "Well, it's just a theory, but it's better than nothing. Here goes. There's a physics theory that I won't go into any details about. . ."

Ginny interrupted, "Thank God!"

"No need to be snippy. Anyway, the bottom line of the theory is that there can be parallel universes. These could be just as real as our universe. There could be an infinite number of them. Some would be very similar to ours. Others could be quite different. The point is that there could be a large number of different versions of us and our histories.

"There could even be an infinite number of you?" Ginny rolled her eyes at that thought.

I agreed and went on. "Now, Jaimie must come from one of these universes. We spent a good bit of the night comparing her memories of events with mine."

Ginny said, "I'll bet that's not all that you compared."

I gritted my teeth and went on. "If she comes from another universe, then it's one where I never returned after Jaimie came into existence. She went into the vanishing cabinet in the Room of Requirement during the Halloween party. When she came out, she was. . . here." I had struggled for a good term for our universe but I had to settle for "here."

Aurora objected. "But, people were going into and out of vanishing cabinets all the time—especially during the war with Riddle. Nobody came from another universe."

I shrugged. "I know. I don't have an explanation."

Slughorn cleared his throat and said, "Maybe I do. That vanishing cabinet is unique. It has a twin. Deatheaters transferred back and forth from its twin. The twin was destroyed after it was discovered."

121

I said, "Then you think that without its twin in this universe, it connected with one in another universe?"

Slughorn agreed. Then I said, "Well, that's good enough for me. So, why don't you just toddle off to the Room of Requirement and scuttle back to Universe Q where you came from?"

Jaimie screwed up her face into an expression of distaste. She said, "Well, I'm not sure that I really want to do that. If there are many universes, I might not want to be in many of them. I think I'll stick with what I have right here."

We all stared at her. Somehow, we all were disappointed. Then there was the problem. What would happen to her? We decided that she could stay at Hogwarts for a while. She would stay in the Ravenclaw house while we thought it through.

Aurora accompanied Jaimie to Ravenclaw while the rest of us stayed and discussed what would happen next. Slughorn said, "I don't see what the problem is. "Our" Jaimie is an accomplished, intelligent witch in this universe. Why wouldn't the other one be over there in her native universe? Such a witch should have no problem getting along here. The sooner she gets off into the world, the sooner she can be a productive member of wizarding society." He pointed off into the indefinite distance somewhere to his left.

I said, "Look, she's had a big shock. She just discovered that her universe—the one she's currently living in has had lots of changes overnight. Some are not so bad. Some are pretty awful. Some are drastic. Some are subtle. The salient point is that all changes are stressful whether good or bad. Many of them, she'll only discover as time goes by. Each will be a fresh shock to her system. We should help her adjust to them." I hesitated and thought. Then I said, "All these changes are sources of grief. Something has died and will never return. For example, her job here. That is dead to her. She will probably grieve that death for a very long time."

Aurora, who had just returned, caught the last of my discussion. She sat and then said, "She could always go back to where she came from."

I shook my head. "It might work. It might not. Would you take the risk?"

Aurora just shrugged.

122

Brewster Grieved

The next day, I was in my classroom teaching my fourth year class. We were discussing the *Winter's Tale* by Shakespeare. There was an intense discussion about the fate of the son, Mamillus. He dies of grief. His mother, Hermione, dies as well of grief. Mamillus has simply died, but his mother Hermione returns to life.

Jessie argued, "Mamillus' death is not tragic because he has no flaw. He is an innocent. He is simply cast away as a disposable prop! How is that fair?"

Burt raised his hand insistently to speak. When I recognized him, Jessie sneered, but he simply said, "Certainly, Mamillus is just a prop. He isn't a character that you're supposed to feel pity for. He just is there to illustrate how serious the dispute between husband and wife is."

Jessie swung her hands wildly to get my attention. I recognized her, but cautioned, "We're not trying to start a war, just bring out the features of this story. Go ahead."

She stood and swung her head as she made her point, "What is the point of killing indiscriminately? Shakespeare isn't a Deatheater! He shouldn't kill just to make a dramatic point."

It was at that point that there was a timid knock at the door. I said, "This is a good point to dismiss you for your next class. Also, I'm declaring this discussion done. Next time, we'll have a quiz on the *Winter's Tale* and move on to our next reading assignment. See you next time."

I opened the door and motioned the lad, who seemed to be a second year off to the side where we could talk as the class streamed out. He handed me a note. It turned out to be from the Headmaster. He wanted to see me ASAP in his office. I folded the parchment and stuffed it in an inside pocket. Fortunately, I had a free period.

When I reached the outer office, Sally just shook her head and said,

"You'd better go straight in. He's in a state."

I wasn't anxious to learn what the "state" was but had little choice. When I entered the inner office, I found Slughorn circling the desk. His hands were clasp behind his back, and his head was pointed up toward the ceiling. He didn't notice that I'd entered right away. I had to clear my throat. Then he noticed me. He motioned toward the red leather chair, and he took one of the yellow chairs nearby.

He said, "Oh, my boy! What shall we do?"

"A good question. What's the problem?"

He stood up again and began pacing. "It's Brewster."

Those words told me everything that I needed to know, but I let him go on. He did. "Mr. Brewster sent me an express owl just now. He wants to see us this evening after dinner is finished. Well?"

I sighed in resignation. "I suppose it was inevitable, but I was hoping to start next week with him. Yes, sure. We can meet tonight. I just hope he doesn't bring Cecily. One Brewster will be plenty to deal with."

Slughorn agreed enthusiastically. "But you'll be there!"

I nodded and thought about how awful it would be.

□

The afternoon classes were no fun for anyone. The fifth years were in a hurry to be done and unhappy that the only thing standing between them and a four day weekend was my class (and the other Friday classes). I could hardly stop thinking about what we'd say to Brewster. It was going to be no fun for anyone.

Dinner was largely untouched on my plate. Slughorn didn't look to have much more appetite despite his well-known proclivities as a gourmet. I ended by simply sitting and staring out over the sea of happy faces. After all, it was TGIF for them. The ordeal ended. Slughorn walked past my end of the head table and collected me on his way up to his office. Neither of us had a word to say.

We walked together up to Slughorn's office. We entered the outer office. Sally was off for the day. Slughorn had his hand on the doorknob to the inner office. Once inside, Slughorn invited me to take the high-backed red leather chair.

He started to ask me for my plan for the meeting. He had hardly started when the inner door swung open behind us. Standing there was an ecstatic Mr. Brewster. He must have caught sight of Slughorn first because he strode directly to the desk, not giving the slightest attention to me. He exclaimed, "I just heard the news! Where's Jaimie, and why hasn't she gotten in touch with me herself?"

Slughorn gestured to me and said, "Have a seat."

Brewster started to sit and was almost resting on one of the yellow chairs when the significance of my presence struck him. He exclaimed, "What the bloody hell! How can you be here? What's going on?"

I said, "It's a crazy story. I suppose that I should start by giving you the good and bad news. From your perspective, it's probably mostly bad.

"First, the good news. Jaimie is here."

Brewster started to speak. I held up my hand, signaling that he wait. I then added, "That is the good news and all of the good news. Then there's the not-so-good news. This Jaimie is not the Jaimie that you know—not the Jaimie that you married."

Brewster's jaw dropped. "How could she not be the Jaimie that I married—unless of course, she is really a polyjuice potion fake." He hesitated. I guess he realized that the original Jaimie was sort of a polyjuice potion fake herself. He then added sheepishly, "I mean a copy rather than the . . . uh. . . original." He hesitated again.

I filled in. "We all know what you mean. I'm not quite sure how to answer you."

He looked up from the floor with defiance in his eyes as he said, "How can you not know how to answer?"

I sighed, and asked Slughorn, "Could you provide us with something to drink. I think this will require some fortification."

Slughorn simply nodded and asked, "Nothing fancy like you have. Would a G&T around suit?"Both Brewster and I agreed. He then waved his wand inconspicuously, and glasses floated in from a corner of the room. They landed on the Slughorn's desk in front of the three of us. I took a sip and was disappointed. I guess when you're used to good whiskey, simple gin is just, well, disappointing.

I began my explanation. "I apologize that I don't know more. It's just the way things happened. I have a guess about why they happened the way they did, but it's just a guess—nothing more."

Brewster said, "Just get on with it. Sometimes you explain the life out of things."

I couldn't argue the point, so I started. "It was Halloween night."

Brewster broke in bitterly, "Why do all these things happen to you on Halloween?"

I just shrugged and went on, "Anyway, the party went fine. I went back to my office. Not long after I arrived, Jaimie walked into the office."

Brewster jumped up and shouted, "Where the hell did she come from?"

"I wish I knew." I started to tell what I did know, but Brewster started

125

to interrupt again. I said, "We'll never finish if you keep interrupting." He leaned back and seemed to be in control. I went on. "She says a lot of things that sound crazy. She says that I never returned after she came to life." Brewster stirred as though he would say something, but he held his peace. I went on. "She says that she went into the Room of Requirement and entered the vanishing cabinet there to get away from Aurora and her crazy schemes. After a long while, she left the vanishing cabinet and walked down to my/our office. When we caught sight of each other, both of us were about as surprised as you come."

Brewster returned to his original point. "How can that be? How can the two of you co-exist!"

Slughorn said, "Wendt has an explanation. It has something to do with knot theory."

I sighed and said, "Close enough. Here's my theory. Bear in mind it's just a theory."

Slughorn said, "Buckle your broomstick seat belt."

I nodded. "Yeh. Here goes. Many physicists believe for a variety of reasons that there are multiple universes—anywhere from many to infinite. They may have somewhat different laws of physics or the same laws, but in any case, there would probably be many universes that were very similar to ours. Probably some would have very similar histories with many of the same peoples and incidents in them. The key is that while some would be very similar to ours, there would still be differences.

"I think that this Jaimie stepped into a vanishing cabinet in a different universe and stepped out into ours. In her universe, I never returned after she took over my body and memories. In her universe, you died in the war against Riddle. Cecily went to live with relatives, but graduated this year from Hogwarts. She never got into chess. Obviously, this Jaimie never knew about you until I told her about you. Here's the thing. She sounds like she doesn't want to play roulette with the various universes by going back into the vanishing cabinet. She thinks this one is OK and will stay here. That's it in a nutshell."

Brewster immediately asked, "How do you know that she is telling the truth?"

Slughorn said, "It's like when Riddle was running around. We tested her memory of key events—things that she would never know if she were an impostor."

Brewster shot back, "But she has a different history than we do. How could she know these key events?"

I said, "She knew them. I said that her history was different but not completely different."

126

He dropped back into his chair and asked for a refill. When Slughorn provided it, he left it untouched. He buried his face in his hands. And said, "How will I ever tell Cecily? The way I knew that Jaimie was here was that she told me. She still has friends in Ravenclaw. A couple of them saw Jaimie staying in one of the rooms."

Slughorn suggested, "Tell her that you two can come and meet *this* Jaimie. We'll set up a lunch date. We'll all go to a neutral spot and talk it through. What do you think?"

Brewster shrugged, "How much choice do I have? I don't have a better idea."

I said, "OK. I don't know what you can tell her to explain why Jaimie hasn't joined you already. I guess a taste of the truth would be best. We'll try to set something up on the weekend, but I can't promise anything."

Brewster asked if he could be with her now. Slughorn and I agreed that might not be an awful idea—that is, assuming she hadn't gone somewhere. I suggested that they stay in Slughorn's office. I would find her in Ravenclaw—if she were there.

I walked there. I ran into Filch on the way. He ran me down and demanded to talk. "Oh, Filch, I'm pretty busy right now."

"Are you too busy to explain why that Jaimie Brewster is staying in Ravenclaw? Did she and that husband of hers have a row?"

I could see that this was quickly getting out of hand. I decided that bringing Filch along was the easiest option, so I said, "Come along. You can ask her yourself."

Filch was pleased as punch to come along, so we took off for Ravenclaw. As we went, he did a running commentary on how to get past the picture that guarded Ravenclaw's entrance. "Now, you see. You'd need to be extry clever. It takes a good wit to sneak one past that painting! Why I remember once that it asked me. . ."

We never found out what the riddle was because we had arrived at Ravenclaw tower just then. The painting asked, "Who shaved the town barber's beard if the barber shaved everyone in the town who didn't shave themselves.?"

Filch cleared his throat and said, "That's oblivious. It was the butcher."

I stared at him and asked, "How do you figure?"

"Well, the butcher is skilled with knives and all such like. It must have been him."

Meanwhile, the painting said, "Then did the barber shave himself?"

Filch declared, "No." Then he hesitated and added, "But the barber doesn't shave himself. So, the barber must shave himself."

I bent over to the painting while Filch was mumbling to himself. I whispered, "The barber is a woman and doesn't need a shave."

The painting said, "You may pass."

Filch scratched his head and said, "You see. I must have been right—we got in."

I just grinned. Inside, we were greeted by benign neglect. I picked a sixth year girl whom I knew from class. She was sitting in the Common Room studying. I asked her, "Judy, would you mind running up to the girl's side of the dorm and see if Ms. Sinistra is there? If she is, please ask her to come down to talk with me."

Judy laid her book down and ran up the stairs. While we waited, Filch said, "I've never been in Ravenclaw before. Interesting to see what the egg-heads are like in their home."

I shrugged. "They look pretty much like everyone else to me."

Judy and Jaimie came down the stairs. When Jaimie saw me, I said, "Would you mind coming with us to the Headmaster's Office for a few minutes?"

She agreed. We left Ravenclaw, and Filch asked, "What brings you back here? You're not teaching? Are you planning to boot Professor Wendt out?" He chuckled as though that were a preposterous idea. In the back of my head, I wondered if it were a completely preposterous idea.

She snapped back, "Maybe I'm going to replace you."

That actually seemed to worry Filch. He looked around as though to see if anyone were in earshot and said, "Don't joke about that. Anyway, you wouldn't last a day having to keep the lid down on the scalawag students in this place." That thought seemed to comfort him. The subject certainly didn't comfort me.

As we approached Slughorn's office I told Filch that this was private business, and he had to scram. Filch wasn't happy, but there wasn't much he could say. He skulked off toward his lair.

I told Jaimie that Brewster was in the office. He wanted to see her. "Don't forget that he is married to another Jaimie. I've told him about you, but. . ." I left the thought unfinished.

We breezed through the outer office and into the inner one. Both Slughorn and Brewster rose. Brewster started to walk toward Jaimie. When he saw that there was no similar reaction from Jaimie, he stopped. She stopped as well. There was a moment when no one seemed to know what to do. Slughorn asked us all to take seats. Brewster pulled a yellow chair up for Jaimie. She thanked him politely and took the proffered chair rather stiffly.

I took a deep breath and said, "This seems to be my show. I guess introductions are in order." I turned to Jaimie and said, "Jaimie Sinistra, this is Theodore Brewster. He is Cecily Brewster's dad. He is also married to a different Jaimie. Mr. Brewster, this is Jaimie Sinistra. She is apparently from a different universe where she is the Hogwarts English literature Professor. She is also single in that universe."

I was stalled at that point. I didn't know where to go from there. Slughorn picked up the thread. "Our Jaimie's step-mum to Cecily. I think that you might meet with her and her dad so that she will understand that this Jaimie isn't Cecily's Jaimie."

Brewster agreed. "Cecily is very close to you. . . er. . . her step-mum. I'd appreciate it if the three of us could get together to introduce you. I think Cecily won't really accept that you aren't her step-mum if she doesn't meet you. Would you do that favor for us?"

Jaimie hesitated and then said, "I can see why that other Jaimie would be attracted to you. Yes. I'll do that. I think we'd probably better not meet again, though."

Gazing at her the whole time, Brewster said, "You look so much like her, but there's something different. I can't identify what. I think it would be difficult for everyone if we spent much time with you who resembles a woman that both my daughter and I love so much."

She agreed. They decided that they'd arrange a meet-up. They'd do that by owl post. Brewster rose and started to leave the office. Slughorn motioned to him and said, "Why don't you use my floo connection. There's no reason for you to walk all the way down to the Great Hall."

Brewster agreed and disappeared into the hearth. I rose and said, "I guess we're done. Have a good evening."

Jaimie said, "Wait! I have some business with the both of you."

I agreed. Slughorn sighed in resignation and said, "Why not? You're here now."

We resumed our seats, and Jaimie began. "I've been thinking about this for the last couple of days." She hesitated and then plunged on, "I think I should be the English literature Professor here." Then she began ticking off reasons on her fingers. "I'm eminently qualified. I've taught it for the last several years here. . ." Her mouth hung open as she thought. "Well, at another Hogwarts anyway. I'm a witch, for goodness sakes." She turned to me and said, "No offense intended."

I scoffed. "None taken."

She went on. "Besides that, I can identify with magical students better than a Muggle can." She turned to me again and placed a hand on my arm as she said, "I know the difficulties you've had relating to your magical students.

"I've not got a job here. This would be perfect for me." She turned to

129

me and touched my arm again. "You're as rich as Croesus. You don't need the job. You could be a consultant for Gringotts." She smiled a wicked smile as she said, "I know that there's someone there who would appreciate your spending more time there."

I grimaced. "Let's not tell tales out of school." I smiled despite myself and added, "Or in school either." She matched my smile at my little joke. I decided that she knew me too well. She had plenty of ready arguments. I started to make my case, ticking off my case on my fingers.

"Clearly, I'm at least as qualified as she is. I too have been teaching for years here. I know *this* Hogwarts better than she does.

"Far from being a disadvantage, being a Muggle is good for Hogwarts. It allows me to give a perspective to students at Hogwarts that they would not get were I not teaching here."

I chuckled. "I am NOT as rich as Croesus. It's true that I am a consultant for Gringotts, but that position doesn't afford me a large salary." I'd mostly been looking at Slughorn as I spoke. I glanced over at Jaimie. She had a reproachful look on her face. I added, "Well, I do have a pretty good income from outside endeavors.".

Jaimie and I scowled at each other and turned to Slughorn. He gazed up at the ceiling—I suppose hoping for inspiration from a benevolent deity. When he looked down, he had a smile on his face. He looked from one to the other of us, and the smile widened. "Here's the deal that I'm going to offer you two. We'll split the English lit classes up between you. Jaimie will take over half of yours, Wendt."

Both of us were on the point of rising to protest. Slughorn cut us off. "There's got to be an advantage to being the Head. I'm not inviting an argument. I'm giving you both an ultimatum. Either you agree to this or you're both out of a job. Period."

Both of us responded almost in unison. "You can't do that. Who would teach English lit?"

Slughorn smiled a smile of contentment. "You both forget that there was not an English lit program before you arrived Wendt. Hogwarts got on for centuries without it. It can get on for a few years without until I find someone I can work with. So, agreed?"

We looked at each other. I asked, "Do you see anything wrong with it?"

She replied, "We'd have to work together so that the program would be consistent." The expression on her face revealed that she wasn't exactly happy about collaboration.

I said, "We'd have to start with MY lesson plans. You don't have yours with you."

She grimaced. I added, "Of course, you could go get them."

She laughed, "You'd like that, wouldn't you. I probably wouldn't return."

I shrugged.

Slughorn asked, "Then it's agreed?"

We both agreed. Then Jaimie said, "Well, as a professor at Hogwarts, I'm not staying in a dorm room. I think that I should have the English lit office/apartment."

I popped up on my feet. "You can't have my apartment!"

She said, "Why not? You've had it for years. You could stay in a dorm for a while."

We both turned back to Slughorn. He rolled his eyes. Then he said, "Wait a minute. I've got an idea." He stood and paced back and forth behind his desk. Then he turned to us and said, "Yes! I think it would work. OK. Here's what we'll do." He turned to me and asked, "Wendt, you stayed with Dursley for a while one year, didn't you?"

"Yeh. We were both in Minerva's doghouse. So?"

He went on. "Well, here's the thing. Dursley is staying in my old apartment. It's really spacious. The two of you could share it. Then Jaimie could have your apartment. Everyone's happy."

I don't think either of us were happy. I'm not sure why she wasn't, but I sure didn't want to have to move out of my place after so many years of living there. Then a thought occurred to me. "Slughorn, it just occurs to me that I don't have anyone to help me with the typical little wizardly things that Minerva and others used to help me with."

Jaimie got a whiff of where I was going with this. She started to object, but I plowed on. "If I have to give up my digs, then Jaimie should have to give up a little something. She should have to provide those little services."

She demanded, "What services?"

I casually said, "You know. Take me by floo or disapparation on the infrequent errands that I have to do, like visiting Gringotts. Then there's the occasional owl post letter that I have to send."

Slughorn nodded. "That seems sensible. I don't see a problem with it."

Jaimie quickly objected. "I could be running errands for *him* every day."

"Oh, I don't think it would be that much."

"Sure, you don't. What if I want to go on a date?"

I sneered, "You don't do dates. You told me yourself."

"Well, I might do."

Slughorn made a decision. "I think Wendt's proposal is reasonable. Sinsitra, you either get on board or you're back to Ravenclaw."

She was clearly not happy, but after a little consideration, she agreed but added, "You don't get to come in the middle of the night with some hare-brained favor."

I smiled. "My favors are never hare-brained."

"Says you!"

Slughorn glared at both of us. "The two of you have taken far too much of my time. Go find someone else's office to argue in, preferably yours, Wendt. While you're at it, divide up your classes and don't bother me again."

She asked, "Is your office OK?"

"Of course."

□□

We reached my office. Jaimie was moving to open the door. I took her arm to restrain her impulse to open the door. I said, "Please just let me go in first, and you stay out here just in case."

"Just in case what?"

"There might be someone there already." I wouldn't say it, but it occurred to me that she might be in a nightgown of some sort. I opened the door and slipped in.

I was greeted by Javeen who rushed up to welcome me with a hug. "Well, finally! I wondered where you were."

I smiled. This was going to be fun. "It's a long story but I've been evicted from my apartment."

She shrieked, "What!"

"Oh, yes. There's a new occupant—possibly as early as tomorrow morning."

"How can that be! You're not fired, are you?" Then she started thinking. "It's not that woman I saw here before, is it?"

"Yes. She's the new English lit Professor. She's taking over the apartment and office."

Javeen was furious. "She can't do that!"

"I'm afraid she can. We were just in with the Headmaster. He approved it all."

A different idea seemed to occur to Javeen, A crafty smile spread over her face as she said, "Well, then. You have no place to stay, do you? You'd be welcome in my little flat—until you get a new place." She quickly added. "And you wouldn't have to be in a hurry to do that either."

I was relieved to be able to say, "Oh, no need, I've been given a new apartment. I'm staying with Dursley."

She quickly said, "You don't have to. And who would do the little magical favors that I do for you?"

I tried to keep myself from smiling too broadly. "I have a new professional personal assistant. So, you can finally have some time for yourself."

She looked down at her feet and said, "It was always time for myself." Then she looked around and said, "I'll collect my things and go."

I hurriedly said, "You can do that tomorrow. As a matter of fact, I have a meeting with my assistant right now. So. . ." She took the hint and went to the floo connection.

She said, "I'll see you tomorrow, right?"

"Yes. I suppose."

With that she was gone. Almost instantly, Jaimie opened the door and entered. She scoffed. "Personal assistant, eh?"

"Well, I just wanted to get rid of her. I didn't want to get into a lengthy debate about what you were and why."

She frowned. "I suppose that I should thank you for that."

"You're welcome."

We sat down and worked on dividing up the classes. We decided that we wouldn't share an age level. If there was more than one class section at a particular age level, one of us would get them all. In the end, she had one more section than I had. We ran out of time before we'd done anything more than review the lesson plans for the next day.

⊡
⊟⊡

The next day, I had a free period at the beginning of the day. It turned out that Dursley did as well. I went down to his office to break the good news. He was actually kind of glad. He said, "Well, I won't be bouncing off the walls of Slughorn's giant apartment anymore."

"Glad to hear it. I'll start moving my things down during lunch. It'll probably take several trips."

Dursley smiled. "Don't worry professor. I'll give you a hand. With the help of magic, we might just finish before lunch is over."\

I gave him my heart-felt thanks. During the lunch hour, Filch dropped by in the middle of the move. He said, "It does me heart good to have you fill in for me as the loco parent for Mr. Dursley. But I don't understand why you would give your apartment to that Mrs. Brewster. Are you trying to break her and Mr. Brewster up?"

I almost laughed as I said, "No. No. It's a long story. Ms. Sinistra is really a relative of Mrs. Brewster. Ms. Sinistra is helping me out with my heavy class load. She's taking half of my workload."

Filch considered that as Dursley and I continued with moving. Then he said, "She is sort of like my Dursley. He came to take some of the drudgery out of my burdensome workload of keeping the old ship shipshape, eh?"

I nodded as I walked down the stairs to the apartment next the Potions Lab. I asked, "Mr. Filch, you wouldn't consider giving me a hand with my stuff?"

Filch pretended not to hear and went on, "Yep! It's too bad that you're almost finished with all that stuff. I'd dearly have loved to take some of your workload."

"Right. The next three loads are probably the lightest." Dursley and I finished up, except that Filch picked up the current issue of the *Scientific American* on my desk to take down as his share.

Javeen arrived during the last load. She looked around the office and said, "Amazing. You'd never know that you'd been here." Then she opened her purse and pulled out an envelope. She handed it to me and said, "Dad. . . I mean the chairman of the board wants to get together with you. What do you think?"

I opened the envelope. It was an invitation to dinner on Thursday at a restaurant. I didn't recognize the name, but I figured it must be the one where we normally met.

Javeen asked, "Pick you up at seven on Thursday?"

I said, "No need. I've got my own way there. See you then." That was the last that I saw her until Thursday. On Thursday, she sent me an owl. The brief note said that something had come up and we'd have to postpone until Saturday night. I thought, "All the better. Maybe the date will keep slipping and slipping."

Gringotts Disappointed

The next day, I volunteered Dursley to help move Jaimie into MY office. Of cousre. She had practically nothing to move. We met her at lunch in the Great Hall. Slughorn had begun lunch as it had rarely if ever begun during my tenure there. He struck his glass with his spoon, rose, and said, "I hope you all are having a good lunch. I have a special announcement to make.

"We have the pleasure this afternoon to introduce you to the newest professor here at Hogwarts. . "

Someone shouted, "You mean Dursley."

Slughorn was unperturbed. He simply said, "The new Assistant Professor of English literature. Some of you will have met her before when she substituted for Professor Wendt. Others may know of her from older siblings. Please give a warm welcme to Professor Sinistra." He led off with polite applause that was mimicked by most of the students. He went on, "That doesn't mean that you are losing Professor Wendt. They are sharing the workload of the English Department. About half of Professor Wendt's classes will be taught by Professor Sinistra. Some have already experienced her classroom style. Most of the rest of you will sooner or later."

Jaimie stood, accepted the applause, and quickly sat. The rest of the meal was ordinary except for the cuisine, which was spectacular. Afterwards, Dursley and I approached her. As we neared, Dursley whistled softly to himself. When we arrived, we were approached by several upper class students who wanted to know more. None of them had seen the two of us together. There were a few comments to that effect. I shooed them off.

We all knew each other, of course. Somehow things were different today. I opened the conversation. "Mr. Dursley and I will help you move down to my office."

She smiled. "You mean my office."

I wasn't going to argue. We walked up to the Ravenclaw tower. She quickly got us in, answering the riddle so quickly that I hardly had heard it before the door was open. Inside, she said, "Come on up with me." As we ascended the stairs, she announced loudly, "Male professors on the floor." Every door opened and heads popped out.

Dursley waved his hand and said, "Move along. Nothing here to see."

We reached Jaimie's room and entered. There was an amazing amount of clothes and other things spread about. Both Dursley and Jaimie levitated lots of clothes. I took a box of books and odds and ends. I said, "I see you've been shopping."

Jaimie just said, "Of course. Professor Slughorn gave me an advance on salary."

Dursley just smiled the whole way to my office. When we arrived, I suggested, "I left a gift bottle of Blue Label for you. I suggest that we crack it open and have a home-warming toast."

Dursley agreed, "Wonderful! There's never been a more lovely tenant of this office!" Then he added, "You're different from the other Jaimie."

She said, "Of course. I'm not her."

He went on. "No, I mean it. There's something different about your hair. it's a different color, and well, I don't know." Then he said something that was totally unexpected. "Would you like to see a movie or some-thing?"

I decided that that was the moment to sneak out. I backed toward the door, but it was not to be. Jaimie noticed. She turned to me and said, "Ex-plain to this very young man why that's not possible."

I smiled sheepishly and said, "Well, I don't really see that I'm such a good person to speak for you."

She snapped back, "You know me very well and you can speak to other men and particularly Mr. Dursley in their language."

Maybe I owed her. So I said., "Let's sit at YOUR desk. I'll take one of the yellow chairs and Dursley, perhaps you'd take the red leather?"

He did. I reminded Jaimie about the office warming gift. She got it out, conjured glasses and ice, and poured us each a portion. Then I started. "Here's the deal, Dudley. Ms. Jaimie is considerably older than you are. You are just in your twenties while she's well into her forties. She isn't as old as your mum, but she's old enough to be your mum. She doesn't want to be seen as a cradle-robber. Besides that." Here I paused for a good sip and a deep breath. "I think that she has kind of given up the idea of ro-mance in her life."

She whipped her gaze around from Dursley to me. "What do you mean, I've given up the hope of romance?"

I looked around to see if she were talking to someone else. Then I said, "Well, you've not dated seriously in all your years at Hogwarts. What else would one conclude."

Dudley broke in here. "Look. Ms. Jaimie, you are as attractive as any of the seventh year girls here. As a matter of fact, much more so. They're all so immature. I wouldn't think of dating any of them. You, on the other hand, are truly beautiful and amazing. Let me judge for myself." He then turned to me and said, "You dated Minerva. She was older than Jaimie when you started dating, right? Did that stop you?"

I shrugged and said, "You've got a point, Dursley. Why don't you give him a shot, Jaimie?"

Jaimie looked from one to the other of us as though we were both due for a berth in Crackerbox Palace. She got up and said, "I'll let you sleep on it. If you still want to go out, we'll see this weekend." She raised her wand and said, "Now, get out the both of you."

We did. We were both bound for Dursley's apartment. On the way down, he said, "Just like old times. Eh, Professor Wendt?"

I frowned and said, "Too much."

□

The rest of the week passed uneventfully. Dursley and I fell into our old habits from the other time that we'd roomed together in my office. Now we were together in his office. Thursday came. I asked Dursley if he still had a date with Jaimie.

"You bet, professor."

"Good. What are you doing?"

His smile was as wide as the Thames. "We're going to a chamber music concert at Albert Hall."

I chuckled, "Really trying to ditch you, isn't she?"

"You bet. She doesn't know me, though. I'm way more determined than your average apprentice janitor."

I corrected, "You mean, junior professor."

"That's just temporary."

"Oh, I think you might just convince old Sluggy that you've got what it takes to keep the job permanently."

Dursley clucked his tongue and said, "You are a hopeless optimist."

I smiled. "I'm a hopeful realist. Now, you show Jaimie a great time tomorrow. I'd like to see you make her eat her words."

"You bet, Professor."

The next day at supper, Jaimie was wearing a skirt with a slit down the

137

side that I could swear that we hadn't helped her move. Dursley was wearing a black suit, shirt, and tie. In another era, he might have been mistaken for Draco Malfoy, but somehow he made the suit look bright and full of joy. Maybe it was his radiant smile.

I, on the other hand, was more than ready to change into casual weekend dress.

That evening sometime in the early hours of the morning, I was awakened by a jubilant Dursley trying really hard to seem like he was trying to slip in noiselessly. Having awakened me, he apologized profusely and insisted that I go back to sleep.

I said, "It's clear that that's the last thing in the world that you want, I'll just get up and pour us a little nightcap, and you can give me the details on how your date went. It's clear that you did something in addition to listening to chamber music."

He beamed. "Yes. It was a good concert."

□□

We walked outside the grounds and disapparated to Hyde Park near Albert Hall. The concert was a string trio with piano. They played several pieces including a Bach piece. During the intermission, we went out to the lobby and shared a drink. She asked me how I liked the first half of the concert.

I said, "The Bach took me back a long way to when I went to a concert of Glenn Gould in Toronto. That was the most amazing concert that I'd ever seen."

Her mouth opened wide and she said, "That's not possible. Glenn Gould must have died before you were born or maybe just after! You're just trying to snow me."

"No way! I saw that concert. I admit that he had given up on concerts that long ago, but this was a special charity concert. I'll always be haunted by the memory of that concert. I'm not sure, but I think he's still alive."

"You're crazy!"

We had gotten rather loud. Someone else had come over and asked, "What's all this then?"

I explained that I thought Glenn Gould was still alive and my friend didn't. He said, "Sure, he's alive. I think he still cuts the occasional album. It's amazing how good he is even in his seventies."

Jaimie's mouth dropped open again. By this time the concert was about to resume, so we went back and didn't talk until after the concert. I invited Jaimie to go to the Leaky Cauldron. We did. The first thing we talked about after getting drinks was Glenn Gould. She finally accepted that he was still

138

alive. She had an explanation. "You know that I'm from a different universe. In that universe, he died in the early '80's. It was some sort of drug overdose or something."

I said, "I thought that only rock stars died that way."

"Gould was strange."

"So, Gould died in your world when you were a kid? That's tragic."

She nodded and said, "Actually, I had just graduated from high school."

I stared at her skeptically. "No way!"

"Sad, but true."

Our discussion turned to other things. I told her about being chased by Deatheaters half-way around the world. We both had had a couple of drinks by then, and she became, well, pretty excited about my adventures. She was disappointed that she'd not even lived through the Riddle wars. It was about that time that she leaned across the table where we were sitting. She put a hand around my neck and pulled me close. She said,"You know, you're not at all what I expected." Then she planted a sloppy kiss, missing my lips a little.

At that point, Tom called, "Last Drink." She insisted on buying us one. She laughed when the drink arrived and said, "This may be the last drink, but it isn't my last drink of you." Then we kissed again. This time, we managed to hit our lips squarely. We dragged that last drink out as long as we could, leaning across the table and holding hands. We closed the Cauldron. We went by floo to her office.

We sat on your sofa snogging for a while, and then I mentioned that for a couple of months I'd slept on that sofa. She said, "Shounds like a capitolish ideaish. We could do that rightsh now. Letsh me get ush a drink to shelebrate the ideash." She tried waving her wand to conjure glasses or something. It didn't work. Instead, a couple of teacups floated through the air and crashed to the floor.

I excused myself from her embrace to sweep up the broken china and dump it in the trash. When I got back she was snoring like a lumberjack. I decided that her idea was not so great for this night, although on another occasion. . .

I straightened her up on the sofa and got her head under a sofa pillow. She muttered something indistinct, and I kissed her forehead goodbye. She smiled. I left and came here.

I said, "Dursley, let's get some sleep. It's good that tomorrow is Saturday." He nodded and headed off to his bedroom with a decided spring to his step. I went back to the sofa where I'd been sleeping.

The next morning, I was up in time for breakfast. Amazingly, so was Dursley. He arrived at the Great Hall shortly after I did. Shortly after that, Jaimie arrived. They glanced at each other sheepishly and sat at their normal spots on opposite ends of the head table even though there was practically no one else around.

Dursley and I returned to our digs while Jaimie was still eating. I took up a spot in what I'd have called a breakfast nook if I were back in the States. There was a knock on the door. Dursley answered it. I continued working on my lesson plans.

I heard a familiar voice talking to Dursley, probably standing in the doorway. "Oh, you must think I'm a lush. You'll probably never want to see me again. I really am not that way! I don't know what happened."

Dursley said, "No."

Jaimie asked, "No to what?"

"Dursley said, "No to everything. No, I don't think you're a lush. No, I don't want to not see you again. . . That is, I *do* want to see you again. As a matter of fact, I thought we might. . . uh. . ."

She asked softly, "What?"

"Go to dinner tonight and maybe a movie."

"You are sure that you're not just taking pity on me?"

Dursley declared, "Never in life."

I couldn't see her face, but I could hear the smile in her voice. Then I remembered about my "date" tonight. I jumped out of my chair and ran to the door to the apartment. "Sorry to interrupt, but I need your help tonight, Jaimie."

She turned a baleful gaze on me, "What!"

"Well, you know, you agreed to take me on the odd occasion to things that I have to attend. Well, tonight is one of those occasions."

Her face went through several emotions in the space of about two seconds. "Oh, shit!" She turned to Dursle., "I'm afraid I did commit to that." Back to me, she said, "This couldn't be postponed, could it?"

I grimaced. "I'm afraid not."

"When?"

"Six thirty."

She turned to Dursley again. "I'm so, so, so very sorry. This is something that I've got to do."

Dursley's smile was as wide as the Grand Canyon. "Don't fret. I'll take a rain check on that date. And soon."

She said enthusiastically, "You've got it."

Then we all stood there for a moment. I realized that my presence really wasn't necessary, so I tried to disappear as unobtrusively as I could.

About 6:15 that night, there was a knock on the door. Even though I was expecting it, Dursley got to the door before I did. There was a quick little snog that they tried to hide from me. Then Jaimie turned to me and said, "Are you ready?"

"Sure. I've got a location where we're going." I handed her the note that had arrived in the afternoon. She glanced at it and said, "Let's go. We'll take the floo connection here directly there."

We stepped out of the hearth into a bar that I recognized. We arrived a few minutes early, but Javeen and her dad were waiting for us. I realized that I didn't have to introduce anyone. We all stood staring at each other. There was a surprise for everyone but me. Neither Javeen nor her dad were expecting Jaimie. Jaimie was certainly not expecting both Javeen and the CEO of Gringotts. I was not surprised by any of them.

The first to speak was Javeen. "We weren't expecting a second guest." She said that with some rancor in her voice.

Jaimie said, "And why not? You are quite aware that I am his personal assistant. Why would he not bring me?"

I was rather surprised by the vehement response, but on reflection, I realized that she was just protecting her position which she'd been occupying for years in her world.

Glorblazz intervened. "Of course, Mrs. Brewster is welcome. Let's go back to the private room where we have a table reserved."

We did that. I thought for a moment about the fact that "Mrs. Brewster" wasn't really present. By the time that we reached our table I had a strategy in mind. I hoped that Ms. Sinistra would go along with it. We were seated and had placed drink orders when I put my strategy into action. I said, "Oh, one little thing that I must point out. I now have two personal assistants."

Javeen's mouth dropped open in shocked surprise, but I hurried on. "This is a distant relative of Mrs. Brewster. They are as good as twins. Her name is, of course, Sinistra since she's never married. She is a great help to me in getting around and doing other things like sending owl mail. She is authorized to stand in for me in all my official roles when I'm unable to perform those duties."

Javeen buried her chin in the palms of her hand and said, "Now we have another."

I asked, "Now, what is the agenda for the evening?"

Gorblazz looked at his daughter who had nothing to say. He took up the question. "Well, Mr. Wendt, I'm sure you remember that before you took your most recent leave of absence, we had proposed a. . . merger. . . It would be very advantageous to both you and Gringotts if you were able to devote more time to us—both me and Javeen."

Javeen rolled her eyes and started to say something when our drinks arrived, and we placed orders for our meal. When the waiter left, she said, "We all know what it is."

Jaimie interrupted. "I don't know what we're talking about."

Javeen snapped back, "If you don't know, then what are you doing here?"

Jaimie's mouth formed a big "O". Then she turned to me and whispered, "You wouldn't really. . ."

I had no chance to answer because Javeen interrupted and said, "He most certainly would. As a matter of fact. . ."

Jaimie interrupted again, saying, "He most certainly wouldn't. If we are talking about what we all know we're talking about, I think it's about time for us to leave." She didn't even consult me by turning toward me as she said that.

Gorblazz took his turn interrupting. "Look. I came here to discuss business and why we want a full-time commitment from Professor Wendt."

At this point, I was trying to work out why Jaimie, who clearly wanted my full time job, would be opposing something that would get me out of her way.

Gorblazz was going on. "In the last dozen or so years, Professor Wendt has provided us with multiple money making opportunities and solved some significant problems that we have had. You simply can't be a part-time partner of Gringotts in this progressively strange universe. For example, what do you think of the feasibility of international trade with the race that you call Ghosts?"

Jaimie immediately shouted, "Who are the Ghosts? You aren't talking about Sir Nick, are you?"

Gorblazz and Javeen shushed her.

I said, "Oh, you probably know them by the name they gave themselves—Souls. The PAK thought that they should be called Ghosts.

"Back to your question, Gorblazz. There are reasons that I can't give you without breaking an NDA with the Ministry that we can't trade with the Ghosts."

Our food was delivered, and we ate mainly in silence. Finally, Gorblazz asked me, "We can't talk you into joining us full-time at Gringotts? We can make it very profitable for you, right Javeen?"

Javeen favored me with a happy smile and said, "I might be your new personal assistant, right Daddy?"

Gorblazz nodded discretely.

Jaimie said, "Absolutely not."

That was the end of discussion. We finished the meal and parted. Jaimie took my hand forcefully and dragged me to the floo connection and back to Dudley's floo connection. There, he greeted her with a quick kiss and tried to talk her into going with him on a date on Sunday.

"No, tomorrow is a school night." She smiled though as she said, "I'm surprised at a Hogwarts professor wanting to go out on a school night. We could go for a walk tomorrow afternoon though." I retreated to a previously prepared position to avoid embarrassing anyone. I needn't have worried. She took his hand and suggested that they take the floo connection to her office.

With that I wondered if I'd ever get my office back.

Over the next weeks, I was a frequent visitor at *my* old office. We had to do planning sessions for coordinating our classes and getting a review of our lesson plans. We originally thought it would be once a week on Saturday afternoons, but soon we were meeting on Wednesday nights as well.

These sessions often went far afield from English literature. I had decided that since this Jaimie was my personal assistant and didn't have access to my memories the way the old one had, I needed to keep her up to date on major events with Gringotts and others.

One time, I showed her an owl post that I'd just gotten from Gringotts. She looked it over and commented, "They seem to really want to trade with the Ghosts. What in the world do they hope to get from them? And what do they think the Ghosts could want from us?"

I admitted, "I don't know. They must have something in mind." I thought about the question and an idea occurred to me. "You know, they might want to trade artistic items."

Jaimie said, "Well, that's just silly. You know that Goblins regard their art as theirs forever. I can't imagine their giving up any of their precious swords or shields to the Ghosts." She chuckled. "And I can't imagine the Ghosts wanting any such items."

"True, but you know that they have substantial collections of human art, don't you?"

She thought and admitted, "You're right. I have seen some in Gringotts back halls. What would the Ghosts have to trade for that art?"

I said, "The Ghosts have all sorts of advanced technology. However, I don't believe that much of it would work around significant amounts of magic."

She then surprised me, "We should bring that up as an agenda item at the next quarterly Board meeting." I hadn't expected the "we".

I fumbled, "You want to attend Board meetings?"

"Of course, I can't be your assistant without actually assisting you at these meetings."

I mulled that over in my head. I wasn't sure that I wanted that sort of "assistance". I tabled it until I'd had time to sleep on it.

She asked, "The Goblins seem to think that you have some influence with the Ministry. Where does that come from?"

"Oh, it's not as preposterous as it may seem to you. In your world, there wasn't all the trouble happening with the PAK and other groups. In this world, there were lots of high level working meetings on how to deal with them. I was involved with a lot of them."

She nodded wisely. "You do always seem to have solutions for problems. Every now and then, I wish I had some of those genes. I can remember the events and even follow your logic, but I never seemed to be able to reproduce your results on my own."

I shrugged. "You're right, I think. Genes."

I took up another topic that had been puzzling me for a while. "I'm a little surprised that you and Dursley are hitting it off so well. Is this thing becoming serious?"

She leaned back in the desk chair that I used to use with MY desk. I was sitting in the red leather chair—nice but not the same thing. She asked if I'd like a drink. "Not Blue Label. I've not got your resources. It's decent whiskey though—Jameson."

"Sure." She conjured a couple of clean glasses with ice and poured from a bottle that she kept in the lower right drawer of the desk. We had a sip, and she resumed the leaned-back position and spoke.

"I don't know where this is going. I told you that in 'my' world, I never had much in the way of romance. I'm not used to this, and I'm just letting things happen."

I grimaced, "Look, there's a lot I don't understand about that. In the first place, I don't understand why you didn't have romance. You're lovely. No. That understates it. You're downright beautiful. You're smart. You've got a sense of humor. You should have had guys tripping over each other to ask you out. Why didn't it happen?"

She took a sip and thought. "Here's what happened in 'my' world. I started off with all your memories—male memories. My experience of dating was mostly by me—that is, you—making contact and getting it going. I guess there's just something in the genes. I was blocked. I couldn't seem to just tell guys that I liked them."

She hesitated for another sip. "Also, I had a hard time accepting invites to do things. I think that came from my male memories. You almost never did that. Also, I hung around Hogwarts too much. There just aren't a lot of unattached guys at Hogwarts."

I took a sip myself. "OK. Where does Dursley fit in? Do you see him becoming a potential. . . oh. . ."

"Husband?"

"OK. Your word."

"He's a nice guy. I like him." She reflected and said, "No. I haven't told him. I guess I assume he's figured that out from the snogging. But, besides that, he's got a sense of humor. He's actually pretty mature. I guess that comes from all the traveling he did staying away from Deatheaters. Of course, it doesn't hurt that he's well-to-do and an assistant professor." She smiled as she thought of something else. "He's damn good at snogging and . . ." She didn't finish the thought.

"Well, that's a pretty good list of characteristics."

She took another sip and asked, "By the way, did you mean it when you said that I was downright beautiful?"

"Of course! I'm not like you ladies who compliment each other when you don't really believe the compliment and are just trying to develop a friendship." I then added, "When I compliment, it's for business."

She said, "Oh." and nodded slowly.

Chess is Not Just for Guys

As I was enjoying breakfast one morning, an owl swooped down and dive-bombed my bowl of cereal. The milk splashed all over me and the main thing left in the bowl was a note. I stared at the bowl, at my milk-splattered robes, and the note. I decided just to take it down to Dursley's apartment. If it were important, maybe I'd forget about breakfast. Otherwise, I could change and return to breakfast.

Back "home" I opened the note. It was from Sissy Brewster. She was following up on the tournament that she was going to play. It went:

> Professor Wendt,
>
> The tournament we discussed starts Nov 17. The first game is that evening. I hope you can come to watch. There are games every day through the 28th. You're welcome to attend any of them. I'd like you to come on the opening day.
> Dad told me about this Jaimie who is at Hogwarts. I don't understand how she could not be my mum. I hope she will attend some time so that I can see her myself.
> Best wishes, Sissy

I turned the note over and over in my hand. The 17th was only a few days away. If I used her to get me to the tournament, Sissy would get to see Jaimie for sure. I decided that I would skip breakfast. Since I tend to procrastinate—especially tough issues—I was satisfied to wait for our week-end meeting to bring it up. That gave me a whole two days to reflect and choose a way to deal with it.

Saturday came, and I had decided that this had to be the first item on the Saturday agenda for the planning meeting. I joined her in her office as usual. It was sad that I was now automatically thinking of it as "her" office. I simply handed Jaimie the note from Sissy and asked her to read it. When she'd finished, she said, "Well. I guess I really have to take you. I'd want to go anyway—just to introduce myself and assure her that I'm not her step-mum. If that's any assurance to her."

I agreed. I added, "I'd like to go to someplace that we can access the internet and find out when the first games start, where the tournament is happening exactly. I'd also like to send an owl post to her to let her know what to expect."

Jaimie agreed to going right after our lesson planning session. She pointed out, "There aren't any internet cafes any more. Your mobile phone is probably a simple flip phone, right?"

I admitted as much. She said, "Well, when I need the internet, which is pretty rarely, I go to libraries. Some are friendly and let you just walk in without a library card to use them. I can take us to one that is that way in my world. I don't know about yours."

I shrugged. "Well, let's just go hunting to see what we find."

"We could just send Ms. Brewster a note asking for details. I'm sure she'd send us everything we need to know."

I agreed. However, I added, "I still want to know about the schedule independently."

Jaimie wouldn't oppose that. So after our review session, we set out to find a library with internet access. We took the floo connection in her office to the floo connection in a bar in Oxford. I paid for a butter beer for both Jaimie and me. We took swallows and departed. Once outside, we went to a local library, the Botley. Once we were there, we went up to the librarian's desk as bold as brass, and I asked for a temporary card.

The librarian was very friendly. She asked where I lived. I answered, "I'm on holiday." That was in a sense true if you considered a nineteen year sabatical at Hogwarts to be a holiday. Sometimes I did—not very often, though.

She asked where I lived. I smiled and said, "The States. I've got my passport with me."

She smiled and seemed as pleased as punch. "So, you even read on holiday?"

"You may be sure of that." I handed her the passport. She gave it a glance. I had the feeling that I could have handed her Minerva's passport and she'd not have paid any more attention to it. She efficiently keyed information into her computer. The nearby printer spit out a temporary card. She explained in way more detail than necessary how the library card worked. Then she asked, "Does you friend want a temporary too?"

I shook my head and asked about using a computer. She smiled and quickly checked something on her computer. Then she took a scrap piece of paper and wrote a computer ID and temporary password on it. We could use any open computer.

We turned to find a computer, but she interrupted us. "Oh, one last thing. The library closes at one PM. Also, if you'd like suggestions of interesting places to see in Oxford, I'd be happy to make suggestions."

I nodded and said, "Maybe. We'll drop by later if we do."

We quickly found an open computer and logged on. A little manipulation of the web browser brought us to the website for the tournament. We found a schedule and details of the location of the tournament. I wanted to print those off. Unfortunately, the detailed instructions from the librarian didn't include how to print pages.

I went back to the librarian to ask about printing. She gave me instructions. It was simple. I printed on one of the printers behind the Librarian's desk. I'd have to pay for them at twenty pence a page. Before I left her desk the librarian asked, "Is she your fancy lady?"

I almost laughed out loud. I just smiled and said, "No. She's just an old friend that I've not seen for several years. She's a local—not Oxford but Scotland."

The librarian hesitated and said, "If you would like a private tour of the area, I could give you a very interesting time."

I opened my mouth, but it took me a bit to come up with a response. The response I came up with was, "That's very kind of you. Unfortunately, we have to move on immediately. I'm sure it would be a pleasure to spend time with you in Oxford. Who knows? Maybe some other time. I certainly won't forget the Botley Library."

She blushed a bit and said, "Sorry. I didn't mean to be pushy. I just thought. . ."

"Don't worry. It was a good thought. Bye."

I printed the pages and returned to collect them. After paying for them, the librarian said, "Don't forget. The offer is always open."

"I won't forget. Have a good weekend."

She beamed as she said, "I hope you have a great weekend!"

We returned to Hogwarts. I composed a note to Sissy, and we went to the owlery to send it off. On the way, Jaimie asked me, "Do you want to go back and try to find that librarian?"

"No. I'm sure she's pleasant and would be decent company, but I'm just not going to invest time in someone who is a dead end."

Jaimie smiled slyly and said, "Oh, she was pretty, and I'm sure not attached."

I shook my head. "You don't have to make fun of me. Maybe someday I'll meet another. . ."

She supplied a name, "Another Ginny?"

"How do you know about Ginny?"

She laughed. "Oh, it was not hard to tell when she was interrogating us that you wanted to be sure to be extra nice to her."

"Maybe I just wanted to be sure to avoid spending a few days in Azkaban."

She shook her head and clucked her tongue. Well, I had to admit that she was right, but not to her face.

□□

We ended up arranging to meet Sissy and her dad for an early dinner on Wednesday, the start of the tournament. We took the floo connection to the Cauldron. I suggested that we stop in at the library again to pick up some suggestions for sightseeing in Lausanne. Then we disapparated to Paris. From Paris we disapparated to Lausanne where the tournament was being held at the Hotel Royal Savoy Lausanne.

On Sunday, Jaimie had grabbed me right after lunch. She dragged me up to her office. When we arrived, she made a proposal. "Have you been to Lausanne before?"

"No."

"Why don't we try to work our classes to have the afternoon off so we can do a disapparation tour of Lausanne."

That was an interesting idea. "My afternoon classes are at one and four. When are yours?"

She beamed. "My only one is at two, but its a double."

I tried to work out what alternatives we could work. She saw my consternation and said, "Oh, let's just cancel them."

I scratched my chin. "I am the department head. I don't think there are any students who would object."

She chuckled. "My double is a seventh year. There's one student in it who would complain."

I grimaced. "She'll just have to get used to a little disappointment."

Jaimie squealed, "Yes!"

After we arrived, we did the disapparation tour. We saw the Lavaux

149

Vineyard terraces. We went to the Lausanne Cathedral and we visited the Christmas markets. The tournament ended at about the peak of the Christmas markets, so we bought some small gifts for my family. Jaimie had thought to bring an extensible handbag. It was largely filled with my presents, so I ended up carrying it through the day. What I bought was mostly consumables—chocolates, cheeses. I didn't attempt wines. No one in my family particular liked them.

Toward the end of the afternoon we went to the Hotel Royal Savoy Lausanne where the tournament was being held. We found the Brewsters at player registration desk .

Mr. Brewster introduced his daughter to Jaimie. It was the most awkward introduction I'd ever endured. Sissy shook Jaimie's hand mechanically and finally said, "You really aren't my mum." Then Jaimie hugged her and said, "No, I'm not. But I wish I were. You're lovely, smart, and a brilliant chess master. I'm looking forward to seeing you play. Why don't we get something to eat. You will need some carbo-loading if you want to be at the top of your form."

That broke the ice. We let the Brewsters lead the way to the restaurant. When we were seated, I said, "I'm rich. Let me pick up the check." No one objected. After we ordered, I asked the crucial question, "Whom do you play to start?"

This was Sissy's element. She started a whirlwind description of the various players, finishing with her first opponent. "He's Gundar, Gundarssen, a Norwegian. He's got a reputation for throwing brilliant gambits at his opponents. He's the one player whom I fear the most. He's not got the highest rating, but he's been rising fast.

"The best five players from this tournament and the other continental tournaments plus a few old has-been fogies get to play in the next tournament. It happens next year. Then the best five out of that tournament compete for the World Championship."

Mr. Brewster said, "You are kind of lucky that you're not in the Asian continental tournament. There's more people in that area than anywhere else."

I replied, "I think it probably evens out. Chess is more popular in Europe than any other continent. I suppose Russia is in the European tournament?"

Sissy said, "They break Russia into two at the Urals. Yes. The European tournament probably has more really good players than any of the others."

Jaimie laughed and said, "Right! It has you."

Jaimie announced that she had the privilege of playing black today. I asked her, "Don't most players prefer white?"

She shook her head with determination, "Yes. But I like to start with black against an opponent that I've not played before. I'll have to play black some time. Since I'm at a disadvantage, I risk less by trying some chancy moves. I get to feel him out."

Mr. Brewster talked about getting into the tournament as spectators. "This venue hasn't got a lot of space for the tournament. Each player is allowed to have half a dozen spectators. We need to get you registered as our spectators for the day. Other family members will be coming other days during the tournament, so please check before coming other days."

I asked, "What does the weekend look like? Expecting company?"

Mr. Brewster sighed, "Don't know yet. I'll send you an owl on Friday to let you know what it looks like for the weekend."

We finished the meal and left for the Conference Center where the tournament was being held. We went to the Registration Table and received badges as official guests of Ms. Cecily Brewster. We all entered the hall. Sissy and her dad went directly to her table. I took Jaimie's arm and said, "Let's take a little tour of the hall."

She shrugged. "OK."

After we got out of earshot, I said, "OK. There are courtesy rules in tournaments. You can probably guess them."

She immediately said, "I will. No talking, cheering, hand-waving, or other distracting behaviors."

I agreed. "That's pretty much it. They are obvious, but they are not easy to remember. Let me remind you of a story from my youth."

She sighed. "If you must."

"When I was in high school, I went to the Ohio State Fair."

She shrugged. "Entertaining?"

"Amazingly so. The most entertaining thing for me was the horse pull contest."

"What happens? Do people pull horses?"

I chuckled. "No. Although a mule pulling contest like that might be entertaining. What happens is that a team of horses pulls a sort of sled with weights on it. The goal is to pull the sled a fixed distance without the sled pausing during the pull. Each team of horses has to do it. The ones who don't succeed, drop out and more weight is added to the sled. Eventually, either only one team can do it or none can. The one who can wins. If none can, the team that pulls the furthest wins. It's incredibly exciting."

She rolled her eyes and said, "I'm sure."

"No. Really. It's so exciting that the crowd gets sufficiently excited that they can hardly keep from cheering their favorite team. That's strictly a no-

no because any noise can distract the team and keep them from succeeding. The tension of not being able to cheer for your favorite but wanting to help them is incredible."

She said, "It actually sounds like it might be interesting. Where can we go to see one of these contests?"

I sighed. "The trouble is that there probably isn't any place you can go. By the time I got out of grad school, there were very few of these contests left in state fairs. By now, I doubt there are any at all."

"Really? Why?"

"Well, when the main source of serious pulling power at farms was horses, these contests were naturals. More than seventy-five years ago, tractors pretty much took over the role of horses. Then horse pulls became the sport of the wealthy old farmer who kept draft horses for a hobby. Now, you can find tractor pulls in some fairs, but you know, it's just not the same. I doubt I could get excited about a tractor pull."

"That doesn't seem logical."

"Probably not, but I don't get excited about car races. I do get excited about horse races. I don't know why."

She smiled. "I take your point. I'm sorry there aren't any horse pulls left. I wish there were." Then she took my arm and said, "Let's go join the Brewsters." She hesitated and said, "Any other words of wisdom for watching chess?"

"Just don't expect to understand it. In most sports, you can pick up the main point of the game pretty quickly and have a decent understanding of what's going on. Chess is different. You really need a commentator. I am not that man. Most tournaments have a commentator when you get down to the end of the tournament. I don't know about this one. Of course, if we had an hour to spare, I could talk about strategy. I could tell you what's going on, but I'm not sure that that would tell you what's going on."

She laughed. "You like paradoxes don't you?"

"Yeh. It's a lucky predisposition—the world being so full of them."

She squeezed my arm and said, "Let's go."

We got to the table where Sissy was to play. Her opponent had arrived. He didn't look that Nordic. He had brown hair cut fairly short. His eyes were brown too. He was about six feet tall. He looked like he thought the game would be great, good fun. He had a broad smile on his face. He shook hands with Sissy and offered to shake hands with everyone else standing around the table. Only Mr. Brewster demurred. His command of English seemed quite good.

I think he was in his early twenties, but I could easily have underestimated his age. He sat at the table, touched the two pawns on the ends of the pawn row and then touched the two rooks at the ends of his back row. Then he said something like, "Good. Good luck, Ms. Brewster."

She seemed more intense than he was, but she still wished him good luck as well. The tournament director announced, "Contestants may now begin."

Sissy was playing black. The first several moves went quite rapidly. By about the tenth move, things had slowed considerably. After a while, I felt a tug on my arm. Jaimie brought her lips close to my ear and whispered, "Biology break." She then dragged me off. When we'd left the hall, she said in a normal voice, "I want to ask you some questions about the game—and have a biology break."

"OK. Go ahead."

She dragged me over to a small sofa in the hallway outside the Conference Center. "Here are a few random questions: How long will the game last? How do I know who's ahead? Is cheating possible?"

I said, "I'll start with the easiest. You've no doubt noticed the double clocks. They keep track of each player's time. Each player has two hours to complete 20 moves in this tournament. If they can't, they forfeit the game."

She broke in excitedly, "Are all games that long?"

"No, it's a decision made by the tournament committee. Lots of serious players play 'blitz' games where the players have five minutes or less for twenty moves."

She nodded. "Go on."

"Knowing who's doing well is hard. Generally, the more pieces you lose, the worse off you are, but there are lots of ways that you can be behind in material, but in the better position. There are a couple of other important factors. Control of the center of the board is considered generally good. Of course, if you're running out of time and have to move quickly, that's usually bad. There's tempo. That's kind of hard to explain. It generally means that you may have a good position and a good plan to get where you want to be, but you may just not have enough moves to achieve your plan before it's over for you."

She made a face at me. "You're crazy."

"You're right. Anyway, you'd think that cheating would be impossible. Everyone can see everything. Chess is a 'total knowledge game' as the game theorists say.

"However, there are technical ways to cheat. You could be wearing a hearing aid that lets you listen to a team of analysts working the position you're in. There are people who legitimately need a hearing aid. It's hard to keep them from cheating if they really want to.

"An American world champion, Bobby Fischer, claimed that the Russians were giving his Russian opponents signals to help them win. He also claimed that some Russians were 'throwing' their games to other Russians as a way of advancing a preferred Russian. He also claimed that the Russian contestants got together and helped analyze each other's games that had been postponed overnight. That's strictly speaking not cheating, but it certainly goes against the spirit of the game."

Jaimie squeezed my arm and said, "I'm almost sorry I asked. OK. I'm going for the biology break. I'll be back here shortly." As she left, I wondered if her world version of me had helped Cedric. If he had, surely she'd know most of this from that experience.

She returned, and we went back into the hall. Over at Sissy's board, we discovered that there had been some progress. She was down a pawn. It seemed like her position was a little stronger than Gundar's, but how could I know? Her clock was only a few ticks behind his although her clock was running at the moment.

After a while, I wished I'd taken a biology break when Sissy's had. I leaned over her ear and whispered, "Biology break." Then I walked away. She followed me. When we got outside, she touched my arm and said, "Wait. What do you think of Jaimie's position?"

"This game has reached the point where I haven't the slightest idea what to think. She's a little behind on time and material, but I sure don't know if that's significant."

She nodded and I found the men's loo.

When we re-entered the hall, Jaimie's game had started to move faster. It looked like no one was going to be in time trouble. Then, there was a long time when Gundar just stared at the board as his clock ran. It ended by his offering his hand to Sissy. She hesitated a moment and then accepted it. There were sighs all around. We all quickly left the hall. Once outside, I hugged Sissy and said, "Congratulations."

Jaimie said, "You tied, right?"

"Sure. That's great against Gundar."

We stood a while talking. Mr. Brewster suggested that we go to the bar and get a drink. Both Jaimie and I declined with thanks. She said, "This is a school night."

Jaimie and I retraced our steps to get back to Hogwarts. When we got to the Cauldron, Jaimie said, "How about actually drinking the drinks that we'll buy from Tom?"

I was a little surprised since we'd just turned down drinks with the Brewsters, but I agreed. She had a Jameson whiskey and I had a JW Black Label. It was a cool evening. We sat by the fire. She said, "I understand what you said about horse pulls."

I had to smile at that. She went on. "At the end when Gundar was sitting for so long on his move at the last move of the game, I thought, 'I could just scream! Why doesn't he move!' Of course, we know why now. I think. Why do you think he spent so much time on that non-move?"

"Oh, I think he was trying to decide if there were any reasonable chance to win the game. He must have decided that there really wasn't. So he just asked for a draw. I'm sure Jaimie was happy to give it. A draw against him while playing black is no small thing."

She touched my arm and said, "I hope we can see at least one game on the weekend. Don't you?"

I smiled. "That would be great. You know that when I was helping Cedric, I eventually got to the point of hating these close games. Anything could happen—especially losing."

She smiled broadly. "But they're so very exciting. I can hardly wait to see another. Can you?"

I laughed. "That would be great."

She looked up to her right and closed her eyes, "Oh, wouldn't it!"

We finished our drinks in silence with our thoughts. Then she rose and held out her hand to me. "Let's go. We're burning moonlight." She was clearly having a great time. Her face was slightly flushed and her hand was cool to the touch. We entered the floo connection and walked out in her office.

She realized that and seemed a bit flustered. "Sorry. Force of habit. I meant to go to Dursley's." She was still holding my hand as she said, "Here, I'll drop you there."

I gulped and said, "No need. I'll walk down. It will help me clear my head out before bed."

She nodded. "Yes. Clear head. Before bed." Then she giggled. I guess it was the rhyme that did it.

I opened the door, looked back, and waved before I went through. She was still beaming.

The next couple of days seemed to fly past. On Friday, I was in the Great Hall for lunch. Toward the end when people were starting to leave, someone sat next to me. It was Jaimie. She handed me a note. It was addressed to her. It was from Sissy. She invited us to come on Sunday to see her play. It explained that Brewster's relatives would be there Saturday.

I asked, "You up for it?"

"Oh, yes. We maybe could do a little sightseeing. What do you think?"

"That would be fine."

She squeezed my arm and said, "See you right after breakfast."

I asked, "Is Dursley going?"

She stared at me a second and said, "No! No. He wouldn't be interested. It's not football or Quidditch."

I said, "Good." Then she left.

Sunday morning, I was up as early as I ever had been on a Sunday. None-the-less, I found Jaimie waiting at the head table having finished breakfast and just sitting impatiently for me. I sat and transferred a sunny-side up egg to my plate along with a couple of pieces of toast and a piece of crispy bacon. I hurriedly had the bacon and eggs as Jaimie sat beside me regarding me faintly disapprovingly for making her wait—I suppose.

I finished, and we left via the Great Hall floo connection. We retraced our previous course. We arrived at the hotel at about 8:30 local time. It was a half-hour before the first game of the day. We went to the hall to see if the Brewsters had arrived. They hadn't. I suggested going to the restaurant for a cup of tea. They had tea available in paper cups. Fortified with hot tea we returned to the tournament hall. The Brewsters showed up slightly after we did.

Sissy hugged me. She shook hands with Jaimie. We caught up with the standings. It turned out that Sissy was in the top three scores. Her dad pointed out that that didn't mean much at this point. She had two games this day. One was at nine and the other was at three.

Sissy handicapped the nine game. "I've played this guy once before in a tournament. He's beatable—especially as black. He depends on one defense. I've got it scoped out."

Jaimie frowned at her and said, "You know that Professor Wendt would call that bad Karma. Don't underestimate your foe."

She lowered her head and nodded slightly, but she whispered, "I'm still going to beat him." She turned out to be right. Even Jaimie and I could tell that he was on the ropes early on in the game. It was almost boring waiting for the end that you knew was inevitable. He strung the game out until he had only two moves left to make. He sat on that next to last move until the clock ran down, and the director declared Sissy the winner. He shook hands with Sissy and sort of slunk out of the hall.

We had an early lunch, picking up some things at one of the Christmas markets and returning to the Brewster room. Afterwards, I suggested going to the Olympic Museum. I was outvoted. We went to the Collection de l'Art Brut. I decided that was the last time that I let the crowd outvote me.

The afternoon game was a very different affair from the morning game. Sissy's evaluation was that she would have to play a genius game to beat her opponent, Dubuffet. She was playing black. The game turned out to be full of surprises. The advantage in pieces swung back and forth. At one point, it seemed like Sissy had victory within her grasp, but Dubuffet weaseled out of the trap. The game reached the end of regulation moves. Both players had time on their clocks. They agreed to postpone resumption until the next day.

We went to the Etoile Blanche for supper. It was nice to find a place with hamburgers even if they weren't quite what you'd find at the TGIF in Dayton, Ohio. After dinner Mr. Brewser declared that it was Sissy's curfew for game days. Neither Jaimie or I argued. As a matter of fact, Jaimie heartily agreed since it was a school night. They disapparated to their hotel. We went outside, and I took Jaimie's hand.

We appeared somewhere. I was pretty sure that it wasn't Paris. It sure wasn't London. We seemed to be on a beach. The sun had set, but there was plenty of light from the nearly full moon. I pondered a bit and said, "We're on a beach in Lausanne."

Jaimie said, "Good. I thought it might be nice to walk along the beach of Lake Leman for a while."

It was cool but we were wearing light jackets. We walked along the beach. The moon was low over the horizon. It cast its silver light over everything. It seemed to transport us to its surface.

I took her hand as we walked silently. There didn't seem to be anything to say. After a while I said, "When we landed in your office by mistake after the first game."

"Yes."

"That wasn't a mistake, was it?"

I couldn't see the color of her face, which was washed out by the moonlight. She squeezed my hand and said, "It wasn't."

I nodded. "That's what I thought."

She stopped walking. I put my free hand on her waist. She inched toward me. We kissed. She backed away and moved closer again. We kissed. It was not enough. I wondered if it had even happened. She must have too because she pulled much closer, and we kissed a long kiss that wasn't enough either.

We stood silent, unmoving for a bit, Then I said one word, "Dursley."

She kissed me again and said, "You." Then she said, "Let's go to the Cauldron." We did. Once there, we ordered drinks and took a table.

I asked, "Why me?"

She laughed. "It does seem almost incestuous, doesn't it."

I agreed. "Yeh. It isn't by any stretch of the imagination, but there it is. I can't help feeling like I'm robbing the cradle or something."

She said, "It's really the other way around. You are younger than I am. The way I get it, you probably missed out experiencing at least four years while your Jaimie was around. I didn't miss any years. So, what are we going to do?"

"In the first place," I hesitated trying to figure out what the first place really was. I went on. "We need to be sure that this isn't just infatuation."

She laughed again. "Right. You're infatuated with an older teacher!"

"Oh, you are so infuriating. No, maybe you're infatuated with a younger man."

She shook her head, loosing some of the hair that was piled in a simple coiffure. "Easy. We just keep seeing each other, and we find out what happens."

She closed her eyes and flexed her lips for a minute or two. Then she opened them and said, "We could sleep together in my apartment. I just take you to and fro via the floo connection in both offices."

I objected. "We'd have to have Dursley's cooperation."

She said, "He's a really nice guy. He won't do anything that will hurt either your or me."

I said, "I have a rule of thumb. I never. . ."

She finished for me. "Make an important decision without sleeping on it. I know." She thought a moment, then laughed. "We could sleep on it in my bed."

"That wasn't what I had in mind."

"I know. Sure. Sleep on it tonight. Tomorrow night, The night after. Then come to me and sleep on it with me."

I said, "We'll talk about it again, the night after next."

She held her hand out and said, "Deal."

I repeated it.

The night after next, I had walked up to her office. She had just poured us drinks—Blue Label. We had just sipped when we heard the screech of an owl outside the window of her office. It had to be owl post. She flicked her wand. The window opened. The owl landed on the desk between us. I sat back in the red leather chair because it must be for her.

To both our surprises, it hopped over to my side of the desk and dropped a letter in front of me. I shrugged and picked it up. I read the direction of the letter aloud, "Professor James Wendt, Red Leather Chair, Professors Sinistra and Wendt apartment, Hogwarts School of Witchcraft and Wizardry, Scotland, UK, Earth."

Jaimie hummed, "Umhuh."

I said, "I guess this decides it. Your doom is to have me sleep with you from now on."

She nodded happily. "Just move your things up here. There's no point in being dishonest about it." She stood and said, "I'll help you. Let's go down to Dursley's and start."

We took the floo to Dursley's office. Fortunately, he was there. I said, "Sorry, Dudley. I'm moving out. Professor Sinistra is the unfortunate beneficiary of the move."

He stood and said, "I knew it. I knew it from the first. I couldn't be lucky enough to be with her very long." He held out a hand and said, "You're a lucky man."

I took it and agreed. He suggested that the three of us walk my things up to my office so that there would be no doubt that there were no hard feelings. Anywhere." We did. We ran into Filch on the way up. He looked from one to the other of us. He seemed to be at a complete loss for words. Finally, he asked, "Is there anything left that I can help with?"

Jaimie said, "Sure. Go on down to Dursley's. We'll join you there shortly. We did. Between the four of us, we finished off the move in two more trips. Filch didn't move a lot in either, but it was good to get his blessing anyway.

When we finished, it was getting late. I pointed out that I'd not read the letter yet. Jaimie sighed and said, "It's late. Read it to me in bed."

I did. It was from Sissy. It was really for both of us. It said that Sissy had reached the second stage of the tournament. She only had to win in the next two rounds to ensure getting to the Candidate's tournament next year. It had some detailed analysis of the match-ups, but the bottom line was that she was confident of getting to the Candidates' tournament.

Jaimie said to me, "I don't give a damn about it as long as you're in bed with me."

All I could say was, "Ditto."

The next day we were greeted by whistles when we entered the Great Hall for breakfast.

Gringotts Advertises

Now that I had an easy way to get around, I made magical trips more often. One of them was in early December so that I could get some gold out of my vault for Christmas presents. Jaimie was actually anxious to go. She told me, "I want to do some window shopping—especially in Madame Malcom's."

I knew that was one "window shopping" trip that I needed to be along and paying special attention. Of course, I had other business to attend to. Sissy had won her way into the Candidates' Tournament. I wanted to get her something as a congratulation gift. I was thinking of something like a self-correcting quill from Weasley's, but I was open to other possibilities.

Jaimie and I went to the Cauldron directly from our office. We had a drink and planned the day. First was Gringotts. We both needed gold from our vaults. I spent some time toting up how much I needed. Jaimie laughed and said, 'Why do you do that?"

"You mean calculate how much money I need?"

"Yes, you've got so much that you could just grab a double handful of 50 galleon coins and be just fine."

I scoffed. "Is that going to be your strategy?"

She sneered. "You know it isn't. I doubt my vault has a single 50 galleon coin in it."

I had already made a list of possible presents for various people, so I was ready to go. So was Jaimie. We walked hand-in-hand into Gringotts. I started for the teller cages. As we were doing that, a Goblin hurried up to us. He said, "What good luck! We were just going to send an owl. Come on down the hall. They're anxious to see you in the C suite."

What else could we do? I looked at Jaimie, and she nodded. It was a long walk back into the depths of Gringotts. I knew the way, Jaimie knew the way. The Goblin assumed as much. We moved as quickly as we all could. We took a turn I didn't recognize. Jaimie noticed my hesitation. She said, "Two years ago, Gorblazz moved his office. I don't know why."

The Goblin said, "It was so that he would have a larger suite. I know. Silly. His suite was just fine. Why do it? It's not far now."

We arrived at the new C suite. The Goblin led us in. I went in first. The anteroom was much as it always had been. I was greeted by Javeen's broad happy smile. Then Jaimie followed me. She was greeted by a scowl. Javeen came around her desk to take me by the arm to lead me to the new office of the CEO. Jaimie took my other arm. We were lucky the door was plenty wide. We all marched in together. Glorblazz caught sight of me and stood. He welcomed me and invited me to take the red leather chair across his desk from him. Javeen announced Jaimie, pronouncing it, "Jay-MEE." Everyone sat. Javeen was at the side of Glorblazz's desk between me and Glorblazz. Jaimie was on the other side. Javeen had a legal pad and quill out to take notes. Jaimie had a legal pad, and I was pleased to see, a ballpoint pen.

Glorblazz began. "It's come to my attention that there is a witch who is going to compete in the Muggle Chess World Championship. The *Prophet* has made a big deal of it and is planning to give the games a full page spread every day of the two tournaments. It's occurred to me that the reputation of Gringotts among wizards and witches around the world would be enhanced if we were to sponsor this young witch. What do you think?"

I said, "It's clear that this unique opportunity for the bank should be used."

Glorblazz folded his hands and said, "We agree. We read in the *Prophet* that Ms. Brewster was a protégé of yours—both of you—when she was at Hogwarts. We thought that you might be able to influence her to accept an honorarium from the bank to use her name in connection with advertising—tasteful advertising—of the bank as the bank of Chess Champions!"

I looked over to Jaimie and asked, "What do you think, Ms. Sinistra? Would that be acceptable?" I winked at her with my right eye, which no one in the room other than Jaimie could see.

She caught on immediately. She said, "I think with our connection with her, she might be convinced to go along with such a proposal." She hastily added, "Of course, it would require some negotiation as to the amount of honararium."

Gorblazz smiled and said, "Of course, Professor Wendt, you'd have a free hand to negotiate as you saw fit."

I said, "Good."

Jaimie said, "I'll get an owl post off immediately we get back to the office to her and her father."

Javeen gritted her teeth at that announcement and muttered, "I should do that."

I didn't pay attention. Instead, I said, "Capitol, Ms. Sinistra." Everyone was smiling except Javeen who seemed to have lost her winsome smile from earlier. I went on. "Ms. Sinistra and I have a little business in our vaults, so if we are finished here, I'd like to be on our way."

Gorblazz hurriedly suggested, "Oh, you could join us for lunch couldn't you?"

I sighed regretfully, "Sadly, no. Our business won't keep. Come, Ms. Sinistra. We really have to be on our way."

We shook hands around and Javeen accompanied us to the bank lobby. She walked us to a teller who had a long line of customers. She moved the line over. Jaimie and I were moved to the front of the line. We asked to be conducted to our vaults. An under-goblin was dispatched and we were on our way into the depths of Gringotts. We retrieved galleons and were on our way to the surface.

Once we were out of the bank, we both had a good laugh. Our next destination was Madame Malkin's. We arrived. Jaimie window-shopped. I watched the process carefully, noting items of particular interest to Jaimie. When that was finished, Jaimie said, "Wendt, why don't you go talk with Madame Malkin. I have a couple of small purchases to make."

That suited me fine. I wanted to talk with Madame Malkin anyway. She turned to me and asked, "I hope you have been noting what Ms. Sinistra is interested in?"

"You can be sure of that. But there's another matter that I want to talk with you about."

Madame Malkin's smile grew and she said, "I hope you're updating your wardrobe. Everything you own is at least four years old and far out of style."

I said, "I'm sure that's true, but for the moment, I have something that should be of more interest to you than my fashionability."

Her brows rose, and she asked, "Really?"

"Yes. Are you aware of Ms. Cecily Brewster's activities lately?"

She said, "Well, if you're talking about her being in the Championship Round of the Muggle World Chess Championship, then yes, I'm aware."

"Good. However, I'm sure that you are not aware of the fact that a certain well-known bank is seriously considering sponsoring Ms. Brewster's run for the world title."

"Really. What concern would that be of mine?"

"Well, if that bank were in another business, say clothes, I would think it would be of a lot of concern to you. But as it is, they are thinking of advertising themselves as the bank that one World Champion contender uses exclusively."

Madame Malkin nodded her head and said, "Do you know if Ms. Brewster has been approached by any other clothier?"

I smiled. "To the best of my knowledge she has not so far been so approached."

She hummed sagely and said, "As a former coach, do you think that you might approach her to suggest that she might become the face of Madame Malkin's clothes. Of course, we'd have to provide her with complete outfits befitting a World Champion."

My smile grew. "I think I can bring that possibility to her attention."

"Thank you, Professor Wendt. Of course, there might be a suit of clothes or two in the offing for her agent as well."

I said, "Good to know."

By this time, Jaimie had made her purchases and packed them into her handbag. She took my arm and said, "I must drag Professor Wendt off. He would stay all day in your shop if I didn't."

We left the shop.

There were other stops on the way home. We spent too much time at Flourish and Blots bookstore. I bought a book for Jaimie—*A Brief History of Time.*

□

Jaimie sent the owl post to Sissy the next day. We got a response the same day. It proposed a meeting with me on the following weekend at the Brewster home. I accepted with the provision to allow Jaimie to participate. It was enthusiastically accepted. They proposed having dinner with them on Saturday at 6:00 PM.

That day, both Jaimie and I had a week's worth of lesson planning to do. We were lucky to finish by mid-afternoon. We had grading to do as well, but we could do that on our own on Sunday. We changed to nicer clothes and got ready for the meeting by discussing negotiating strategy. It might seem strange to have a strategy when we were planning to give away the farm, but we did.

We arrived just before six. The greeting was warm. Dinner was not up to the standards of Hogwarts, but it was the most welcome meal I'd had in a long time. A meal not prepared in a professional kitchen like Hogwarts or a restaurant is special because of its imperfections. The roast beef that's a little overdone or the baked potato that is served plain without a sauce is a welcome rarity.

We helped clean up. I insisted on washing up the old-fashioned Muggle way. No one seriously objected. After the meal was over, we went to the Family Room to negotiate.

I opened the discussions. "Here's what I've been chosen to do. I negotiate the terms of an agreement between Gringotts, International and you, Cecily Brewster. You're an adult, so you can sign contracts, negotiate on your own, and make all decisions yourself.

"I wouldn't recommend it though. Your dad is pretty smart. I'd listen to him carefully if he has advice for you. Here's what I'd suggest.

"First, I'll tell you my philosophy as a negotiator for Gringotts. This was not dictated to me in whole or in part by any representative of Gringotts. Jaimie and I came up with it."

At that point, Sissy asked us, "Are you two. . . uh. . ." She couldn't quite finish the sentence. I finished it for her. "In love? Yes. Living together, yes? In my office? Yes."

Jaimie said, "He means in my office."

Everyone laughed at that.

I went on. "OK. Now that we've had our fun for the night. I'll go on. Here's my philosophy of the goal for negotiation. We think that the best contract gives you, Cecily, half of the value brought to Gringotts by the advertising.

"Second, we don't know what that is right now. We'll only have a chance to learn that after the advertising starts. So we have to have a different theory to start with. Here it is. You should have enough to let you work on your chess full time. You should have enough money to let you travel to tournaments. You should have enough money to hire a governess for your sister and brother. You should actually make a salary that might be like your Auror salary if you'd gone that way.

"So, here's where you come in. What do you think you'd need for those goals?"

The Brewsters looked at each other. Mr. Brewster said, "Let me get my record books." He left for upstairs. He returned in about fifteen minutes with a roll of parchment. He glanced down the roll and said, "I think that Cecily could go to half a dozen tournaments throughout the world for about forty thousand galleons give or take. I've never tried hiring a governess. What do you think? Another twenty thousand?"

I asked, 'Let's make it a round fifty thousand for salary?"

Cecily said, "That sounds reasonable."

Jaimie said, "Good. Then sleep on it. At least one night. We'll get Gringotts to write up a draft copy. You can look it over and suggest changes. You'll have to do your banking exclusively with Gringotts"

Mr. Brewster said that was what they did anyway.

I went on, "That's not all. I've talked Madame Malkin into being a sponsor for you. I can't negotiate for her. You and your dad should go to talk with her. You might not get much money, but you'll get some nice clothes from her."

We finished the evening before nine. As we left the house, I asked Jaimie, "We could see a movie."

She nodded slowly. "It is kind of late."

"Let's find a *Times* and see if there's anything interesting."

We found a grocery store. It had several newspapers. We bought one that had film listings. We searched them and decided to see *Unstoppable*. It turned out to be a movie about a runaway train that couldn't be stopped by normal means. We found it to be an exciting story. I found it to be a great movie to cuddle with your girl friend on the back row of seats in the cinema. It had a number of opportunities for snogging during the tense moments. Actually the tense moments were not super tense, but we didn't care. They were good enough as excuses.

We got home shortly before midnight. We ended up sitting on the sofa in *our* office snogging. At one point, I made a point, "Jaimie, you are the most beautiful woman that I've seen in the world."

She laughed and said, "Now when you say things like that I just think that you're trying to get me into bed."

I laughed too. "But I have no problem getting you into bed. I have a problem being able to be with you and not say that. I am so happy to be with you that I can't help myself."

She laughed again. Then she said, "Well, you're right. You don't have any trouble getting me into bed." With that she stood and we went to our apartment.

165

Christmas at Hogwarts

We had a great time during finals that fall term. Jaimie and I planned our exams together. We also graded together. I told Jaimie that. She took my hand. "Do you hear what you're saying? It shouldn't be that much fun." She was laughing as she said it. Somehow I doubted her sincerity. I had to join her in her laughter, though. It really was a lot of fun doing it with her.

I'd never had help in this really difficult part of teaching—coming up with fair grades. Composing fair exams is perhaps the hardest part of the process, but grading them is also excruciating. Grading multiple choice tests are easy. Grading fill-in-the-blank tests are a breeze. Grading essays is a whole different beast. It's completely about judgment. Nobody has an easy time at that. Having a second pair of eyes read those essays and give their judgment is heavenly. Where you agree, you can be confident of your judgment. Where you disagree, you have the opportunity to argue your case and come to a consensus that you can be confident of.

Every day during finals season, I kissed Jaimie goodnight with the most earnest thankfulness that she was there—for both grades and for bed.

The annual Christmas party was one that I enjoyed more than any other that I'd experienced. Christmas with Minerva was frequently wonderful. It was occasionally painful. Being a Muggle mixing with wizards among your in-laws could be just that. This by contrast was completely happy. Jaimie and I danced most of that night. That dance didn't end when the party ended. Between sets we circulated around and spoke with our friends —both staff and students.

At one point Nicholas Brahms and his wife Aurora came over and talked to us. Nicholas (the B. G.) asked me, "You and Aurora dated on one or two days a year. One of them was Christmas. How does it feel dating someone who is effectively Aurora's twin?"

Jaimie poked me in the side and asked, "Yeh. How does that feel?"

"Well, I suppose it's ironic. When Aurora was trying to get me to be her boyfriend, I fought it like the plague. Now, I couldn't be happier that someone so closely related to her is with me."

At that point, Filch noticed us talking with Aurora. He came over and said, "As Dursley's in loco parent, I'm still unhappy about you and Ms. Sinistra being uh familiar-like!"

Jaimie sighed and said, "Just drop it Filch. I'm happy, Wendt's happy. I bet Dursley isn't unhappy. You're the only one dragging this out."

He grumbled a little and then said, "Well, if you invited me up once in a while for a wee dram of your whiskey, I'd be. uh. Happy, too."

Toward the end of the party, Slughorn joined us. We were dancing. He stepped up to us and said, "May I cut in?"

I couldn't blame him. He was going to dance with the prettiest girl on the floor. They finished the slow dance. He bowed and backed away. I rejoined Jaimie for what turned out to be the last dance of the evening.

I asked her as we began the next dance, "Is he a good dancer?"

"Not especially. He danced with me to invite us up to his office the first thing tomorrow morning after breakfast."

"It's a little early for grades to be due."

She shook her head. "I don't think it's about grades."

"Then we'd better make the best we can of this evening—just in case."

□

That evening we did have a spectacular after-the-party party. We had to be on time for breakfast because it was the last meal before students took the Hogwarts Express back to London. It was usually an especially fine breakfast. This was no exception.

Slughorn gave the usual pre-Holiday speech. It's been a great term. Enjoy your Holiday. Look forward to seeing you all the next term, etc.

We had something special planned for the Holiday. We were to stay at Hogwarts. In my whole career, I'd not done that before except for my very first year at Hogwarts.

During breakfast, we defied fate by sitting together at the head table despite the fact that our assigned seats were far apart. No one made a fuss. I asked Jaimie if she had a memory of that from Wendt in her world.

She smiled and said, "You're thinking of seeing a Pegasus."

I nodded. "Yes. That was special. I'm glad you have that memory. I never know which memories you have and which you don't.."

She smiled happily. "That's something we should take some time to

167

explore while we're here. We could make a game of it. I describe a memory and you see if you remember it."

"It works both ways. I could describe memories, and you tell me if you've had them."

We actually managed to while away the breakfast without thinking of the upcoming meeting. Of course, Slughorn didn't let us forget. He was one of the last to leave the Great Hall. He tapped me on the shoulder as he passed me on his way out. I said, "I know. I know. We'll be there in a minute."

We took our time walking up to his office. We found Sally in the outer office—no surprise there. She invited us to enter the inner office. After we entered, she started to close the door behind her. I asked if she weren't going to join us.

Her response was just, "Are you kidding?" Then she closed the door.

Slughorn invited us to sit. I let Jaimie take the red leather chair. I took a yellow. Slughorn offered drinks. We accepted. It was Johnny Walker Blue Label. "Was that a good sign?" I wondered internally.

Then he began. "I know that you two have been. . . uh. . .you know, sleeping together."

I agreed. "We haven't made a secret of it as Minerva and I did long ago."

Slughorn nodded, "Yes. I knew about that, of course. I never made an issue of it since you were discreet."

Jaimie said, "There isn't a prohibition against it in the teacher's handbook."

Slughorn grimaced, "It was never an issue before. People were discreet."

I asked, "Not that it should make a difference, but have there been complaints?"

He frowned at me. "Not as such. However, there are complaints about all sorts of things that you never heard before. Filch is too hard on kids. English literature is not magical enough. Why do I have a Muggle secretary? The list goes on and on."

I chuckled. "So, you want us to voluntarily stop sharing our office?"

He grimaced again and drew out the "no's". "Nooo. Nooo, nooo. I don't know." A thought struck him, "How do you manage sharing the office part? Do you share your desk?"

Jaimie actually laughed. "We took a page from Dursley. We moved a desk from the Room of Requirement."

I agreed. "I use it. We have scheduled office hours so that neither of us has to be in the office for office hours while the other is there for office hours."

He said, "Smart. I guess I wouldn't expect anything else from the two of you." Then he went back to the reason for the meeting, "Here's the deal. If you just make it obvious that you two are not living together, I think everything would be all right."

Jaimie was starting to speak but Slughorn interrupted her. "I don't mean that you can't sleep together. I just mean that you have to hide it. You don't even have to be perfect about it. Merlin's Beard! The two of you are smart! Why didn't you figure it out on your own?

"Here's what I suggest. Wendt, you go back to staying with Dursley—at least on paper. You have your office there as before. You could work out the same sort of arrangement that you have with Ms. Sinistra for office hours, I'm sure. You can continue to stay with Ms. Sinistra any night you want. I just ask you to go there by floo connection from Dursley's office. I'm sure that Ms. Sinistra can manage that." At the end of that pronouncement, he looked from one to the other of us seeming to defy us to object. I didn't have an objection.

Jaimie asked, "What about between terms? Can we stay together more openly then?"

Slughorn looked like he was going to pull his hair out. "Yes, I suppose so, but only if there are no students present and you move stuff between the offices through the floo connection."

We agreed. Slughorn released a sigh of relief. Then I asked, "So this new policy starts with the new term? What's happening with Professor Dursley?"

Slughorn nodded his head and flicked his wand at the door to the outer office. When it opened, he shouted, "Sally would you send in Professor Dursley?"

She did. While he was coming in, Slughorn said, "I arranged an appointment with Professor Dursley as well for this morning. I told Sally to hold him in the outer office until I called for him.:

Jaimie got up from the red leather chair to make room for Dursley. Dursley shook his head and said,, "Keep the seat. Ladies first."

Slughorn provided a glass of Blue Label for him and said, "This appointment would ordinarily be private between you and me."

As Slughorn said that Dursley grimaced and said, "Here comes the ax."

Slughorn laughed the first hearty laugh heard in his office this morning. "No. no. I just summoned you to announce that the Potions Professor, Professor. Química, is still recovering from spatter goit. He promised me that he would be back in less than two months. I can't wait that long. By then, a lot of the term will be passed. Professor Dursley, you are now the official Potions Professor for this year. Sally has a contract for you to. . ."

At that moment, Sally entered the inner office with a couple of sheets of parchment. She placed them before Dursley and Slughorn and said, "Please review them and sign when you're ready. You can take a couple of days if you want, Professor Dursley."

Slughorn nodded. "We'll finish this interview privately, but I just want you and your friends to know that I'm very happy with your performance the first term. If you keep up your performance through the rest of the year, you can count on getting one of these contracts in May. Now for the reason that the English Department is here.

"We're going back to the old housing model. Professor Wendt stays with you. Professor Sinistra stays in her apartment. Do you understand the arrangement?"

Dursley looked from one to the other of us and said, "Let's see. You want us to move Wendt's things back to my place openly."

Slughorn said, "Yes, preferably at the beginning of the school year— maybe on the first full day of school next term."

Dursley went on. "And he'll stay with me and we'll share my office as before?"

"Slughorn nodded, "Right."

Dursley puzzled a minute and then had a thought. "Right after I help Wendt move down via stairs. I help him move up via floo?"

I said, "Right you are."

He nodded and said, "Congratulations, Professor Sinistra for getting Wendt out of your hair."

She laughed. "Oh, I'm not sure that I can keep him out of my hair completely." With that she flipped her head, sending her ponytail over her left shoulder.

Dursley said, "I can't blame him."

Slughorn said, "I think that finishes my business with Wendt and Sinistra, right?"

We channeled the Weasley twins saying, "Right you are." in unison. We rose and left the office. By this time, the hallowed halls of Hogwarts were completely empty of students. They were on the Hogwarts Express that was audible leaving the station.

□□

We spent the rest of the Holiday exclusively at Hogwarts. We did do some Christmas shopping in Hoggsmeade.. We also went to a chamber music concert in London on Boxing Day. Meals during the Holidays were held in the Teachers' Lounge. The elves set up a long table with places for twelve even though there were never more than nine actually present at any meal there. If there had been even just one or two more people staying over, we'd have had to eat in the Great Hall as I'd experienced before.

We occupied our time by planning the next term together. Those plans were just outlines for the term. We also planned the first month in more detail. Finally, we planned the first week in great detail. We discussed the possibility of mounting a joint play in the spring with students from both our classes. Because of the disruption the previous term, we'd not been able to do a play. That was a real disappointment to some students and a real source of joy to most.

We also took walks around Hogwarts grounds, the lakeshore, and even the Forbidden Forest. It was cold and cloudy most of the time. There were occasional snow showers, but nothing really serious. I enjoyed walking in show showers. We were never tempted to make snow angels. Instead, we walked and enjoyed the slow filtering of snow flakes down from the grey thin clouds above.

One day as we walked along the lakeshore, I decided to play the little game of memory that we had talked about during that breakfast at Hogwarts. I asked, Jaimie, "Do you remember the nuclear submarine here during the invasion of the ghosts?"

She answered, "Sure. I remember the CPO Brown who risked his life to save us from nuclear disaster. How did he come out?"

I asked, "Don't you know?" Then I thought about our different histories and said, "Of course you don't. You've not been back on the Ohio since that war, have you?"

She said, "You're right. Except that the submarine was the Wyoming. You have?"

"Too many times. Anyway, it was CPO Green on the Ohio not the Wyoming."

She thought about it. I went on. "CPO Green was fine the last time I saw him. With radiation, you're never sure until the end of your life if you've been affected. Even then, you don't always know."

We continued walking and playing the game. She wanted to know if I remembered when Ohio State won the NCAA basketball tournament three years before. I sadly had to admit that not only I didn't remember that, but I wasn't even alive then. I added that Ohio State had lost rather embarrassingly.

She laughed. "Too bad. They won in triple overtime over Florida."

Finally, we decided that we needed to return to the castle. On the way, Jaimie said, "I've got a bad feeling about the next term."

I agreed. "Oh, you can say that again. I'm always worried when the students return."

She scoffed. "I understand that. But, I'm not talking about students. There's something else. I don't know what it is, but it's out there."

We didn't talk about it again during the Holiday, but I didn't forget.

We went to a chamber orchestra concert in the Albert Hall. We had just been seated. The conductor came out and brought the orchestra to attention. He then started the performance. As we sat and listened, I noticed that Jaimie was disturbed. Finally, she took my hand and stood. We worked our way past a couple of seated people. She hurried us out of the hall and then out of the building.

Once out, Jaimie released the tears that she had held back. She sniffed and said, "I'm sorry. I just couldn't forget that one time long ago that you and Professor Dumbledore had gone to a concert here. It was just everything—his death, your capture, and torture that night. I'm sorry that we didn't get to see the rest of the concert."

I took her hand again and started walking into Hyde Park. We walked silently for a while, then we disapparated. We landed outside the Leaky Cauldron. Inside, I paid for a drink and we took the floo to her office. I'd already begun thinking of it as her office again.

The New Term

It was beginning of term dinner in the Great Hall. That was the official beginning of next term. Jaimie and I hadn't officially moved my residence yet. Everyone had always enjoyed the beginning of the Winter Term for fairly obvious reasons. There was nothing new. No new warnings about the 3rd floor corridor. The fateful Tri-Wizard Tournament was not about to restart. It was just ordinary school. There was only one more term left before summer holiday. There was only the trivial non-announcement that there was a new permanent Potions Master, Professor Dursley who had been promoted from permanent temporary Professor of Potions to permanent Professor of Potions—without a pay raise. Of course, only Dursley, Filch, Sally, and I knew that.

A student stopped Jaimie on our way out of the Great Hall. She cast a furtive glance at me, hesitated, and decided to proceed with her question. "Have you moved Wendt out yet?"

Jaimie answered, "What house are you in?"

She just shook her head, unwilling to say more. Jaimie said, "Good. Don't admit it. Otherwise your house would loose ten points for impertinence."

We returned to her office untroubled by other interrogators. Once we were there, we had a drink to "celebrate" the beginning of the new term, did some snogging, and retired to our bed. That night, it felt right to just hold each other close rather than make love.

Sometime in the middle of the night, Jaimie woke so violently that I too awakened. She was shuddering and cold. I held her. "A bad nightmare?"

She nodded silently and then said, "Yeh. I dreamed that I was inside some sort of pyramid. I was being chased by something. I couldn't identify it. I just knew that it was bad—really bad. I kept trying to find a way out, but couldn't find it. Finally, I reached the outer wall of the pyramid. I used my wand to blast a hole in an exterior wall of the pyramid. It was just large enough for me to squeak my way out of the pyramid. The problem was that whatever was chasing me was right behind me. I turned and used the defindo spell again and again blindly pointing my wand into the hole I'd just come out of." By the end of the recital of her dream she was shaking with sobs. I held her for a long while.

Then I asked, "Do you think it means anything?"

She soundlessly shook her head against my chest. She was so troubled by the dream that I was sure it must mean something. I could only hold her until the sobs subsided and she slipped back under the covers. I continued to hold her until I fell asleep.

□

We awoke to a bright clear day. We had breakfast—hot, scrumptious, filling. We went off to classes.

At noon we ate quickly and headed up to Jaimie's office, accompanied by Dursley. The three of us started moving things down to Dursley's office. I don't know how he does it, but Filch always seems to have the pulse of what's going on in Hogwarts. He joined us on the first trip down. He offered to help He actually took a small load on the next two trips. When it was over, he drew Dursley aside and said in a stage whisper, "There you are. I knew that this Wendt-Sinistra thing couldn't last."

After we'd taken the last load Filch went back to work. Dursley, Sinistra, and I went through the floo connection to undo what we'd just finished doing.

That evening, I told Jaimie, "I'm going to stay in Dursley's apartment tonight. I want the move to be technically true even if we don't live there more than one in a hundred nights.

The next night, Dursley took me up to Jaimie's office through the floo and wished me a good night's sleep. Jaimie took my hand and said, "I wouldn't bet on it."

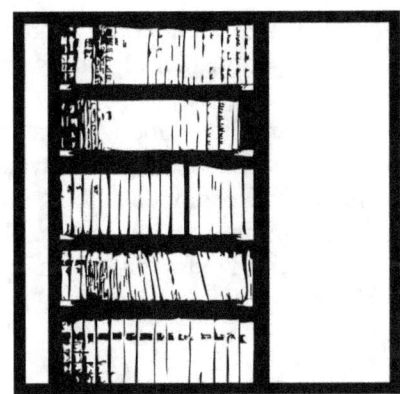

The Lieutenant Redux

It was Tuesday and only a couple of weeks since the beginning of the Winter Term. I was in my shared office in Dursley's Potions Office. There was a whoosh in the floo connection. I wasn't expecting anyone. Dursley was in his classroom.

Jaimie ran out of the hearth, looked around the office, spotted me, and came to me. I rose to greet her properly. She beat me to it, kissing me quickly on my lips. She took my hand and dragged me back to my desk. She pulled up the red leather chair, sat, and rapidly began speaking. "There was a knock on our office door." So, it was now **our** office door. I rigged for a crash. It came as she proceeded with her story.

□

It couldn't be a student. I was exasperated at the idea that it might be Filch again, so I gritted my teeth and said, "Come."

The door opened and I saw someone that I had never met. He seemed to be mild-mannered, almost shy, but I had a bad feeling. I immediately reached into my handbag for my wand. I had it in my hand and was bringing it out as he said, "I don't think that will be necessary to you."

My heart was strangely warmed as he said that. I found myself agreeing with him. I said, "I think you're right." With that I laid the wand in front of me on the desk in easy reach. It took all my will power to do that, but I was relieved when I had.

Then I began to think calmly. I asked, "Please take a seat." I indicated the red leather chair. He smiled and took the seat. I offered something to drink. "Will you have water, pumpkin juice, tea, something more serious?" I quickly added, "I think I have some Blue Label here."

His smile didn't falter. He said, "Tea would be good. I think I just can't quite imagine pumpkin juice." I did pick up my wand and conjured two cups of tea.

He took a sip and said, "Earl Grey. Good." I was not ashamed to reach into Wendt's drawer for the Blue Label. That was what I called the drawer where the whiskeys were kept. He dipped into it much more frequently than I did. However, I did keep his stock up to date. Today was a day that required the Blue Label. I materialized a glass with ice and poured a moderate amount, I then focused my attention on him. I immediately realized one thing.

"You're a Muggle!"

He mildly agreed. "Yes, I am."

That realization reactivated my concern. "Who brought you here?"

Again his answer was mild, "I."

I shook my head in confusion. "No, I believe that you had your own reason for coming. I meant, who brought you past the spells intended to repel Muggles?"

"No one." That frustrating, impossible, self-satisfied smile reappeared as he said that.

"Someone must have. Do you not know who it was?"

He shrugged, "No one did."

I took a swallow of the Blue Label. The sharp tingle that went down my throat emboldened me. "How did you get here?"

"I walked."

"Along the rail line?"

"No. Through the forest."

I couldn't keep my eyes from widening in surprise, "The Forbidden Forest?"

"There weren't any signs."

This was next to impossible. "Did you run into the Aracnamanchulae?"

Again the frustrating smile, "It wasn't that hard to avoid them."

"What about the Centaurs? They are very jealous of their territory."

He just shook his head. I asked about vampires and werewolves.

He shrugged and asked, "Are there any of those in that forest?"

I wondered about that, but I hadn't heard of any. I took another sip and said, "Not that I'm aware."

"Well, there you have it. It wasn't that hard getting through the forest."

I then asked if he'd gone through Hoggsmeade. His reply was, "Yes. I stopped at the Hogshead for something to drink and a sandwich. The local ale isn't all that good."

In frustration I asked, "Aberforth didn't recognize that you were a

Muggle?"

"The subject didn't come up." He expanded on that. "He didn't seem troubled when I paid with US dollars."

Now that I thought about it, it didn't seem that strange that Aberforth would accept anyone who seemed harmless and had good money. I pursued the main question. He might have gotten into the Forbidden Forest and gotten around the usual dangers. Maybe he walked into Hogsmeade and directly into The Hogshead without running into anyone. Maybe no one was there, and he got served. Then he walked on toward Hogwarts, but how did he get past the main gate? It is heavily defended against more than Muggles. You just don't walk into Hogwarts unless you've got legitimate business here! I asked, "How did you get into Hogwarts itself?"

He was nonchalance itself as he said, "I walked in through the front door. By the way, the glass cylinders with colored stones that shift about is an impressive work of art."

How could he just walk into Hogwarts and critique it as though it were just a museum to art of the past? It almost diverted me from my main point. I asked, "It should have been impossible for you to reach a point where you could see that 'work of art'. How did you do it?"

He smiled, but this time it was not an insouciant smile. It seemed sympathetic. "I actually don't know. I just knew that I needed to come to Hogwarts, so I went. I walked up to the main gate. It seemed like the gate was very narrow, but I found the way through. Then the main entrance was not so narrow. I walked through without a second's hesitation."

I shook my head in disbelief. "OK. Was I the person you wanted to find?"

"Oh, no. I wanted the owner of this office – Professor Wendt." Then he showed his first sign of surprise. "This is your office, isn't it?"

I nodded.

"Why is his nameplate still on the door."

At last, a question that I understood and for which I could provide an answer. "Oh, the 'maintenance engineer', Filch, hasn't got around to it yet. Everyone knows this is my office, so I haven't been pushing him much to do it."

I went back to my questioning. I said, "I'm going to have to call the Aurors in if you can't give a sensible explanation of how you got here and why you're here."

He just stared at me. I nervously prepared to answer the unasked question. I decided that I didn't want you, Jim, to have to deal with that calm anomaly without warning or preparation. "Wendt has taken a leave of absence. He's unavailable to help you." He showed no other reaction than to

177

continue to stare. I was about to ask him to leave.

Before I could do that, he spoke. "You are not what you appear to be."

I couldn't help flushing despite the fact that I'd faced that statement more than once in my history. I tried to speak in a calm, even voice, but I couldn't quite pull it off as I said, "I don't know what you mean."

He smiled an irritatingly knowing smile, "Yes, you do young lady. You know quite a lot about Professor Wendt. As a matter of fact, I think you have some of his personal memories in your head."

I tried to react as though I were scandalized, "I hope you're not implying that Professor Wendt and I had an illicit relationship."

His smile widened. "Not an illicit relationship. You have his memories in your mind, don't you."

This time I couldn't prevent myself from flushing beat red. I couldn't think of anything to say, so I just sat there trying to decide what to do. Before I had an idea he said, "I suppose you'll have to do. I need your help."

I opened my mouth to ask how I could possibly help him. He spoke first, "You can help me find the . . ." He hesitated as if looking for a name that he'd not heard in a long time. Then he went on, "the B. G."

I then asked a question that I should have long before, "Who are you?"

He answered, "I'm Lieutenant Minns."

Once the name was named memory flooded into to my mind along with the name. I said, "You're Philip Minns!"

His smile was extremely quick. It appeared and disappeared in an instant. "Yes, I once was Philip Minns. I am now the Lieutenant—again. So, I need to see the B. G."

Enough memories had returned that I knew that there was no way that he could know about Brahms's nickname. Strangely, the way that he said it, I could tell that he didn't know that the abbreviation was an abbreviation. I remembered enough about Minns that my earlier fears were rekindled. "You've got to tell me what you want before I let you see him."

Minns was deadpan as he said, "I can only tell you that I need to see him."

"Well, you're out of luck then." I added, "Until I know more."

He said, "I need him to send a message for me."

This was like pulling teeth. "What is the message?"

He looked at me intensely for a moment and then said, "I'm going to ask the people that you call the PAK what help they need."

I don't know what I was expecting to hear. It certainly wasn't that. It so startled me that I just blurted out, "How in the world could you help the PAK?" It was preposterous. I knew that Minns was brilliant and had amazing intuitions, but how could he help a race that traveled faster than light routinely, that had defeated the Souls, that had what seemed like unlimited resources.

He just shook his head and said, "I don't know."

I pondered what to do. I decided to see the Headmaster. I grimaced and said, "Come with me." I finished my glass of Blue Label and led Minns down to Slughorn's office. His personal assistant, Sally, told me that we could go right in. We did.

Slughorn stood up as we entered and greeted me with pleasure, "Professor Sinistra, how can I help you?" He looked at Minns more carefully.

I introduced him. "This is Lieutenant Philip Minns."

The expression on Slughorn's face soured. "I've heard of you, haven't I?"

I nodded and explained, "He is from one of Wendt's adventures."

The sour smile turned into a frown. Under his breath he said, "Why is it always me?" Then he said, "Please sit. What would you like to have something to drink."

Minns said, "Nothing." I agreed.

Slughorn said, "I'm going to have something stiff." He didn't specify what, but a glass went flying through air and landed on his desk. He took a swallow and then said dejectedly, "What is it?"

I explained what had happened so far. Slughorn looked from one of us to the other throughout the explanation, his frown growing more dour throughout. When I'd finished he said, "I should just order you off the grounds never to return, but I've got a feeling that I won't be able to succeed at that. So, let's just go see Brahms and get it over with. We might as well collect his wife while we're at it."

I gave a brief prayer of thanks that Slughorn had decided to do exactly what the Lieutenant wanted and thus not involve you until absolutely necessary.

We did collect his wife. I went up to the astronomy tower while Slughorn kept Minns company at the base of the tower. I called to Aurora, "This is Jaimie. Come on down, we need you."

She got up from her desk and approached. "What is it?" She seemed to have a premonition of trouble. She asked, "It isn't Nick is it?"

"It's complicated. Just come on. It's nothing bad." I added under my breath, "I hope." When we joined the others she took one glance at Minns and instantly pulled her wand.

Minns raised his hands in the universal gesture of peace and said, "I mean no harm to you or anyone you care for."

I wondered about that, but Aurora lowered her wand and said, "We'll see. What are we doing with you?"

I said, "I don't want to go through that any more times than I have to. Let's just go find your hubby." It was a brisk walk. Only Slughorn showed signs of lagging behind. We reached the Shrieking Shack where the Boy Genius had his business. We rang the doorbell.

He checked us out on the video monitor and said, "Look what the wind blew up on our doorstep." He then unlocked the door remotely. We went up to his main workroom. He asked for an explanation. He and his wife listened intently as I gave it for the third time.

By the end of my story Brahms was leaning forward on his swivel chair. He asked, "What makes you think that I can communicate with the PAK?"

Minns simply said, "I don't think you can." Then he added, "However, I happen to know that the PAK left a communications channel with the central command of NATO. I also know that you can hack into their systems and use that channel."

Brahms folded his hands and rested his chin on them. "Why would you think that?"

Minns said, "Do you doubt that you can?"

Brahms laughed, seemed to look inward for a moment, and then said, "It would be an interesting challenge. Why would I want to?"

That seemed to puzzle Minns for a minute. Then his eyes lit up. "There's something terrible happening. The PAK know about it, but they don't know that we can help."

Brahms opened his mouth to say something. Then he shook his head and said, "Of course, you don't know how you know. You just know."

Minns simply nodded.

Brahms laughed and said, "Well, you've come to the right person. I just happen to run a security service that has a contract with NATO. I might just be able to do it. What precisely would you like me to send to the PAK?"

He reached into his breast pocket. Out came a slip of paper, which he handed to Brahms. Brahms unfolded it and read, "We can help with Kali. It's signed Lieutenant Minns."

Aurora asked, "What is Kali?"

I asked, "Who is Kali?"

The B. G. said, "Kali is Death, Doomsday."

Minns said, "Yes, that's right, isn't it? I hadn't thought of that before."

We all said, "You hadn't thought of that before!"

The B. G. said, "This doesn't seem to be a particularly dangerous message. Of course, if the PAK believe you, and it turns out that you can't help, what do you suppose they will do to us?"

Minns nodded and said, "If I couldn't help them, I wouldn't say so."

I asked, "What can you do?"

Mimms shrugged. "I don't know now. I will know when I have to."

The B. G. nodded. "I need to consult with various authorities. I am not going to send your message on your say-so alone." He turned to Slughorn, "Can you put the Lieutenant up for a day or two somewhere inconspicuous?"

He scowled. "It seems like all that I do is provide homes for indigent geniuses." Then he looked around and said, "Minns come with me. We'll find a place for you. I'm thinking that Slytherin would be good." Then we all left.

Minns mentioned on the way back up the hill to Hogwarts, "I left my luggage just inside your door, Professor Sinistra." So, everyone except Aurora accompanied me up to my office. We arrived, Minns picked up his backpack, and he and Slughorn departed my office.

Then, I took the floo to your office.

I thought about what I'd heard for some time. I was so deeply into consideration that I forgot that Jaimie was still there. She cleared her throat once or twice or maybe more. Then I offered her something to drink.

She shrugged. "This is so awful that I just want some cheap whiskey. Or Maybe Jameson, if you've got it."

I reached into my whiskey drawer and pulled a bottle of Jameson out. "You're in luck. Here it is." She conjured a couple of glasses with ice. I poured. I then took a sip and said, "I'm thinking. Please let me continue." She did. I closed my eyes and thought. I don't know how long it lasted, but I did come to a decision.

I said, "Send an owl post to the Minister of Magic."

Jaimie conjured a quill and parchment. "Saying?"

"Saying that we need to contact the PAK. We need to meet as soon as possible."

Jaimie asked, "With whom?"

I shrugged, "The usual suspects: a representative of the Ministry, a representative of HMG, I suppose someone from the States. Maybe NATO."

Jaimie scoffed. "You're not asking for much."

"Oh, we've been here before. I think they'll come. As a matter of fact, we'll have to beat them off with a stick."

"What about the B. G. Doesn't he have to be there?"

I thought a while. Then I said, "Not now. He's our backup in case we can't talk the powers into going along with us. I think it's better that he not know about our ideas." Jaimie opened her mouth to object. "Or that we know about his—for now."

She took a big breath. "OK. I'm out of my depth here. I was never involved with any of these groups and even my Wendt wasn't involved with most of them."

I chuckled. "Oh, you'll get used to flying under the radar."

Under her breath, she said, "That's what I'm afraid of."

How are the PAK like Zombies?

I was waiting in the entrance to the Ministry of Magic along with Jaimie, Aurora, and Slughorn. How was it that we just seemed to keep arriving here to talk about the PAK? This time there was a difference. We were inviting ourselves rather than our being invited. The Ministry was not in as big a hurry to meet with us. We had arrived on time, but no one was ready for us.

Slughorn grumbled. Jaimie and I held hands in silence. Aurora just paced glumly. About every ten minutes, I went to the receptionist to inquire about when our meeting would start. Of course, she had no idea. We were eventually invited into the Conference Room. We all had been there before —even Jaimie. We walked directly in without having to be directed.

We were the only people there at first. Almost immediately after we arrived, others started to flow in. The first was Ginny Weasley. She smiled at me and said, "It's been a while. I need to get you an invite to my wedding." Then she looked over at Jaimie and said, "I'm glad you're here. You will never understand Wendt without being in these meetings."

She smiled. "Yes. I'm glad I'm sitting here next to him." She took my hand. "Of course, you're inviting both of us?"

Ginny turned pink and said, "Of course." The pink clashed with her red hair. She seemed ready to say something but didn't.

Then a man whom I'd not met came into the room. We all stood. Ginny introduced him. "This is the head of the Auror Bureau. His name is Martin Gardner." Then Ginny went around the room introducing us all. Martin repeated each name more than once, saying, for example, "Good to meet you Professor Wendt. I've heard of you and your associates. Professor Wendt we owe you a debt of gratitude."

After the introductions were over, we all sat and waited for all the other people whom we expected to arrive. We waited with bated breath. We waited. Finally, the Minster of Magic arrived with her personal assistant. She nodded at all of us. Of course, she knew us all. She started off promptly.

Her automatic smile turned to a grimace. "Let me make clear what's going on here. You, Professor Wendt, are here because you've got a reputation for being right. You've got a half-hour to convince me that this crazy proposal of yours has merit." She looked around at us and said, "Your clock is running. Get started."

Everyone turned to me. I had been thinking about this moment for a while, but I had thought that I'd have to prove how urgent it was, not that it was real at all. I took a moment to re-orient myself to my new task. My eyes might have closed while I breathed slowly through my mouth. I felt what I thought must be Jaimie's hand on my wrist, but it was the wrong arm. I opened my eyes and realized that it was Ginny who'd nudged me. She whispered, "Go."

I nodded my head, satisfied that I'd got the best approach I could on such a change of plan. I looked around the conference table and said, "Some of you will be familiar with the incident that happened more than seven years ago. Understanding it is essential to what I'm going to say." I faced the Minister of Magic, Pamela, directly and asked, "Have you read the report *The Legacy Incident* that was written and distributed to the Seven I's working group?"

Jaimie asked me, "What is this Seven Eyes business?"

Ginny assumed an air of superiority and said, "You don't know about the Seven I's?"

Jaimie gasped and asked, "Has that anything to do with the Evil Eye?"

Ginny laughed and said, "No, it refers to five Muggle intelligence agencies and the intelligence branches of the Aurors of the United States and England."

Jaimie just squeaked a soft, "O".

Pamela wrinkled her brows in consternation and looked to her PA. "Did we read that?"

The PA flushed and said in a whisper, "I read the report and forwarded the executive summary to you. Do you remember that?"

Pamela grimaced and turned back to me. "I just read the executive summary. It would be good if you reviewed it for the people who didn't get to read it." Of course, there was only one person present who hadn't at least read the executive summary, Slughorn. I supposed that one was enough, so I started recounting the main events of the incident.

"This happened about a year after the Ghosts were expelled from the

Earth. That is likely why the incident so quickly got the attention of the authorities in the States.

"What happened started when a US soldier was severely wounded in Iraq in the explosion of an IED during the fight with ISIS." Everyone in the room except the PA oggled me—including Ginny.

She said what everyone else was thinking, "What's an IED?"

I was puzzled by her puzzlement. "Didn't you read the report?"

She smiled sweetly. "It must have been above my pay grade."

Gardner frowned and said, "Apparently, it was above my pay grade, too."

The PA cleared her throat and said, "Well, sir. Actually, a copy was filed with the Auror Office. You may just not have got round to it yet."

There was embarrassed silence for a moment. Then I went on. "Well, anyway. The soldier was transferred to a hospital in the States, dedicated to treating trauma. IED stands for improvised explosive device. It is ordinance that is manufactured in the field. Usually, it consists of some explosive that is surrounded by shrapnel. The shrapnel could be anything that is hard and small, including gravel. There is a detonator attached and the whole is housed in any old container that comes to hand. They're pretty cheap to make and. . ."

I was interrupted by Pamela who said, "We're burning daylight here. Get moving."

I went on. "Anyway, the soldier's brain was struck by a piece of shrapnel. The doctors in the field hospital thought that he would not survive long. In San Antonio where the hospital was, he made a rapid and surprising recovery. Barely a week into his recovery he was up out of his bed, active, reading voraciously. Then he disappeared."

Ginny slapped her hand onto my arm, "Was he a wizard?"

"No. At least, not in the normal sense of the word. No one paid much attention to his disappearance. Lots of soldiers go absent without leave every day.

"Then a similar case showed up from Iraq. He had the same amazing recovery."

The PA said, "And he disappeared as well."

I nodded. "This got the attention of the staff at the hospital. Having one severely wounded soldier disappear from your care might be chance. When it happens twice in a short period of time, it starts to seem like carelessness." Ginny chuckled.

I went on. "Then a third showed up. This time, the hospital took special precautions with him. There was a guard posted outside his room at all hours."

Ginny excitedly exclaimed, "He disappeared too."

"Right-o. Then, a fourth man showed up in the hospital. The staff brought in outside help. They got the three men put on the FBI's most wanted list. They brought in Military Police. They made sure that there were multiple security cameras watching all exit routes from the floor of the fourth man."

Pamela was beginning to show interest. She asked, "They caught him, didn't they?"

I was happy to smile and say, "No. He got away like all the rest."

Pamela scoffed. "I know they're all just Muggles, but how could they let him get away?"

I was the only Muggle in the room, but I decided to let the slight pass. I said, "Nobody knew. It was at that time that more groups were called in. They were the United State National Science Foundation, the US Federal Bureau of Investigation, and Minerva and I. We recruited several other people from Hogwarts.

Pamela who was always wanting to leap ahead said, "Then you found the four criminals." Ginny rolled her eyes while facing me and not visible to Pamela.

Ginny nodded as I said, "We started off with no luck at all. Then something happened that attracted our attention. The ISIS group had lost about one half billion dollars worth of gold." Most of the eyes in the room bulged at that. "We thought that that might just have been pulled off by the four."

Ginny said, "I don't know much about ISIS, but I think that's supposed to be a really tough group. Surely, the four weren't responsible for that!"

I said smugly, "You're right. It wasn't the Four. It was one of the Four."

Gardner said, "That's impossible. I think it would take a team of wizards to do that."

"I'm afraid it was one. His name was Minns—Lieutenant Phillip Minns. After a while everyone both in their group of four and outside it were referring to him as the Lieutenant. He was the leader of the group—as much as anyone was."

Pamela asked, "What do you mean, 'as much as anyone was'?"

I took a deep breath and plunged ahead. "Later when we interviewed them, they all swore that there was no grand plan, no leader. Each man just did what they thought needed doing."

Pamela smacked her forehead with her hand. "That's impossible. How could anyone lead a group like this without coordinating? How could they just know what needed to be done!"

I shrugged. "I don't know. I do know that everything that they did sure

186

seemed like they were working by themselves."

Gardner rested his chin in his hands, shook his head, and said, "What in the world did they do with half a billion in gold? I suppose we'll never know."

I shook my head and said, "Actually, we did find out what they did with that money. They spent most of it."

Ginny leaned over to me and said, "Well, give! How can you spend that much money?"

I said, "Well, they spent most of it making a ship."

"That must have been some ship. I don't think Muggles spend that much money building cruise ships."

"Where did they build that ship?" someone asked.

"They rented an empty warehouse in Kansas, USA. They had the parts fabricated in Sweden."

Gardner asked, "How many people did they hire to help assemble it?"

"None. They built it all by themselves."

That silenced them for a bit. "What happened to the ship?"

I smiled. "It was a space ship. They took off and flew somewhere out of our solar system."

Slughorn leaped out of his chair. He had been sitting quietly listening all along. With that last statement, he rose quickly and paced. "I've known you a long time Wendt. You are always dependable, but this is a bridge too far. Where could you go outside the solar system?"

I shook my head. "I don't know where they went."

I thought a moment and then corrected myself. "Sorry, the Four didn't actually fly away. They sent four children."

That brought real reactions. Pamela asked, "And you let that happen!"

I said, "It's not that simple. We didn't find out that that was on the program until almost the end. We had caught up with the Four. You'd think that we'd be able to follow them. Somehow they kept evading us at critical times. We did discover that they were visiting homes where children who were disabled in one way or another lived. On the last day, the Lieutenant rented a car, drove to the kids homes, and collected them."

Pamela shook her head, stood, and paced while she practically screamed. "How did you not prevent that happening?"

I answered, "We tried everything we could. We even had the American military involved—helicopters, tanks, soldiers. We couldn't prevent them from delivering the kids to the warehouse. When we caught up with them, we couldn't get to them. They had some sort of invisible shield that prevented us from approaching the ship."

Ginny said, "Couldn't you disapparate into the ship?"

"Minerva and I decided to do just that. We were. . . uh. . . that is, I was afraid of what might happen if we tried to disapparate around that shield. We didn't because Minns let us in."

Everyone exclaimed, "He what!"

"Yes, he let us in. He offered us a deal. If we would promise to talk to the kids, we could see them and even take them back if we wanted to."

Slughorn was on his feet again. "Why in bloody hell didn't you take them back to their parents?"

I shook my head. "I couldn't. None of us could. The kids were somehow cured of their disabilities. The blind boy saw. The deaf girl could hear. The. . ." I was overcome for a moment by the memory of the Downs syndrome boy who talked with us.. "The cures were reversible. No one wanted them reversed. Even their parents accepted our decision."

We were all silent for a while. Then, Pamela said, "An amazing story. Do you have an explanation for it?"

I chuckled. "Not one that I could give you in thirty minutes."

She went on. "So."

I went on. "I told you that story so that I could prepare the way for the punch line."

Pamela interrupted again. "What happened to the Four, as you call them, after the ship took off with the children?"

"They went back to normal lives. They had enough money left to pay all the fines and even a little left over. Think about it. They did absolutely nothing illegal, other than stealing gold from ISIS. Somehow that doesn't feel all that bad."

Pamela said, "What about . . . oh, I don't know. There must be something about moving gold around to different countries that's illegal."

I shrugged. "I'm not a lawyer. I don't know. Maybe something. Why do we care?"

Pamela said, "So, what's the significance?"

I took another deep breath. "Well, in those seven plus years, we've not heard anything more from any of the Four . . . until now. The Lieutenant walked into Jaimie's office without a word of preparation."

Ginny asked, "Do you know how he got to Hogwarts?"

"Sure. He walked."

Ginny was skeptical. "Really. How did he get there?"

"He walked through the Forbidden Forest. Then, he walked through Hoggsmeade. I think he stopped for a drink there. Then he walked up to the castle. Finally, he walked to Jaimie's office, looking for me. He knew how to find her office."

Ginny shook her head. "If I hadn't used the word impossible so many times today, I'd use it now. I suppose it wasn't for a social call?"

I scoffed. "You bet it wasn't." I turned to Jaimie and asked her, "Tell what Minns had to say."

She said, "Really not much. He just said that we had to get in touch with the PAK. He wanted to send the message that he could help them."

That message forced everyone to drop back in their seats to think. The silence was broken by Pamela who asked, "He used the word PAK?"

"Yes."

She turned to me to ask, "Did you ever use that word with him?"

I laughed. "Do you really think that he kept in touch with me?"

Ginny said, "I'm pretty darn sure that you haven't."

Pamela looked at me and asked, "Just how would she know?"

I just shrugged.

Pamela asked Jaimie, "Just what was the thing that the Lieutenant had in mind that he could help the PAK with?"

"I asked him that question myself. He claimed that he didn't know.. I think he was being honest."

Pamela glanced at her watch. "Well, I've given you more time than a half hour, and I don't have a better idea of whether I've wasted the time or not.

"God knows that if even half of the things you've told me are true, this Lieutenant is an amazing man. On the other hand, how can I believe someone who doesn't seem to have any idea what's going on?" She turned to me more directly, "Why isn't he here to speak for himself?"

We'd reached the point that I was more than a little afraid of. I said, "To be honest, He didn't ask to come. As a matter of fact, I haven't seen him."

Gardner asked, "Then why did you come?"

"I have a bad feeling that whatever his reason for coming out of the woodwork is, it's important. He's got his own plan. I want there to be a backup just in case."

Pamela asked, "Do you think that we can get in touch with the PAK?"

Jaimie said, "It was pretty clear that the Lieutenant thought that there was a back channel communications method. I'm pretty sure that you've got access to it."

Pamela shook her head. "We'll think about it. If we only knew what was so important, it would be a lot easier to work with you. Let's suppose for the sake of argument that there is a back channel available to us. That back channel is not going to be easy for us to use. I've got to have something more to bring to the table than that this Minns says that he can help the PAK." She laughed. "What would you say, if you were, oh, let us say

189

the Prime Minister. Would it be something like, 'Oh, we've got this genius who wants to help the PAK. And, yes, he doesn't know what we will help them do. How about our giving them a call?'"

What could I say? I decided on, "Thanks for your time. If the Lieutenant decides to open the bag, we'll let you know. In the mean time, you should think about what might happen if we do nothing."

Pamela said, "God, every time you come here, you bring us something like this. Take your partners in crime with you and. . .and. . . I don't know!" Then she led her PA out. Gardner followed. Ginny held back a minute and said, "Can I at least come along on whatever happens?"

I asked, "Whatever is going to happen? Nothing might happen."

"I don't know, but I'm pretty sure it won't be nothing."

Then the rest of us left. On the way out, Jaimie took me by the arm and whispered, "I'm glad that Ginny is getting married."

The Boy Genius Plays Through

Nicholas Brahms is the only person at Hogwarts who communicates regularly by written note, delivered in the Teachers' Lounge to the recipient's pigeon hole. It's true that on rare occasions other people use that means of communication, but it is so rare that all the notes that I've received that way from the Boy Genius outnumber all notes that I've received that way from everyone else.

It was only a couple of days after the meeting in the Ministry of Magic that I received a note from the B. G. It said, "Professor Wendt, please join me in my office for an interesting meeting about our mutual friend tonight after dinner. B. G." I turned the note over and wrote a brief note to myself, "Who else invited?" I check the mailbox after my last class in the afternoon. My next stop was dinner.

All of the possible cast of characters for this meeting would be in the Great Hall for dinner, but we all had different seniorities, We all would sit a distance apart. I decided to wait till after dinner to find out who else was going to the "party."

After dinner I left directly for the Shrieking Shack. It quickly became apparent that Slughorn himself, Jaimie, and Aurora were headed there as well. We tried to extract from Aurora why her hubby had called the meeting. She claimed to know nothing more than we did.

At the Shack, Aurora used the key code to let us in. When we reached the Control Room, we found the Boy Genius there by himself. He greeted us. "I'm glad you all came together. That saves time letting you in individually. I think it's time for a pow-wow on what we've been doing about Minns and the PAK."

I started to object that he had no idea that any of us were doing anything. Brahms cut me off, "Don't be facetious, Wendt. In the first place, I can't imagine your not getting together with your wizard and witch buddies at the Ministry to get them apprised of what's going on. And in the second place, I've heard from one of the meeting attendees about the meeting."

I laughed, "Is there any reason for this meeting, then?"

"Sure there is. I'd like to get a second take on the meeting. Also, I thought you lot might want to hear what I've been up to."

We all agreed to that, so he began. "Here's what I've heard about your meeting. You tried to convince the Ministry to pull some strings and get them to use the officially non-existent communication channel that the PAK left us to pass Minn's message along. Is there anything else that I should know?"

I looked around at my fellow attendees at the meeting and said, "I guess the only other thing is that the Minister was not very encouraging about the prospect for getting in touch with the PAK." I then looked at the rest and asked, "Anything else?"

Everyone shook their heads. Then Brahms started his announcements. "It's a breach of the Official Secrets Act that I'm going to tell you this, but that point disappeared in the rear view mirror long, long ago. It turns out that I'm a contractor for MI6 and a few other government agencies. So, I know a back door or two into the most secure systems.

"The authority that I told Minns that I'd have to consult was myself. After consultation with myself, I decided to break into the system that connects to the comm channel to the PAK. I won't say that hacking in was easy, but since I designed the system, I had a leg or two up on the problem. It didn't help that I had to keep my labors secret from my employees. Interestingly, one of their continuing assignments for me is to monitor for intrusions of that very system.

"Anyway, I sent off the message as dictated by Minns. Based on how the Ghosts respond to messages, I didn't expect to hear anything back for weeks if not months. Instead, the return message arrived in less than twenty-four hours." He paused—for effect, I guess.

He got it. Nearly everyone demanded, "Well?!"

"There will be a mission arriving within a week. Further messages will arrive as the arrival gets closer." He paused again and added, "The response was phrased in such a way that a casual reader might suppose that the initiative for the mission was totally on the shoulders of the PAK."

I scoffed, "Nice of them to think of that."

"Yes, it was." Jaimie said. She scratched her right ear and said, "What do you think happens when they arrive?"

I said, "I suppose they ask for help. Then who knows." I went on, "I suppose that they'll ask for Minns. NATO will approach the Seven I's. The

Ministry of Magic will meekly raise its hand and say, 'Maybe we can help find him. Then, the Ministry will get in touch with one or more of us."

Aurora said, "I suppose this will end up as an extraterrestrial mission. Who is willing to go?"

Jaimie immediately jumped up, raised her hand, and said, "I'll go."

Everyone stared at her—not least of all I. I said, "You will not! You have no idea what you're getting into. You've never been on one of these expeditions."

She made a face at me, put her face into mine, and said, "You are not going to go out and get yourself killed without me."

I was equally determined. I leaned into her and said, "Well! You're not going to go out there and get yourself killed PERIOD!"

There were a few uncomfortable silent moments. Then Slughorn stood and said, "Well, I'm not going."

Aurora softly said, "I am going."

The Boy Genius added, "Then I'm definitely going."

I had cooled off a little. I looked around at everyone and summed up. "Then we have time to think."

The B. G. shook his head and muttered, "About what?"

"Preparedness for emergencies. I'm going to bring my Glock in my mokeskin purse. Certainly all wizards and witches should bring their wands. In addition, they should bring Peruvian darkness powder in something that is undetectable and tamper-proof. Maybe there are other things we could do?"

Slughorn said, "Maybe some potions would be useful?"

Jaimie asked facetiously, "Maybe a love potion?"

Everyone laughed, but I wasn't so sure that was a bad idea. What I said was, "polyjuice potion—not the new improved variety? Maybe Veritas serum?"

Jaimie asked, "Who would you use those on? Would they work with non-humans? We know polyjuice potion, old or new, doesn't."

I shot back, "In an emergency I'd probably want to try almost anything."

Slughorn said, "I'll talk with Dursley to see if he has any suggestions." He hesitated and added, "You might want to take a bezor or two along to protect you from poisoning. I don't know how it would work in the case of atmospheric poisoning, but I can heartily recommend it for all other poisonings."

193

□

The next couple of days we returned to business as usual. I conducted my classes. Jaimie conducted hers. We coordinated our lesson plans. We even sometimes graded each other essays.

The one thing for which we never had enough time—sometimes not any time—was being intimate together. We could usually spare time for a drink and some snogging. Then we'd fall into bed, exhausted. Sometimes just before falling asleep, she'd say, "Are we really going to travel in space?"

I'd given up on trying to convince her that she was not going to come with us to wherever we were going—that is assuming that we were going anywhere. So, usually, I'd just say, "Probably." This time, I answered differently.

"OK. Let's start with past history. In your world, nobody traveled off-planet let alone to a different solar system."

She put in, "What about the moon?"

"Sure, sure. I meant excluding the immediate neighborhood of Earth. So, just let me go on." She had a hand on my hip. She gave it a nice tweak just then. "Yes, that was nice, but I'm trying to treat you question seriously."

She nodded with a serious frown on her face. I went on. "OK. You've never been in space. God! How I wish the Jaimie buried in my head were here for this trip rather than you." She gasped. I hugged her and said, "Honey, having her along could be the difference between coming back and not coming back." She nodded. Her tears made my face moist.

"You don't know anything about what real space travel with aliens is like." I hesitated as I thought about the two expeditions that I'd been on. That brought Minerva to the forefront of my mind. I fought the tears that wanted to come.

Jaimie sensed that I was disturbed. She held me closer until I began again. "OK. Space travel with the PAK is sort of like being on a sailboat crossing the Pacific. The vastness is so great that you just don't appreciate it. Except when a big storm comes through, you might as well be on a large lake. You have your cabin. You have a galley where you can fix yourself something to eat. You have a meeting room slash game room slash mess hall. You have one or two showers. And by the way, your cabin is just big enough for two people, a clothes closet (small), and a little room for a few (very few) personal belongings. There's an engine room, of course. There's a locker where tools and space suits are kept."

Jaimie said, "Doesn't sound too bad."

194

"No, it's not, if only you could travel with other people whom you totally trusted. The trouble is that there are guaranteed to be at least two aliens with you who are very different from you—different in every way. They have different physiology. Since we're going to be with PAK, let's talk about the PAK. They're not going to breath the air we do. More important, we're not going to breath the air they do. So, somebody's going to have to wear a space suit almost all the time. Guess who it's likely to be. We were sort of lucky in previous trips. The PAK wanted us to be comfortable for their own purposes. Maybe not so much this time."

Jaimie was very quiet. I went on. "The flights are long. One of our biggest problems was avoiding terminal boredom. You probably won't believe it, but one of the top things we did was to have a chess tournament. We were serious. We jury-rigged computer-based chess clocks."

I paused. "On one flight we were convinced that we were going to die at the end of the flight. I used to joke that I didn't know which was worse —the boredom or the excitement."

She rubbed the back of my neck. Then she asked, "Do you really want to go on this expedition?"

I shook my head. "I don't think that I'll have much choice. Either I'll be required to go or I'll be required to stay. BUT, you could have a choice. Please, please think seriously about what you want to do."

She shook her head decidedly. "How can they possibly force you to do what you don't want to? It does matter whether you want to go or not."

I sighed in grief. "Maybe. The last expedition, the PAK told us who would go. They vaporized a fair chunk of the south Indian Ocean to incentivize NATO and me to take part."

Jaimie asked, "How would that incentivize you?" Then she answered her own question. "You mean they would do that in the English Channel or the Med if you didn't go along."

I grimaced. "You've got the idea."

I said, "Just for the record. I'm glad you're here and not 'my' Jaimie. Even if we get parted permanently by this, I'm glad we were together." That sort of finished the night for the both of us. We spooned until we fell asleep.

In the morning, she kicked me out of bed and said, "Get moving. I've got some last minute preparations for class, and I want you in Dursley's apartment before I start. God, it's hard enough working with you in the room when it's just grading fill-in-the-blank tests, let alone grading papers."

I laughed. "You mean you didn't finish that last night before we went on the extended discussion of the 'Final Frontier?'"

She stuck out her tongue at me and said, "A girl's got to have some fun, doesn't she?" I got up out of bed and was hustled off to Dursley's floo connection. He wasn't up yet. I tried to quickly and silently shower and dress before he was up.

The Ministry of Magic Has a Problem

The next day, I was having lunch when my worst nemesis appeared in the air above my head. It was a bright clear day. The transparent ceiling was so clear that for a moment, I thought the owl had descended through the ceiling to drop its letter into my bowl of bean soup.

I picked it up, wiped it dry with several napkins and put it in an inside pocket of my robe. I knew it must mean trouble. But, dog-gone it, I was going to finish a good meal in the Great Hall before I submitted to whatever terrors it held.

After I left the head table to go to the office that I shared with Dursley, I discovered that a couple of other people were following me. There was Slughorn. He caught up with me first. He said, "That letter that fell in your soup seemed ominous. Let's go up to my office to open it." He seemed to think that it was addressed to the both of us. I decided not to challenge that assumption. Who knew? Maybe it was.

On the way, Jaimie caught up with us. Then there was Aurora and finally, Dursley. When he caught up, he asked, "Hurry up, I've got a class starting in fifteen minutes." By this time, we'd reached Slughorn's office. Sally had gotten there before any of us. She nearly always had a working lunch at her desk. That doesn't mean that she packed her own—just that she went down to load a plate with Hogwarts provender and returned to her desk to work on mail or planning the next school party or fund-raising or whatever. When we arrived, she took one glance at us and said, "This looks juicy." Then she opened a desk drawer to find a notepad and pen.

Slughorn opened his mouth—maybe to object, but he relented. We all entered his office and found chairs. I got the red leather chair—I guess because I had the letter. Slughorn just shrugged and said, "Open it."

I did. Then I read aloud. I decided that the best way to protect myself from the censors of England was to read word by word without editing content until I'd finished. Then I could go back and say something like, "I'm going to redact this sentence and that one and so forth."

What I read was, "Professor Wendt, you are requested and required to present yourself at nine AM tomorrow morning to the Minster of Magic's Conference Room. Certain developments involving PAK diplomacy are to be discussed. We will need your experience guided by intelligence to analyze these developments. Please invite Professor Slughorn, Professor Brahms, and Mr. Brahms to accompany you. Best regards, Pamela Moertl, Minister of Magic." I commented, "No response was requested, I suppose that means that we don't have a choice."

Slughorn said, "Sally, please post notices about classes being canceled in the classes involved. If you can find a substitute for anybody, please do so."

Sally just shook her head. "No, Professor, we don't have anyone on the sub list except for English literature, and she has classes at the same time as Wendt."

Slughorn just shook his head in resignation, "Why is it always me?"

Sally asked, "Anything else?"

We all looked at each other. No one said anything. Sally said, "Then you'd better get to your classes."

□

The next morning, after an early breakfast—at least early for me—I headed for Slughorn's office. We'd decided to take the floo from there. Aurora was headed there with her husband. Jaimie accompanied me to the door of the outer office. When everyone else had entered, she put an arm around my waist and we kissed. She whispered intensely in my ear, "Come back before you leave!"

I shook my head and said, "They wouldn't send us out without letting us pack."

She just said, "I don't trust the Ministry as far as I do the *Prophet*."

I said with more confidence than I felt, "Don't worry. I won't leave without seeing you again." With that, she turned away from me rapidly and hurried down the stairs.

In Slughorn's office, we grouped ourselves in pairs—Slughorn with me and Aurora with the B. G. We entered the floo and emerged in the Minister of Magic's office. I didn't know that Slughorn had the password for her floo. Interesting. Aurora and Brahms followed us closely.

Slughorn noticed the small conference table in the Minister's office and said, "We could just meet here, couldn't we?"

The Minister just said, "We have other guests coming. We will meet here briefly, though. I want to present a unified front to our other guests. They will no doubt want. . ." She stopped and realized that we were all still standing. "Please sit."

When we were, she went on. "Want something to drink?"

Slughorn asked, "You don't have a glass of sherry to spare, do you?"

Pamela's assistant had entered the room soundlessly. She waved a wand and a glass appeared. She retrieved a bottle of sherry from a cabinet. Meanwhile Pamela looked at the rest of us questioningly. Everyone else shook their heads.

We sat around the small conference table except for Pamela's personal assistant. Pamela started her sales pitch. "All right. It's obvious to us at the Ministry that the reason that the PAK are coming is that they need help. That means that some number of people are going to return with them to whatever problem is coming up. Every one of the Seven I's want a hand in that. We've got to present a united front to be sure that wizards and witches are well represented."

I laughed. "Does that leave Brahms and me out?"

She shot a glare in my direction and continued. "We want people whose interests are aligned with wizarding interests on that flight."

Aurora contributed, "And we can guess who they are. Could it possibly be the five of us invited to this little meeting."

Pamela said, "Can you think of a better group? Except for the Headmaster, you've all been on previous expeditions. You know your way around space. The wizards are accomplished in potions, transfiguration, and other specialties. The witch is an astronomer. The Muggles are brilliant."

I summed up, "So, we're supposed to work together to push the four of us as sort of mission specialists to go wherever the PAK are going?"

Pamela smiled and looked up to her right. "I didn't think about it that way, but. . . yes. You are."

Slughorn said, "Well, you've got the wrong man. You need the current potion-master of Hogwarts."

Pamela's smile faded, "And who is that?"

"Why, Professor Dudley Dursley."

Pamela stood and paced for a couple of minutes. Her assistant interrupted her to say, "Please. Our meeting is supposed to start in a few minutes."

Pamela held up a hand. "Yes, yes. I'm thinking." Then she said, "All right. It has to be Dusley then." She turned to Slughorn and said, "OK.

You're here to testify about how the great potion-master that Dursley is. Yes! That's it!."

Slughorn agreed. "The funny thing is that I would be completely prepared to give you that precise advice without any urging from you."

Pamela waved the comment away, saying, "Whatever. Let's go to the Conference Room." She was taking the lead, but stopped at the door. "Is everyone on-board with me?"

No one said anything. She tried a different approach, "Does anyone disagree with me."

I had been searching my morality to decide where I stood. I decided that her goals coincided with mine. Also, I couldn't find anything explicitly immoral about having a planning session up front of a meeting. As a matter of fact, I did it all the time. I didn't say anything. No one else did. Pamela murmured, "Silence betokens consent." The way she said it, it sounded like a magical incantation. We walked the short distance down the hall to the Conference Room. She whispered, "I don't want everyone entering at the same time. Joyce and I will enter together. Wait three minutes. Then Mr. and Mrs. Brahms come in. Wait another four minutes and then Wendt and Slughorn come in." Then Joyce without any urging opened the door. She let the Minister enter before her.

The rest of us waited silently while the minutes crawled by. Then the Brahmses opened the door and entered. Slughorn grumbled, "Just watch. All the good refreshments will be gone by the time we get in." Eventually the time ended. I held the door for Slughorn, and he entered. I closed the door behind me.

The first thing I heard was the Minister saying, "Well, I should have guessed that Wendt would be the last. Is your time more important than ours, Professor?"

I shrugged.

The Minister went on to do introductions of the various people in the meeting. She asked each of us to give a short introduction of ourselves. She said, "I'll begin and we'll work our way around the table. I'm the Minister of Magic, Pamela Moertl." She went on to introduce her personal assistant. "This is my personal assistant, Joyce Poynter."

The next person around the table wore a business suit. He appeared to be around six feet tall. His mostly black hair was streaked with grey as was his mustache. He said, "I'm Morton Ponsonby-Jones, the Assistant Under-Secretary for Exterrestrial Affairs. I speak for the Ministry of Defense as well."

Next to him sat a woman dressed in a dark suit and black blouse. She wore her brown hair in a pony-tail that reminded me of Jaimie. She said,

"I'm a consultant for the US NSA. I have a role similar to the Ponsonby-Jones. My name is Laticia Trent. I've followed your exploits among the PAK and Ghosts with a great deal of interest Professor Wendt." I shuddered at the idea that she was maybe someone who knew more about me than almost anyone alive.

Next was a man in a uniform. I thought it was US Air Force, but I wasn't sure. He was about the same height as I am. He was the only person in the room who wore a smile. When he spoke, I thought I recognized an upper midwest accent. "I'm Major Stephens. I'm in the astronaut candidate program. I'm here to try to get a few steps ahead of my colleagues." Well he might smile. He was in a perfect place to do that.

Next to Stephens was a short, stocky woman. Her long blonde hair was braided and fell over her left shoulder. She wore a geometric print dress. It was a sort of checkerboard pattern. She said, "I'm Andrea Dupres. I represent NATO central command." Her accent seemed to me to be central European. However, I couldn't be sure.

Next was Slughorn. He simply said, "I'm Horace Slughorn, the Headmaster of Hogwarts School of Witchcraft and Wizardry. My field of expertise is Potions."

I was next to Slughorn. I said, "I'm James Wendt, Professor of English literature at Hogwarts."

Aurora was next. "I'm Mrs. Aurora Brahms, Professor of Astronomy at Hogwarts."

Finally, there was the Boy Genius. He said, "I'm Nicholas Brahms. I run an internet security company."

Next to him was the Auror Ginny Weasley. She said, "I'm a senior Auror of the Ministry of Magic. My name is Ginevra Weasley."

Trent immediately asked, "I understand why everyone is here except for Professor Slughorn. What is his role?"

The Minister had her answer ready. "Professor Slughorn is the ultimate authority on Potions. They can be very useful in interrogation, impersonation, and other similar. . . uh. . . activities."

Trent didn't show any response. After a moment of silence, the Minister went on. "This meeting was requested by the Muggle services represented here. NATO, the members of the Seven I's, and others want us to prepare for the arrival of the PAK. We don't know how long it will be before they arrive, but we shouldn't hesitate to prepare for their arrival. We want everyone here who has information about the reason the PAK are arriving to reveal that information now."

We all looked around at each other. No one volunteered any information. So, the Minister said, "We will stipulate that there was a message four days ago from the PAK. I have a verbatim copy of the text here. It says,

From: PAK Central command
To: NATO Secretary General

Re: Visit to Earth of PAK Military Research Unit

Please be prepared to contribute to resolving a developing situation that is too sensitive to name in this transmission. There will be guidance given on our arrival of the skills of those who will be needed to accompany an expedition we are mounting to deal with this situation.

Again, no one said anything. Finally, the Minister said, "We have some information that is not generally held among the Seven I's." That caused some commotion.

Dupres expressed a feeling that was pretty general. "Why haven't you raised this before?"

The Minister smiled. "We didn't know what other groups had. I wasn't going to be the first to contribute information. Here's what I have." She looked over at me.

I looked around at my Hogwarts friends. Everyone found something very interesting on the tabletop or their blank notepad. So, it was up to me. I said, "We at Hogwarts had an unverified report. . ." At that point there was a knock on the door. It was repeated.

The Minister swore under her breath and said, "Come in." The door opened, and the receptionist opened it just enough to stick her head in. She said, "There's someone here whom I really think you ought to see." There was a happy broad smile on her face.

The Minister said, "Not now, Melanie."

Melanie replied in a voice that was almost a whine, "Really, Pam. This is someone that you just *have* to see."

The Minister's lips compressed and she squeezed out, "Not now."

Melanie would not be gainsaid. In a sort of singsong plea she said, "Now is the time, Pam."

The Minister nodded. Melanie's face resumed her happy smile. She opened the door wide, and ushered in Lieutenant Philip Minns. Everyone's attention was riveted on him. The Minister said, "Send for Aurors, Melanie!"

Minns said, "I really don't think that's necessary, do you?"

The Minister cautiously asked, "Why not?"

His smile was utterly unperturbed as he said, "I don't intend any harm to anyone in this room." I believed what he said.

Even the Minister seemed convinced. She said, "I suppose so. Why are you here and who are you?"

Minns said, "I am Lieutenant Minns." With that, the Minister reached into her purse, but left her hand there. Ginny had her wand in her hand as quickly as I'd ever seen anyone pull a wand. Aurora had pulled her wand out but then dropped it onto the table in front of her. Slughorn made no motion. I knew it was hopeless to pull my Glock out. I'd probably not be able to do it. Even if I did, what would I do with it?

I was the first to speak. I started to ask, "Why are you. . ." However, Trent asked, "Are you armed?"

The Minister came to herself, left whatever she was reaching for inside her purse, and asked, "How in the world did you get here?"

Minns smiled that infuriating, disabling smile of his and said, "It wasn't that difficult. I had no trouble finding the phone box in the park above us. I took the visitor entrance through that phone box. I'm afraid I didn't use a real galleon in the coin slot, but it seemed to work anyway. The receptionist in the Atrium was very anxious to help. She pointed out the proper elevator to use and the correct floor for the Minister's office. Since the elevator is self-service, I. . ."

He was interrupted by Ginny. "That elevator should only work for magical people."

Minns laughed. "I'd have walked up the emergency stairs if I'd known that."

Ginny grimaced. She looked at me. "You helped him!" The accusation was as biting as any that I'd ever suffered.

I shook my head. "No. I had no idea he was coming. I might not have come if I'd known he was going to be here."

Ginny lifted her wand hand and gasped as she started to point it at Minns. Then she lowered her hand to the tabletop, but she didn't release the wand from her grip.

I relaxed. I had an idea that as long as I didn't attempt to harm him or get in the way of his purpose I could act. I said, "Why *are* you here?"

Minns scanned the room quickly. There were no empty chairs. He looked at Joyce and said, "Do you mind if I take your chair? I don't think your boss will need you for a while."

Joyce stood and said effusively, "Of course, not, Lieutenant. Please take my seat. I'll just go outside and wait with Melanie."

Minns took her chair and began speaking. "You are here to plan a re-sponse to the PAK even though you don't know what the PAK want. I know a little of what they want. I can help you do that planning."

Trent said, "I don't think we ought to share any information with you." It was not said belligerently. It was just matter of fact.

Minns said, "Of course not. I'm here to share information with you. You don't know why the PAK are coming to Earth. I know that they are coming because there is a terrible threat that they face. They have come to seek help of me."

Stephens asked, "How do you know that?"

Minns laughed gently. "I know that because I invited them to come to get the help that I can provide."

Ponsonby-Jones asked, "How could you possibly do that? There is only one link to the PAK. It is controlled by us!"

"You're right. I used that link."

Ponsonby-Jones' lip trembled and he squeaked, "That's not possible."

Minns asked, "How do you think I knew about the PAK coming?"

Trent grimaced, "OK. You have the advantage here. You know what's going on. How about sharing it with us?"

"I just did."

Her face showed disbelief. "Come again. I didn't catch what the danger is."

Minns said, "I don't know the details either."

The Minister leaped to her feet. "How can you not know what is going on! Did you just guess about it! Have you lured the PAK to us on a wild goose chase!"

Minns was utterly unmoved. He simply said, "There is something terrifying happening. We can help resolve the problem. I'm not guessing or wrong."

The Minister looked a plea to me. I sighed and said, "Some of you may be aware that there was an incident about four years ago involving a Lieutenant Minns and three other US Army officers.

"I was involved in an investigation of their involvement in the incident." It struck me how uncomfortable it was trying to give an evaluation of a person present in the room. Would he contest anything I said? So, I tried to make what I had to pitch my statements to be about their team, emphasizing that Minns was the leader of the team.

"You can check what I say against the formal report that we issued. It's available to the Seven I's team."

Stephens asked, "What's the title of the report?"

"The Legacy Incident."

He asked, "Don't you mean the report about superluminal objects?"

I chuckled. "No. That was a less complete report meant for wider distribution."

Stephens exclaimed, "There is no way that they could have done that!"

"None-the-less, they did build it. I don't mean to say that they built it from scratch. They had a lot of help along the way. However, I do mean to say that the design for every aspect of the craft—electronics, HVAC, structural engineering, even material design, and so on came from them. They hired electronics firms, boutique fabrication plants, and so forth. They built components, but the components were designed and assembled by those four people."

Stephens pressed on, "That sort of effort would have required tens of billions of dollars of funding, at least. It took us more than half a dozen years to design and build the system that took Neil Armstrong to the surface of the moon and back."

I smiled. "They actually had a fairly large budget. It was over a quarter of a billion dollars. They did hardly any testing along the way. Their designs just worked from the beginning."

Stephens interrupted again. "Where could they get that kind of money without someone noticing?"

I chuckled. "Actually, we did notice. They got the money from ISIS. . ."

Stephens sneered. "I wasn't aware that ISIS had a space research budget."

"They didn't. They stole nearly a half-billion dollars worth of gold from ISIS."

Stephens was becoming more and more agitated. He stood and practically shouted, "I can't believe this. ISIS is a real bad-ass organization. Could four Navy Seals have looted their treasury of that much gold? No. Not in a million years!"

Ponsonby-Jones smiled and whispered, "Maybe four Royal Marines could have."

I said, "You're right four people didn't loot the ISIS treasury. One man did. He's here before you right now."

Stephens' mouth opened and refused to close. He seemed to be beyond further protest. However, someone else spoke. Trent had been nodding throughout the discussion. She said, "I actually did speed-read the report. That is what was reported. It was jointly authored by someone from the NSF, the FBI, a US Army Colonel, Wendt, and a few others. Some of them are here now."

Minns spoke for the first time. "What Wendt said is substantially correct."

Trent nodded. Then she said, "All right. We don't have an agenda for

205

this meeting. Are there action items for us or anything else that we need to deal with?"

The Minister said, "My thought was that it is very probable that the PAK will request that a team return with them to deal with this emergency. I think that we should come up with a prioritized list of candidates who could be called on when necessary."

Stephens said, "I, for one, am ready to serve. I've been training for space flight and have a long record of piloting aircraft of all sorts."

Dupres said, "Although I don't have a specific candidate in mind, I think that all the Seven I countries should have at least one candidate on the list. I think we should go back to our organizations and conduct a quick search for reasonable candidates to be presented with CV's at our next meeting."

The Minister said, "Noted." Then she said, "We actually have a variety of people who have real, successful experience at interstellar travel. No other organization has that. In addition, we should include as many magically talented people as we can so that we can have the best chance of responding to unexpected circumstances as they arise."

Ponsonby-Jones broke in. "Intelligence is at least as valuable for responding to the unanticipated as magic ability is. We need to consider IQ in our selection process."

At this point, Minns stood. He spoke softly, but suddenly the hubbub of whispering and Ponsonby-Jones fell silent. Minns said, "I think I can save you all quite a lot of time and angst. I'll put it simply in a syllogism.

"First, let me point out something that very few of you are aware. The PAK are coming as a result of an invitation that I issued. The invitation stated that I could help with their problem." Dupres started to say something, but Minns cut her off. "Please hold all questions for the end of my comments.

"Consequently, the PAK will require any team that accompanied them to include me." There were rumblings of whispers in the audience but no one spoke openly.

"Second, I will not go with the PAK unless the full team meets my criteria."

At that statement, Stephens asked, "What are those criteria?"

Minns simply said, "I can not state them in a way that you could apply them." That left Stephens confused.

Minns went on. "I will give you a preliminary list of the required members of the team. They are: Mr. and Mrs. Brahms, Professor Wendt, and Ginevra Weasley. They are all currently in this room."

That statement resulted in an uproar. Everyone had one objection or another. Minns raised his hand. Silence descended. He said, "I don't rule out additional team members. However, I can't guarantee that the PAK will accept more or that I can accept more from the candidates that you propose."

Stephens asked, "How can we propose candidates if we don't know your criteria?"

Minns said, "I don't know."

In her contrarian way, Ginny asked, "How do you know that we'll accept the invitation?"

He replied, "Will you?"

"You bet your bottom galleon I will!"

I asked, "Do you have a guess as to how quickly the PAK will arrive?"

Minns said matter-of-factly, "Probably, the day after tomorrow."

Stephens just threw his hands up and said, "I still submit myself for the team."

Minns replied, "Not this time."

Dupres asked, "How do we submit candidates to you?"

"Have them present themselves at the park above our heads at four PM each day until the PAK arrive." He then turned to the four lucky winners in the room and said, "You should prepare to leave on a moment's notice. Be prepared for an owl from the Ministry of Magic with details at any moment."

There was still grumbling, but everyone was anxious to leave. The Muggle representatives wanted to get in touch with their countries to try to get reasonable candidates to the park as soon as possible. Those of us who had been hand-picked to take the long voyage were anxious to get back home to prepare. The Minister and Poynter were anxious to get back to the Minister's office. It didn't look like Minns was particularly anxious to do anything.

We were all hurrying out of the Conference Room when Pamela cornered the four candidates in the hall. She made an invitation that we couldn't refuse to join her immediately in her office.

When we were seated around the conference table, she said, "Some ground rules. I want a report about everything that you learn before leaving. Also, I want a complete report after you return."

I pointed out, "You can set all the ground rules you want, but only Ginny is bound to abide by them. She's only obligated because she works for the Auror Office, which reports to you."

Pamela was unhappy, but what could she do? She said, "You work for Slughorn. Slughorn works for the Board of Directors of Hogwarts. I'm the chair of that board."

I grinned. "Don't take this wrong, but Hogwarts is not my only job. Maybe I shouldn't speak for the Brahmses, but. . ."

Aurora said, "Don't forget that Nicky has an independent business. He makes quite a nice salary, thank you."

Ginny looked around the room and said, "I could leave the Auror Office at any time and work for my brother in his business. That assumes that I just want to take a vacation, which is what working for George would be. I could start my own business."

Pamela looked even more unhappy. "OK. It's only reasonable for you to write a report and submit it to me."

Ginny said, "That's the spirit. We'll be in touch before we leave."

Aurora asked, "Can we use your floo connection to go back to Hogwarts?"

Pamela nodded and asked me, "Do you want a ride home?"

Aurora asked me, "Do you want a lift with us?"

Ginny said, "No, he doesn't. I'll take him home. I've got something to talk over with him anyway." The Brahmses left first. Then, Ginny reached for my hand.

I gave it to her, but said, "I'm staying with Dursley in his apartment off the Potions classroom." She made a big "O" with her mouth and asked, "You're not in your office?"

"I'm afraid not."

She asked, "Surely, Jaimie's not there?"

I just nodded mutely. At that moment we walked into the hearth of Pamela's office.

□□

The next step dropped us in Dursley's office. Ginny commented, "You weren't kidding." Then she had a thought, "Are you and Jaimie, you know. . ?"

I said, "I won't dignify that with an answer."

She smiled. "You are! You know, it would make it easier for me if I could tell Harry that you and she were. . ."

Just then, Jaimie came through the floo and almost knocked us over. She looked at the two of us and said, "I know there's bad news. How about just giving it to me right now."

I said, "Yes. The bad news is that Minns has insisted that his team consist of the Brahmses, Ginny, and me." With that, she frowned and said, "You are coming up to our office right now." She turned to Ginny and said, "Goodbye, Ms. Perfect." Then we went through the floo to "our" office.

When we arrived, she threw her arms around me and kissed me seriously. We were on the couch. She asked, "When are you going?" There was no preface to the question.

I answered as simply, "Three, four days."

I felt a tear roll down her cheek. "I'm not going am I?"

I shook my head.

She said, "Refuse to go." I started to answer. Then she said in almost a wail, "Oh, I know you can't do that." She sobbed and said, "You've been twice. Your luck has to run out sometime."

I wanted to assure her that my going was very safe. She hadn't been on one of those trips in her world. I could lie and try to console her. I couldn't force myself to do that. I tried to spin what I said to make the pain less. I finally said, "You're right. This is dangerous. There are good witches going along. Lieutenant Minns is going. He's really amazing. There's no one that I'd rather have on my side in a fight."

She sobbed again, "I don't trust him."

I suggested that we have a drink. She asked, "Blue Label?"

I nodded. She let me get the glasses and the bottle. I poured and ice materialized in the glasses. She took one and drank deeply. She nodded. Then she said, "Let's not waste any of the little time we have." I took her hand and we went into the apartment. We made love. It wasn't tempestuous. It was almost desperate. We knew that we might never see each other again. I suggested calling in sick and walking in the Lake Country the next day.

Jaimie reminded me that it would be cold and maybe snowy. I laughed at snow. I said, "All the better. We'll really forget what's coming." She agreed.

The next day, bright and early we told Sally that we were taking a sick day. She nodded and said, "So, English literature is sick today."

We took the floo to an inn near one of the lakes. I reserved a room for us that evening. Then we disapparated to a trail head that the inn-keeper suggested. We walked until noon, hand in hand. As noon approached, Jaimie suggested having lunch at the Cauldron. I agreed. "I've spent many a wonderful lunch, dinner, and night there. Since I may never see it again, it would be nice to have a last supper there."

Jaimie frowned at me. "Let's not be too disheartened. We may yet spend many more hours there." We disapparated outside the Cauldron and Jaimie led me in.

We were greeted by Tom, the bartender and owner with a complaint. "I've not seen you in an age. What has happened to you?" Then he turned to Jaimie and asked, "Aren't you that Jaimie that's married to Brewster?"

She quickly assured him, "She's a cousin. Many think that we have an uncanny similarity. Let me assure you that we are worlds apart. I've met Ted Brewster. He's nice, but I'd not choose him over Wendt here."

Tom was still uncertain but accepted the obvious fact that I wouldn't have an affair with the other Jaimie in such a public place.

The Cauldron was especially full with the lunch trade. I assured Tom that we were not in a hurry and would be glad to sit at the bar and nurse a drink until a table opened up. While we were there, sipping on our drinks and chatting, an idea occurred to Jaimie. "I don't have a photo of the two of us together."

I laughed. "There isn't anyone in the universe who does—or could."

Her happy smile turned downward. She said in all earnestness, "I want one. Today." Then she followed up. "I liked that one that you took of you and Minerva together. You took that at the photography shop here in Diagon Alley."

I agreed. "Yes. After lunch, we could go there and get a snap made of the two of us."

We were seated and had a pleasant lunch, almost forgetting how close we were to being separated. Then we entered Diagon Alley and found the photographer's business. We explained that we wanted a photo made of the two of us—today and printed before the day was over if at all possible.

He said, "I have appointments until four PM today. I can fit you in, but I can't guarantee that I'll get you prints before I close at six." It must have been easy to see the disappointment on both our faces. He added, "I can rush it to you by owl post tomorrow morning for sure." We still showed disappointment. He asked, "What's the rush about?"

Jaimie said, "My fiancé has to leave for the States tomorrow early. I want for him to have a copy before he leaves."

The photographer looked genuinely concerned. He thought for a bit and then said, "I'll stay late to print it if I have to. You come here at closing time and if you'll wait, I'll make the prints for you."

We thanked him profusely and promised we'd be back at a quarter to six. We then left and faced the problem of what to do until four. I suggested going back to the Lake Country to do some more hiking. Jaimie wasn't excited at the prospect. Then I had an idea. "Take us to Harrod's."

She asked, "You mean the department store?"

"Yes."

We arrived and I led her confidently to the jewelry department. When she saw where we were going, Jaimie clapped her hands together and asked, "Are you going to get me a string of pearls or a diamond bracelet?"

I smiled and said, "Just observe." We walked up to a sales person. I said, "We're looking for an engagement ring. Could you show us some!" With that Jaimie squeezed my arm as though she were going to wring all the blood out of it. She was speechless for the moment. The saleswoman led us to a display case. She showed us dozens of designs. In the end, Jaimie and I couldn't decide. I glanced down at my wrist and exclaimed, "We've got an appointment in two minutes. We've got to get going!"

Jaimie dragged me away and said, "Let's find a quiet corner. That poor photographer agreed to go out of his way for us. We need to be prompt. The design of the floor was so open that it was hard to find a spot. We settled on a ladies dressing room. We walked in hand in hand and reappeared just outside the Photographer's storefront. We walked in five minutes late.

The photographer was helping someone else, so I didn't feel too bad about being a little late. When the photographer finished, he came to us and said, "Sorry about that. Another rush job. Let's go back to my studio."

In the studio, there were a number of backdrops. As we were looking at them, he said, "I've photographed you before, haven't I. I never forget a nose."

I shrugged and said, "Yes, you did."

He scratched his head and said, "You wanted something special, didn't you! Let me think. . . Yes, it was a photo where there was no movement except in the shadows in the background—shadows of leaves. Is that what you want now?"

Jaimie said very decidedly, "No. I want a regular wizard photo with lots of movement." Then she giggled.

Meanwhile, the photographer slapped his forehead and said, "Yes, I remember. You were with a different young woman, weren't you?"

Jaimie had decided to be impish. She said in mock shock, "Did you get a picture made with another woman!"

The photographer supplied the answer, "Yes, he did. That was a long time ago. Did you ever get married? I seem to remember that she was reluctant."

I nodded. "Yes, we got married. She died several years ago."

"Oh. I'm sorry. I didn't mean any harm."

Jaimie assured him that she was completely aware of the "other woman." We found a different backdrop and posed for the picture. The photographer said, "OK. How much movement do you want?"

I asked, "What do you mean?"

Jaimie said, "Oh, he means how much time should the exposure be? What I have in mind could last ten seconds."

The photographer suggested that we practice what we were going to do. Then he could time it to pick the proper duration. We posed ourselves facing out toward the camera. The photographer then said, "Action."

I didn't know what Jaimie had in mind. It turns out that I didn't have to. She took my chin in a hand, turned my face toward her and kissed me. The photograph had us do it a couple of times. Then he said, "I think I've got a good shot here. Let me go ahead and develop it right away. That way, we'll know for sure."

Jaimie asked, "Don't you have other jobs to print?"

The photographer smiled, "Yours is more important. Is this for a special event?"

Jaimie asked, "Would you say getting engaged was special?"

He smiled, "Pretty special. Let's see the ring."

I said, "Sorry. We were shopping for a ring before we came here. We didn't decide on one yet."

He persisted, "But this is THE day, right. This is the day that you popped the question."

I agreed. Jaimie said, "You know, you didn't actually formally say the words to me, did you?"

I frowned. "I guess not."

The photographer quickly said, "Perfect. Why don't you do it right now, right here. I'll catch it on film. Perfect for the grandkids."

Jaimie squeezed my arm and whispered, "IF you get back to have kids and grandkids."

We posed again. This time, it was for real. We were sitting on the bench we'd used before. I didn't try to think of fancy words, I just sat with both her hands in mine and said, "Jaimie. You are the last woman in the world that I thought I'd have a chance with. I want you for my wife forever. Will you be?"

She turned a shade of red that surprised me and nodded and cried and said, "Yes."

The photographer said, "Perfect. I'll have both the photos out in a bit. How many do you want right now?"

I said, "Two each."

While we waited, I said, "Let's go to the inn. I want to consummate this before we run out of time."

She nodded. When the photos came out, we had a choice of several of the first shot. We agreed on one. The other was a one-off. We were out of the shop by 5:30. We went back to the Cauldron and used their floo connection to go to the inn. We had a decent meal there. Cuisine was not their forte, but it didn't matter. It was our engagement day. We couldn't have cared less.

We went up to our room. The first thing that Jaimie did was to drag me

212

to the bed, pull me down, and reach into my pocket. I smiled, "What do you think you'll find there?"

She pulled her hand and my purse out. She said, "This."

I stared at her. She was very methodical. She commented as she opened my purse, "I see that I can open this purse even in other universes." She started taking things out. There was money of varying nationalities and denominations. There was a pocket knife. There was the Glock, of course. At that point, she commented, "We'll deal with this later."

Then out came my leather card case. It had two clear plastic sleeves on the outside. On the inside there were two pockets where more cards could be placed. The outside pockets had the old picture of Minerva and me that had been taken at the very photography shop that we'd used that afternoon. In the other one was a photo from our wedding.

It caused me a twinge of regret when Jaimie took both those photos out of the clear sleeves and transferred them to the inside. They were replaced with the two photos we'd made today. I took the card case from Jaimie's hand and admired the pictures for a moment. Then I returned it to the purse. Jaimie put the rest of the contents back in the purse. Then she reached into my pocket for something else. This time there was no doubt for what she sought.

That night was one of forgetting—forgetting what would undoubtedly happen in a day or two, forgetting that we might never share a bed again, forgetting our fears. The next morning, we slept in. We hadn't meant to, but we were forgetting things. We could forget that we had classes that day. We showered and dressed slowly, trying to draw out our forgetting.

There was a tap on the door. I shouted to Jaimie who was still in the WC that I would get the door. It was probably the bill. I opened the door.

On the other side was an owl. It had a small note in its beak. I took the note and apologized for not having an owl treat. I walked into the WC with the unopened note. Jaimie gave a little falsetto scream. I opened the note and read aloud.

"Professor Wendt, your ship has come in. Please proceed to my office suite as quickly as feasible. Come prepared for extended travel. Yours always, Pam"

Jaimie said, "Presumptuous slut, isn't she?"

I said, "I've got to go back to my office right away. I haven't packed everything that I will need."

"Hurry. We'll have to go from this floo."

213

I said, "I'm ready to go. I'll take my bag down to the front desk and settle the bill."

She said, "Then, GO."

I did. At the front desk, I discovered that the inn didn't accept credit cards, so I had to dig into my purse for wizard money. I found a hundred galleon note. I gave it to the desk clerk who fumbled for change. Jaimie had just arrived at the desk at that moment. I said to the clerk, "Just keep the change as a tip. Share with our maid, please."

Jaimie took my hand, and we almost ran to the floo connection. We stepped in and stepped out in Jaimie's office. I said, "Didn't you get the wrong office?"

She said determinedly, "No! There are things here that you will need. Get that purse out now!" She sat at her desk.

I did. She quickly untied it and started taking things out. All of the money went into a pile on one corner of her desk while she commented, "I doubt they take those in PAKLAND." Then she put my credit card on the opposite corner of the desk. No comment. The leather card case went on that pile. She commented, "I don't want you to forget me."

"God, the only way that you could get me to forget you would be to kill me."

She quickly commented, "Bad Karma." Then, she had my Glock. She quickly removed the clip. It was empty. Deeper in the purse she found a box of bullets. She efficiently loaded the clip, drove it home into the handle of the Glock, set the safety on, and reached into a desk drawer. Out came two boxes of bullets that I remembered that I had kept there and not looked at for ages.

She emptied what was left in the purse. She sorted the rest of the contents into the stay or go piles. In the end, she loaded the go pile into the purse systematically. She picked up my bag and walked into the apartment. She said, "Let's pack clothes from your closet here." We did.

Back in the office, she motioned with her head at the floo connection. I put the purse into my pocket and picked up my bag. We walked to the floo. I took her into my arms and started to kiss her. She shook her head in disgust. "You've still got things at Dursley's that you need to pack, right?"\

I thought. I supposed so. We stepped into the floo and emerged in Dursley's office. He was there. When he saw that Jaimie was staying, he asked, "How was your little holiday?"

She said, "Great. We can talk later. Right now, Wendt has to finish packing for a long trip." I did. When I thought I'd gotten the few things I needed, she said, "Forgetting something, aren't we?"

I was puzzled. She said, "Don't you want to take your Kindle computer. It will work just fine where you're going."

"Right as always, your majesty."

She smiled for the first time in a while. I found the Kindle and then we really had to go. I walked over to Dursley and we shook and hugged. I said, "Please say goodbye to everyone for me—especially Filch. I don't want him to think that I forgot him."

Dursley agreed and said, "I'd never hear the end of it, if I'd let you go without remembering him."

I said, "Here, let me give you some party money, so everyone can go get drunk at the Broomsticks." I had my purse out when I remembered that there was no money in it. I swore silently.

Jaimie realized what had happened. She said, "What Professor Wendt wants to say is that I'll be hosting a big party on his behalf. Now, we HAVE to go."

This time, I had her in my arms and kissed her thoroughly. Then I took her arm and we walked into the floo connection.

Rendezvous on the Beach

We stepped out into the Atrium of the Ministry of Magic. The receptionist at the Visitor Desk called over to me. "Yoohoo, Professor Wendt. I have your visitor's badge here."

She trotted over to me and pinned on me the visitor's badge, fully filled out. She said, "You're expected in the Minister's Office Suite whenever you arrive." She looked Jaimie over and said, "If you're with Professor Wendt, I suppose you don't need a visitor's badge."

We walked off toward the elevators. Jaimie muttered, "Now that you get invited to see the Minister of Magic, you're all popular."

I laughed. "Maybe I'm just the latest craze. You know, I was called in some four or five years ago. I had a fleeting popularity back then as well."

In the Minister's Office Suite I was waved through to the Conference Room without another visitor's badge. I wasn't all that excited to get there in a hurry. We walked into the Conference Room and found that the Brahmses were already there. The Minister entered almost immediately after me. She looked around and frowned as she said, "Why is Minns not here?"

Just then, the receptionist opened the door and announced a visitor. He entered the room. I'd not met him yet. He introduced himself. "I'm the Naval Attache to the US Embassy, Thomas Wilkin. We received word that the PAK want to meet up as in the past—at sea. We've decided to make the USS Ohio available for that meet-up. It will rendezvous with you as before. I'm informed that you can make your way to the coastal location where you'll be picked up by the sub. It is headed for that location at flank speed. Their executive officer informs me that they expect to arrive there around mid-afternoon. Lieutenant Minns will make his way there on his own."

Just then, the door opened again, and Ginny entered, saying, "Sorry, I'm late. There was some last minute business that I had to attend to." She sat and looked around the room for the first time. Upon seeing Jaimie, she said, "As the security officer here, I have to ask you to leave this meeting."

Jaimie's lips compressed, and she seemed ready to say something. Instead, she got up, took my hand, and led me outside. There she said, "I love you. You have to return." We kissed and she walked off toward the Reception Area. I returned to the Conference Room.

Pamela was saying, "You have a little time. Apparently, only the four of you are going with Minns. I suggest that the three who have traveled with the PAK before brief Ms. Weasley. Do some brainstorming on preparations that you can make before you have to leave for Scotland. You still have some time left, and my staff will do anything to help you that you want. I'll get out of your way. Good luck." She went to the door, opened it, and turned back, saying, "I think you'll need it."

Ginny stood, walked to the whiteboard, and said, "We've already discussed what we should bring along. I've got my wand, of course. I have Peruvian darkness powder, Polyjuice, Veritas, even some of Dursley's cursed love potion. Anything else that you can think of?"

I said, "It's probably going to be a long voyage. We should bring anything that we can use to pass the time—games, compact books, etc." Then a thought occurred to me. "We should bring some compact exercise equipment."

Aurora said, "I've brought some strong elastic bands that I use for doing stretching exercises. We could all probably use them."\

I said, "Good. What else?"

Ginny asked, "Wendt, are you bringing your Glock?"

I nodded.

The Boy Genius said, "How about pads of paper and pencils?"

Everyone agreed. The B. G. said that he'd stuff as many as he could in his bag.

I said, "How about simple drugs—pain relievers, tooth paste, even cosmetics. We may be away for months."

Ginny gulped and said, "Right. I need to visit my apartment."

Aurora asked, "Everyone has clothes that are comfortable, loose, and easily washable?" Of course, the everyone that she was talking to was Ginny.

Ginny said, "OK. We've got two hours to finish preparations. Let's meet at the Cauldron for lunch. We'll go from there to the shore."

As we left the Conference Room to go, it occurred to me that I didn't have a way to get to the Cauldron. I opened my mouth to say something when Ginny anticipated me. "Wendt, why don't you tag along with me. You're probably as prepared as anyone, aren't you? No errands to run?"

I agreed. She smiled and said, "Then let's go. I'm taking the floo to my apartment."

"Are we using the one in Pam's office?"

Ginny stared at me as though I'd proposed going into the lady's loo. "Nooo. We'll go down to the Auror Office." I'd been there before and actually took the lead in heading for the Emergency Exit that she always used to get between floors. We went directly to the floo connection. Someone noticed us and asked, "Wendt's back in town?"

I answered, "No."

We arrived at Ginny's apartment, and she said, "If you want something to drink, go in the kitchen. I'm rummaging in my bedroom for stuff." I decided to just wait in the living area of the apartment. She quickly finished and returned. "OK. Well, we have over an hour before we have to get to the Cauldron. What do you want to do?"

I looked around the apartment. There were the usual things—bookshelves, sofa, chairs. There was no TV. I grimaced. I sure didn't want to sit around here and think about things. I said, "Let's go to the Cauldron. Maybe the Brahmses are there."

Ginny agreed. We entered the floo. She clasped my hand, and we were in the Cauldron. Tom greeted us as usual. We picked a table and ordered a drink. Ginny asked if Tom had Blue Label. The answer was no. She asked me, "What are you drinking?"

"Jameson. I've started drinking it. You have that, don't you, Tom?"

Tom agreed. Ginny asked for the same. She named the T. Rex in the room. "Well, this is uncomfortable. How will things be when we get on the rocket?"

I chuckled. "They don't use rockets. Their means of propulsion seems to be to use magnetic fields against planetary and solar magnetic fields to accelerate and then some sort of geometric drive to achieve trans-light speeds."

She laughed. "And you think magic doesn't make sense."

I started to object, but then I remembered that she lives on arguments. Instead, I said, "What are you going to eat?"

She asked, "Will I get air-sick?"

I couldn't help smiling. "Do you fly a broom?"

She threw her head back and laughed. "I retract the question."

I said, "You won't. That's one thing they know how to do." She laughed again and patted my hand. I gritted my teeth. We spent the rest of the hour sipping our drinks and waiting. Then the Brahmses arrived.

After a tasteless meal, we left for the rendezvous on the beach. Ginny and I went second. We landed and found Minns waiting for us. It was 1:30. We joked about the possibility that we'd freeze before the Ohio showed up. It was a running joke.

I asked Minns, "It's only us now. What's going on? Why did you get involved? How did you get involved?"

Minns shrugged his shoulders about a millimeter. "You know better than that. I never knew until the end."

Shortly after that, Minns commented, as though he were mentioning that there was some snow in the air, "The Ohio is here."

We all looked around. I couldn't see anything. Then, the B. G. said, "There's a rubber raft out there." He pointed off to the northwest. Yes, there was a rubber raft propelled by an outboard motor. It quickly grew as it neared. When it arrived on the beach, we were assisted on-board by CPO Green.

I greeted him. "Mr. Green. It's always good to see you." We shook hands. I added, "It's good to see that you're still around."

"You too, sir."

Minns didn't need any assistance getting onto the raft. Ginny didn't either, but the rest of us took a hand gladly. We were greeted on the deck of the Ohio by a small party. Two of them had assault rifles unslung. The third was a lieutenant. He said, "Welcome aboard. When we are possibly going to have aliens on-board, we take precautions. I will guide you down to Officers Quarters where you will stay until we rendezvous with the aliens. Please don't wander off. The guards are to be sure that you don't get lost."

Three of us had been this way before and knew what the drill was going to be. Minns seemed completely relaxed and comfortable. Ginny was either nervous or excited—maybe both. We reached the Officer's Mess. The hatch was dogged behind us. The lieutenant announced, "Please remain here in Officer Country until we rendezvous with the PAK. The XO will join you at meals and be your liaison with the captain." He passed us on the way to the hatch. He turned and said, "I believe that some of you have been on-board during similar situations. Please be kind enough to help your companions when necessary. If something serious arises, use the intercom to communicate with the bridge."

Ginny said, "The welcome was not so warm."

The Boy Genius said, "Oh, it was about par for the course. I think they were almost as friendly the first time we were on the ship."

Aurora and I agreed. Minns sat at the table and asked, "Anyone care for a friendly game of twenty questions?" No one was interested.

Ginny asked me, "Don't you have some sort of card game that you like to play?"

"Sure. It's called 'Back Alley. . .'" I was interrupted by the appearance of the XO.

He walked to the head of the table and said, "I think that you have all met me except Mr. Minns. I, Commander Wainwright, am the Executive Officer, of this ship. You all are our guests on this cruise. We expect you all to respect the conditions under which you are permitted on this ship. You will not leave the immediate area of the officer's quarters. You will not interfere with the operation of this ship. You will follow all orders given you by the officers of this ship. Is that clear?"

Everyone nodded.

"Very well. We will have our evening meal almost immediately. We expect to rendezvous with the PAK ship in approximately twenty-two hours. You will have to sleep as well as you can manage in this mess hall this evening. Is that clear?"

Everyone nodded.

"Finally, any breach of these conditions will result in your being handcuffed to your chair. Any attempt to leave this area of the ship may result in your being shot and possibly killed. Is that clear?"

That was abundantly clear to everyone.

"Then let's proceed to dinner."

We had a good meal by Muggle standards. Afterwards, Ginny suggested a discussion of what the spaceship would be like. Minns summed it up very succinctly when he said, "Look around you. This is what life in the spaceship that we designed was like." There was elaboration from the Brahmses about the spaceships that we'd been on. One important addition that Minns hadn't discussed was spacesuits.

The B. G. explained. "Something that you've never done is to wear a spacesuit. The ones the PAK have are not like the clunky ones that our astronauts wear that are cumbersome in zero gravity and really difficult to deal with in Earth gravity.

"The PAKs have spacesuits that perhaps weigh twenty pounds, wouldn't you agree?" He looked at Aurora and me. We nodded. He went on. "They recycle air so that you could wear them almost indefinitely without taking them off. They somehow absorb urine and remove everything but water. Don't gag. You can drink the resulting water. They are transparent or opaque depending on your preferences.

"They monitor environmental conditions inside the suit and display readouts of those conditions on the clear helmets when commanded to."

Ginny smiled. "It sounds like they are little spaceships on their own."

The B. G. said, "Except that they don't have propulsion, you're right."

Minns said, "That was spacesuits as they were several years ago. The PAK are ingenious. They may be rather different now."

Ginny asked, "I'm rather surprised at how unfriendly the captain and crew of this ship seem. Were they that way before?"

Aurora said, "They were very careful before, but they were not openly hostile. I would have said that they were actually friendly. Don't you agree?"

Both her husband and I agreed. Minns said, "The difference between previous trips on this sub and this one is my presence. If I were in the captain's place and knew about me what you all do, I'd probably do exactly the same thing."

Ginny asked, "Wendt, do you agree about the captain's attitude?"

I said, "Let me tell you what Phil Ballard who was on our original team that was trying to capture Minns had to say about Minns. We worked with Ballard back when Minns and his people were running around causing havoc. He gave this advice to the FBI team that was trying to arrest Minns. 'This is probably the most dangerous man you will ever meet.'"

She turned to Minns and asked, "Agree?"

He smiled that gentle smile of his and said, "It would be hard to argue against it. On the other hand, I'm only dangerous to people who are dangerous."

I said, "That's why it's nice to have him along."

Ginny muttered, "Some people might say that I'm dangerous."

I muttered, "I'd be first in line."

□□

The rest of the night was quiet, boring, and mostly sleep-free. The next morning, breakfast was early. That was good. We needed something to break up the monotony. It was decent, nutritious, and not up to Hogwarts's standards by a country mile.

The cook had joined us for breakfast. The XO had not put in a second appearance since the previous night. I asked what the menu for lunch would be—I was that bored. He said that it would be a surprise.

Lunch was a surprise. It was bean soup made with "navy" beans. There was freshly baked bread. There were cut up vegetables. It could have been worse.

During lunch Ginny asked about the smell. "What is that awful smell that seems to be everywhere? I know that it's not the lunch. It tastes too good."

Aurora answered. "Sorry. It's the ship. Somehow the filtration doesn't remove all the odors. You get used to it—eventually."

Ginny sneered. "I don't want to 'get used to it'. Will it be the same on the PAK ship?"

We all said that the PAK ship was almost odor-free. Ginny was doubtful but our insistence won her over to cautious skepticism. Minns said, "Our ship was completely odor-free. We tested it for a couple of weeks. We filtered all odoriferous chemicals out of the air."

Ginny said, "That was your ship—not the PAK ship."

At 2:30 the ship's intercom sounded. The captain came on and announced. "We've reached our destination. All passengers should prepare for imminent departure."

I commented, "I don't know which is worse—boredom or terror."

Aurora replied, "Keep those thoughts to yourself, please."

The next hour was as long as any on this trip. Then the captain came on the intercom to announce, "Will our guests please follow officers to the deck to prepare to leave the ship?"

Within moments, the XO arrived along with two armed guards. He said, "Please follow me without any delays." We worked our way up to the deck of the sub. When we stepped out onto the deck, the sky was overcast. I couldn't see a spaceship. In those last minutes, Wainwright stepped next to me and said, "Good luck and Godspeed, Mr. Wendt."

I could only thank him. Then Ginny exclaimed, "Look!"

Space Again

Everyone looked up from the deck of the Ohio. There was an airship breaking through the cloud cover. It quickly descended until it was hovering overhead. It was very similar to the craft that had picked us up twice before. A section of its underside cracked and swung down so that it almost touched the deck. I took a step toward the ramp, but Ginny beat me to it. She ascended quickly. The rest of us were not far behind. After we were all in, the ramp raised and rejoined the deck seamlessly. Ginny turned and said triumphantly, "At last!"

I said morosely, "Yeh. At last."

We were hardly in when a disembodied voice spoke. "Welcome to the Reliant." It quickly added, "That is the closest English equivalent to our name for this ship.

"Most of you have cruised on a ship much like this. There are differences, however. First, I assume that those that have traveled on such a ship as this will help instruct those who haven't. Therefore, I will only discuss new features of this ship.

"The most striking is the addition of a human autodoc. It is located next to the galley. It has the capability of diagnosis of most human diseases, both genetic and pathogen-caused from blood samples. It has a whole-body MRI scanner. This is used to determine the location of injuries and diseases such as cancers. It can synthesize treatment regimens for each of those. In the cases where it cannot treat ailments unassisted, it can give precise descriptions of how crew members can aid in the treatment.

"Less striking, but more useful are the improvements to environmental suits. Those are mostly evolutionary, but everyone should use one to train themselves on these suits with the assistance of previous users. I believe that previous users will be able to train themselves without assistance.

"We have installed controls that prevent the ship from being hijacked by overenthusiastic passengers. The ship is currently being remotely controlled. You can feel free to enter the bridge area and observe instrument readings and settings. However, there is no way to control the ship from within without assistance from without.

"We have improved the cruising speed of the ship considerably. We expect to be able to arrive at the PAK home world sometime late tomorrow. Please become accustomed to living in the ship. It will be your base of operations for quite some time. If you have problems or questions, don't hesitate to call out. Your living space is monitored continuously for speech."

Brahms muttered, "No doubt."

Ginny laughed. "Duly noted."

Minns said, "Let's see those spacesuits." It was an eminently practical suggestion. We headed for the locker that contained spacesuits and miscellaneous tools. We entered. However, the spacesuits were not immediately obvious. However Minns found them. He picked up what looked like a small sleeping bag. He unrolled it and discovered a transparent suit. The design had changed significantly since I'd last used one. All the parts of the spacesuit were connected by a narrow dark flexible rod. It made the spacesuit look vaguely like a skeleton.

Minns handed it to me and said, "You've got experience with these. Model it for us."

It was hard to deny his request. I'd worn spacesuits as much as anybody. It had a fairly obvious helmet at one end. At the other was the end of the "skeleton." I put a leg into one appendage that must be intended for a foot and leg. As soon as I put the second leg in, the legs sealed to the body part of the suit. It pressurized and then depressurized. After depressurization, it was almost impossible to feel the legs. I then touched the flaps of the legs. The body of the suit unfurled from the rod. It had arms into which I pushed my arms. They sealed themselves to the body of the suit, which pressurized and depressurized as the legs had. All that was left was the helmet. I pulled the helmet over my head. When I did that, the helmet sealed itself to the body of the suit. The helmet pressurized and was hardly wider than my skull. There was a voice that sounded in my ears. It said, "Suit status good. For details ask for details."

I said, "Air status." The voice was a soothing vaguely female voice.

It said, "Statistics over your left eye. Generally, good. Partial pressure of oxygen is 0.2 bar. Partial pressure of nitrogen is 0.3 bar. Recycling efficiency 99.8%."

Ginny asked, "What did she say?"

"Oh, boring statistics on my air supply." I went on, "You saw almost everything you need to know. The suit practically suits you up on its own. I'll take it off now and see how that goes." I decided to reverse my steps. I pulled up on the helmet. It asked, "Ready to unsuit?"

I said, "Yes." It then unsealed. The helmet easily came off. The seals at the arms released. They pressurized and easily removed. The other seals released. The legs pressurized and my legs came out of the suit easily. I said, "Well, there you are. Easy on, easy off." I added, "Everyone should put one on and wear it a bit—maybe walk around."

Minns took one off the shelf. We all watched in amazement as he unrolled it and suited up in less than five seconds. He stretched as though he were a ballet dancer. When he finished, he took off the spacesuit and said, "Amazingly flexible." I wasn't sure whether he was talking about the spacesuit or himself.

The rest of the team took turns with a spacesuit. Everyone wanted to do it by themselves. I'm not sure why. My speculation is that they wanted the maximum amount of help if something went wrong. Ginny was the third person to don a spacesuit. She did it with amazing agility—not like Minns but quite easily.

By this time we were pretty hungry. Aurora was elected to operate the food printer. She'd done it the most in previous flights. It worked almost identically to how it had worked in the past. It just had a wider repertoire of meals. We voted and agreed that Chicken Cacciatore was a dish that would test the meal printer's metal.

It came out completely satisfactory—not Hogwarts, but good. Then the B. G. raised the question, "What is the problem that is troubling the PAK?"

Minns smiled. "I don't know."

I was exasperated. "You know. You've got to know. Back on Earth you couldn't admit to knowing. You didn't want to reveal what it is. Maybe the PAK didn't want you to. Here , you're safe. We'll know in a couple of days at most."

"I don't know what it is."

I knew he was telling the truth. He has a way of convincing that leaves no uncertainty. I tried a new tack. "OK Guess. You're maybe the smartest person I ever met. What do you think it might be?"

"You mean guess?"

"Yes, if you have to."

He considered. Then he said, "Here is my guess. It's necessary that it is broader than just the PAK world or even worlds. They wouldn't do this—send for me if it were just something that they could fight out on their own turf. This is a much bigger fight than just our corner of the Galaxy. I don't know what it is or where it is, but I'm pretty sure we're not done traveling

225

when we reach the PAK home world. They even hinted as much."

Aurora brought up the question of cabin assignment. "We've got three cabins and five people. I suppose it's Nicky and I in one, Minns and Wendt in another, and Ginny in the third." She popped up before anyone could comment and dragged her bag to one of the cabins. They were all equivalent, so I certainly didn't care who had which cabin. Minns picked a cabin and moved his luggage into it.

Meanwhile, Ginny didn't move from the table. She looked over at me. She said, "That Minns is spooky, isn't he?"

I chuckled. "Yeah, you could say that. You know, you never had to try to arrest him."

She sat for a while longer. Then she said, "Do you really want him as your roomie?"

"Well, I guess I'll have to."

By this time, Aurora and the B. G. had left their cabin. They overheard enough to answer an unasked question. Aurora said, "I am not rooming with you Ginny so that Wendt can room with the B. G. This might be our last time together. I'm not going to miss sleeping with my husband."

Ginny said, "Wendt, you can room with me." She was looking away from everyone. "We can work out details as we go."

I said, "OK. If it's really OK with you. This might be just as creepy for you as being with Minns would be for me."

She shook her head. "No. It'll be alright. Move your stuff into my cabin." I did. That was pretty much all any of us could take for the day. We decided to get as much rest as we could manage. We went to our cabins. I sent Ginny off to the WC while I changed into my shorts and T-shirt that I usually wore to bed. She returned, and we traded places. That night was a little strange, but we both managed to get to sleep. I'd commandeered the upper bunk. Ginny had complained, but I was adamant.

□

The next morning we were preparing mentally for arrival at the PAK system. In a way we got a reprieve just before lunch. The ubiquitous translated PAK voice announced, "We have a minor problem. We have to delay your arrival by two days. Please don't be alarmed."

That was comforting. The B. G. announced to no one in particular, "I wish they would just keep us out of the loop altogether. If they can't let us know what's happening, they just shouldn't tell us anything."

Minns said, "Would it make a difference if we knew everything?"

226

I said, "Oh, probably not. It just scares us to death that we don't."

The rest of the day was just the boredom that was more frightening than the excitement. We read. We played cards. We waited. When the day finally dragged to its end, we prepared for the second night on the ship.

Ginny got back from the WC and took the lower bunk. It was quiet for a few minutes. Then I heard Ginny moving on her bunk. That went on for quite a while. Finally, I asked her, "Something wrong?"

She said, "No. . . Well, yes. I just can't stand the suspense of waiting. You know that I can face some pretty scary things. I faced the Deatheaters, the Ghosts, all sorts of criminals. I just haven't faced the totally unknown." She was quiet for a while. Then she asked, "Do you know what would help?"

"What?"

Again there was silence for a while. Then she said shakily, "Could you come down here and give me a hug."

I laughed and immediately regretted it. "Sure. Sorry. You just surprised me. Sure." I jumped down from the upper bunk. She was out of her bunk and had her arms around me. I put my arms around her and could feel her shaking. It subsided. I started to release her.

She shook her head. "Would you hold me until I fall asleep."

I nodded. She slipped down onto her bed. We both leaned back onto the bed. She'd begun shaking a bit. I held her tight, and the shaking subsided. She fell asleep, and I decided that I couldn't disengage her without waking her, so I closed my eyes and let sleep come.

The next morning, we had breakfast together. Ginny offered to make breakfast. She was chipper and even joking a little. Aurora asked her how she'd slept.

Ginny shrugged. "Oh, the first night it was not great—you know, the first time in any bed is bad. But last night I slept a lot better."

That day, I proposed that we play cards—Back Alley Bridge. The Brahmses knew the game from before. Ginny was a quick study. Minns wasn't interested. He borrowed my Kindle so he could do some reading. Ginny and Aurora were partners. The B. G. and I were partners. The B. G. and I won the first set of games. In the next set of games, Ginny began getting a feel for the game. She and Aurora kept the score close until the last hand when I took a chance on a difficult bid called "Boston." We almost made the contract, but almost doesn't nourish the canine, so we lost. Ginny kidded me about my reckless bidding. I said, "Well, nothing put at hazard, nothing won."

The B. G. and I selected the menu for the night. It was Cornish hen. Ginny asked, "Considering that last game, shouldn't it be crow?"

That evening, when we all went to bed, I held Ginny again. We lay in bed. She wanted me to spoon her. I gritted my teeth and spooned her. She said, "Tomorrow we meet the PAK."

I said, "We'll be OK."

"Still." She paused and went on. "Kiss me goodnight."

"OK." I brushed her hair to one side of her head and kissed the back of her neck. "See you tomorrow." She nodded mutely, and we fell asleep.

□□

Breakfast was a very different meal the next day. No one wanted anything heavy to eat. We all ended up with scrambled eggs and toast. No one wanted to clean up the dishes until we knew what was going to happen. Finally, I collected them and stuffed them in the dishwasher. It was ultrasonic and very quiet. We waited in silence for the end of the suspense. It didn't happen until the afternoon.

The anonymous voice of the PAK announced at 1:23 PM ship's time, "We will be flying past the PAK home world in about a half hour. The main video screen will show it as we pass. Be sure to be watching."

Ginny said, "I thought that was where we were going."

Minns said, "I never thought it was the final goal, but I thought we might at least go into orbit."

We all stayed in our seats. As the ship's clock reached 1:50 PM, we all were sitting on the edge of our seats. The large monitor on the wall switched on. In the center of the screen was a bright point that quickly grew to more than a dot—to a small circle that was multi-colored—to an ever-larger circle that had large swathes of tan and blue on it. It completely filled the screen and continued to grow. We then began to move further away from the planet. Then around the edge of the planet appeared a huge crater. It overlapped one of the blue areas that I guessed was an ocean. The part of the crater that overlapped the "ocean" was only faintly visible. We rapidly receded from the planet. The terminator of the dark part of the planet was quickly dominating the part of the planet we could see.

I suddenly realized that there was a hand squeezing my hand. I looked down away from the screen and saw Ginny's hand on mine. She asked, "What is that crater? Is it natural?"

Minns said, "I really don't think so. Did you notice the sharp relief that the rim of the crater had? Also, the sharp central peak?"

She nodded.

"Those couldn't survive long in an atmosphere. Sure, it might be only a few hundred years old, but I don't think it was a few hundred days old."

228

The B. G. was nodding as he said, "With their level of technology they'd have prevented it from happening if it had happened in the last couple of hundred years—maybe the last couple of thousand."

Aurora agreed as well.

I looked up at the ever-present observer above our heads. "You wouldn't mind elaborating how that happened." I was answered only by silence.

Minns said, "Apparently, all will be answered when we arrive where we're going."

Ginny asked, "If that crater happened recently, how many people were killed by it?"

Aurora said, "Well, there must have been one god-awful tsunami. The seismic shocks must have been pretty terrible, too. But where in the world is the shroud of dust from the pulverized crust?"

The B. G. said, "Maybe it really is hundreds of years old?"

Both Minns and Brahms's wife frowned at him. He relented. "OK. OK. But how in the world did all that dust get vacuumed out of the atmosphere?"

No one had an answer. Also no one had any idea how long it would be before we arrived wherever we were arriving. As a matter of fact, we arrived within a few minutes. THE voice said, "We are about to rendezvous with asteroid. 3155-07-14.00274. You can see the approach on the monitor in the mess area."

We were all there already, so all we had to do was look up. The monitor lit briefly and then showed a scene that could have come from our solar system. There was an asteroid that had what seemed to be a hole. The interior was brightly illuminated in a light that was slightly orange-tinged. We approached quickly. When we almost reached the point of entry, we realized just how huge this asteroid was. Our ship was dwarfed by the entry area. When we were in, an inner iris opened. We entered it.

Inside there was a larger cylindrical area where there were a number of docks for ships. A few were occupied by ships. There was one ship that was obviously much larger than ours. We docked.

Finally, the bag would be opened. Whatever was inside would come out.

□
□□

We pulled forward to one of the docking ports. When we arrived, there was an announcement on the intercom. It said that we should leave the ship and proceed to a meeting room. There was a schematic diagram of the area around our docking port with a route laid out. The announcement reminded us that the atmosphere in this facility was normal for PAK and would be poisonous for us. Therefore, we had to suit up and stay suited up except when we were in "our" ship.

The ever-present voice concluded by saying, "Please have a meal and suit up so that you can leave the ship at 9:00 ship's time." That gave us almost two and a half hours to do those things.

Minns spoke first, "I suggest that we have a discussion before doing anything else." We were already all seated around the Mess Hall/Conference Room table, so we remained seated.

I said, "Go ahead. It sounds like you have an agenda in mind."

He sort of shrugged and rolled his hand open. Then, he said, "I propose that we have a contingency plan ready that will handle . . . uh . . . most unforeseen circumstance."

The B. G. said, "It sounds like you have one in your hip pocket. Why don't you just explain it?"

Minns said, "Well, no. It's more that I think we should inventory what resources we have available and make sure that we maximize them before we leave the ship."

I said, "So, you want us to go around and list resources that we have right now? What about people who might not want everyone to know what capabilities we have?"

Minns grimaced and said, "Well, let me start us off. Then perhaps you all can follow suit. Do you remember when we were all in Witchita, Kansas? You, Wendt wanted to talk with the children of whom we were guardians."

I nodded, understanding. "Sure I remember them. Are you asking if we can use the same way that we wanted to approach them for interview purposes?"

Minns actually seemed relieved. "Exactly what I was thinking."

Ginny kicked me under the table. It brought a couple of tears. Not all of them were tears of physical pain. I went on. "You weren't there, Ginny, but let me assure you that Aurora would agree with me. She might fill you in on details later."

She almost snarled, "You will fill me in on details before very long."

Minns then asked, "Ginny. Are you able to use the techniques that Thomas R. used a number of years ago so sadly?"

Ginny's face lit up. "You bet your bottom galleon I can." She added, "Wendt, you have what I think you Americans call the equalizer?"

I just nodded. Minns seemed to be catching all the references. I just hoped the PAK weren't as well. They had studied the Earth pretty thoroughly before our last encounter. Who knew how much they'd learned about witchcraft and wizardry?

We had a meal and started suiting up. I was glad that we'd practiced this process thoroughly. I wished that we'd practiced it and gone into the airlock of the ship. That was the way that we were to gain access to the rest of the base. We were to enter the airlock two at a time. That was the limit for how many people could use it at once. We would empty the airlock. Then we would open the outer door. Outside the door, the centripetal force of the rotating asteroid would give us a mild gravity of about a quarter of Earth's gravity. We would enter the station's airlock for our dock. We'd closed the outer door and flood the lock with the poisonous atmosphere that they used. Meanwhile the lock, which doubled as an elevator, would take us down to the first level of the station proper.

If all went well, our suits would provide us with nice breathable air while keeping the hydrogen sulfide atmosphere out. That sounded good in theory. I'd never had to depend on a spacesuit for more than a couple of minutes of poisonous atmosphere or a couple of hours of vacuum or a relatively innocuous planetary atmosphere. Now, it was real life and death.

There was a little argument about who would go first. Minns wanted the honor. I argued that he was the most indispensable member of the team and so should go last. He argued that he was the one most able to adjust to unexpected conditions quickly. Therefore, he should go first to scout out possible problems. In the end, I won the argument. I wanted the B. G. and me to go first. Ginny's ire was up with that suggestion. She clinched it by saying. " Every team of two should have a witch along. You and I go first, buster. I go because I'm a witch. You go because you're the most dispensable."

So, it was that Ginny and I entered the airlock at 9:50. I started the cycling process. At one point the memory of my maneuvering the PAK body in that confined space returned to me with force, and I almost discovered what it would be like to throw up in a space suit. We finished the process. The airlock of the station was controlled from inside. Someone cycled it and opened the outer door. We entered.

I involuntarily took a deep breath as the outer door closed, and the lock began filling with deadly gas. Ginny seemed unfazed by the experience. She just smiled at me and rubbed my arm. It was amazing to me that that felt almost like a bare hand doing it. I think I turned red. She asked, "You're not nervous are you?" I just shook my head in denial as I felt my face redden even more. She looked puzzled but said, "Sure."

Meanwhile the elevator was descending. It stopped. The door opened. There were two PAK standing there waiting for us. One said, "Welcome."

231

He held out a hand. I'd seen more than a few PAK in the past, but none had walked up to me and offered to shake hands. I didn't feel all that comfortable about it, but I held out my hand. We clasp hands. The other offered me his hand while Ginny shook hands with the first of them. In the mean time, I heard the B. G. call out, "You two all right?"

Ginny replied, "We just left the elevator and were greeted there. Yes, we're OK."

He said, "Good. We're on our way down."

While we waited, one of our hosts said, "Would you prefer to wait here for the rest of your party or would you like to proceed to the Conference Room?"

Both Ginny and I said something so close to unison that you'd have thought we were channeling her twin brothers. It was the single word, "Wait." While we did, I looked at the two PAK who were with us as I never had before. True, I'd had to struggle to get two dead PAK into the airlock of a ship that was pretty similar to the one that I'd just left. You'd think that their appearance would have been burned into my memory. Not so. I was maybe trying to purge that whole incident from my memory.

Now, I had time, and I had inclination to study them. The two were taller than both Ginny and I, but they seemed lighter. Perhaps it was a higher percentage of muscle over fat—if that distinction made sense for PAK. The head was set on a shorter nick. They had two eyes, one mouth. Two nostrils that were set wider apart than we humans' are. There were two appendages that I supposed were ears on the sides of their heads. The ears seemed capable of independent movement. Their color was a shade of orange that might have gone well with the light of their cooler sun. The arms and legs seemed proportioned to their height as though they were humans. I had no idea what the gravity of their native planet was, but it seemed unlikely to be much different from ours.

By the time that I'd finished the assessment, the elevator doors opened, and the Brahmses emerged. There were greetings and the repeated offer to go to the Conference Room that was declined with thanks. We checked on Minns who was waiting for the elevator to arrive on the exterior level. It wouldn't be long before we'd have to move on to the Conference Room.

The elevator opened and Minns exited, looking as cool and calm as I was worried and nervous. We proceeded to the Conference Room where there were already three PAK seated around a Conference Room table that could have come directly from the Gringotts Board Room. There were things in this room that you wouldn't find at Gringotts. There was something that looked vaguely like a standard white-board. It probably would have served that way, but I was pretty sure that it was a video screen as well. Maybe you'd have found something like it in an Apple meeting room. There were not any obvious controls for it.

There was a sort of sideboard. I could imagine it loaded with a tray of snacks and beverages. There were none in evidence. Apparently, one of the people who were seated when we'd entered the room noticed the attention I paid it. He or she said, "I see that you were wondering if there would be refreshments. I'm sorry that we can't offer you any. Therefore, we won't partake either. We can have what I suppose you'd call a 'biology break' whenever you like. You'll have to go back to your ship for that. Since you can all go up or down at the same time in the elevator, you should be able to get into your ship a good bit faster than you exited it.

"Since we're all here, we'll start. I'll introduce us. We already know what your names are, but I think it would be good if each of us took a few of your minutes to give us all background on you."

It was so obvious that no one objected. The PAK speaker began. "My name is . . ." Here he pronounced a word that I think I never could have said. He went on, "Because our names don't translate to English, each of us will pick an English name that we think is appropriate to our role. Call me Ahab."

I don't know if he expected the laughter that accompanied the announcement, but he didn't seem troubled by it. I quickly said, "I apologize for any . . . embarrassment that our reaction might have caused. You chose a name that has a lot of cultural resonance with us English-speakers. Are you aware of those connections?"

Ahab answered, "Yes, I am. I chose that name because of those resonances. I am Ahab. I'm sure the Ahab you are thinking of is the man who captained a sailing ship on your Earth seas. That captain declared war on a whale who took his leg. I am the captain of this space station. Someone far more precious to me than my leg was taken from me by . . . by . . ." I found it hard to tell if Ahab's voice was shaking with emotion. The translator not only translated the PAK language to English, it blocked extraneous sounds —like the captains PAK statements. However, I am completely sure that his voice did shake. He was saying, ". . . my love." With that he turned his head.

No one said a word. His head turned back and he said, "I will have that creature."

The PAK next to him said, "I'm sure Ahab could and will say much more, but not now. I won't insult your ears with my name. The English name I've chosen is Spock. I was the original director of this base. I ceded that position to Ahab for reasons that we will cover later. This base was a research and development facility. Our main emphasis was the development of space vehicles. I have been lucky in that I have not lost anyone near my heart. I am ready to support his goal completely."

The next PAK said, "Call me Warren Buffet. I am the closest thing that we have to a CFO. In one sense my role—obtaining resources for this base's mission—is obsolete. On the other hand, I continue to oversee the operations of the base and make sure that critical resources are available to the important teams."

I chuckled. Everyone looked over at me. Ahab said, "Well, why don't you explain that laugh and introduce yourself as well."

I nodded, and realizing that the nod might not be understood, I said, "Yes, I will. OK. First, it occurred to me that the roles that you three have could be summarized as corporate roles in this way. Ahab is the CEO, Chief Executive Officer. Spock is the CTO, Chief Technology Officer. Warren is the CFO, the Chief Financial Officer."

Everyone smiled or made appreciative sounds. I went on. "My name is Wendt. If you would like a functional name that translates to PAK for me, I can suggest one."

No one said anything, so I went on. "I teach the literature written in the English language and, actually, others. My students are immature humans. I also am a consultant."

Ginny impishly asked, "With who do you consult?"

"I consult on banking issues."

Buffet asked, "Which banks?"

I was forced to say, "I'm not at liberty to divulge that information."

He nodded innocently and added, "Anything else?"

I laughed at that. "Come on, you must surely know that I consulted on those two expeditions to destroy the Ghosts."

Buffet and Spock had a strange expression on their faces—that is strange even for aliens. I was to learn why they had that unusual expression later. But for now, Buffet said, "I didn't know that. I suppose that explains why you are here now."

Aurora went next. She said, "My name is Aurora. I suppose that you could call me. . ."

She was interrupted by Spock. "Are you northern or southern?"

Aurora was dumbfounded temporarily. Then she said, "Perhaps, you should call me Dawn if your translator doesn't know the other meaning of the name."

Ahab said, "That would be acceptable. Dawn, it is."

She went on. "I am a teacher, like Wendt. I teach astronomy."

Spock said, "That sounds like a pun to me."

She said, "Perhaps it is. My father wanted me to follow my heart. It lead me to astronomy."

Ahab asked, "Were you on the expeditions with Wendt?"

She agreed that she was.

Then, the B. G. said, "My name is Nicholas Brahms. I am an expert in information handling."

Spock nodded and said, "Perhaps after this is over, we should consult. Are you another expeditionary?"

The B. G. replied, "Guilty."

Ginny was next. She said, "My name is Ginevra Weasley. Perhaps you should just call me Weasley. Weasels are small . . ."

She was interrupted by Spock. "We are aware of the reference. I believe the name Weasley would be no problem for our translator."

She went on. "My role is . . ." She hesitated as she thought. Then she said, "My role is security."

Ahab asked, "Security against us?"

Ginny said, "Security for my crew."

Ahab nodded. "An honorable calling. Were you involved with your war against the Ghosts?"

She smiled. "Yes, I was."

Ahab just said, "Good."

Finally, it was Minns turn. He said, "You may call me the Lieutenant— Lieutenant Minns."

Ahab said, "You're the one who offered his services to us. That includes the rest of the team, right?"

Minns agreed.

Ahab asked, "How much do you know about the problem we all face?"

Minns said, "Nothing."

They all seemed to be speechless. Eventually, Ahab stood, paced, and asked, "How did you know to contact us? This is almost insane. You must have known something about it."

I found my speech. "Let me try to explain what can't be explained. The Lieutenant has a long reputation for knowing things on an instinctive basis that he should know nothing about. We were all aware that he had no idea what was going on. We all chose to come because we trust him."

Buffet said, "I am an expert in the allocation of scarce resources. I would not allocate a. . ." Here he made a noise that the translator did not make an attempt at. He kept going. "to this crazy enterprise. Still, here you are and we are putting a great deal of our hope in you."

Minns chuckled. "I knew exactly what I needed to know. I knew that you were in desperate need of help. I knew that I could provide it. I knew that the rest of the team would be crucial to providing that help."

No one found those statements comforting in the least, but we were stuck with them. Ahab said, "Well, I, at least, know what the problem is. The three of us will describe the situation. Then you can judge whether you really can help. The story is long. If any feels that you need a biology break, we should take it now."

We all looked at each other. No one seemed in desperate need. I said, "I think we can carry on for an hour or so. Then, perhaps, we could take a break."

Ahab said, "Very well. I will begin the story. I was originally the captain of a space warship, the Tecumseh. Most of you have been on such a ship during the second of your expeditions that we launched to destroy the Ghosts. Do I need to describe what that ship was like to the others?"

Ginny looked at me and said, "I've had a brief description, and I can get more details when I need them."

Minns said, "I've seen enough to think that I have a good idea of what that is like."

Ahab said, "Good. Then, I'll begin. You may interrupt with questions as you see fit. Also, interrupt when you need a biology break." We all nodded. He then began. "I was the captain. I was assigned to go to the world of the Ghosts in order to destroy it."

I interrupted him. "Why! Did the Ghosts break the pact that you had with them?"

Spock asked, "Why do you think that there was a pact?"

"It's simple. You didn't destroy them when we were on that second expedition. That was years ago. You must have come to an agreement. What happened?"

Buffet said, "We did come to an agreement. They accepted the terms of our agreement."

The B. G. said, "Then they broke the agreement. I never really trusted them completely, but they seemed to honor their agreements with us and never lied to us. What did they do?"

The three PAK looked at one another. There seemed to be some silent communication between them. Spock answered the question. "Well, technically, I suppose, they didn't break the agreement."

Ginny slammed her flat palm on the table. "Then why did you break the agreement?"

Spock said, "Well, remember, I said that they technically were keeping it."

Aurora asked, "How did they 'technically' not break the treaty?"

Ahab answered, "They continued to explore space."

The B. G. said, "How about explaining what's wrong with exploring space."

Ahab shot quick glances at his associates and said, "What was the purpose of that exploration other than looking for species to colonize?" It seemed like a question, but the speed with which he proceeded with his answer showed that it was not a question at all. "They couldn't conceivably colonize an empty planet. They need intelligent species to conquer to colonize new planets."

I started to object, but Aurora interrupted me. "Without faster than light travel, they couldn't transport any reasonable number of non-ghosts."

Ahab continued forcefully. "The only purpose of that exploration was to wait until we got lazy and then resume colonization."

I wasn't done. "Well, haven't you ever heard of exploration for simple knowledge' sake? Anyway, someday they could obtain Faster-Than-Light, and then they could expand by colonizing the old-fashioned way—transporting complete persons."

Buffet said, "It's never happened in our experience that anyone spends the resources necessary for exploration without colonization being the eventual goal."

Spock added, "Besides that, do you have any idea how old the Ghost race is? Why just to cross the nearly thousand light years to colonize the planets they have. . ."

Aurora finished the idea. "It would have taken thousands of years. And that's just to cross that much space. To colonize as you go, it would take far longer than that. Perhaps, tens of thousands of years."

Buffet said, "Considerably more than that."

Ahab said, "If they haven't developed FTL yet, they won't ever."

I said haughtily, "So, you just decided that you'd short-circuit the process. They were going to break the treaty sooner or later, so why not just get the jump on them and do it right away?"

Again there was a brief silent consultation among them. I decided that it was deciding who would take the burden of answering. It turned out to be Spock. He said, "It seemed the only logical thing to do."

Through this entire discussion, Minns had been silent. I wondered if he'd already known where this argument was inevitably going and had decided not to prolong it. Well, I was not through. "So, you, Ahab, won the contest to decide who would rid the universe of the scum Ghosts? How long did it take? Years? Months? Given the speed with which we arrived here from Earth, I think it might have been measured in weeks."

He looked at me and said, "We never did it."

"What? They surely didn't beat you." A scary idea occurred to me just then. I said fearfully, "Did they? Is that why we're here? Did they develop some super weapon that threatens even you?"

There was a look in Ahab's eye that I'd not seen yet. I didn't know what it represented, but in that moment, I feared that he would do something like leap across the table at me. Instead, he stood and said, "No, they didn't. I'll tell you what did happen."

Minns said, "I think that it would be a good time to take a biology break. It's been a while since we ate. A meal would be a good idea as well."

A quick glance around showed that the rest of us felt that way too. I agreed, "Sure. We'll take an hour break and be back to hear what you did do." We all stood. I said, "I think we can find our way back to our ship on our own." I added, "With you permission."

Ahab just said, "Of course."

We left together. We entered the elevator together. We exited together. Then Aurora said, "Let Nicky and me go first. We'll get lunch started." We agreed. They cycled through the airlock quickly. Then Ginny and I followed. Again, Minns brought up the rear. Lunch was already well on its way to being ready when we arrived in the galley. The Brahmses had decided on vegetable soup and sandwiches for lunch. They had the food printer do a stack of ham, turkey, cheese, and bread after the vegetable soup. There was a little good-hearted squabbling about their choice of swiss cheese, but we were all happy to have food that looked pretty much Earth-normal after spending the morning in an alien space station.

Ginny sat next to me and asked for a better description of the PAK warship. I sat for a few minutes trying to come up with a comparison that would mean something to Ginny. She thought I was welshing. "Are you going to break your promise?" With that, she got up and walked into the galley to get something. I joined her. What she was getting turned out to be a glass of J. B. Blue Label.

My mouth hung open. She said, "You look surprised."

"It never occurred to me that the food printer could manage something like Blue Label. How does it taste?"

She took a sip and nodded appreciatively. "Try a sip."

I did. It wasn't quite THE Blue Label, but it was quite decent. I said, "To get back to your question, no. No. I'm trying to think of something that you might have experienced as a comparative." I thought of something that might work. "Have you ever been on an ocean liner?" I quickly interrupted myself. "Of course, you haven't. Witches don't travel by boat."

She laughed. "Of course, I have. Don't you remember my visiting your room on that ship?"

I was forced to laugh, too. "Sure, I do. How could I forget it? But you didn't really do any sailing. Also, you didn't spend any time outside that cabin."

Her face colored. "You don't know, do you, that I seriously considered staying with you in that cabin."

"What? Did you really? What would you have done? Never step out of the stateroom? Had all your meals by room service?"

Her smile was radiant. "Would that have been so bad? Maybe I'd not have gotten out of that bed. Now what does a cruise ship have to do with a battleship?"

"Well, they both are very large metal vessels. They both are designed to keep air in them. They have large mechanical engines that drive them through whatever they're in. They both have large crews. They both have a Control Room that is directed by a captain who rarely is seen by most of the crew." I paused for breath.

She asked, "There have to be big differences."

"Oh, yes. Cruise liners have thousands of passengers. Battleships have lots of weapons—sometimes, including small fighting vessels. Cruise liners are designed for luxury and comfort. Battleships are designed to be deadly."

She took another big sip and asked, "What would you have done if I'd declared that I would stay in your cabin?"

I scoffed. "You'd not have done that."

"Don't be so sure. What would you have done?"

"I think I'd have been stuck. I guess I could have gotten a ship's officer to kick you off. If you'd been determined, I don't think they could have done anything. You could disapparate around the ship. You could have walked up to a buffet and eaten yourself sick. I think I've heard of people stowing away on large ships and not being discovered."

She laughed. "That's exactly what I would have done."

Just then, the B. G. showed up and said, "We've got to leave for our meeting."

Ginny asked, "A last sip for you before we go back to work?"

I took the glass and finished it. She tilted her head and complained, "You are greedy."

I said, "American sign of respect. I don't want you to fall asleep during the afternoon."

We all had visited the ship's WC and re-suited. Then we were off to the airlock. We started to go in the same order as before. The B. G. grabbed me and let the rest go in before us. He held me outside, and once we were in the airlock, he took off his helmet and signaled me to do the same. I did. Then he said, "You and Ginny. Dumb."

I said, "Probably right." I shrugged and said, "She surprised me. I don't know what I'll do."

He just shook his head and said, as he started to don his helmet, "Don't be dumb." We both did and cycled the airlock.

They waited for the two of us before taking the elevator down. We arrived. No one was waiting for us. I reflected on how trusting they were. I said so.

The B. G. said, "Don't you think they're monitoring us and what we do?"

I had no answer. Anyway, we arrived at the Conference Room quickly. The three PAK were waiting for us. Everyone entered. I allowed the ladies to sit first. The B. G. sat beside Aurora. I sat beside him. He nodded approvingly.

Ahab looked around the room. I suppose he was verifying our attention was on him. How it could have been otherwise was beyond me. It's not every day that you are sitting across the table from aliens who are probably three times smarter than you and at least twice as physically powerful. Then he began.

"As you doubtless remember, I was telling you how I commanded a ship on its way to kill the Ghosts!" The translator gave real emphasis to the last words. He went on. "We were less than a day's flight from their home star system. I was sitting on the command chair on the Bridge when my executive officer came to sit beside me."

He knelt beside me and said, "We just received a priority message from Central Command. I've verified that it is genuine. It has all key data intact and validated. You can view it on the command screen in the secure message window."

I opened that window and saw a message that I had thought impossible. It read in part, "Captain Ahab, you are required to return to Home Planet immediately at the highest feasible speed. The Home Planet is under attack by forces unknown. There will be no further communication until you arrive within our system to maximize the surprise factor for our attackers. Best of Luck, Admiral Lutz, for Central Command." There were a few other details such as ideal approach vector to the home system.

I sent the XO back to his duty station. I ordered the Helmsman to set a course back to the Home System. He asked, "Sir, please repeat that order. I'm not sure I heard it correctly."

"Set course back to the Home System. I'll give you final approach vector information shortly." He acknowledged, and we executed a turn that was felt throughout the ship.

I then spoke to the engineer at his station. "Mr. Scott. How much faster can you push the engine?"

He answered, "Give me a moment to assess the status of the engine and power supplies." He consulted the monitor screens at his station. Then he answered, "We could do +25% safely."

"What if I wanted to push us beyond that. How much could you give me with small risk?"

His mouth snapped shut. He was that shocked. "Sir. How much risk do you want to take?"

I said, "I can accept 5% probability of serious engine damage by the time we arrive."

He took a deep breath and said, "I could give you +35% but I wouldn't like it."

All I said was, "Do it." Then something happened that I'd not experienced before. There was a groan of stressed metal that permeated the ship. I stayed on the Bridge throughout the thirty-plus hours that it took us to reach the point where we would change our course to match the final approach vector. At that point, I spoke to the crew. The essence of what I had to say was:

"I'm sure that you all realize that we have done a radical change in course and that we have accelerated drastically. I can now tell you that yesterday, I received an urgent message that announced that our Home System is under attack. We were ordered to return as quickly as possible. We are changing course to match the suggested approach vector that was sent to us. We have not heard anything further. Everyone should be prepared for a pitched battle. We might all die fighting the ship. I expect you all to serve in your posts with distinction as you always have. Good luck to us all."

With that, I ordered the helmsman to execute a maneuver that changed our course into something more like a spiral approach. There was still more than an hour until we entered the inner system. We would be approaching the Home World from out of the plane of the ecliptic at about 115 degrees from the direction to the Ghost home world. I wondered how we'd find out

241

what was going on. I didn't have to wait long. We were still more than a quarter of an hour out when the XO brought me another coded message. It said:

"Captain Ahab, the Central Command has surrendered. The Home World has sustained a gigantic nuclear explosion on the continental shelf of the Alpha continent. Tsunami's have decimated most of the harbor cities of the world. Your ship is needed for rescue missions on the coasts of the Delta continent. You will be allowed to enter the atmosphere there by the invaders if you make no effort to attack them. You are required to acknowledge your consent to this arrangement and accept rescue assignments. All your subsidiary craft will be dedicated to rescue missions as directed by the continental authorities. They will be in contact with you as soon as your acknowledgment is received. Regards, acting POTPAK, Central Command."

I said, "XO. Send acknowledgment. Obtain instructions for rescue operations. Then join me and section heads in my Conference Room." I then turned to the Engineer and said, "Reduce to sublight and join me in the Conference Room."

In the Conference Room, the section heads quickly assembled. When everyone was there, I began. "The war hasn't been going two days and we've lost. Our assignment has changed. We're now on a search and rescue mission." There was universal dismay in the room as people internalized what that meant. After giving them some time to react, I took the next essential steps.

"Central Command is overwhelmed and has referred us to the Delta Continent leadership to assign us specific goals. In this environment we must do lots of thinking on our own. So, I turned to my staff. I'm going to call on each of you to report what you can deduce from the information that we have collected ourselves on the approach. First, Helmsman, on our current course and speed how long do we have before we arrive at the Home Planet?"

His answer was quick and confident. "We are now traveling at approximately one-half light speed. We have more than twelve hours before we arrive. Of course, we could increase that speed immensely and arrive as soon as you wish."

I turned to the Chief Engineer, Mr. Scott. "How are our energy reserves?"

His answer too was quick and confident. "We have 71% of full reserves available."

242

"Can we work that up higher? We're in a hydrogen-rich environment, aren't we?"

Mr. Scott answered, "Yes, sir. We should have no problem getting as close to 100% as you want."

I thought a moment, weighing the advantages of having 100% energy capacity vs. the time wasted collecting it. I said, "I'll give you two hours. How much energy can you collect in two hours?"

"I can get us above 95%."

"Do it."

He rose to leave. I interrupted him. "We're not done here yet. Sit back down." He opened his briefcase to get his tablet, on which he began keying. I'm sure it was orders to the engineering department.

I asked, "What kind of tragedy are we likely to find?"

I was a little surprised when the weapons officer rose confidently. He went to the white-board with his tablet and brought up an image projected on it of the hemisphere where the big attack had happened. He said, "You can see from the semi-circular impact crater on the coastline that the weapon detonated maybe twenty or thirty kilometers out to sea—still on the continental shelf.

"We flew through the gamma-ray shockwave. We weren't able to do much in the way of measurements, but it's quite clear that the weapon was a proton-proton fusion weapon. I personally think that the weapon was very like our anti-inflaton weapons. The total energy released was probably around ten million megatons.

"The models that we've developed for such weapons on planetary surfaces like ours show that the casualties from direct blast and radiation would be 100%. For this target on our planet, the radius of total destruction would be over 300 kilometers. My estimates of direct deaths would be about one to two percent of our home planet's population." Although everyone should have been expecting something like that, there was still a dismayed gasp at the figure.

He turned to another topic. "We are fortunate in that we have very good tsunami models for our planet. We've been able to predict quakes that could cause tsunamis far in advance. The vast majority of the areas that would be affected by tsunamis would have been able to do almost total evacuation before the tsunamis struck. Only the coastal areas immediately beyond the direct blast area would have tsunami casualties.

"My estimate is that the affected areas would be those closer than 1000 kilometers from ground zero. The resulting death toll would probably be another two to three percent of our population."

Somone asked, "What about direct quake damage?"

"Surely, the vast majority of the planet would be quake-impervious buildings or would have evacuated substandard buildings. Deaths would be very minor. No, the biggest potential for deaths is the huge amount of radioactive dust blasted into the upper atmosphere. Besides radioactivity, it would obscure the sunlight. I don't know . . ."

The science officer stood. "We have been scanning the entire system for Cherenkov radiation, indicating FTL drive use. We've found a small comet in the outer system that is being pushed toward our planet. At first, I thought it might be the basis for another attack. Then, I realized that our enemies could do far worse than that if they wanted.

"I think that the defense force is planning to break it up into small fragments and dump them into the atmosphere over the cloud of dust. That much water vapor along with some liquid water would precipitate the dust into rainfall over an ellipse extending a little over a two thousand kilometers away from the target area. The radioactivity would be confined to that ellipse and the long term dust in the upper atmosphere would be small. The surface area affected would be about a million square kilometers—only a few tenths of a percent of the surface area of our planet. Most in that area, could be evacuated. Again, the deaths would be small."

I said, "These are only rough estimates. It sounds to me like we might be talking about five to ten percent of the population as casualties."

The consensus in the room was agreement on that level of casualties. Then I came to the hardest part of the meeting. "So far this has been academic. We have to face that everyone in this room and in this ship will know people who are dead now. Many will have relatives who are dead now." I hesitated as the truth of that hit me personally. I was overcome with a wave of grief. Then I went on. "We must adjust our expectations for our performance. I still expect everyone to perform at their personal best. However, we as leaders must be prepared to deal with the effect on those we lead.

We must be prepared to relieve crew members who are overcome with the terrors that we will all face. The future of our race is at stake. My quarters are always open to those who wish to request to carry on at a lower level of responsibility temporarily."

I looked around the room. What I saw was, I hoped, determination in all eyes. In the hours and days that followed, I felt waves of hopelessness, anger, fear, and rage sweep over me. I was determined of two things. One was that I would perform my duty as effectively as was PAKly possible.

I dismissed the staff to go to their posts and prepare to follow instructions that would come from Regional Command. Meanwhile we would proceed to get into position to carry out those orders. When I reached the

Bridge, I spoke on the intercom to the entire ship. "We have lost the battle. This ship is now on course to assist in rescue of people trapped by the tsunamis on the coast of the Delta continent. We will receive specific coordinates of people to rescue. Each deployable ship will receive coordinates in their guidance system. All pilots and crews, prep for deployment within the hour."

We had almost an hour before we arrived on station. All crews would be ready when we arrived. We had fifty-four deployable ships. We arrived on station. We were forty kilometers above the surface. Our ships scattered and began rescue operations. We operated around the clock for over one hundred hours. By the end, we'd rescued almost a quarter of a million people

When we had rescued the last, we were given two days of rest. Every person on the ship did their best to locate their relatives and closest friends. I called my spouse. There was no answer. It didn't surprise me. A lot of the phone system was still being repaired. I knew where she should have been. I started there.

In the recovering public transportation system, there were priorities for fleet personnel. I bumped a regional politician who was also trying to find someone that he cared about. He was unhappy, of course. He said something along the lines of, "You selfish bastard! I'm more important than you! I directed the rescue of millions of people. You've only gotten a few hundred thousand out. I bloody deserve this!" His face was contorted into a mask of pain by this time.

I said, "You can have the next flight to Sebastapol. I'm on this one." He was smart. He knew that he'd never convince anyone to replace me. The flight was fast. I arrived and began my search. The first step was the database of dead persons in the government house for the city. Thank god she wasn't there.

Then there was the database of rescued people. She wasn't there either. That meant that she was in some hospital. She was unconscious and hadn't been identified yet. In the triage, life was more important than identity. There were thirty hospitals in this city. I memorized the map of the city and set off for the closest. On the way, I worked out the optimum route through the list of hospitals to minimize travel time. Sometimes I could catch a bus, but almost always, I had to run between most of them. The city spread over

245

fifty kilometers. Just running the distance cost me three hours. In each of the hospitals, I went to the back room where the rooms are all monitored. I sat at a monitor and looked at the faces that showed up on the screen. Sometimes it wasn't possible to identify a patient on the video. I'd go down to the ward to see for myself. Usually, I could just walk in. Sometimes, not.

Once, the patient was in an ICU. The doctor didn't want me to go in. "I'm the husband of one of the patients."

He looked at me in puzzlement. "You can wait to see her."

"No. I can't."

He could see the desperation in my face. "OK. Go ahead."

I walked in. The patient had bandages that obscured most of her face. She was unconscious; I approached her cautiously. When I was within reach, I touched her wrist. Then I closed my hand around it.

It wasn't her.

I moved on to the next hospital. At the twenty-fourth hospital, I found her. She was in the ICU. I didn't stop for permission. I ran in. She was unconscious. She was in a body cast. Her wrist told me the tale. I cold feel HER pulse.

It faltered and then failed. The time that I begged the doctor to bring her back was wasted. She was lucky to have survived as long as she had. I like to think that she knew I was there at the end. I like to think that I'll catch the bastard who killed her. I like to think that he will lose what he cares most about in the universe before we're through.

In the Conference Room there was nothing but the profound silence that you normally encounter in the vacuum of space. Ahab said, "I'll let Buffet take over next. He was on the Home World when the bastards arrived."

Buffet nodded. "Yes, I used to be the Chief Financial Officer of the home world. I was called in when this event happened as part of the ruling cabinet of our world."

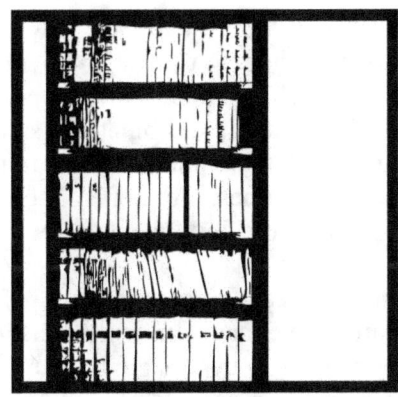

When Kali Came A'calling

It began one day in an asteroid research unit in the outer belt of debris left from the formation of our solar system. Ever since we developed FTL flight, we have been working on ways of detecting ships traveling faster than light. Our interim answer was Cherenkov detectors spread through our solar system. The ones installed on one of our asteroid went off.

We barely had an hour before the projected course of the object would be into the inner system. There are tens of thousands of intelligent species within two thousand light years of our planet. Of course, you're one of them. Of those tens of thousands, only a few hundred have space travel within their system. Again, yours is one of them. Of those few hundred only several dozen have interstellar travel. Yours is not one of them. Of course, the Ghosts are one. Of those several dozen, fewer than a half-dozen have faster than light travel. The Ghosts are not one of those. We are. The others are at the outer limits of our exploration.

The arrival of one of those ships in our system is extremely rare. It's only happened a couple of times to the best of our knowledge. Therefore, we assembled the cabinet as quickly as we could. It was done before the ship entered orbit around our world—just. We have developed procedures to handle this situation. Near space transit control attempts to develop contact with them. We can deduce new languages quickly if its speakers try for communication. The crew of this ship did.

They were past masters of "first contact". We had effective communication going before the cabinet meeting had ended. I said to the rest of the cabinet. "I don't think that it's a good idea for us to communicate directly with these aliens." Everyone agreed. Then, of course, I was appointed to take the "point" on communicating with them. I told the technical operator who had brought the message to send back a message that I personally would be the point of communication with them. I went on. "Tell them that I will be prepared to talk with them in twenty hours after I've made preparations. Set up the link to my office and my office only."

Then I sent her off. I turned to the cabinet and said, "My goal will be to strictly limit the contact with these aliens and try to get as much information from them as possible." There was general agreement with that approach. We adjourned the meeting, and I went to my office to prepare for my "first contact."

That afternoon, the technical operator came to my office and setup the hardware for a direct hardware connection to the translator so that it would be very difficult for these aliens to bypass the link and gain access to other parts of our network. The operator and I tested the link to the translator. She told me that after the translation had been perfected, they'd sent an opening statement. She said, "I have the transcript here." She handed it to me.

I asked her, "You've read it, haven't you?"

She nodded agreement.

"Good. Then give me the executive summary." She looked surprised. I assured her, "I'll read it myself. I just want an independent opinion of what they have to say."

She still hesitated, but I was insistent. She started a little uncertainly, "Well. Uh. The message basically asks for access to our premier research library. They say that our reputation as the best scientific authorities in the known galaxy is unchallenged. They want to improve their understanding of a few obscure cosmological issues."

"Really? Do they specify what they are?"

She shook her head. "No." Then she added, "They claim that only a few top cosmology experts would understand the points."

"Hmmm. I've got a bad feeling about that. Sounds like the only obscure points are their real motivations."

She gasped and said, "Just what I thought." She sat in my red guest seat unbidden—not that I minded. Then she leaned over my desk and said, "I don't trust them." More softly she asked, "What are you going to do?"

Her intense gaze surprised me. I shrugged. I hadn't thought about it. After a moment's thought I said, "Have any aliens used our research libraries before?"

She twisted her head a little and said, "I don't know. BUT, I'm going to find out right now." With that, she got her tablet out of a pocket and keyed a few words into it. Then she said, "There have been half a dozen alien missions granted access to one or more of our research libraries. Three were mathematics. Two were cultural history—strictly limited to civilizations that we had discovered. One was chemical."

"Did we make any requirements of them?"

She referred to the tablet again and said, "They just had to list the libraries for which they wanted access."

I nodded. Then I said, "Would you mind helping me work out the requirements that we will place on them?"

A look of surprise crossed her face followed quickly by one of pleasure. "Of course, if I can be of any help, I'd really, really like to."

"Yes, you can. I think that anyone applying for access to our libraries needs to fill out an application, don't you?"

She nodded vigorously. "Yes, sir, I DO."

□

The next day, the technical operator, whom I'd had transferred temporarily to my department, and I were sitting in my office. I asked her to make contact with the aliens. They responded almost instantly. We'd limited the communication exclusively to verbal.

The voice on the other end of the connection was high and imperious. I could hardly believe that the translator had gotten those intonations into the speech, but it had. "Are you ready to grant us the access that we desire?"

I answered smoothly. I hoped the translator didn't insert too much oiliness into my words, but if it had, there was nothing I could do about it. "We require all peoples who get access to our libraries to fill out an application. It's really just a formality. However, it's something that everyone— including natives have to do." With that, the technical operator, whose name turned out to be Sandy, looked like she was about to break out into loud laughter. I raised a digit to my lips, requesting silence.

The voice on the other end said, "Please transmit the application to us."

I nodded to Sandy. She had her tablet open in anticipation of the request. A few keystrokes and she nodded to me. I said, "You should have received it now."

There was silence for a brief period. Then the imperious voice said, "This is what you call a formality."

I tried to sound like a faceless functionary as I said, "Yes, sir."

"But these questions are . . . detailed and largely pointless."

I said in my most serious tones, "Really! They are all necessary to evaluate your needs and satisfy minimal prudent requirements to grant you proper access."

The voice said, "Let me just cite one or two examples: 'Where do you come from? Specify precise spatial coordinates. Give a brief outline of

249

your cultural and scientific history.' Why in the world do you need all those details?"

I said, "Really, I'm just a subordinate. I don't make up these question?"

Sandy almost fell off her chair. She looked at me and mouthed, "You made them up." I shrugged.

The voice went on. "Or another: 'What precise fields of research are you interested in?" Or: 'Specify the precise research question or questions that you want to answer. Please, provide an executive summary of the hypothesis that you are investigating.' You don't need to know those answers."

I tried to sound as serious as I could. Really, it was very serious. I was not going to let unknown aliens troll in our libraries without knowing their real goals. I said, "I'm afraid that I do need those answers. If you want access to our libraries, you're going to have to give us good, convincing answers to those questions."

Sandy gave me a manual sign of approval.

The alien voice said, "This will take some time."

"We are, if anything, patient. Take your time. We'll be here."

The alien's final words were not re-assuring, "We'll see about this." With that the connection was broken.

Sandy released a sigh of relief. "Good for you, sir. You're spot-on. We do need those answers and frankly." Here she shuddered. "I hope they don't satisfy you. I've got a bad feeling about them."

I said, "It's been a hard meeting. Would you like to go to lunch with me?"

Her face lit up, and she enthusiastically agreed to lunch.

□□

The next day. Sandy and I were trying to get some work done. Neither of us could do much. Every opportunity that we had we speculated on what answer the aliens would give us. Before the day was over, the completed form was returned. Sandy read the answers:

Q: Where do you come from? Specify precise spatial coordinates.

A: Our home planet is located about nine thousand light years from here. We will base its polar coordinates on a system where the origin is a line proceeding from your planet to the black hole at the center of the galaxy and the plane formed by it and the velocity vector of your star. The right ascension 0.0834 radians. The altitude is 0.0024 radians. The radius vector to the central black hole is 21,687 light years.

Sandy said, "Well! We must have quite a rep. Right?"

I grumbled. "Maybe I would prefer to have a less prominent reputation." She nodded. Then she went on.

Q: Give a brief outline of your cultural and scientific history.

A: Our small empire, consisting of eighty-five planets was assembled over the last sixty years. Our goal is to improve the life of the inhabitants by controlling over-population. The empire was assembled by our leader Kali who has combined the best of the sciences and cultures of these planets to permit the expansion of his goal of universal population control.

We both said, almost in unison, "Oh my god!" I added, "What in the world does that mean? Read on."

Sandy said shakily, "Yes, sir."

Q: What precise fields of research are you interested in?'

A: Nuclear Synthesis in the early universe, particular its effects on the early expansion phase of the Universe.

Q: Specify the precise research question or questions that you want to answer.

A: We want to understand how inflaton/anti-inflaton synthesis occurred during the era before quark confinement.

Q: Please, provide an executive summary of the hypothesis that you are investigating.

A: We believe that inflaton/anti-inflaton synthesis can occur in stable very high Z nuclei that would have been present in the early universe. We also believe that inflaton/anti-inflatons are Majorana particles that can be manipulated to achieve brief super spatial collapse followed by super spatial expansion.

After the last answer, I said, "Oh, shit."

Sandy blinked her eyes rapidly and held them shut for some time. She exclaimed, "We can't give them access to our libraries!"

I nodded slowly. "Yes. you're right. Call an emergency meeting of the cabinet in my name."

"Yes, sir!"

□
□□

The next morning. Sandy had miraculously gotten the meeting convened. I spoke first. "I've been in contact with the aliens. I made up a new application for aliens who want to use our research libraries. They have filled them in. Here they are. I think they speak for themselves."

Sandy distributed copies. The cabinet should have only required less than a minute to read and internalize the application. Instead they all sat in different attitudes of thought. Finally, they each said, "We can't let them have access to anything."

The Science department head said, "What they are asking for could be used to build a weapon to completely destroy our galaxy. It could convert our galaxy into a quasar that would be hundreds of times more massive than the largest we know about. Forming that quasar would release energy at a rate tens of thousands of times greater than our largest known quasar. It probably would kill every intelligent species out to the Andromeda Galaxy. It would make life extremely contingent throughout the Local Group of galaxies. I would destroy all our libraries before I would let them have access to them for one second."

I commented, "I like the way you use understatement so effectively."

The prime minister instructed me to send him his application back marked rejected. I waited for the meeting to end. He shouted at me, "Now! Do you think there's a bloody minute to lose." Sandy and I left. We arrived in my office.

She asked, "Ready to send the rejection notice?"

I nodded.

A few keystrokes and within seconds there was a request from the aliens for discussions. The same voice as before demanded to know why we had rejected the application.

"All I can say is that my superiors decided to deny your request."

There was silence for at least a minute. We were about to break off the contact when a different voice came on. It was much deeper and deliberate. "Tell your superiors that they should reconsider their decision. If they don't, they will regret the consequences." I immediately told Sandy to try to get the cabinet to continue their meeting to let me report this latest event. "I'm on my way up there. Get in touch with them and follow me up."

"Yes, sir."

She did keep them from adjourning. When I arrived, the cabinet members were literally sitting on the edge of their seats. The Prime Minister said even before I could sit, "They threatened us." It was not a question but a statement.

"Yes. They did. There was no specific threat made, but just an indefinite one."

The Prime Minister said, "We've been expecting that. We've started planning a response. What do you suggest?"

I looked around the cabinet to gain time for thought. Sandy entered the room, giving more diversion that gained me a little more time for thought. It really didn't take much thought. I said, "We should do whatever we can to prevent them from getting access to our libraries."

The PM nodded agreement. He turned to the Science Head. "What sort of security do we have at the libraries?"

The Science Head said, "We can prevent unauthorized access through imposing cyber controls. However, even the most stringent controls can be overcome. The subornation of a single person with access would make them moot."

Everyone chewed on that for a time. Then the Armed Forces Head said, "I really hate the idea, but I don't see any alternatives . . ."

The Science Head said, "If it looks like we will lose control of the libraries . . ."

I finished, "We destroy the library."

The Science Head added, "It won't be as easy as you think."

I scoffed. "I never said that I thought it would be easy."

The Science Head responded, "The library system—although it has separate specialized libraries—is connected in a network of backup servers. You can't just destroy one class of knowledge without destroying it all." There was a hushed silence in the room.

Finally, the PM spoke. "In other words we have to destroy not just our science, we have to destroy our culture to protect the Local Group of galaxies."

The Science Head said, "Right now, yes. Perhaps we could compartmentalize knowledge more to protect it. But that is a discussion that can't even begin in the time that we have."

I asked, "What can we do?"

The Science Head said, "We designed the library to be virtually impossible to destroy. Physically, it's distributed and buried deep in the world. The individual components were designed to be able to survive any natural disaster short of our sun going nova."

Sandy asked, "Didn't you consider the possibility that you'd want to destroy it?"

The Science Head just shook his head. The Armed Forces Head asked, "What weapons that we have could destroy it?"

The Science Head thought a moment. "The weapons that we were planning to use to destroy the Ghosts could be dialed down so that they didn't destroy our world."

The Armed Forces Head said, "Those weapons are currently on the way to that planet . . ."

The PM immediately interrupted him to say, "Call them back immediately!"

The Armed Forces Head turned to his aide and said, "Do it." Then he turned back to us and said, "Those weapons are in storage as well at a couple of military bases—none in space other than . . ."

The PM interrupted again. "Get them out of storage and mounted on spaceships." He turned to the Science Head, "Get the co-ordinates of those library system locations immediately."

The Science Head turned to his aide, who just nodded briefly and started working on his tablet. The PM had been going on. "I want those ships backed out of the system and prepared to launch on warning."

The Armed Forces Head said, "My associate and I have to go to get those plans in motion. With your permission?"

"Yes, yes. Go immediately." They left the room so quickly that they didn't hear the next question the PM had. "What about defensive forces for the planet? We may never get to the point of needing to use these emergency plans."

The Science Head said, "I think I can answer in a general way. It's practically impossible to defend from an attacker who has FTL propulsion. We don't yet have systems that can detect FTL travel until after the fact. We mainly use Cherenkov radiation. That travels at the speed of light. We have detectors spread throughout the system. They can detect position and velocity, but typically only ten or fifteen minutes after the craft has passed them. That's why your ships with FTL missiles would be effective to destroy our library locations—if they're in place in time."

The Commerce Head asked, "How long will it take to get them in place?"

The Science Head said, "A rough guess would be a couple of days."

The Cultural Head asked, "When are we going to tell this Kali that we aren't intimidated?" That question could be the one that the fate of our world turned on.

While we were thinking, Cultural Head asked, "Did you say, 'Calley'?" He spelled it.

I corrected, "No. It's spelled K . . . A . . . L . . . I."

There was another moment of silence, and then he said, "I think we might just have an expert on the cultural roots of Kali. Apparently, they start on a obscure planet called Earth. They hardly have travel within their own system."

The PM frowned and said, "Well, we're burning time here. Can you get him onto a conference call?"

"I think so. Give me a couple of minutes." We did.

The call came through in the late morning just before I was to leave for lunch. I'd have gotten the call anyway, but I might have decided not to answer right away. Instead, I did answer. The call requested voice only. I agreed. The person who called asked me what my area of specialization had been when I studied the Earth. He asked the question with all the casualness that I would have used if I'd asked a human what professional sport was his favorite.

I replied, "The culture of the Southeast of Asia."

He then said, "Are you familiar with the name Kali?"

I stopped my mouth from forming any reaction. However, I said, "Yes. Kali is the personalization of what the people of earth frequently refer to as Armageddon. It's the ill-informed idea that the Universe has 'Ages' a little over 28000 Earth years long." I prepared my muscles to remain untensed when I said the next words, "I believe that the current age of Shiva is about to end and the new age of Kali, the Kaliyuga, will begin shortly. It will be marked by the remaking of the heavens and the world."

He asked, "Who is Shiva?"

I said, "Shiva is the 'Destroyer'. "

I couldn't resist the temptation to ask the question, "Do you know someone who regards himself as . . ."

He didn't allow me to answer the question but provided an answer himself, "I know of someone who might regard himself as a . . . a . . . a."

I said, "The word that you're looking for is 'avatar'. You know someone who regards himself as an avatar of Kali?"

He said, "Yes. I suppose that might just be true. Were you on that expedition to Earth—the second one that tried to find the World of Ghosts?"

"We found it. We just didn't destroy the World of the Ghosts. Was this avatar of yours on that expedition?"

"No."

"Can you tell me how he found out about Kali?"

"No. This is Cabinet business. Don't share this conversation or anything you deduce about it with anyone."

I could only agree to that.

I ended the call. The PM said, "That could just be coincidental."

I sneered. "Of course. It was just a coincidence that this Kali is supposed to re-make the universe just now and just as 'our' Kali shows up ready to turn our galaxy into the black hole to end all black holes, hmmm."

The PM asked, "You've been talking with this Kali. What do you think? Can we stall him for a couple of days? Can you convince him that we might just give him access to the libraries if he is just patient?"

I glanced over at Sandy. She knew me well enough that she could communicate fairly well with me without words—even without noticeable gestures. There was no question in this case. The slight tick in her lips told me. I said, "I'd say one day. Not more."

The PM said to the room in general, "Wait and see if we can push it for a couple of days?"

The SM said, "What would it gain us to disappoint Kali right away?"

The PM said to me, "You two go down and talk when you have to; keep Kali off balance. Give us as much time as you can to get ready to destroy our history."

Sandy and I went down to our office. We arrived and I shook my head. We sat. There was a call that showed up on my tablet. It was a collect call from Kali. Sandy reached out and put her hand over mine. No words were necessary. I nodded. The voice that I'd only heard briefly once before came over the speaker. "You're not going to let us have access to the Library are you?"

I didn't say anything. Sandy's hand tightened around mine. That was the last that I heard from Kali. Ten or so seconds later the emergency alarm blared. Then an announcement sounded. "There was a fusion explosion on the coast of Continent Alpha. If you live downwind from the blast, evacuate immediately. The resulting seismic waves will be of magnitude fifteen. Check the local seismic forecast and evacuate all buildings that are not capable of withstanding the shock. If you live on a coastline, check the local tsunami forecast, and evacuate as appropriate."

It was all good advice. I wondered how many had been killed by direct blast, etc. Sandy gave me a minute to absorb the shock and said, "We are not downwind from the blast. This building will stand the shock. The margin of safety is two magnitudes. We don't live on a coast. We're safe. For now." She still was holding my hand.

I said, "Call the PM's office."

I didn't finish the thought before Sandy said, "We got an email from the office of the PM. We're to evacuate to . . ." A tear appeared on a her cheek. "It's just you."

I was sitting in my new temporary office. I'd been there for a little over an hour when the call came through from the PM. It was a conference call. Everyone was on the call. The PM spoke. "They have threatened to continue this war. The next step will be another strike. That would fall just short of killing everyone on the planet. We've managed to hold the casualties to less than five percent. That has cut our resources for rescuing people to the limit. The next would kill another twenty percent. We're done."

I couldn't believe my ears. "You can't do that."

"The weapons didn't get off the ground. We can't stop them from accessing the library. All we can do is hope that he doesn't figure out how to destroy our galaxy. If the Tecumseh gets here in time to destroy the Library, we will probably all die in the battle that ensues. It will arrive within a day or two."

I said, "There's nothing I can do, is there?"

"I don't think so. But we won't make any rash assumptions."

I nodded and said, "Right."

Well, there was something I could do. I made a call to Sandy. It was the first video call I'd been on in quite a while. It was a nice change. She smiled when she saw me. She asked, "What can I do?"

"Come here." She started to object. I simply said, "It doesn't matter any more. Come here."

Her smile actually became broad, "Yes, sir."

I said, "We're burning our bridges behind us here. It will either be OK or we're dead. So, why don't we make it, 'Yes, dear.'"

She said, "Yes, dear."

That was the end of Buffet's statement. He looked over to Spock and said, "You're up."

Spock's Story

Spock said, "It must be time for a biology break. You normally have three meals a day. Why don't you have a meal. Then you can return if you want to continue before the end of the day."

We all looked at each other and I got appointed to decide. "We will have a meal. I think we've had enough to chew on for the day. We'll be better taking this up tomorrow." No one objected. We returned to our ship. I'd begun thinking of it as "our" ship sometime during the day. The Brahmses fixed the meal. It was vegetable beef stew, cornbread, and chocolate brownies for desert. I dialed up some ice cream for my brownie.

The discussion around the dinner table was pointed. Aurora asked, "What in the world are we doing here? It seems darn hopeless." No one had an answer. She turned to Minns. "Don't you have an idea?"

Minns simply said, "Not yet."

Ginny exclaimed, "Not yet! How can you not have any ideas! You got us here." Minns shrugged. That was pretty much the end of conversation other than "pass the pepper."

After cleaning up, we took to suggesting things to do while we waited. The BG said, "Let's go back and hear Spock's story."

Everyone else looked at him as though he were crazy. Ginny asked me, "Does that Kindle thingee of yours have any crossword puzzles in it?"

I thought it did. I got it out and found a book that I'd downloaded a long time before this trip that had a couple of hundred pages of them from the New York Times. I said, "Sure. Do you want to work on one?"

She said, "Yes. Let's make it a game that we can all play. We start working the puzzle. Each player gets a clue to solve, one at a time. We do all the Across ones first. Then we do the Down ones. If a player can't solve it, the next player gets a shot at it and so on until everyone has had a chance. Then we move on to the next. Once we've gone through all the clues, if there are still unsolved ones, we go back and start over until the puzzle is solved or we're all stuck. The one with the most right wins."

I objected, "If Minns plays, he'll get all of his right. It won't be fair."

Minns said, "I'm not any better at crosswords than any of the rest of you. I'm only good at the things that . . . well, have to be done for the common good."

Ginny scoffed. "Says you now."

No one else objected, so we started. After a couple of rounds through all the clues, there were a lot of unsolved ones. We improvised. We decided that it was all right to look up one clue answer at a time and go again. By the end, we'd looked up five words and the winner was Aurora. By then, we were ready for sleep.

When Ginny and I were ready for bed, she just took me in her arms and said, "Let's just sleep tonight. I'm too tired even for spoon." I didn't argue.

The next morning, we were out of the ship in a hurry. In our Conference Room, Spock started the meeting abruptly. "There's not a lot to add."

□

After I left the meeting to obtain locations of library server facilities, I caught up with The Armed Defense Head. I had a request for him. I asked, "After you get the military moving to prepare to destroy our library facilities, I want to talk with you about defense strategies." He agreed.

Later that day, we met—after the attack—in his office. He was having a working lunch. He was straight-forward. "You'd better have a damn good idea. Even if all the military does is rescue, we're up to the crowns of our heads."

I said, "Would you like to be able to track FTL ships from behind?"

He leaned back and stopped eating to think. "From how far away?"

"It's only a hypothesis, but I'd think long after the ship has left the area."

He closed his eyes, and his lips moved silently. Then he said, "That would be something. You think we can do that?"

It was a statement—not a question. I nodded. He smiled. He leaned forward and said, "We're up to our ears and will be for a while. As soon as it cools down—if we're still alive—I'll send you to a weapons research facility that we have. For now, keep developing your idea as much as possible. Now, get out and go volunteer or something."

I went out and worked the idea that I had.

Each day, I monitored reports from the library system of who had accessed it and what information had been taken. A clear pattern arose. The first day, there was an unauthorized access of huge amounts of data that involved quark confinement, inflatons, anti-inflatons, inflation in the early universe, high Z nuclei, and many other topics. As the days went by, there were follow-up inquiries that went into other areas.

When the Tecumseh arrived, there was a discussion in the cabinet about whether they should vaporize our libraries. On one side was the PM and the CFO. The rest of the cabinet didn't want to destroy it.

What the CFO said is a good representation of the arguments for destruction of the library system. What the Armed Forces Head said was a good representation of the case against. If it were presented as a debate, it would have gone like this:

The CFO said, "We know that the Kali researchers continue to plumb our database. They must be stopped now while there is still time."

The Armed Forces Head said, "They already have the key information that they need. To destroy the database would be to put an end to our society needlessly. We don't know that the information they are gaining now will substantially change the future!"

The CFO said, "We were already agreed to destroy our library."

The Armed Forces Head said, "That was old news. Things are different now."

Then I said something that tipped the scales. "We don't have a way to track FTL ships, so when they leave, we can't do anything to stop them."

The CFO asked, "So?"

"I think I know a way to track them. It will take some time and a dedicated team, but if we succeed, we can track Kali down and maybe stop him."

The PM said, "Come on. We couldn't stop him on our home ground with all our resources. What makes you think you could do that on neutral location?"

"It was easy for him to attack us, because we couldn't track him effectively. I bet that he doesn't have a way to track us. We will have turned the tables on him. Defense against FTL ships is nearly impossible. If we are on the attack, he'll be on the defensive."

That quieted the room. The PM asked, "What do you need to build this tracking capability?"

I smiled. "For one thing, I need our library." The PM had been standing in his excitement. That caused him to drop into his chair, close his eyes, and think. After a bit, he said, "You win. What do you need?"

I had thought this through already. I answered directly, "I need a deep-space facility. We have at least one that is still intact – the Asgard. I need connection to the library. I need a team of physicists and engineers and maybe a few mathematicians sprinkled through. I need incidental resources that won't become clear until I begin."

Resignedly, the PM said, "Yes. Yes. Name who you want."

"I want the CFO. He needs to be present at the facility. He has to have all the authority that he has now. I want the best ship's captain that we have."

The PM sighed, "Yes, you can have Ahab from the Tecumseh. What else? Do you want the Armed Forces Head?"

I shook my head. "No. There will be others."

The PM said, "Well, get up there right now with your team."

I said, "As far as we know, our enemy doesn't know about Asgard. Let's keep it that way by not sending anything up there until Kali has left the system for sure."

The PM shrugged. "Why don't you just take the whole cabinet with you."

I scoffed. "You'd just get in the way."

The CFO said, "Well, I'm not going without my assistant."

It took another week before Kali's ship left our system. We immediately transferred operations to Asgard. It wasn't that we weren't working while on the ground. We were using the library system to research, plan, and design. When we arrived, I took control of the fabrication facilities. We had nearly complete plans for a proof of principal device.

The first day, I met with the Tecumseh's chief engineer, whom I would have chosen to head the engineering team even if he weren't already on Asgard. We had a one-on-one meeting to discuss what I wanted. He asked, "OK. I can tell from the plans what you want us to build. The specs are crazy. Maybe we can do it, and maybe we can't. It would help to know what it's for."

I stood agape. Then I answered him. "Isn't it obvious?"

"Well, not exactly. I mean. I know what the components are. You want four gamma-ray lasers that operate in the one pico-meter range. That's . . ." He thought a moment and then said, "Yes. that's possible. You want it to be stable to one part in ten to the eighteenth. Now, laddie, you're starting to tread on the outer edge of miraculous. You want semi-transparent mirrors for those gamma-rays. Now, you've stepped over into the impossible. Have you got any ideas about how you make those?"

I looked down at my feet for inspiration. "You know what the device is, don't you?"

He was beginning to be a bit touchy. "Of course, I do, you nitwit. You're building a gamma-ray interferometer. What are you going to do with that, hmmm?"

I started to speak, and then his eyes narrowed, and his mouth opened wide. He said, "You're going to measure the geometry of space with that. It would make a standard gravity wave detector look like a wooden yard-stick."

I nodded.

He went on. "With that, you could see where an inflaton/anti-inflaton drive has traveled."

I added, "And where it's going and how fast."

He scratched an ear and said with a satisfied smile on his face. "You could follow one damn rat-bastard into hell."

I simply said, "Something like that."

⊞

Then we got a message from Mr. Minns. It seemed nothing less than mirac-ulous. It was so much so that we had an impromptu cabinet meeting to try to decide what to do.

The PM convened the meeting and asked THE question, "Should we allow this Minns to come here? What are the dangers? What are the advan-tages? I am inclined to dedicate a small ship to picking him up and bring-ing him here."

I said, "Think about it. A world that barely has space travel is going to be capable of helping us against those . . . wholesale merchants of death. They're not sending a fleet. They're not sending a single ship. They're sending some kind of magician who knows we have a problem. If he can help us, he might be worse than this Kali."

The Armed Forces Head sneered. "How could he be worse than Kali?"

The PM stared at the images of the cabinet on his video screen. No one had further comments. How could they? What we'd said really covered it all despite how brief the discussion had been. The PM waited a good while just to be sure. Then, he went around the virtual table polling each one. "Finance. What say you?"

The CFO took a deep breath. "The only downside that I can see is the diversion of the resources to pick up this person. Is he worth even that

262

small effort. On the other hand, we don't have anything better to do with that single ship, do we? Go."

No one said anything. The PM turned to me, "Science?"

I said, "I think we can't afford to turn down any offer of help. Go."

"Military?"

He threw his hands in the air. "We're in hell. Even if the guy just lifts us to Purgatory, we're better off. Go."

"Culture?"

"Go."

"Education?"

"Go."

"Medical?"

"Go."

The Armed Forces Head said, "OK. Is that it?"

The PM said, "I've not given the word yet." There was a pause. Then he said, "Go."

The Head of Military asked, "What about precautions?"

The PM asked, "What do you suggest?"

"Two ships—not one. One for our friend. One to operate the ship remotely."

I said, "We make sure that the ship for our friend can't be operated by him." The Head of Military agreed.

"Also, we take them to Asgard." That was said by Head of Culture.

The PM asked, "What is that?"

Culture smiled—the first that I'd seen in that sort of meeting in a long time. He then said, "I just thought it would be appropriate to the situation. It comes from the world that Minns is coming from. It refers to the mythical realm of the Norse Gods—the hardest realm to approach. I thought that might be a good name for the research asteroid where we're working on the tracking technique."

The PM said, "Right. Do it. Quickly. Sure, rename it Asgard.

"Now, how is the tracking hardware coming?"

I dialed up the chief engineer. "I need you to join this conference call with the cabinet."

He acknowledged the call and set up his tablet to join the conference. When he was on he asked, "What's up?"

I said, "The PM wants to know how the program is going."

"Well, sure. Now. Here's the thing. We've got a prototype working."

The PM asked, "So, you're ready to outfit a ship with it?"

"Wo, wo, wo. I said we had a prototype. It's large. It's larger than most ships. We've only tested that it does basic functions. It generates the proper

263

gamma-rays. The semi-reflective mirrors are semi-reflective. Sort of. The detectors have the necessary resolution—at least some of the time. We haven't even taken it into space and tried it out."

There was another long pause. I said, "Well, we'll never finish if we don't get back to work."

The PM said, "I sure hope we don't have any more business." No one said anything, so we were adjourned.

Our Role

Spock said, "That brings you up to date. Questions."

I said, "Well, probably only a couple of dozen. Let's start with the big ones first. What do you think this Kali is actually going to do with the information he stole from you?"

Spock replied, "Well. He was not very explicit about what he was going to do, but the questions that he asked were clear. He was going to build a weapon. He already had in his possession a weapon that could level a continent, reduce a planet to a cinder, even cause a star to go nova. He was looking for something bigger.

"Was he just trying to turn the Milky Way galaxy into the largest quasar ever? Or did he really want to bring about Kaliyuga—the end of Time and the beginning of a new Universe? From our perspective, does it matter?"

Ginny asked, "If he set off his doomsday machine how long would it take before the Earth was gone?"

Spock sighed. "I don't know. You could make an argument for three possibilities.

"One: He just wants to kill everyone in our galaxy and nearby galaxies by a gigantic supernova that is millions of time larger than the largest ever observed and create a black hole that is ten times larger than the most massive black hole ever observed. The shock wave of destruction would move at the speed of light and would reach our part of space in about 30,000 years.

"Two: If he really wants to create a "Big Crunch" followed by a "Big Bang", one possible rate of speed for the shock wave to reach us out here in the outskirts of the galaxy—30 light years per second—would reach us in less than an hour.

"Three: The theorists say that a higher number is correct, 3000 light years per second. Even if the thing is set off at the other side of the galaxy, it would take less than a minute to reach you."

That sobering thought didn't stop the BG from commenting, "If he's out to destroy the universe, it would take take anywhere from a year to as much as a hundred years. Of course, if he were considerate enough to set it off as far away as possible, it might not reach us for a hundred years. We'd all be dead of other causes."

Aurora said, "Don't try too hard to make us feel good."

Spock probably thought he was being consoling when he said, "Well, whether sooner or later, we'd never know it when the shock wave hit." With that, Ginny gasped and turned away.

Minns was the first to recover from the multiple shocks we'd had. He said, "We need to find Kali and stop him."

I said, "Well, finally, we know what you're here to do. Tell us your plan."

Minns didn't blink an eye when he said, "You just heard it."

Spock, who had exhibited amazing equanimity throughout the last two days, finally seemed to hit the end of his seemingly unlimited quantity of calm. "That's it. When you said that you could help us, I thought you had something more in mind than what is obvious to everyone around this table."

He was not disturbed in the slightest. "You're right. It is obvious. We will do it."

I began to recall everything I knew about Minns. I stood and started to pace. "You don't know Minns like we do. If he says that he's going to do something, you should take him seriously. He frequently doesn't have a detailed plan. He seems to improvise, but our experience with him is that he constantly pulls rabbits out of his hat." I looked to the Brahmses for confirmation. They just stared blankly.

Aurora did say, "What Wendt just said has been true." She said it in such a deadpan way that I wondered if she even believed it herself but was just trying to cheer us up.

Spock went on. "Well, the simple plan is not quite so crazy as it sounds. Mr. Scott, our chief engineer has a team that has been out doing field trials of his latest version of a tracking device. You'd probably call it a beta test. With luck, we'll be ready to start outfitting all ships with the device within a few days."

Minns nodded, "Good. Our ship needs to be the first. We'll leave to pursue Kali as soon as it's ready."

Everyone was shocked. The silence was palpable. Spock said, "What do you plan to do when you catch up with him?"

The answer was simple to the point of being ludicrous. He simply said, "We'll stop him."

Spock said, "We'll have to pick a ship and crew to help."

Minns said, "I already have my ship and crew."

That was so laughable that I laughed. I said, "Even though we've only reached lunch time, it's been a long day. Let's go back to the ship, have lunch, and take a nap."

No one objected. We left.

After we'd arrived and removed our suits, we started lunch. No one was very hungry. The menu for lunch was soup and salad. We all left soup in the bowl and salad uneaten. Even before we cleaned up, I went after the T. Rex in the room. "Let's have this out, Minns. We all know that you never revealed—maybe never knew what your next step was back in the day. OK. I accept that."

I stood and began pacing. He had just put me, Ginny, and the Brahmses in a position where we could be partly responsible for the end of the universe or at least the end of life in our galaxy. I was trying to find words strong enough for my anger and feelings of betrayal. "You . . . you . . . You got us to go along on this quixotic quest utterly unprepared. If we were just talking about the damn Ghosts conquering another race or the destruction of a planet or . . . or . . . or a star going nova and incinerating every planet . . . If that were all we were talking about, I could have forgiven you, but this is the entire universe. If we screw up, if we didn't bring enough people or the right people, if we could have done something more, but didn't . . . We'd be guilty of criminal negligence. We'd be the stupidest, most evil, most . . . Oh, I don't know." I had run out of things to say. I got my breath and said, "Well, say something. Say anything."

He looked me in the eye and said, "If I said something, would it make any difference?"

I leaned over the table and said, "Take that stupid look off your face and put something else in its place that shows some remorse!"

I tried another tack. "Why in the world didn't you bring some more firepower with you? Why not bring Renaldo or Connover or . . ." I struggled to remember the name of the fourth of them and then thought of something better. "For God's sake, what about those kids that you sent off to some distant planet or the others who were already there when they arrived. If we had a few of them, you could have finished Kali off without breaking stride."

Minns just sat.

Just then, the BG raised a hand almost timidly and said, "Maybe what we've got—who we've got—is all we'll need."

I looked at the two of them one at a time back and forth and tried to stomp off to my cabin. It wasn't easy. The flooring was a sort of rubbery material that was a little springy. At least, I could slam the door of the cabin behind me.

I heard the door open behind me. I was so disturbed that I couldn't sit. Someone put a hand on my shoulder. Then she said, "Let's sit on the bunk." We did. She sobbed.

I thought she'd come to soothe me. I put my arm around her and after a minute said, "I think I've said everything that I can."

We sat that way for a while. Her sobbing relented, and she began speaking. At first, it was just fragments of sentences broken by tears. I thought I heard her say, "Harry." Then her words started to be whole thoughts.

"I'll never see George again." She took a deep breath. "I'll never see Da again." There were more tears. "Mum." She broke into something that was almost a wail. She sniffed back a few tears. "I'll never make love again." Her tears returned in force. Her hand wormed its way into mine. I caressed her side. How I wished that I could relieve her grief. There were no words.

I started to say, "It will be OK." The words died in my mouth. That would have been the grossest lie. There was nothing that was going to be OK out of this situation. We were all going to be witnesses to the end of the universe. What I did say was, "This is going to be terrible."

Somehow those words seemed to release something in both of us. My caress, that I'd never stopped, moved down her side to her hips. She turned her head to me and opened her mouth but not to speak. Her mouth smothered any words that might have been forming in my throat. She was still wearing the bottom part of her space suit. I struggled to get it off. Even with her help, it seemed to be impossible with just four hands. Under that was a pair of jeans. Under that were her panties. Under that was our goal. I don't know at what point my jeans and boxers had come off. I didn't care in the least.

It was not the most wonderful sex I'd ever had. It was the most satisfying. I wanted to blot out the end of everything and everyone that I loved. That did it for the moment. We lay in each others arms for a while and then I took her again. This time, we used muscle memory from years before. It was close to the most wonderful sex I'd ever had. It was not satisfying. We finished leaving me wanting more—wanting somehow to go back to those times years before when the weight of all of creation was not on our shoulders.

Then we napped. Actually, it was more like meditation in a completely relaxed body. I could think about what was coming without fear. I didn't have a way to save anyone. I just wasn't afraid.

Eventually, Ginny short of shrugged her shoulders and said, "I'm hungry." I glanced at my wrist and said, "We could get something to eat even though it's not exactly dinner time."

We rolled out of the bunk and started arranging our clothes. She ran a brush through her hair a couple of times. I think neither of us were anxious for what we would face when we opened the door.

Outside, the three were seated around the dinner table. They were eating sandwiches. Aurora said, "Looks like you got a nap in. Good idea. Nicky and I did, too." She colored a bit, and then she added, "There are plenty of sandwiches. Go ahead and dig in."

After dinner we played cards for a bit. The BG went into the Bridge of the little ship, saying, "I want to see if I can bring up a view of the exterior of the asteroid."

□

The next day, we got notification that the engineering staff was going to have to make some changes to the interior hardware of the ship to accommodate the new tracking hardware. We would have to don spacesuits and let the engineers replace our air with their air.

Ginny and I helped each other on with our suits. There was a lot more skin contact than was strictly necessary for the operation. We were especially careful when putting on the leggings part of our suit and the helmets. We left our cabin and found the rest donning their suits in the Conference Room. No one said anything.

An engineer asked for permission to enter. We cycled both airlock doors open and stood back as our air whooshed out of the airlock. The engineer attached a hose to a port on the outside of the ship. Then he asked if we wanted to leave the ship while they worked. The BG quickly said, "We want to stay." The engineer shrugged and cycled the lock closed. He then opened a valve that let his atmosphere fill the ship. He opened his suit up and took off the arm sections and the helmet. Then he opened up the main console on the Bridge. He had a small toolbox. We watched him remove a cable, attach it to some kind of junction box, attach another cable that seemed to be loose to it. Then he attached it where it had been. There were a couple of further changes that he made. Then he put the console back together. He flicked a couple of switches, and the console lit up. He made a couple of adjustments on a console. Then he flipped the switches again. He was finished.

269

The next day, we were summoned to a meeting—same place, same time as before. This time, it was Ahab, Spock, and somebody who was identified as military. We decided that a good nickname for him would be Grant. Ahab started the meeting.

"The tracker is working. We've installed it on my ship and your ship. We've already identified the original direction that Kali took. We want to get going as quickly as possible. We've got our ship prepped. We'll have armaments on yours shortly. We'll bring your ship on-board ours so that you can keep your native atmosphere."

I was ready to go. Well, no. I wasn't ready to go. I wasn't really anxious to be running down the guy who could end the universe and had made mince meat of the PAK home world. The thing was that it was inevitable, so I had to go. I was nodding all along.

Then, something went wrong. Minns said in that damn irritating reasonable voice of his, "We're going by ourselves."

The PAK have very good hearing and excellent reflexes and are very quick on the uptake. None of them blinked an eye. Instead they all said, "You're coming with us. Tomorrow. We're loading up your ship right now."

Minns said, "Very well. We'll leave in two days. You won't."

Spock stared at him very long. No one said anything. Then, Spock said, "You're very sure of that?"

Minns didn't say anything. I looked at one and then the other. Then I said, "I'd not be so sure that he's not right. You know how he got here."

Spock nodded and said, "I think we're done here. We don't need anything from them other than to be in their ship tomorrow. We can discuss strategy once we're in space."

We went back to our ship. We all looked for something to do. I got out my Kindle and started to look for something to read. Someone poked me in the back of my neck. She then whispered in my ear, "Fancy a nap, hmmm?"

I nodded. Once in our cabin, we forgot our problems for a while. Then she whispered in my ear, "What do you think is going on?"

"You don't know Minns. He has some sort of Zen awareness thing. He picks up all sorts of microscopic clues and stitches them together with some intuition and you can pretty much depend on them as gospel."

"So you think that somehow, these PAK are going to let us go on our own? I sure wouldn't."

I was distracted for a while as someone nibbled on my ear. When she'd finished provoking a reaction from me, I said, "Yes, I don't have the foggiest how he's going to manage it, but we're going on our own, the day after tomorrow."

That night as we slept in each other's arms a deep shudder rumbled through the ship. I said, "Dress and on with your suit." She followed directions and was suited up before I was. We kissed just before we both donned our helmets.

Back in Space

The intercom sounded and an announcement followed. "All personnel: The station is under attack by unidentified forces. All personnel to their battle stations. All non-essential personnel remain sheltered in place."

I shook my head and asked the rhetorical question, "Are we non-essential personnel."

Minns said, "Mr. Brahms, we need to have a conference on the Bridge."

I suddenly realized that Ginny was next me. I took her hand. She asked me, "Is this the end?"

I squeezed her hand and said, "I don't know. Could be."

She asked, "What are Minns and Brahms doing?"

I whispered, "Don't ask. I think it's better the fewer people who know."

That day, the two of them were working on the small Bridge continuously. We brought them in sandwiches and fruit cups several times through the day. In the mean time, there were explosions that sent shock waves throughout the asteroid and our ship. I decided to go outside to see if I could learn anything from what was going on in the docking areas.

I did. Half a dozen times during the day, the iris of the inner lock would open revealing a glimpse of the outside. Each time, a powerful laser at the opposite end of the dock fired down the axis of the docking area and out through the open irises. Usually, it hit something. Following closely behind a ship exploded out. There were explosions that I saw out the open iris until it closed.

I came back in for dinner. Minns and Brahms joined us for that meal. I told everyone about the apparent battle going on outside. I finished by saying, "Well, you were right about one thing, Minns. We're not leaving today."

He said, "I think we'll have sufficient control of this ship to leave sometime early tomorrow."

Ginny asked, "Without Ahab and his ship?"

Minns said, "Definitely."

Aurora asked, "Should we try to sleep tonight?"

The BG said, "Get as much as you can manage, but be ready to leave at a moment's notice. We'll be flying through a barrage when we do."

After we cleaned up, the BG and Minns returned to the Control Room. We sat around the for a little while talking about the end of the world. After that conversation quickly wound down, we just sat for a while. I finally said, "Let's just call it a night."

In our cabin, we kissed and sat on the bunk for a while. Neither of us wanted to make love, but we did want to lie in the bunk holding each other. After a while we fell asleep.

□

The ship was ready to fly. I was seated in the co-pilot seat. Minns was beside me in the pilot's seat. I was where I was because I'd used a similar ship's weapon system once before. Everyone else was back in their cabins strapped into their bunks. Minns was briefing me before the take-off. "We're likely to have missiles launched against us. Our only defense is evasive maneuvers and decoys. We'll use the ship's offensive missiles as decoys. Their FTL drive will look like our ship's drive. With luck, we'll escape."

I looked at the weapons console. There were ten missiles available. The launch controls were pretty clear. I nodded. Then we moved away from our dock, rotated, and saw, in our forward-looking monitor, the iris open. There was a brief view of the dark of space. Then there was a flash of light that filled the forward view. Minns commented, "There was a missile just outside that the laser vaporized." As he said that, the interior of the asteroid disappeared and we were surrounded by the black of space.

The ship rotated and changed direction rapidly. The gravity couldn't compensate quickly enough to keep us from feeling the maneuver. Minns twisted the ship around again and said, "Fire a decoy." I couldn't do that immediately, because the firing control system wanted a target. Minns said, "Override fire control."

I found the override and fired the missile. Minns swivelled the ship around the same direction as the missile went. We saw a flash. I guess the enemy missile hit its mark. We sustained our course for almost a minute. Then Minns said, "Fire." There was no mis-step with fire control. The missile launched immediately. We didn't see a flash. I don't know if it was a miss or not. Almost immediately, we slewed sharply at a large angle. I instinctively fired before Minns said a word. We saw the flash.

There were a series of swift turns and the occasional decoy fired. We were down to three decoy missiles left. I said, "We've got to get out of here. We're almost out of . . ." At that moment there was a sharp shudder that went through the ship and someone was screaming. "Up. Damn you, get up!"

Ginny was shaking me, saying, "Come on. You've got to get up. You're having a nightmare."

I groggily mumbled, "OK. OK. I'm trying." I found that I had rolled over in my sleep so that I was wedging Ginny against the cabin wall."

She said, "It's about time. You were having a nightmare."

I shook my head as I rolled out of bed and thudded to the deck. "Sorry. Sorry. Right." I glanced at my watch. It was 5:14 AM. She muscled past me and said, "I'm up. If you want to catch a little more sleep, go back to bed. I'm dressing and going out to the galley."

"I think I will."

She asked, "What were you dreaming?"

"Oh, just that we were leaving the base and were under attack from whoever is out there."

She refused to let me get some more sleep. She said, "Who do you think it is?"

I was pretty much awake, so I rose shakily and started dressing. She asked, "I thought you were going to catch some more sleep?"

"Well, someone keeps talking to me and preventing me from doing that."

She showed no signs of remorse. I went on. "Think about it. I think there's only one reasonable candidate."

She narrowed her eyes as she stared at me. "You don't mean Kali?"

I scoffed, "Not Kali himself. I suspect that he left some sort of automated satellites or maybe a couple of small ships that were keeping an eye on the PAK. If anything suspicious were happening, they'd take action."

"But why keep an eye on the PAK?"

274

I finished dressing and started suiting up. Ginny asked, "I suppose we should suit up?" She started doing the same.

I said, "The PAK may be the only ones who know about Kali's plans. We're the only ones who represent a threat to him." I couldn't help chuckling.

She asked, "What?"

"Oh, it's kind of ironic that I'm thinking of the PAK as 'us'." She chuckled too. We had both gotten to the point that we were suited up except for donning helmets. She put her arms around me. I kissed her.

She said, "Help me with my hair." I helped her get her hair stuffed into the spacesuit. She asked, "Why didn't they attack sooner?"

"I think they noticed us when we entered the system. They probably tracked us to this asteroid, but they were waiting for re-enforcements to arrive to attack."

She nodded, causing some of her hair to escape from the spacesuit. We weren't really in a hurry. I kissed her again just before we both put our helmets on. She used the *Imperturbable* spell and whispered in my ear, "I love you." I nodded in response.

We finished putting the helmets on, and the seal hissed closed. The electronics activated, the heads-up display appeared, the suit radio was on. From here on out, everything we whispered would be heard by everyone in the ship and probably in the base who were wearing spacesuits.

We went out into the common area. Minns and Brahms were sitting at the table drinking coffee. Brahms said, "We're prepared to leave any time."

Ginny asked, "Are we waiting for anything?"

Minns said, "There's a lull in the battle. When it hots up would be a good time to go." Somehow I was kind of hoping that wouldn't be soon. Ginny looked like she might be having the same thought.

She asked, "Should we get Aurora up and make sure she's in a suit?"

Minns shook his head and said, "I think the fighting won't resume for a few hours. Nicholas and I will get some sleep—in our suits. You might want to do the same."

I admitted that we were pretty thoroughly awake.

⌑

It was actually in the early afternoon when another barrage began. Minns was out of his cabin almost instantly. The Brahmses were not far behind. Minns said, "Nicholas and I will take the controls. Everyone else should just stay in the Conference Room. We'll keep you up to date as much as we can."

275

They entered the Bridge and closed the hatch behind them. Ginny asked me, "Is this much like your dream?"

Aurora looked the question at me. I answered them both. "I had a dream last night. We flew out of the asteroid and then were attacked. The answer is, 'No, my dream was very different. I was on the Bridge.'"

Aurora said, "I have a bad feeling about that. In my experience dreams like that come out of more than just the subconscious of the dreamer."

I shrugged. "To quote Minns, 'Would it help to know?'"

Aurora said, "It would help me feel better to know."

Just then, the intercom came on. I recognized Minns voice asking, "Flight control, Ship 4432 requesting permission to depart."

A cool voice responded, "Permission denied. Please prepare to be boarded."

Minns said, "Permission denied. Open the iris gate in ten seconds, or we will fly through it."

Ginny asked, "Can we do that?"

I said, "We can fly into it. Whether we can fly through or not, I can't say."

The voice then said, "Permission granted." With that we felt the ship rotate to align with the passage out. Then we accelerated. There was no collision."

Minns came on the intercom. "We've just exited the asteroid. We will be cruising in the system for several days before exiting the system."

Aurora asked, "What's going on?"

Minns said, "We'll discuss details within an hour."

It was a very quiet hour. Somehow everyone had the idea that silence was absolutely essential. The BG came out. He said, "Minns is watching the store while I give you the low-down on the plan for the next couple of days. Here's the good news/bad news:

"Good news: we got out with our lives. More good news: it's unlikely that anyone will find us until we start using the FTL.

"Now for bad news: we've got to use the FTL sometime. The current plan is to use the sublight drive at a very low level initially and gradually increase it as we get further away from the asteroid. When we're confident that nobody is watching, we'll switch to FTL."

Aurora asked, "What if Kali's people find us?"

The BG said, "That's why we have to have a constant watch so that we can move if they do find us."

Ginny asked, "Everyone?"

"Yes."

"You're going to have to give us a demo of what to do if we are spotted."

The BG agreed. He had us crowd into the Bridge and then began explaining. "If the ship detects anything close by going FTL, there will be a verbal alert." He then touched a control on the weapon monitor. That opened a little control box. One button in it was labeled "Demo." He pushed it. A siren sounded and a voice that sounded a lot like the BG's said, "FTL Detection."

Aurora said, "How likely is it that we'll detect FTL ships coming from behind?"

Minns said, "Since anyone would have to slow down to rendezvous with us and missiles would have to go sub-light to be sure to hit us, there's a good chance that we can detect the Cherenkov radiation from them before they arrive."

Aurora scoffed. "Great. What do we do then? Say our prayers?"

Minns pointed at a button on the weapons monitor. "You push that. It throws the ship into a random series of high acceleration maneuvers that will keep us safe for a while. Maybe we can escape with our lives."

Ginny nodded. "A good idea."

We went back into the Conference Room where the BG put together a schedule to watch the FTL detector. I asked, "I don't quite understand it. Don't we want the quickest possible reaction? Surely, once the detector goes off, automatically starting evasive maneuvers surely is better than depending on human reflexes."

The BG said, "Not really. The human reaction time is an advantage, really. You see the detector was kludged together in a hurry. I don't trust it fully. If it is triggered accidentally, I want a little time to be sure that it's not a fluke."

That was encouraging. The schedule let Ginny and me get some sleep in together. That first night was another nail-biter. Ginny was very tense. She held me close and whispered in my ear, "Tell me this won't be our last night."

I wasn't completely sure that it wouldn't be, but I said with total assurance, "No, it won't be. As a matter of fact, let's put a little bet on it."

Ginny answered cautiously, "What kind of bet?"

"Oh, nothing serious. If it turns out to be the last night, I owe you a night where we do anything you want. Of course, if I win, you owe me." In response, she hit me on the shoulder, relaxed, and said, "You are such a moron." We kissed and dropped off to sleep.

It turned out that we had not spent our last night together. The next day, Ginny had the first watch and I the second. I spent most of the first watch in the co-pilot's seat. When the watch changed, we switched seats. We talked about old times during most of those watches. The future was so depressing that we didn't spend much time on it. The present was a decent topic for conversation but it didn't last very long. We'd talk about our delight in each other's company. That couldn't last very long. Then we were back to the past.

The past divided itself into two realms: Minerva and post-Minerva. Pre-Minerva was tricky. Ginny could talk about her various infatuations: Dean Thomas, Harry, and amazingly, me.

I knew it might be bad Karma, but I couldn't resist asking her, "Just when did you get interested in me?" I'd asked her that before, but the answer was always so satisfying that I couldn't keep away from it.

She put on a sort of thinking expression and opined, "Well, fascination with you was growing so slowly that it's hard to know, but . . ." At this point, the answer was usually different. This time, she said, "You remember when the Ghosts were running the show on Earth, and you were in the abandoned Ministry? I was controlling the operation from across the street."

"Of course."

"Well, by that time, I was definitely finding you hard to keep out of my mind completely. I'd not think about you for days on end. Then, something would happen to make me think of you. Suddenly, for a day or two I'd just be thinking about you all the time.

"Of course, I'd got to that state after the mission to France to find and recover Merlin's Sea. I saw you every day for weeks, and I began to understand why Minerva was in love with you. I started to think about you in romantic terms. I was so very foolish.

"You and Minerva had been an item so long without getting married that I assumed that you'd always be available. I know that it was crazy that I didn't tell you that I liked you. You'd think that it would be a snap for me. I've always been bold about all sorts of things. I guess I was just enjoying having a crush on you so much that I didn't want to take a chance of screwing things up by telling you.

"Then, damn you, you two got married at the end of that war. Who was ever to guess that it would happen?"

I knew that anything I said would be "wrong." I didn't want to admit how long it was after that that I fell for her. Of course, the real answer was

278

that I hadn't thought about her in romantic terms until she practically dragged me into bed with her after I'd decided to return to the States after Minerva's death.

What I actually said was, "You remember about Sally's wedding?"

She scoffed. "Sure, the Muggle bitch who was her Maid of Honor, who gave you that Dursley love potion. There was one more reason to hate Dursley."

I went on. "You spent all that time with her and me. It was becoming obvious that you didn't like her very much."

She exclaimed, "Didn't like her very much! I'd have turned her into a ferret if she hadn't been Sally's MOH. Even before she gave you that love potion, I knew that she was angling for you. The idea that she could get you away from Minerva, and I couldn't even get a smile out of you was just too much. I started making lists of dark magic spells that I could use on her. I think I must have come up with a dozen different ways to use the Imperious Curse to send her far, far away.

"You know, once I had lunch with my sister-in-law, Hermione. I almost got her to tell me in detail how she had obliviated her parents and sent them to Australia to keep them safe. I just might have done it too. Australia would have been just right for that bitch. I started to talk to Hermione about it."

I was a more than a little surprised and asked her, "What stopped you?"

She shrugged, "Oh, when I brought the topic up, Hermione was very embarrassed that I even knew about what happened. She begged me not to take her in for trial for doing such a horrible thing. I think she thought that as an Auror I was cleaning up old cases. What were you going to say?"

I was hoping that she would get so wound up in that incident that she'd forget why I brought it up. So, I had to go on. "I began to think that you were pretty when you flared up every now and then. Of course, it was amusing too that Haley didn't have the slightest idea that you were un-happy with her."

Ginny chuckled. "Yeh, she was so besotted with you that she was oblivious to everything else. You should have seen the expression on her face when I released you two from the *Petrificus* curse up in the Astron-omy Tower. When she saw it was I who'd frozen you two, you'd have thought that her best friend had tossed her off the Tower." She thought a second and said, "Sorry. It just occurred to me that that was how Dumble-dore died."

I must have had an expression on my face because I was thinking of that too.

She asked, "You thought I was pretty when I was furious?"

"Of course, it's your best quality. I should think about ways to enrage you more often so I can see you that way."

She shook her head in disbelief. "How would you do that?"

"Oh, for example, when we get back to Earth, I could give Jaimie a kiss that would knock her socks off."

Ginny's face contorted, and she seized my collar as though she were about to wring my neck. She said in a low, desperate tone, "If you do that . . ." Then her face changed and she said, "You were just trying to get that expression right now."

"It worked."

"If you ever do that again, I can't be held responsible for what I do."

She relaxed her grip on my collar and I promised, "I won't do it again. Life is too short for taking risks like that."

It turned out that while we were snogging before sleep, we were interrupted by a knock on our cabin door. I said, "Oh, hell! What is it?" I started disentangling from Ginny.

The answer was given by Aurora. "You two lot, just stay put. You don't need to come out or even . . . uh stop snuggling or whatever. Nicky says that Minns has given the OK to take off. He and Nicky will take the next two watches. We'll be far away before anything happens." She added softly, "I hope."

Ginny whispered in my ear. "If anything is likely to happen, it will be soon."

I nodded silently. She went on, "Maybe we'd better take opportunities when we can."

I replied with a caress and what followed.

To the End of the Galaxy

The next morning at breakfast everyone was around the table. The BG was speaking while we ate. "Over night, we've picked up the trail of Kali's ship. We've been following it long enough to establish where he's going— sort of. He was traveling at a very high inclination to the plain of the galaxy."

Ginny asked, "What does that mean?" She quickly added, "I know what the galaxy is and sort of what the plain of the galaxy is, but 'high inclination?'"

Aurora answered, "We didn't talk about that in astronomy class. The plain of the galaxy is extremely flat and contains most of the new bright stars. The higher the inclination, the further away from that plain you are. So, I have my own question now. Have you identified where we're going? If we were going somewhere in the galactic plain there would just be too many potential targets to narrow it down, but out of the plain of the galaxy, you might be able to do it."

The BG answered, "No. Here's the short story. There isn't a star within the most probable cone of travel in which the ship we're tracking is traveling. If you go to a larger, less likely cone, there are only a couple of stars that have planets in the habitable zone of their star. They might be the target, but I've got a hunch that they're not."

Ginny asked, "So, you don't have a hint of where we're going?"

"That's about it."

I asked, "How long will it take to get to the nearest possible star in your list?"

He had to think a minute and then said, "We're in the neighborhood of ten days."

I followed up with, "If we're not going to a star with habitable planets, do you have any idea where we could be going?"

He shrugged and said, "It could be someplace like a fleet base that's like the one we came from—an asteroid or maybe something constructed from scratch. We probably couldn't detect that until we were much less than a light year away. We could get there today or in a month."

That was something to chew on along with breakfast. Ginny nudged my knee with hers. She just repeated, "Could be a month."

Over the next week or so, nothing changed. We continued on our course. Every day or so, there was a revision to the possible star systems that we might be going to. By the end of that period, there was just one possible system left. It had no habitable planets. It had a couple of gas giant planets. Any moons they had were not in the habitable zone of the star. The BG finished that report with a cheery challenge. "Would anyone like to bet me that we're going there?"

There were nothing but glum looks and expressions of displeasure around the room. After I took my watch on the Bridge, Ginny joined me. She commented, "I don't know about the Brahmses, but I'm glad I have something to look forward to at night."

I agreed.

But she was still glum. She said, "Why don't you organize some sort of games like you claim you did on previous space journeys?"

I thought about it for a while. I think it's a measure of how well we were suited to each other that she waited patiently as I thought. Then I said, "You know, there's a different sense in the air on this trip. Except when we were facing imminent disaster, people were not depressed and were quite willing to have mildly entertaining pastimes. Even when we were facing disaster, it was only personal disaster. It wasn't all that you touch, all that you see, all that you taste, all you feel, all that you love, all that you hate, all you distrust, all you save, all that you give, all that you deal, all that you buy, beg, borrow or steal, all you create, all you destroy, all that you do, all that you say, all that you eat, everyone you meet (everyone you meet), all that you slight, everyone you fight, all that is now, all that is gone, all that's to come, and everything under the sun will be . . ."

She interrupted me at that point. "Wait a minute. I've heard that list before. Isn't that from a Weird Sister song?"

"No. It's from one of my favorite songs by Pink Floyd called *Eclipse*. Anyway, with all that and more at stake, it can be hard to get excited about a game of chess. Just wait, we may reach the point of boredom when we'll be ready for a chess tournament or something else."

She frowned. "So, we're stuck here watching the big board for something that almost certainly won't happen for days if not weeks?"

Then, an idea struck me. "You know what my Kindle looks like?"

"You mean your paper tablet?"

"No, my Kindle."

She was a bit uncertain but said, "I think so. What do you want me to do?"

"Go get it from our cabin."

"Where is it? I don't think I've seen it for a while."

"Oh, I'm sure it's in my duffel bag. Just go rummage around. I'm sure it's in there."

She took a sudden, deep breath. "Are you sure that you want me poking around in your stuff?"

I was surprised by the question. "Sure. Of course. There's nothing in there that I don't want you to see. Come to think of it, there's nothing that I own that I wouldn't want you to see."

She nodded slowly, saying with apparent wonder, "Really?"

It was my turn to wonder. "Of course. I'd trust you with everything that I have. You should know that. That's always true—always has been, always will be."

She stared at me, licking her lips. "Even letters from Jaimie?"

"Well. Not letters from her to me. I don't have any, but if I had written any to her, I'd trust you with them." With that, she walked off with a cer-tain spring in her step. I thought about that while she was gone. She didn't know me as well as I thought. I never said or wrote anything that I would be ashamed for anyone to see—especially Ginny.

She returned, all smiles, with the Kindle. She asked, "OK. What are we doing?"

I turned on the Kindle and opened one of the several crossword puzzle books that I had loaded on it. I suggested, "Let's work some cross-words cooperatively. Whoever is not on watch, will fill in answers, give clues, and help solve. Whoever is on watch will help solve clues." Ginny agreed and we started working them. It was a little rocky at first. Working out a procedure for the person who was not on duty was a little tricky. We were able to work two or three each joint shift that ran about ten hours.

Some examples of problems were that Ginny (and honestly I as well) didn't always say the clues clearly and didn't make clear which of the homonyms for a word was the one used in a clue. One particular bumpy patch almost ended our game.

I had been getting irritated at Ginny always giving the square on the puzzle that the clue matched up with. For example, Ginny would say, "Twenty-three down. Common printer format. We have blank 'D' blank."

I finally said, "I really don't want to hear what square we're working on. It just confuses me." Now, actually, if I'd had an eidetic memory the "23-Down" could have been useful. I don't have an eidetic memory. I was just frustrated every time she did that.

She used her huffy voice to say, "Well, pardon me. Don't you like playing with me?"

Eventually, she stopped giving the square location—most of the time. After several days we reached a sort of standard that worked pretty well. A typical dialog would be like this:

"The clue is 'bird that appears in the Arabian Nights." It's a three letter word that begins with 'R'. That's all we have."

I would answer, "Let's try 'ROK'."

"I don't think it's a 'K'. The letter next to it is an 'R'."

"OK. Then it's a 'C'."

Things went smoothly then. There was one exception to that smoothness that we never resolved. At first, we hardly ever finished a puzzle. There would be some clues that we just never could get. After a while we decided to have "hints." The person not on watch would pick a hard clue with lots of letters—our favorites were the phrases that completely crossed the puzzle from edge to edge. Then she'd find that word in the puzzle solution and fill it in. Having one extra letter in a word would let us solve lots of other clues. Those in turn would let us solve other tough clues. So, we could always solve puzzles that way. Once we had solved a puzzle, then we could score it. The scoring worked like this:

- Determine the number of clues.
- Determine the words that were wrong. Every word that was looked up was counted as wrong. If one letter in a word was wrong, both horizontal and vertical words were counted wrong.
- Determine the number of words that were right.
- Divide the number right by the number of clues. That was the percentage.

That was one rubric for getting a score. There was another one that I preferred. It worked like this:

- Determine the number of squares in the puzzle (kind of time consuming I admit).
- Determine the letters that were wrong. Every square in a word in which we already had some correct letters that was looked up was counted as wrong. If a word were misspelled, only the wrong letters were counted. So a misspelled word with one letter wrong was counted as only one wrong letter despite the fact that it was in two words.

At first we argued the virtues of each. For example, I would say, "Look, if a letter's wrong. That's all that's wrong. Why count both words wrong?"

"Oh, come on. You have two spelling errors, not one."

"OK. Then think about this. When you look up a twenty-five letter word where you've got two letters already, you only count that as one error even though, there are twenty-three letters and probably four or five words wrong."

We went on and on. Finally, I suggested calculating scores on puzzles that we'd finished by both methods just to see how each rubric worked. We did that for four puzzles. They all had scores in the 90's by both rubrics. We finally decided on Ginny's rubric, for two reasons. One was that she was just a pain in the ass when she was onto something—like an old dog that won't let go of a bone. The other was that it was pretty hard counting up squares in my rubric.

□

Round about the time that we came to that decision on scoring, Aurora made an announcement at lunch. "We just eliminated the last star that could have been on our course. We're in unknown territory now."

I commented, "Shit."

Aurora said, "Now, now, you're always so upbeat."

Ginny rubbed my shoulder and said nothing.

Aurora asked, "So, where do you think we're headed?"

The BG said, "Well, we're pretty sure that the ultimate goal for Kalli is to find a source of very high Z atoms. We know there's an island of stability for them around Z of 126. We also know that the best know source of them is neutron star collisions—either with black holes or other neutron stars. So, he should be looking for near future or near past collision candidates."

Aurora asked, "Is there a collision remnant on our path, do you think?"

The BG just shrugged.

Aurora said, "You know the probability of one of those remnants being this far off the galactic plain is minuscule."

The BG seemed miffed, "Prove it!"

Aurora rolled her eyes. "OK. First of all, even on Earth we've been detecting these collisions often enough to know that within a billion light years or so, they only happen . . . oh, say a half dozen times a year. Now, the half-life of those semi-stable high Z nuclei is only a couple of million years at most. So, the number of collisions within the last couple of million years is around ten million. That's ten million within one billion light years. The average distance between them is around five million light

285

years. There's probably only one or two within the local group of galaxies! You tell me what the chances of one being far away from the galactic plain is."

The BG sort of mumbled a bit and asked, "Does that mean that we're safe from his finding one?"

I said, "I don't think he'd be heading so far from his home if he didn't hope to find something out here."

Finally, Minns weighed in. "I think that whatever he's looking for, it's inside the outer edge of this galaxy."

Ginny said, "And that means that we have to keep our watches going. We were watching for our nearing a star. What are we looking for now?"

Minns answered, "The trail ending—in which case, he's close by and we need to be on alert. Or, it takes a drastic change in course. In that case we need to look for a destination at that point. So, we have to stop ourselves to search."

An idea occurred to me. "Why doesn't Kalli go to the black hole in the center of the galaxy. There must be tons of collisions there. He could just wait for one."

Aurora clucked her tongue and said, "Wendt, Wendt, Wendt. There are so many reasons. In the first place, there aren't that many collisions. The detritus from collisions can be observed even from Earth. There just hasn't been much of anything happening in the last million years or so. Second, a neutron star colliding with a black hole that size, just won't produce much of anything. It's got strong enough gravity itself that it won't be torn apart by tidal forces at the event horizon. It just disappears down the rabbit hole before anything happens."

I was feeling kind of stupid. I tried to resurrect my self respect with a different idea. "Well, our ship is run by inflatons. They're generated using these high Z nuclei. Why doesn't Kalli just get them the way we do?"

Aurora had an answer, of course. "We use very small quantities that are generated using inertial containment fusion reactors. The quantities are large enough to drive our ship or Kalli's. They're not enough to collapse the universe by many orders of magnitude."

Ginny asked, "What's an infernal confinement fuse reactor?"

The BG answered that. "Oh, it's an old idea to use lasers to squeeze fuel pellets down to densities high enough to create nuclear fusion. Someone had the brilliant idea to put pellets of uranium in them instead of Tritium. Some of the squashed uranium comes out as element 126 or its close cousins."

Ginny just squeaked, "Oh."

I whispered to her, "We can discuss that in bed tonight."

She hissed back, "Discuss that with yourself if that's the way you're going to use precious sack time!"

I suppose it's needless to say that there was no talk of Uranium pellets or inertial confinement.

□□

The next day we returned to the routine that we'd followed for a number of days. However, at lunch, Ginny asked, "I've heard of all those games you played when you were in space. Why don't we do that now?"

The BG said, "We have four who could play at one time. We could maybe do your Backstage Bridge, couldn't we Wendt?"

I answered, "That's Backalley Bridge as you surely know. But that is a good idea." I turned to Minns, "Do you know the rules of ordinary whist?"

He nodded. I went on, "Well Backalley has a bidding stage that's similar to ordinary whist. No suit is mentioned. That is determined randomly in the initial deal.

"The play of the hand is very similar with a few minor differences: You can't lead trump until it's already been played."

Minns nodded and said, "Interesting. So, only after someone has trumped another suit."

"Right. There are two additional cards that are always trump and are normally the jokers. They are labeled the 'Big' and the 'Little'."

Minns said, "The hierarchy is obvious. I suppose there are exceptions to these rules."

I smiled wanly, "Sadly, more exceptions than one might like. A normal game consists of 18 or 26 hands depending on . . ."

Minns interrupted, "Of course, you start with dealing a single card and each hand consists of one more card until you hit the maximum and then you . . ." At this point he interrupted himself. "I see from your reaction that you start with the maximum number of cards and work your way down hand by hand."

I said, "Usually. But your first guess sometimes happens as well."

Minns said, "Scoring is surely different from whist."

I shrugged. He went on. "Well, the best way to learn exceptions is to play a game. I'll observe and ask questions when necessary."

The four of us who knew the game played and Minns observed. At the end of the first half of the game, Minns said, "I think I've got it. I'm sure there are other very specialized exceptions to the rules of whist. I can play. I'll be a good sport when one of the exceptions arises, so you needn't hold back from taking advantage of my ignorance."

That was ironic. The idea that anyone could take advantage of Minns was laughable in the extreme. All this had happened during Minns turn at the watch on the Bridge. I'm pretty sure that we weren't in as much danger with all of us in the Conference Room as we were when anyone else of us was on watch in the Bridge.

We played a couple of games of Backalley in the morning and the evening interspersed with other diversions.

□
□□

Then one afternoon while the BG was taking his watch, and I was reading an old *Scientific American* on my Kindle, an alarm went off that I'd never heard before. The ship almost lurched to a stop. That was really unusual. The accelerations on that ship were normally so gradual as to be imperceptible.

Minns was the first to react. He was up and heading for the Bridge while I was just rising, even though he had been in his cabin napping. He arrived first. I was second. The ladies arrived last and could only stand at the door and try to peer over my shoulders. Minns asked, "We're completely inert, right?"

The BG agreed. Then Minns said, "OK. Wendt take the weapons console and scan the area for ships or anything that is likely artificial."

The BG said, "Look in the infrared first. We're so far away from all stars that anything warmer than background has to be what we're looking for."

Minns said, "Kali may simply have changed course. I can't imagine why he would if he'd not found something here."

I took the co-pilot seat and began working the console. I changed the mode from visible to infrared and started cranking the focal point around to cover all directions including behind. I slowly worked my way through the sky surrounding us. It was a slow and arduous process. As I scanned, I reached a point where the section of sky covered included part of the Milky Way Galaxy arrayed before us like a milky lake. That lake made it really hard to see any close-up objects that were bright in the infrared. I exclaimed, "This is hopeless. What's part of the Milky Way and what's not?"

Minns, looking over my shoulder said, "It's time to announce our presence." With that, he worked on his console.

I asked, "What are you doing?"

"Just activating the ship's radar. I'd been holding off because Kali might still be in the area. It's become time to do some active searching."

I felt a squeeze on my elbow that startled me. I realized it had to be

288

Ginny. I couldn't help smiling. I heard her voice whisper in my ear, "Well, finally, we're doing something other than hunker down."

It didn't take more than a few minutes for Minns to say, "We've got something. It's less than a hundred thousand kilometers away." Then he spoke to me., "Here are coordinates. Center your display on them." He gave me two strings of numbers. I entered them in the pointing app for the telescope. It slewed around, and at the center was a small blob. I didn't have to be told to increase the magnification.

I said, "Let's see what we have here." I increased the magnification to the maximum. What appeared on the screen was a roughly cigar shaped object that was still not really well resolved. It seemed to be covered with craters. I announced, "An asteroid."

Aurora who was apparently also looking over my shoulder said, "I'm not so sure. Those things that look like craters aren't. If they were, you'd have overlapping craters, craters within craters. You don't see that. I think this thing is artificial."

Minns agreed.

That left us with the question of what to do next. There were two preferences. One was to move closer slowly and improve our view. When close enough, we'd fly around it observing from all perspectives. The other preference was to move closer rapidly, searching for an entry point if it were really artificial. Minns and Ginny were in the fast track camp. The rest of us were in the slow and cautious camp.

Minns almost never argued for his preference whenever issues came up. He just acted if he thought his view were crucial. Ginny, on the other hand, was almost always very vocal. She stated her essential argument at the beginning. "We've been killing ourselves to get to Kali, why would we want to take chances by taking our time!"

I summarized, the alternate view. "We probably have only one shot at getting this right. Let's make sure that we don't throw away that chance in our haste."

We ended up compromising. We approached rapidly, but circled the asteroid completely to view it from all angles. In the process, we found something that was evidently a large airlock.

The BG looked at the airlock and made observations—evidently designed for ships, we've not been challenged despite how close we are, it's probably a deserted facility. Then he said, "Then, why am I scared to go in?"

I said, "That's easy. IF it's deserted, it's deserted for a reason. That reason may still be present."

Aurora said, "Thanks for those cheery words."

289

I went on. "We're going in, so we should be prepared for whatever we find. Let's sit down and plan."

No one objected.

We actually had dinner first. I'd never seen people dawdle so much over their beef stew, which, by the way, was as good as any I'd had at Hogwarts. Eventually, we realized we couldn't wait longer.

Somebody handed the white-board marker to me. I said, "Why is it always me?"

Ginny said, "It's because you're such a sweet-heart."

I grimaced and said, "I think this planning should have four phases: Risk assessment, Risk management, plan for entry and exit, and objectives. Let's start with Risk assessment. We'll start with brainstorming. You've all done it before except you, Minns. Do you need a primer?" Before he could answer, I answered for him. "Of course, you don't. So, let's start." "Risks", I wrote on the white-board.

They started coming in: Disease, hostile aliens, poisonous atmosphere, etc. Someone mentioned "arrogance." I then asked for management ideas. Mostly they were obvious. The spacesuits that we had would protect us from a lot of risks.

On the topic of hostile aliens. I asked who had weapons with them. Ginny just raised her wand. I said, "Right. Both of the witches have wands. I have a Glock. You've all seen that haven't you?"

Everyone except Ginny raised a hand. Minns said, "As a member of the US military, I probably know more about your Glock than you do. You can give Ginny instruction on your own time."

Ginny scoffed at that remark. "You bet he's on top of that." It's an indication of how serious this planning was that no one made the obvious double ententre.

Minns followed up on the "arrogance" hazard. He said, "The chief arrogance hazard would be to commit too many people to exploring this asteroid. We should have Wendt and Ginny do the exploration."

Aurora asked, "Why them?"

Minns nodded and started his perfect argument. "It would be arrogant to assume that the boarding party could handle any possible threat. We need to reserve the minimum talent base to complete our mission even if everyone died in the boarding party."

Aurora said, "That all may be obvious to you why that makes Wendt and Ginny the ideal boarding party. Elucidate."

290

Minns shrugged. "Of course. The talents that we need at minimum to complete our mission are: one witch, me, the technical knowhow of the BG." Aurora's stare was read correctly by Minns, who continued, "Aurora, you are the one to stay on the ship. If we lost you, the strain of grief on the BG would be too great for him to function effectively."

Ginny looked at Aurora and said, "You can't argue with that logic, can you?"

Aurora grimaced but accepted her fate. I went on. "How do we get in?"

That had everyone stumped for a moment. Then the silly suggestions came: blowing a hole in the airlock, searching for a hidden keypad, and so on.

After a while both Ginny and I stood quickly and exclaimed, "Of course." We looked at each other. She said, "You go ahead."

I answered, "No, you."

She smiled broadly and said, "*Alohamora.*"

Aurora laughed. Even the BG smiled and said, "It's worth a try."

Only Minns seemed baffled, but he quickly recovered, "Magic spell to open doors, right."

I shrugged. "Sure."

We then went into detailed planning. I guess more accurately we started listening to Minns' plan. He said, "OK. There are a few things about this installation that are pretty clear:

"First, there's a ship-sized airlock because they needed a large airlock to move all the equipment they needed in efficiently. The interior is probably rotating to provide gravity. It's a lot easier to get a ship and contents rotating at the right speed than individual pieces of equipment one at a time.

"Inside the airlock, there are airlocks that give access to the habitable parts of the interior. So, you'll have to use your spell multiple times. I don't know how you'll close the airlock after you get through. Maybe it will close itself automatically, given enough time.

"Once you get inside, you'll be looking for a Control Room. It may be locked. You'll have to use your magic spell again. You may need light. Can you provide that or do you need to bring one of our light sources?"

Ginny said, "I can provide light."

I said, "Maybe we'd better bring a flash for emergencies." Ginny frowned but didn't object.

I asked, "What is this facility?"

Aurora immediately flung her hand up and said, "It's obvious. This is an astronomical observatory. It's in deep space—really deep space. It's got antennas and telescopes all over the place. What happened here? It's like this observatory is abandoned. What reason could there be?"

The BG said, "That's what we hope to find."

I asked, "Are we ready to go?"

Everyone looked at Ginny. She nodded. Then they looked at me. I sighed and said, "Yep."

Ginny and I looked at Aurora. She gasped and fumbled an answer, "Well, yeh, I suppose."

We turned to the BG. He shook his head. "We'll never be ready completely. Let's just go."

Minns nodded. Then he said, "Let's go. Ginny and Wendt, suit up. The rest of us will too. I'll maneuver the ship close to the airlock. Then I'll suit up. Then you go."

Ginny and I went to our cabin and started suiting up. We had gotten fairly proficient—especially at working together on it. There were always the occasional pinches and caresses that made the task pleasant. We finished and arrived on the Bridge. Everyone was suited up by then. I said, "Ginny and I will get in the airlock and wait for your go-ahead."

Minns nodded. We entered the airlock and closed the inside hatch. Then we cleared the airlock of air. There was a camera in the airlock. Minns noted that we were ready to open the outer hatch. He just said, "Go ahead and open it up."

I opened it and discovered that we were only a few meters from the asteroid's airlock. It was so wide that I couldn't see the edges of it. Ginny had her wand out of her fanny-pack. She apparently could control it through the spacesuit material. She apparently spoke the spell silently because the iris of the outer hatch opened so smoothly and rapidly that I almost didn't notice the change. I said, "Well, I guess we've got to launch ourselves toward the wall of the airlock and try to hang on there before opening the inner door."

Ginny sighed. "I guess you're right. Here I go." With that she grasped the edge of the ship's airlock and pushed herself toward the left edge. She landed, and we discovered that the wall of the inside of the airlock was rotating. It produced a very mild gravity that held her to the wall. I followed and landed on the same wall near her. Then she opened the inner hatch of the airlock. When she did that, the outer hatch closed as quickly as it had opened, and the inner hatch opened. Atmosphere immediately filled the airlock.

The cavity beyond the inner airlock door was large and dimly illuminated by indirect lighting. At that point, I tried to talk to the people on our ship. No one answered. Ginny tried as well. There was no response. Then I said, "I guess radio doesn't penetrate the walls. Well, we're really on our own for now."

Ginny asked, "What next?"

I looked around the interior and noticed that the interior was wider than the airlock. I said, "They must dock ships away from the center of the cavity so that there will be some gravity to help people maneuver. There's a ramp over there. Let's walk down that. How about turning on the light of your wand?"

She did. The ramp was wide enough for two to walk abreast, but we didn't. We reached the bottom and started walking toward the center of the cavity where there seemed to be some docking ramps. We reached one. It seemed to have an airlock that we supposed led into the interior of the asteroid. Again, *Alohamora* got us into that airlock. The inner airlock door led to another ramp down. There had been dim illumination up until that point. From there on, there was no illumination at all.

I said, "Well, it's time for me to get out my Glock."

Ginny giggled nervously and said, "I don't usually like the fact that you have that Glock, but right now I'm all in favor of your getting it out."

"Agreed." I opened my fanny-pack. My mokeskin purse was inside. I opened it. The Glock inside had a clip with bullets. I checked the clip and the safety. I closed the purse and then the fanny-pack. I said, "Lead on."

Then we proceeded into the endless dark.

We both took a deep breath and took one long step forward.

I said involuntarily, "The long dark of Ultima Thule."

"What?"

I whispered, "Did I say that aloud?"

She said in a normal voice, "You certainly did. What is Ultima Thule?"

"Well, this seems like a good place for that name. Ultima Thule was the farthest point to the North. We are pretty darn far in the North of the Milky Way galaxy."

"Really? The galaxy has a north pole?"

"Yes, it does. Just ask Aurora."

Ginny just harrumphed. "That would be something to explain in bed if you have nothing better to do."

We were in a long wide corridor. Ginny's wand light didn't illuminate it to the end. Ginny said, "I'm going to make the wand brighter."

I immediately grabbed her hand and said, "I'd not risk more light just yet." She shrugged, and we walked on. Before long we passed a door that had some sort of label on it. She asked, "Go in?"

"I suppose." She then opened the door with the *Alohamora* spell. I had

293

expected that when the door opened a light would go on. It didn't. Ginny's wand revealed a small room with something like a desk, a chair, and a computer monitor. There was a metal plate that might have served as a keyboard where a keyboard would have been on a human PC.

I said, "Checkpoint Charlie."

Ginny stared at me. I explained, "That was a point that controlled access between East Germany and West Germany. I bet that if this place were functioning, we'd have to check in here."

She nodded and said with a sigh, "I suppose this place is completely deserted."

"Probably, but we've got to keep going." Again she nodded. We went back to the hallway and kept walking. We came to another door. Ginny opened it. Inside was a similar office setup except that there was more to it. More chairs, desks, computers, and so on. There was nothing that was living or had been living.

We passed other doors and a crossing corridor that we bypassed for the moment. At the end of our corridor was a very large door with a transparent window. The interior was completely dark, so we had no idea what the interior was. This time, the door opened of its own accord, sliding into the walls. We entered. From Ginny's wand light we couldn't tell much about the interior. We could barely see the far walls. They had things on them that might have been posters.

Ginny said, "We need more light." With that she said, "Lumos Maximus." The room was lit in a weird, intense, fluorescent light that made every shadow as dark as space and every exposed surface was bleached almost white. As we looked around, it was hard to recognize things in that crazy light. The first things that were recognizable were the tables and chairs designed for creatures not that different from us humans.

Then we saw an indistinct pile of something along the far wall. As our eyes adjusted, I recognized a pool of something that looked a lot like . . . blood . . . and . . . bodies." Ginny gasped and buried her face in my chest. She didn't say anything for a while.

I asked, "Can we try moving on?"

She nodded mutely. I turned her around toward the door that we'd come through. We walked out. Once outside, she said, "What do you think would have happened if I'd thrown up?"

I couldn't suppress a laugh. "Yeh, it would be interesting to know what our suits would have made of us both throwing up."

"You, too?"

"Sure. Do you think I could look at all of those bodies and not be ready to empty my gut."

She managed a weak smile. Then she said, "Yeh. Let's just not go through that big room." I agreed. We tried one of the cross corridors. At the end of it was another large room. We went in carefully.

I said, "Let's try bringing the light up slowly, eh?"

"Right-o!"

The lights slowly got brighter. Eventually, they were bright enough to see that we were in another large room—a really large room. It must have been twenty meters tall. There were two cranes suspended from the ceiling. There were industrial grade workbenches scattered around the room. There was something that looked like a polished mirror on one of the benches. It was huge! We walked around some, but didn't find anything like a creature.

She asked, "Are we done?"

"We've not tried the other end of this corridor."

She took a deep breath. "How are you? Do you need a biology break?"

"I'm still good—probably for a couple of hours."

She nodded. "Let's keep going then."

We left the Workroom of the Gods—that was what I had decided to call it. I mentioned that to Ginny. She laughed, but said, "You are crazy."

"Absolutely straight."

We walked down to the end of the corridor. This time Ginny had to use the *Alohamora* spell to get us in. I'd slipped the Glock back into my fanny-pack. I brought it out before we went in. Ginny asked, "What's that about?"

I shook my head. "It's just a bad feeling I have."

She nodded and lowered the brightness of her wand. We entered the room with wand and Glock raised. The first shocking thing was that there was light in the room even without Ginny's wand. It came from a far corner of the room. It was a medium-sized room as rooms on this asteroid went. It almost looked like a cubicle farm. There were rows of what looked like computer monitors. They were all dark, but there were several especially large monitors that were on. They showed views of the exterior of the asteroid focusing on the telescopes and antennas.

I gritted my teeth and soundlessly nodded my head toward the light in the distant corner of the room. We slowly approached, casting frequent glances to our sides as we went. We reached the edge of the one lit cubicle. We hesitated, rounded the corner, and entered through the opening in the cubicle. Inside, there was a monitor that was lit. It showed some sort of scatter graph. There was a body slumped over the desk that the monitor was on. I tried to motion Ginny to stay where she was. Then I approached the figure from one side. Despairing of something intelligent to say, I simply said, "Hello." There was no reaction. I said, "Hello" one more time. I was preparing to poke the figure with my Glock.

I didn't have to. The head rose and shook itself. It turned on its shoulders and caught sight of me. I repeated, "Hello. I come in peace." The incongruity of my holding a gun on the creature and talking about peace struck me and almost caused me to laugh. I slipped the Glock back into my fanny-pack and extended my lowered arms, palm up. I hoped that it would take the nearly universal sign of friendship the right way. It stared at me for a moment and said something as well.

I repeated my greeting and added, "I'm James Wendt."

It said something. I had no idea what it was, but I hoped the translator built into the suit was trying to make sense of the sounds. Ginny contributed to the conversation with her name. I decided to start explaining why I was there in conversational English and hope that the translator would eventually pick up enough of its language to give us an idea of what was going on in its head.

After about ten minutes, it was translating about half of what it said into comprehensible English. It was also giving a try at translating what we said. We heard a sort of consecutive translation of our words. The conversation went a little like this. I tried to reproduce what the translator said as clearly as possible:

I said, "We're here looking for someone named Kali."

It said, "I am astronomer/astronaut. This is observatory. We are peaceful."

Ginny said, "We want peace, too."

It said, "Why are you here?"

I said, "We want to prevent Kali from breaking the peace."

It said, "I want, too (to?)."

That went on for a while as the translation became more literate. I finally said, "We are from a spaceship parked outside your airlock. We need to return to it for food and rest. Please wait for us to return."

It said, "When you return, I will tell you why we are all dead."

I said, "We should be back within twelve hours." I didn't know what the translator would make of that time period, but the alien seemed satisfied. We worked our way back to the main corridor.

Ginny said, "I can disapparate us back to the airlock."

I thought and then said, "I'd like to reserve that for real emergencies."

"Suit yourself."

We opened the outer lock hatch and re-entered our airlock. After closing the outer hatch, the inner opened almost instantly. Everyone was huddled in the small Bridge. Aurora spoke first, "What's going on? We figured that radio wouldn't penetrate the asteroid. But it gave us quite a fright when we couldn't talk with you for hours on end."

I said, "We'll talk about that after we've had a biology break and have started some dinner." We threw in a shower with the biology break. To save time, we helped each other. Ginny commented, "I'm not sure this cooperative showering is helping us finish faster."

When we got out, the questions bombarded us: What did you learn? Are there people on board? Is it an astronomy station or something else? Etc.

Ginny and I had agreed in the shower that we would tell the story straight through without questions until the end. It's lucky we agreed to that. We'd be talking still otherwise. We took turns telling the story. Our procedure didn't earn us many friends, but in the end, everyone had their critical questions answered, such as how many aliens are there, were you threatened, how much time do you need tomorrow?

I spoke for both of us when I said, "We're going to get a good night's sleep and go back the first thing in the morning."

That evening, we de-compressed in bed. Ginny said, "I've never seen so many dead in one place since the last great battle at Hogwarts when Riddle was defeated." She sobbed, and I held her for a while. Then we fell asleep while I spooned her.

The next morning, Aurora declared that she and the BG would go over. Her argument was that it was safe now, that getting a second perspective would be good, and that she was better equipped to handle a session with an astronomer.

Minns vetoed that categorically. He said, "I gave the reasons for Wendt and Weasley to go yesterday. None of that has changed. We don't know precisely how dangerous it is over there. Shut up and sit down." Actually, he wasn't that abrupt. He said to Ginny and me, "Get up and get going." We did.

However, the BG and Aurora insisted on going. Minns didn't try to stop them.

When we opened the inner airlock door of the asteroid, we were greeted by a good bit of light—still indirect. When we passed through the second airlock, the interior was lit. Actually, a path was lit for us to the observatory Control Room that we'd been in before.

And I Alone Have Escaped . . .

The Control Room was well-lit. The alien was sitting up at his desk. There were guest chairs in his cubicle. He even had a mug of something steaming at his desk.

He greeted us, "Welcome."

It was the first time that we'd been welcomed in a long time. "Thanks. Here's the thing. Do you know someone who calls himself Kali?"

That brought the conversation to a sudden halt. Then he said, "What do you know about Kali?"

Here might be the point where everything was poised on a knife edge. Ginny looked at me. I wet my lips and said, "Kali is going to try to destroy the universe."

The alien shook his head in a sort of sideways shake. I didn't know what it meant. It probably didn't matter, because he said, "Yes, he is. So, why are you here?"

I said, "We're here because we want to stop him. We know practically nothing about him. We want to know as much as we can. Please tell us everything you can. There is nothing too trivial to help us."

The alien said, "Let me start by telling you a little about me."

□

I am a member of a race that has been traveling in space for thousands of years. We have colonized a few planets outside our system but we have never had building an empire as a goal. About a hundred years ago, one of our scientific organization decided to sponsor an observatory in ultra-deep space. We took an asteroid from one of our star systems. It was partially hollowed out and the interior loaded with equipment and supplies. We

298

didn't mount the extremely sensitive sensors and mirrors on the outside until we were deep into interstellar space. After the asteroid was supplied and outfitted, we started the long trip well out of the plane of our galaxy. Such a large "ship" could not be moved much more than a hundred times the speed of light by our technology. We slowly moved it out to its current position. We have many kinds of sensors here from long wave-length radio to gamma and xray. We do gravitation wave observations along with two other small observatories that are separated from us by a couple of hundred kilometers. We set about doing a systematic observation of the entire universe. From our ultracold location almost in intergalactic space, we are able to make incredibly precise observations. In short we were an academic community with little to do but pursue our peaceful researches.

That peace was disturbed by the arrival of Kali. His ship was incredible in its size and armament. We never had an opportunity to gauge its true size, but we were able to measure its mass from the gravitational force it exerted on our station. It's mass was more than fifty times that of our asteroid. Our extremely sensitive instruments were thrown so far off adjustment that my chief of optical telescopes stormed into my office only minutes after Kali's ship arrived. Let's call her after one of your great astronomers, perhaps Hubble. Anyway, Hubble stormed into my office complaining. "Do you know that there is a huge ship that is so close to our station that my main mirror is bent completely out of shape!"

I was about to say something consoling when our communications officer called. He said, "Professor, we have an urgent message from the commander of the ship that is resting not a single kilometer off our asteroid."

I said, "Tell me the gist of it."

The communications officer—let's call him Marconi—said, "The message is from someone who calls himself Kali. He says that he insists on meeting with the director of the observatory immediately."

I thought about it. It had to be his ship that was causing the distortion of the telescope mirror. I supposed that the sooner that I met with him, the sooner we'd have the ship out of the way and could re-adjust the mirror. So, I said, "You can reply that I'm ready to meet him whenever he wishes. Get in touch with observatory maintenance and make sure that the airlock is ready to accept a shuttle."

This Kali was a mystery to me. What in the world could someone who had a giant ship want with us? We are—well, really—were academics. What could we possibly provide anyone other than fellow academics. If they were some impossible shipload of astronomers, all they need do would be to read our scientific papers. If they want raw data, I would have said, "Go find it for yourselves."

I'd hardly finished thinking that when Marconi was calling me. I was rather testy at this point, "What is it?"

Marconi said, "I've just opened the airlock for Kali's shuttle. I've sent a maintenance person down to meet him and conduct him to your office. I think he'll be at your door in a few minutes."

"Thanks." I had hardly switched off my phone when there was a knock at my door. Hubble was still there. I decided that it would be better to meet Kali one on one, so I sent Hubble back to her lab with the assurance that I'd insist that Kali move his ship back—way back. I opened the door. It was filled by the nearly giant proportions of the creature who stood at my door.

He didn't wear an environment suit of any sort. His skin looked more like a spacesuit exterior than anything else. As a matter of fact, your space-suit looks far more like skin than his skin does.

The three of us were caught in an unusual tableau for a moment. Then I invited Kali in. That allowed me to quickly introduce Hubble and let her leave. Kali moved ponderously out of the way to allow Hubble to leave. I looked around for a place for Kali to sit. No chair in my office would ac-commodate him. I looked around for something for him to sit on. He solved the problem by saying, "What I have to say will take only a minute. I wanted to say it to you in person, though. We need the research results of your station. I expect you to make them available to me and my staff im-mediately and without reservation." With that he turned and left my office.

I wasn't worried—yet. Still, I did have a bad feeling. He did have a big ship and was potentially a threat to our entire base. I sent for my second in command. She showed up in my office almost immediately. We'll call her the XO. She spoke before she'd even taken a seat. "What do they want?"

I said, "They want unlimited access to our research—published, in re-view, and currently in progress. He didn't give me a hint as to what he's looking for. I want you to take the point on supervising and 'helping' with their access to our research."

She nodded, "Would you want anything withheld from them—very carefully and very secretly?"

I couldn't decide. I opened the bag completely. "Frankly, I have no idea what to withhold from them and even if we should. Our research is normally shared freely. On the other hand, I had a very bad feeling in the brief discussion with this 'Kali'.

"By the way, do you have any idea of what that name implies, if any-thing?"

She shook her head. I always had a little trouble talking science with her. She was very appealing. I always found my thoughts drifting to other things beside the topic at hand. She said, "I suppose we could do a culture search in the general information database."

I didn't think it could do us any good, so I said, "Don't bother. Just monitor very carefully what they are interested in." I dismissed her and hoped rather than believed that this Kali would find what he was looking for and would leave our station.

□□

The XO came to my office several days later. When she entered, she said, "Let's keep this completely confidential." I agreed.

She inspired a deep breath. Then she leaned over the table toward me and whispered—yes, whispered—as quietly as she could, "What do you guess they are looking for?"

I started to ask, "Who?", but it was perfectly obvious whom we were discussing. So, I guessed. "Maybe, the distribution of intelligent species across the galaxy." I hadn't the slightest idea where their interests might lie, but this guess would at least make a certain amount of sense for a large, well-armed ship. Of course, I was wrong.

The XO said, "They want to find binary condensed objects."

I almost laughed. "No, really! And I thought that they might have some nefarious purpose. This sounds completely like a pure scientific curiosity. So, it's good for us. They'll get their list. It will be long. That's not my field, but my guess is that there must be a couple of million in our galaxy alone."

The XO said, "Well, you're right about one thing. There are about that many binary condensed objects."

I said, "That should keep them busy for quite a while. But, I've got a feeling that you wouldn't be here talking about it if that was the whole story."

She leaned a little closer. That made me a little less inclined toward scientific issues and more toward personal issues. "The thing is that they have a rather more specialized interest than that. They want to find binary condensed objects that have collided within the last million years."

That sort of changed the object of my interest from the XO to her state-ment. I said, "That definitely isn't my field of study, but I doubt that there have been more than a couple of those anywhere in our galaxy in that time."

She said, "I can tell you the answer to that definitively. There aren't any."

I paused to think. Then I asked, "Have you told them that?"

"Not yet. Their crew is not that great at doing astronomical searches in our database. I am great. There's nothing, zero, zilch."

"They'll find that out pretty soon."

"I'd give them a couple of days. They could do it faster if I didn't send them down a couple of false paths."

I took her hand in mine. "They'll find that out and then leave, right?"

She shook her head. "I wouldn't bet on it."

I said, "Well, what's the worst that they could do? If there aren't any, there aren't any."

She squeezed my hand and said, "If they were reasonable, nothing. I've just got a bad feeling that they aren't reasonable. Still . . ."

I said, "I know this is crazy. We'll be laughing about it in less than a week, but there's something that I'd kind of like to tell you. It's just that . . . well, just in case there isn't a week from now."

She completely surprised me by smiling and nodding. "I know. At least I think I know. You don't need to worry about being . . . oh . . . embarrassed. I feel the same."

I still felt embarrassed anyway. But I managed to blurt out, "I kind of like you. As a matter of fact I've got a lot of affection for you."

She smiled even more broadly. "You know, I like you too. And, just in case—you know, something were to happen—I'd like to spend time with you while we've still got it to spend."

At that point, I was grinning like a lorax.

The next several days, I did some things that I would never have believed that I would ever do. First, I sent a message to the military headquarters of our republic's space forces. I requested that they be on alert to evacuate us in case of 'trouble.' Then, I had the one ship that was always docked in our port readied to leave on a moment's notice. It was not large, but in theory it could accommodate the entire staff and enough supplies to get us to the nearest outpost of our republic—that is, the nearest outpost other than our own. I had that done as surreptitiously as possible. Finally, I started paying the XO visits in the evenings.

After a day, Marconi got in touch with me, saying that there was a sociologist who wanted to do a video conference with me and the XO if possible. I summoned her immediately. She was already on the way to my office for lunch. We'd been having them regularly.

It was actually the military who set up the direct video conference. Thank goodness, they did it on a secure connection and with header information that made it look like I was going to be talking to sociologists.

When they came online, I was greeted by three military types. I couldn't have told rank or even branch of the service from their appearance. The one in charge announced that he was the Director of star base epsilon—the closest to us. He did most of the talking.

He asked, "Just what is going on at your base? Is there a major failure imminent in one of your systems. Your message was very vague."

I introduced my XO and then said, "We have guests. They came in a ship that is larger than any I've ever seen. They are not from any world that I've ever heard of. They don't seem to be regular military, but they do have some unusual demands. We've not denied them anything so far. They've not asked for anything very far out of the ordinary, but both of us think they may demand something that we can't provide. We expect that soon."

The XO said, "It's hard to know with them. I personally expect that request to come tomorrow."

The Director swore and said, "Well, you could have notified us sooner."

I started to agree, but he quickly went on. "Never mind. What is, is. We'll send a ship that can give them something to think about. However, we can't be there for several weeks. Can you hold out that long?"

The XO started to say something. I cut across her. I said, "I think you'll be coming to rescue survivors if anything happens."

The Director swore and said, "Are you sure about this?"

"We're not sure about anything," the XO said.

"We'll send a rescue ship. If you're right about their formidable force, we'd have to send a fleet to intimidate them. I have three suggestions:

"One, stall for time as much as you can.

"Two, quietly have your crew position emergency supplies throughout your installation.

"Three, call a fire drill or something.

"Four, pray."

I thanked them, and the video conference ended. I stood and drew the XO to me. "Spend the night with me."

She nodded silently.

It was two days. There was a thunderous knock on my office door. I said, "Come."

The giant that I knew as Kali opened the door and entered. He stood as before. This time, the conversation was much longer. He began, "You have been trying to cheat me."

I swallowed to clear my throat and said, "I don't see it."

"Your crew has not been helpful to my children."

The statement confused me. It must have been evident on my face—alien or not. He said, "You have been trying to fool my people into thinking that you are helping us. You aren't."

I said, "We've given you access to everything we have."

"You haven't given them what I need. You have been stalling."

At that point, I had to decide how to proceed. Did I try lying or did I try to be truthful—mostly? I decided on as much of the truth as I could stand to tell. I began, "I have told my people to make your researches their lowest priority." I swallowed again. "I have called for assistance from . . ."

Just then, I heard a voice that had become dear to me announce brightly, "I'm coming in. I'm dragging you away to lunch . . ." She had just entered my office and seen my guest.

He turned and said, "Ah, good. I was going to have your superior call you. Luckily, you came on your own."

While his back was turned to me I tried to mouth, "Go! Now!" She turned rapidly and got a step or two off.

Kali said in such an imperious voice that it would be hard not to obey. "Stay." She turned and stood her ground. Kali turned back to me and said, "Here's the thing. There are no colliding binaries in the galaxy in the last million years or so."

I started to breathe a sigh of relief and offer my condolences when Kali said, "I want to know if there are any that could have collided so recently that you couldn't have observed them because of the limit of the speed of light. Or, even better, if there are any that will collide shortly."

My XO, bless her heart said quite matter-of-factly, "We couldn't possibly know that. They're too far away, and decaying orbits are very hard to compute."

He laughed. At least, I think it was a laugh. It seemed to be quite genuine and even good-natured. It was as though he were including us in a very funny joke that only he understood. He said, "I admire your XO. She has courage and is smart. She deserves to be remembered." With that, he pulled a strange double-bladed knife from his belt and flung it without looking. It drove straight and deep into her brain. She collapsed without a sound. I suppose death was nearly instantaneous. My reaction was. I leaped over my desk and ran to her. By the time I reached her, she was definitely dead. I pulled the knife out of her head and threw it with all the force I had at Kali. The throw was off the mark. He deflected it with an arm to his feet.

I might as well have been dead myself. I shouted at him. "What are you waiting for? Kill me, too."

He smiled and commented, "You two might well have been well-matched." Then, all business, he said, "No. I don't want to kill you. I needed both of you. I decided that I needed one as an object lesson in my seriousness. I needed the other to carry out orders efficiently. Her last comment decided me. She would probably be too much of a nuisance to stay. She would be the object lesson. The lesson is that there will be no more quiet resistance. If you don't cooperate and cooperate right now, I will start killing your staff. We'll start at the bottom of the hierarchy and work our way up."

I stayed knelt beside XO. I gave in. "You have it. What do you want?"

"She told you didn't she?"

"Yes, you want the locations of all possible condensed object collisions in our galaxy, including ones that are just imminent. You understand that is a very difficult request?"

"Of course, I wouldn't be here if it were easy. Now, move."

I had to put away grief for a while. I swore though that if there were a way to have revenge, I would.

It was less than an hour when I had collected the heads of departments and lead investigators. I didn't waste time on greetings or providing refreshments. I began straight in. "Most of you have been working to some extent with our 'guests'. Most of you know what they want. We're going to try to give it to them as quickly as possible."

Someone raised a hand. I interrupted him. "No questions until the end and only absolutely necessary questions then. Some of you may be aware that my XO was killed by the leader of our 'guests'. He has promised that we will all die eventually unless we cooperate completely.

"This meeting is to plan the attack on our problem."

Some idiot said, "You mean Kali?"

I didn't honor that question with a second's attention. I went on. "We need a list of likely candidates for the collisions that Kali wants. I want precision measurements of all candidates taken. Hubble will obtain them. Then each will be assigned to a team to do the computations to project the time of collision. If the projected time is clearly more than a year in the future, set aside that candidate and take up another one. We will continue until we have eliminated all candidates or have two or three that will have happened in the near future to a hundred thousand years in the past.

With that someone asked, "Why not longer?" Those words were hardly out of his mouth when he rescinded them. "Never mind. If they happened longer ago, we'd already know about them."

Then I turned to the Director of Computation. "You will allocate all available computer time to this project. Choose the optimum number of candidates to investigate at one time. I want results as soon as possible."

I turned to the Head of Stellar Dynamics. "You will have to make up teams to build simulations to compute the results we want. You're free to use whomever you wish. Form them into whatever teams you want, and lead as you please." He nodded.

I turned to my personal assistant. "You will be responsible for collecting all progress reports and collating them. I want to be able to report our present status to Kali whenever he wants and as accurately as I possibly can."

He said, "So, I'll be the project manager for this effort?" I nodded. "Then, I'll need a representative on every team who will be responsible for reporting milestones and any progress. Each team will do a rough project plan as quickly as possible and communicate it to me. As you refine your plans, I will need them. Is that understood?"

I turned to the head of facility services. "In addition to your normal duties, you will be responsible for keeping food service open and running at all hours. Food services will include providing meals to the various teams in their work areas."

Filch, the facility manager, almost cackled, "You can bet your life. We'll not let you down."

I said, "I'm betting all our lives. I will be available at all times in my office or in my suite. You may all enter both without warning. Now, what essential questions do you have?"

A quick survey of the room revealed no questions. We all left the Conference Room silently.

My team was efficient when it needed most to be. It was less than a week before we had results. Kali seemed to know something significant had happened almost before I did. He showed up in my office shortly after my personal assistant came with results. He'd printed them on paper rather than showing them on a monitor. He had hardly finished handing them to me when Kali muscled into my office.

He said, "Impressive. You see, you can produce results when you need to."

I grimaced. Praise from a murderer was not to my taste, but I said nothing. He was also a psychopath in my books. I said, "Yes, there are three candidates. One is near the far edge of the galaxy. That collision happened about 75,000 years ago. There's another one that's quite close. It will happen in ten years, roughly."

Kali smiled, "But you've saved the best for last."

"Right. To the best of our ability to calculate, it happened within the last year, although it might be about to happen. It's located just inside the near edge of the galactic bulge. It's less than 14000 light years away."

He immediately demanded details. "It's a strange one. It's a black hole/neutron star binary. The neutron star is only a little less massive than the black hole."

Kali exclaimed, "Wonderful, almost ideal!"

I frowned. "Please, just take the results, and go your way."

His joy seemed to know no bounds. "Oh, I want to reward your team for its great work. Gather them together in your cafeteria."

I shook my head in disbelief. Surely, he was joking. I, and I'm sure everyone else, would treat his disappearance as perfect reward, but he would not be gainsaid.

He had what I took to be a smile on his face as he said, "No. No. I want to see them all and thank them personally. Gather them together."

I called my Personal Assistant in and told him, "Get on the public address and request everyone to come to the cafeteria."

He asked, "Many of them are exhausted from lack of sleep. Surely this could wait?"

I nodded in Kali's direction. He just made a silent "O" with his mouth and then said, "Right away."

The announcement went out. There were a couple of calls that came in begging off this, but my Personal Assistant was insistent without actually using Kali's name.

Kali, my Personal Assistant, and I walked down to the cafeteria where people had already started gathering. The cafeteria was set up with tables and chairs occupying about three-quarters of the room. One end was raised. We used it as a stage for the odd gathering and the occasional theatrical. Almost everyone looked bored, tired, and/or resentful of disturbed rest. They were all gathered among the tables and chairs. Only Kali, my Personal Assistant, and I were on the stage area. I spoke first, "This is a time for thanks and congratulations. You've done an amazing job—better than I thought possible. With this, I believe that Kali wants to provide you with his personal thanks. I'm sure he and his associates will be leaving shortly afterwards." There was a sort of murmur that passed through the staff.

At that, several of Kali's retinue showed up and entered stage left—as though on cue. He stepped forward and said to my Personal Assistant, "Why don't you step down there as well. You deserve my thanks as much as any of those."

At that moment, alarums began ringing in my head. I started to say something, but my Personal Assistant was already off the stage, and Kali was speaking.

"I want to thank you all personally for the excellent job that you have done for my cause. I also want to express my feelings for the meaningless delays that you've imposed on me. For that, here is my thanks."

At that instant, I realized what was about to happen—not in detail, but the broad outline. I turned and was about to tackle him when he spoke a word that my translator didn't render although I already knew what it meant. He said, "Fire." His henchmen raised concealed weapons and began firing rapidly. There wasn't a person standing within five seconds of the command.

Meanwhile I had thrown myself at him. He grasped me in his huge hand and lifted me high by my shoulder. The pain was excruciating, but I will not forget his words ever, "Your punishment for your intrigue will be to know that you have brought on the deaths of all your companions." Then he threw me to the floor next to my dead friends. He turned rapidly and was gone.

My team was strewn around me. I held my eyes shut for hours. Finally, I opened them and started the job of cleanup. The Director of an installation like this has to know something about the operations of all departments—including the medical department. I knew that the theory was that in case of a team member's death, the body would be sealed in a special, large impervious bag. The bag would be put in a holding area near the surface of the asteroid that was open to space. The temperature there was close to absolute zero. The body would be well preserved for whatever future purposes were required.

That was the theory. In practice, no one believed that more than a dozen deaths could possibly occur in our installation. So, there were only a dozen of these bags available. I started the lonely process of putting my associates in bags and transporting them to the surface of the asteroid. It was hard in every way: hard physical labor, hard mental labor, hard spiritual labor. It took me a day to finish eleven bodies. XO had been the first several days before.

I had originally planned to move all the bodies to the surface. I began the process on the first for whom I didn't have a bag. It was much harder in all ways, physically, mentally, spiritually. I stopped before I got it out of the cafeteria. The rest of my time here has been spent in the communications cubicle, in touch with Epsilon Base. I go directly into the galley when I have to eat. That hasn't been much lately.

And I Alone Have Escaped.

I listened to the story with growing fear. They had given Kali what he wanted most! The BG was talking to the survivor. "I know this won't mean much to you, but I will tell you anyway.

"Kali is the name of a god in one of the religions of my home planet. He was to recreate the Universe from scratch sometime around now. He probably thought your XO's death was just pat of a necessary part of his role. If he succeeds, your team would only have died a few weeks early."

The alien stared and shook his head violently. "How does he intend to do that?"

Aurora said, "You must be familiar with the use of inflatons to provide faster than light travel."

He closed his eyes and said, "Of course, of course. That's why he wanted to know the locations of condensed object collisions. He is going to harvest element 126 and use it to generate huge amounts of inflatons and anti-inflatons."

Aurora said, "He intends to collapse half the universe in what we call the Big Crunch."

The alien actually laughed. "So you have a name for it. Very descriptive it is. I like it."

I asked, "Is there a name we can call you by?"

He said, "I will let your translator pick a name from your culture to translate my name. My name is," Here there was a strange sound that the translator rendered as "Picard."

Aurora said, "I think Kali thinks that he's going to crunch the entire universe. How can he do that with both inflatons and anti-inflatons being generated?"

The BG answered that. "I think he will generate the inflatons in a very narrow beam and the anti-inflatons in a very wide beam. Eventually when the two coalesce the universe will be much smaller than it is now. The energy density will be very high, and the next Big Bang will begin." He hesitated and added, "There is a preponderance of matter over anti-matter in

309

the universe. Possibly, the decay of inflatons will happen much faster than anti-inflatons."

Picard shook his head. "Does it matter? Both would be equally disastrous for all creatures in the universe. I personally prefer the narrow beam/wide beam approach."

I asked, "Do you want to come with us? We have room in our ship. If our atmospheres are compatible, you wouldn't even have to wear a space-suit. It would be a chance for revenge against Kali."

Picard frowned, "No. I think that I would just slow you down. Don't worry about me. A ship from my civilization should arrive in a week or so. They can help clean up the bodies. You can be my agents of revenge."

I asked, "Do you want us to contact you when it's done?"

He chuckled. "Not necessary. If I get back home, it will be proof that he failed. That's enough for me." He gazed at us for a moment. Then he said, "You don't have a second to lose. Go now with speed. Go with power. Go with God."

The BG asked, "Do you know where Kali is going next?"

He nodded. "I don't have the coordinates. He took them and it might take days to find them in the computer files we have. I do know that it's somewhere near the closest edge of the central galactic bulge. Sorry I can't be more helpful."

Aurora said, "We can track him. That's OK."

We got up and left. When we were out in the main corridor, Ginny started running. She called behind, "He said not to waste a second." So we arrived at the inner airlock. The inside door opened as we approached. The outside door was already open. The pressures were equalized, so there was no harm done. We ran up the ramp to the inner surface. We reached the ramp up to the outer airlock. When we got to the top, the inner door was already open. Ginny commented, "Our friend down below must be helping us along."

I asked, "You mean, Picard?"

"Of course."

When inside the airlock, the inner door closed. A voice sounded through our translator. "I'm not going to pump out the airlock. I'm going to open the outer door a little and let the atmosphere bleed out into space. That should be quicker. Grab a handhold." We did, and the center of the iris door opened a little. There was a rush of wind that tried to drag us to the opening. Then it opened completely. I gave a sigh of relief that our ship was there.

Minns' voice sounded in our helmets. "I've opened our outer lock door. Please leap as accurately as you can toward the opening. After the first has arrived, the rest can leap gently in the right general direction, and the first will catch you."

Ginny immediately said, "I'm going first." Her leap was dead center. She disappeared inside the lock, and then she stuck her head and a hand out. She said, "OK, next up. I'll catch you."

Aurora went next. I was afraid that she had not leaped hard enough, but she was caught by Ginny. Ginny said, "You next Wendt."

I said, "Let the BG go next. Two of you go in, and I'll come last."

Ginny was angry, "You don't have to be the hero every time."

"You're right, but I'm coming last this time."

She used an expletive and said, "OK. BG, you could jump a little harder than your wife did."

He jumped and was caught by his wife. Minns said, "I'm closing the lock and two people will enter. Then when the lock opens, you come next, Wendt."

After the lock re-opened, I saw Ginny waiting. She said, "Don't daw- dle." I didn't. I was in the lock. The outer door closed. Ginny ripped her helmet off and then did mine. She kissed me as though she hadn't seen me for a month. Meanwhile the inner lock opened.

Minns said, "We're on our way." There was no sense of acceleration, but I knew that we were probably already out of sight of the Ultima Thule and Picard.

Star's End

The first thing that we did after starting to follow Kali was to try to estimate where he was going. As before, initially there was a very wide target area. However, this time, we were going into the body of the galaxy, and there were thousands of stars in our first error circle. What made it even more frustrating was that none of them were in the near edge of the galactic bulge.

We had a little impromptu meeting when this became clear. I asked the question, "Do we stay on the current course or try to get to the general area of the binary system where we think he's going?"

Aurora answered, "We don't know exactly where the binary system is. We could spend weeks trying to find it while he arrived and ended the universe. I say that we keep following his ship."

Ginny said, "We could end up just missing him time and again until everything disappeared."

Those seemed to be the only arguments. I asked, "Vote?" Minns disapproving look told me that it was a silly idea, and we'd hear nothing more of it.

The BG summed things up, "Then we're going to stay on the trail of Kali's ship?"

Minns just nodded. The weeks saw slowly improving estimates of where we were going. The error circle shrunk so that there were a thousand or so stars in it. Then there were several hundred. Then there were just over a hundred. Then we were in the dozens. By that time, we could identify inhabited systems. There was only one just outside the error circle. Finally, there was one star dead center and one other on the edge of the error circle. It was a giant star.

Aurora commented, "That's a main sequence super giant. I estimate it's mass at least fifty times the sun's. It doesn't have any planets in the habitable zone. There's a bunch of junk out where the Kuiper Belt would be for our star. What the heck is Kali doing at that star?" Then she asked, "How long before we get there?"

The BG said, "Tomorrow. Is this it? We need to plan for the coming battle."

We were all around the Conference Room table. Minns said, "When we catch up with Kali, we'll have two opportunities to deal with him. The first one will be to use the missiles onboard our ship." He turned to me and asked, "I can count on you to be the weapons officer and fire them?"

I wasn't quite sure whether it was a question or a statement. I took it as a question. "Yes. I'll be on duty when we arrive. Do we fire everything we've got in the first salvo?"

Minns said, "No. Two will either do it or no number of missiles will. I'm sorry. I don't think they hold much hope for us. No offense intended."

I laughed, "None taken. I'm just pulling the trigger. I didn't design or build them."

Then Minns surprised me. He looked directly at me and said, "Something you have to understand is that you kill with your mind not with your missiles. You have to be totally committed to the mission if you're going to accept it."

I felt well-critiqued. I said, "You're right. I will be prepared."

He simply said, "Good." Then he turned to the ladies. "Our main chance is for you to disapparate us onto the ship where we'll launch our main attack."

I said, "Wait a minute. Do you think that you can defeat the entire crew of that ship single-handed?"

Minns simply said, "No. I'll have the rest of the crew with me."

I sighed. "No problemo."

□

Ginny and I were doing our normal double watch. I was on the weapons console. Ginny and I were gazing into each other's eyes. She said, "This is getting boring, but this might be our last watch—ever."

I nodded and put an arm around her shoulder. I pulled her close and we kissed. It wasn't a passionate tongue in the other's cheek sort of kiss. It was just to remind us that we were together. Our kiss broke.

Minns came into the Bridge and said, "We've got to slow. We're really close to the star now, probably only light hours away." Ginny dialed back our speed to barely faster than light.

313

I still had her in my arms when an alarm sounded.

I shouted for the BG. "Not heard this before. What's going on?"

Everyone clambered for a spot on the Bridge. The BG glanced at my monitor and said, "We're under attack."

I exclaimed, "What! Where. There aren't any Cherenkov detector alerts. Who's attacking us?"

Aurora's eyes widened and she said, "The star."

Ginny said, "Huh! How could a star attack us?"

Aurora said, "The star's way bigger than it ought to be, and its growing!." She was right. The star was expanding before our eyes.

The BG said, "That star is going supernova." He leaned over me and worked my console. He drew a box around a small part of the center of the star and keyed a command into the console. Then a new number showed on the display.

Aurora said, "That part of the star is traveling toward us at 92% of the speed of light. No supernova ejecta travels at a quarter of that speed. What the bloody hell is going on?"

I couldn't keep my mouth from gaping open. I said, "That star isn't an ordinary supernova. It's Kali. He's detonated most of the star."

As I was saying that, Aurora slapped her head. "That light is only slightly behind the shock wave. That shock wave will hit us in less than ten minutes! We'll never survive the impact. We can hardly stand the radiation that's hitting us right now. We've got to get out of here."

Minns said, "If we stop following Kali's ship, we'll never find him again. We've got to stay on our course."

Ginny still had the con. She looked the question at me. I said, "We stay on course until we only have a few seconds. If we haven't turned away from the star by then, we swing around and go to maximum speed."

Ginny's voice turned intense. She demanded of Aurora, "How can we only have minutes left? Look at the size of the star. It would fill the screen if it were really that close to us. The surface would have to be going many times the speed of light to expand to fill our screen in a few minutes."

Aurora said, "No it wouldn't. I don't have time to explain. Just look at how fast the sphere is expanding."

Ginny gulped. "Right." Her hand hovered over the joy stick that could turn the ship on a dime by overriding the autopilot that was following Kali's trail.

The alarm became more strident and Ginny's hand rested on the joy-stick. I asked Aurora, "How long?"

"Not sure. Maybe two or three minutes."

I looked at the navigation display. The center point was no longer pointing at the center of the star. The alarm stopped and was replaced by a voice that said, "Radiation intensity exceeds design limits by five percent." The aim point was now pointing at one of the edges of the sphere. I realized in a shock that the point that it was pointing at was now actually inside the sphere of the star. The disembodied voice said, "Ten percent. Hull integrity approaching compromise."

The aim point at the center of the navigation display turned so far away from the star that it wasn't visible on the screen. However, the relentless voice said, "Thirteen percent. Hull compromise in ten seconds. Nine. Eight. Seven." Then the voice said, "Ten percent. Hull integrity about to be breached." I kissed Ginny. Her tongue found mine. The ship said, "Radiation within design limits and falling."

I took over the navigation monitor from Ginny and directed the view to the rear. The disk of the star was shrinking on the monitor rapidly." I took a breath and realized that I'd not breathed in several minutes.

□□

We had a postmortem on what happened to the star that we'd just escaped by the skin of our teeth.

The BG began it by asking, "What was the purpose of blowing that star up?"

Aurora said, "I think they were testing their weapon—very much scaled down, of course."

Ginny said, "I think they were trying to decide how the effect of anti-inflatons scaled with the number generated."

I said, "I think they were seeing how much they could stress the anti-inflaton generator before it collapsed."

The BG said, "I think all of those would have come out of that test."

Minns said, "Those are all things that would come out of that test, but perhaps they were looking to obliterate their trail so that they couldn't be followed."

I added, "And perhaps obliterate those following at the same time."

The BG wondered if there would be more tests.. We argued a variety of answers. There were arguments for no more tests. For example, he's crazy and he'll see this one test as good enough.

Another argument was that at least one more test was required at a larger scale. It had to be large enough to collapse a globular cluster. That was Aurora.

Another argument was that there was the one more test of Aurora and one more in pure vacuum of the same size.

315

I ended it by asking, "Would the number of tests make a difference to what we do?"

That night Ginny wanted to talk in bed. She said, "That talk of the number of tests got me thinking. I think there will be no more."

"OK."

"Then the end could happen any time. It could happen tonight."

"I suppose so."

"We'd never know it, right? The shock wave would travel much faster than light. It would hit us and we'd be compressed into the size of the period at the end of sentence before we realized anything had happened."

"Probably much smaller." Her eyes flashed briefly. "Yes, yes. you're right. Damn perfectionist!"

She began shaking. "Then we don't have any time to lose. I want to make love every night."

This was something new. I'd heard her hint verbally about making love. She hinted physically in an unmistakable way, but she'd never said it outright. I hugged her and caressed her. She still shook for a while. Then it subsided and she fell asleep. I chuckled to myself, "So much for love-making every night."

However, after that night, we did make love every night. Sometimes it was grand and loud. Sometimes it was soft, accompanied by moans. Sometimes it was just foreplay.

The Black Hole

We took more than a week to approach our goal. It was not visible on the navigation monitor at all. We'd been picking up the radio pulsar that was in the cross-hairs of our navigation for a couple of days before we arrived. It had a huge Doppler shift in the pulsar frequency. Our radio antenna didn't have good resolution, so frustratingly, we couldn't be sure that it was what we were headed for. However, unless we were stopping for another test, it had to be our goal.

The BG had been improving the space geometry detector so that it could detect the amount of space compression Kali's ship created. This gave us a rough idea of his speed. We had been looking for a deceleration to signal that we were getting close. We also had a rough idea of the distance to our goal by the power of the pulsar. Both of those signals gave us a few hours warning that we were getting very close. When we were that close we could use our x-ray detector to get a more precise fix on its location.

We knew that Kali's ship was close, but it was hard finding it. Even if we'd used radar, it would have be tough discriminating the echos of all the debris that filled space around the black hole. At least we knew that the collision hadn't happened yet, but it couldn't be far off. The Doppler shift of the pulsar had been increasing very quickly.

We held meetings three times a day. On one, Aurora asked the question, "How long until the collision? I don't have a way to calculate it. Does anyone else?"

The BG asked, "Can you calculate the frequency just before collision? That ought to be possible."

She thought and said, "Yes. There are so many factors that come into play, like frame dragging. But I'll try." After a few minutes and the use of her calculator, she said, "Given that the rotational speed can't be more than the speed of light, but is probably not much less, the rotation rate would be around a thousand per second."

The BG said, "We're clocking at about eight hundred per second right now. We can monitor it. By the time it reaches nine hundred, we're really close. Also, the spatial distortion detector should start registering something close to that time as well. We ought to be able to predict pretty close when the collision will happen."

I asked, "How will we find Kali's ship in the blast debris of the collision. We haven't been able to find it now when there's not much debris flying around—relative to after the collision?"

The BG said, "Let's review what we know is going to be happening. What is Kali's ship going to be doing?"

Aurora answered, "Flying through the debris at high speed. It will probably collect element 126 using a powerful magnetic field to separate other isotopes."

The BG wrote that on the white-board. Then he said, "They'll be cruising rather fast." He wrote that on the white-board. Then he said, "They'll be generating a pretty powerful low frequency signal. It's too bad there's so much electromagnetic radiation flying around from the neutron star."

Aurora said, "What are you talking about? The neutron star and all it has will be swallowed by the black hole, never to emerge. There won't be much EM radiation around after the collapse of the neutron star into the black hole is complete."

The BG said, "Then we can track Kali's ship by the radio waves it generates?"

Aurora said, "You bet."

I said, "And we won't be generating much EM radiation, right?"

Aurora agreed. "Right. He would have a hard time tracking us even if he suspected we're out here."

Minns said, "Then all we have to do is to wait for the collision."

Ginny asked, "We don't know how long it will be before that collision occurs, right?"

Aurora answered, "That's right. We can tell when it's close, but that's about it."

Ginny sighed, "Great! It's a waiting game then." An after-thought occurred to her. "Is this going to be another titanic explosion like the supernova?"

Aurora said, "I don't think so. The black hole will swallow most of the energy—except for gravitational energy. It interacts so weakly with matter that we'll never feel it."

We discussed our plan of attack. It came down to the following:

First, we'd try a frontal attack with the inflaton missiles that we had onboard. If that failed, Aurora and Minns would disapparate onto Kali's ship and try to destroy it. If that failed, Ginny and I would disapparate over. If that failed, the BG would ram the ship and detonate every remaining missile in our armament.

The biggest point of discussion was how to communicate during the attack to be sure that we didn't trip over each other. The BG pointed out that once onboard Kali's ship we probably couldn't communicate by radio.

Ginny had an idea. "Here's what we should do. Each boarding party will have a witch. Every ten minutes. The pair will disapparate out of the ship and have a brief discussion of what has happened and how to proceed."

That sparked a discussion of what a brief discussion consisted of. I offered, "It should include where the team landed. That is, were they in the engine room, crew quarters, cargo hold, or (ideally) the Bridge. Second, what has the team accomplished, third, do they need help, and fourth, how long to the next report."

People estimated how long that would take. Estimates varied from two minutes (Ginny) to ten minutes (Minns). We decided that a minimum of five minutes was what we should expect.

Next we considered how long between reports. The results were even more varied. Ginny said that we should expect reports when they came. After all, the team might be pinned down in a fire fight. I said, "No matter. We need to know a maximum time. We need to know when to move on to the next stage of our plan."

There was a vote. Ginny was still for an hour. I was for twenty minutes. The BG favored a half hour. Aurora agreed on a half hour. I wondered why. Finally, Minns was for forty-five minutes, but he revised that to a half hour to make the decision process easier. We settled on a half hour.

Then there was the argument about which team would go first. Both Ginny and I wanted to go first. My argument was that you sent in the most expendable first. Aurora was for her team, arguing that you sent in the best first when it would be most likely to make a difference. We finally decided on Minns and Aurora first and then, Ginny and I.

□

That night in bed Ginny asked me, "How much time do we have after the collision before Kali has enough of element 126 for his doomsday device?"

319

I shook my head. She said, "Well, just in case things get moving too fast, I want you to know that I love you."

I almost laughed. How she could think that I didn't know that was incredible. I didn't though. I said, "I love you with all my heart."

Her head nodded just perceptibly. After a bit she said almost under her breath, "I thought so."

The next few days, the revolution rate of the neutron star increased slowly. On the third day, it was up to 832 per second. Aurora commented that the rate should begin increasing quickly. We sometimes let that frequency play on a speaker. Ginny, who has perfect pitch, said it sounded like G#.

Two days later, the tone was just under 900 per second. Aurora announced, "Tomorrow or the morning after at latest."

That night we decided to play Backalley Bridge. We hadn't in quite a while. The partnerships were obvious: Ginny and I; Aurora and Nicholas. It was a close game. If it hadn't been, I think we'd have kept playing until we hit a close game. Gnny and I had a narrow lead going into the final hand. As luck would have it Nicholas dealt and thus had the final bid. Since we all understood the mathematics involved, I trusted Ginny to bid appropriately. Nicholas bid so as to win by a point if his team made their bid. He just barely made the contract. His team won. We all thought it had been a good game. We all felt like it was time to stop while we were all ahead.

Ginny and I made love that night. We were both convinced it would be the last time.

The next morning, Ginny and I took our usual double shift.

□□

When it happened, we happened to be gazing into each other's eyes. A luxury that we allowed ourselves for a few minutes each hour. The space distortion detector went off. We might not have realized otherwise. The alarm sounded throughout the ship, so everyone quickly joined us in the Bridge.

However, before they arrived, Ginny and I kissed quickly. I kicked Ginny out of the weapons console seat. The BG took my seat. The BG had set up a radio wave detection alarm. We were now waiting for Kali's ship to start collecting heavy elements. Everyone expected it to happen quickly, so the Bridge was crowded for a couple of hours. Then everyone sort of gave up and we went back to our normal routine. Aurora and the BG finished their normal shift. Then Minns took over.

The next day we finished our joint shift with Ginny sitting in my lap. Nothing had happened. I was beginning to wonder if we were wrong about

320

the way that we could detect Kali collecting element 126. I was wrong. During Aurora's shift the electromagnetic sweeping mechanism on Kali's ship started and we got a clear signal. Our radio telescope quickly identified the location of Kali's ship.

We had a quick meeting in the Conference Room. I asked, "It time to set our attack plan in motion?" I polled our crew sequentially:

"Nicholas?"

He answered, "Go."

"Aurora?"

"Go."

"Ginny?"

"Go." The answer came without the slightest hesitation, full of determination.

"Minns?"

His answer was almost a drawl. "Go."

I then answered for myself, "Go."

We all suited up. I took the weapons console seat. The BG took the command pilot seat. The plan was that we would approach Kali's ship as closely as possible. We would approach sublight. If we were detected, we'd begin the assault. If we weren't, we'd go to rest at one hundred miles and begin the assault from there.

It took us a few minutes to arrive there. When we had, we had a quick meeting on the Bridge. Minns and Aurora were standing in the airlock with the inner door open. The BG was in the command chair. I was at the weapons console. Ginny stood behind me, a hand holding my arm. I was about to set up to fire when a thought occurred to me. "We should move after firing in case Kali's ship survives and has missiles capable of tracking the missiles' trails of geometric distortions."

Minns immediately agreed and said, "We should move fifty miles or so at a random direction using sub-light engines. Agreed?"

No one disagreed. So, Minns took the command chair to execute the move once I'd fired. I began the firing sequence. The monitor had a section set up for firing missiles. We had eight missiles on-board. The monitor showed icons for all of them. I tapped one. It turned from white to green and a small text box opened beside it. It contained the number 0.00. A question showed up above, "What fraction of power?" An on-screen key pad appeared. I entered, "1.00"

Ginny gasped, "Are we too close for that much power?"

I said, "I don't want to take a chance with too little. Now watch this." I tapped another missile icon. Again, I entered, "1.00" Ginny just said, "Shit."

"Now, now. If this prevents our having to go over there and punch some noses, it's all to the good."

She mumbled, "Just so long as we don't punch our own noses."

I looked over at Minns. He nodded. I pressed the green circle with an "X" inside. At the same instant several things happened. The tactical screen filled with white. We felt a full G of acceleration that drove us toward the back of the ship. There was a shock wave that hit the ship. The tactical screen cleared quickly, and an alert sounded. Four tracks showed on the screen, which rapidly shifted view to try to track the missiles. Then a gigantic explosion filled the screen. The shock wave from it was weaker than the earlier one. It must have been really far away. All of that happened in about three seconds.

Minns said, "Well, that answers the question of whether our missiles were successful. We'd better go." He got up from the command chair and motioned for the BG to take it. He did. Meanwhile Minns took Aurora's hand and said, "Put us in the cargo hold if you can."

She gave him a dirty look as if to say, "You'll be happy if I just get us on the ship." Then they disappeared. On the ship, we all released our breaths that had been held since before the shot that we took. Then we waited. I started a timer on the tactical display. It reached five minutes. Irrationally, I expected a report then. Of course, it didn't happen. The clock passed ten minutes, fifteen, twenty. Then the radio sounded.

It was Aurora. She said, "We think we're outside the Main Bridge. We landed in the cargo hold—miraculously. We've been working our way in toward the Bridge. Every bulkhead has been locked. All of the ship's lights are off. I've had to use my wand. It scared me to death. It makes us an obvious target for anyone who cared to shoot at us.

"We used the *Alohamora* spell to get out of the cargo hold. I decided to turn off my wand light when I went through the bulkhead. I stepped out. I didn't hear anything, so I barely lit my wand and signaled Minns to come out. He stepped out and said, 'There's no one here in this passage.'"

Minns added, "The whole time, we hardly saw a soul. I think they are either planning a bad surprise for us or don't care—one or the other."

Aurora went on, "We wandered around a bit, trying hatches that didn't lead us anywhere. Minns sense of direction kept us heading toward the Bridge. We actually saw a crew member that I stunned as soon as I saw him."

I asked, "What makes you think you're outside the Bridge and not an engine room or the weapons hold?"

Minns said, "For one thing, the *Alohamora* spell didn't work. That's an area that they want to keep people out of at all costs. It could be any of

322

those, but where they're located in the ship—amid-ships makes me think it's the Bridge. We're about to go to the other side of the bulkhead."

I answered quickly, "Whether it's the Bridge or not, report back in less than thirty seconds. If you don't, Ginny and I are coming over immediately."

Aurora announced that they'd been and returned. She announced, "It is the Bridge, but it's strange. I expected a crew to be manning the Bridge. Instead, there was only one person. He looked a lot like the description that we had of Kali."

I said, "One person can fly this ship just fine."

Minns said, "No. Not that ship. It had a number of duty stations. I'm sure that as a lifeboat one man could fly it, but you couldn't FLY it with one man."

Brahms said, "It sounds too good to be true. Go back and try to stop him and report back in not more than ten minutes—even if things are going swimmingly.

Aurora agreed. This time she announced their departure. I reset the timer and hoped for I knew not what. If they were back quickly, surely it would be because they had a problem. On the other hand as the timer passed five minutes, everyone on the Bridge were counting the seconds along with the clock.

□
□□

At seven minutes thirty-seven, Minns came back online. "We've hit a snag. I want some advice. We want to disapparate to our ship so that Wendt and Weasley can all come onto the Bridge."

"What!" I exclaimed.

Aurora just said, "It's complicated. It will be much easier if you are there with us."

I looked over at Ginny. She nodded urgently. She was right. Time was wasting. I said, "Come. We'll go back with you and do whatever's possible."

The BG stared at me and said, "I don't like it. It sounds screwy to me."

"You're right. What's the worst thing that could happen, though." Of course, I could think of a few worst things that would be worse than things were now, but I didn't have any time to talk them through. The next instant, Minns and Aurora appeared.

The BG asked, "Come clean now. What's going on?"

Aurora said, "No time. The four of us are going. If you don't hear from us within an hour, do you worst."

The BG grimaced and said, "I swear. If something goes wrong, I'll kill the lot of you."

Ginny whispered in my ear. "I hope so."

Then we all joined hands and disappeared—except for the BG.

We landed in a spacious room that had at least a dozen large-screen displays high up on the wall. The images included one of the silhouette of the black hole and another of a large expanse of densely star-packed space. The other displays were blank or they showed something in parts of the spectrum that my eyes couldn't perceive. Beneath this large displays were work stations with smaller monitors. There was a giant chair, almost a throne. Before and below it was a large monitor that might have been as large as the displays high on the wall.

There was a giant who seemed to be almost slumped into his "throne". He slowly swung his chair around to face us. When he saw Ginny and me, he actually laughed. Then he said, "Your friends will tell you why it's in-evitable. The universe is going to be re-built in the image of Kali."

Minns said, "Briefly, Kali has set up his Z-126 collector so it's impos-sible to turn off. It is buried in the core of our ship, almost under our feet. How can we stop it?"

Aurora said, "Move us out of the cloud of debris from the collision."

Kali laughed again. Minns said, "Kali has moved all the Z-126 out of the drive of the ship into the collector, haven't you?"

He smiled, "Very perceptive of you." Then he laughed again.

I said, "Let's use the sub-light drive to send this ship into the black hole."

There was just the slightest amount of uncertainty in Kali's voice when he said, "You don't know how to use this ship's controls."

This time it was Minns who smiled. "I think you'll help me."

Kali's mouth fell open. An arm lifted and a finger pointed at the dis-play before him. Minns almost chuckled. "Of course, the concentric circles are a joystick. The vertical bars are thrust and fuel reserves. There's an au-topilot, too. Let's use that. We can set the target to be the heart of the black hole."

Kali gasped and seemed to be struggling to seize Minns by the shoul-der, but he could hardly extend his arm a centimeter toward Minns. Mean-while, Minns had completed the autopilot configuration. The ship's engines fired and we could feel the thrust. It was difficult to stand against it.

Kali managed to gasp and force out, "No!" Then after a few minutes, he sighed. "It's still inevitable. You haven't moved the ship enough. We'll collect enough Z-126 before we fall into the black hole." He actually man-aged a weak chuckle.

Minns started to say, "I'm afraid he's right."

At that moment, a voice sounded in the room. I suppose it must have been from a radio receiver. I couldn't believe the words I heard:

"To the last I grapple with thee: From Hell's heart, I stab at thee; For hate's sake, I spit my last breath at thee."

One of the blank displays above our heads showed a ship fast approaching. It was coming over the horizon of the remains of the neutron star. Almost immediately there was a terrible crash. We were all thrown to the floor by the shock. Even Kali went down.

Our acceleration increased. Apparently, the ship was being pushed toward the black hole.

Kali seemed unhinged by the event. He ran to the control console and moaned, "NOOOOO!!!"

Minns said, "I think the ship is going through the event horizon in a few minutes. We've got to get back to our ship." He looked to Aurora. "Can you do it?"

The answer was, "We'll sure try." She turned to Ginny and said, "Take my hand. I'll take Minns. You take Wendt's. We'll disapparate at the count of three."

Meanwhile the ship groaned under the force of the colliding ship and maybe the tidal forces of the black hole. Ginny took my hand. I heard the dual voices counting three. Then we were all standing on the Bridge of our ship.

The BG asked, "What happened?"

I said, "We're safe. Give us a few hours to rest, and we'll debrief."

As it turned out, the debrief didn't happen quite that quickly. Before we'd had time to get the debrief started, we received a message by radio. There was a PAK fleet that had just arrived. They were looking for a lot of things that weren't around any more. They wanted to find Captain Ahab and his ship. They really wanted to find Kali and his ship. None of them were anywhere to be found.

The BG was on the Bridge. He fielded the questions. Of course, he was the least well prepared. He talked them into setting up a video conference call to debrief us all. Getting it set up took a good bit of a day. For one thing, the fleet and we wanted to stand off from the black hole. With the recent neutron star collision, there was way too much high energy debris around for anyone to be comfortable. We'd tolerated it when attacking Kali because we didn't have any choice. We had a choice now. So we all backed off about half a light year and stayed close together.

Then there was setting up the video connection and getting all the interested parties together. It turned out to be that evening. It was strange having both PAK and humans around a virtual table without either wearing a spacesuit. I think the PAK were expecting to be mostly listening while we reported. They were wrong. We had appointed Minns to do most of the talking although all of us expected to be questioned at one point or another. Minns started.

He said, "Let's level set here. We both know a lot about what the other group has done. You know that we left your research facility. We followed Kali to his next destination, which you did as well. How did the battle end?"

One of the PAK answered, "We defeated Kali's ships. It took us three days. Then we assembled a 'fleet' to follow Kali and you. We arrived at the astronomical observatory and found the director, who was happy to help us."

Minns asked, "How did you get here? You surely followed his trail to the supernova star. We only barely were able to continue the trail there. By the time you arrived, the trail near the star must have been obliterated."

Another PAK started to answer, but was cut off by the lead PAK. He muted their mike and a discussion ensued. Ginny asked, "I suppose they're trying to decide how much to reveal?"

Minns agreed. Meanwhile, there was a heated discussion going on with a lot of gesticulating. Finally, they unmuted and the lead said, "We decided to split into two groups. The larger force would follow Kali's trail. One ship would go directly to this black hole which was apparently Kali's final destination."

Ginny started to ask something. The PAK interrupted her. "The director of the astronomical observatory had worked out the precise location of the final destination by the time we arrived. Our decision was based on the hope that we could catch up with him before he reached the black hole. Ahab volunteered to take one ship directly to the black hole as a precaution. Did that turn out to be necessary?"

Minns explained, "As a matter of fact, it did. We were ahead of you, but we didn't have the advantage of knowing the precise location of his final destination. We followed him to the supernova. He detonated it just before we arrived. Fortunately, we were able to follow the trail by going through a high radiation area just before the physical shock wave arrived.

"We arrived at the black hole shortly before Kali could set up the extraction process for collecting Z-126. We waited until it started. We knew it had because . . ."

He never finished. He was immediately asked, "Why did you wait?"

I thought about that question. I've been bothered by it ever since. It was not a thought out decision. It just seemed obvious to all of us that we should wait. Was it because of fear? Did we hope that he'd back away from the awful act that he was about to perpetrate. Then we wouldn't have to attempt the extremely dangerous acts that we eventually did. I finally decided that it was the reluctance to strike first. God knew that Kali had provided plenty of provocation and offenses and deserved the fate that finally overtook him. Somehow, I just couldn't strike the first blow. I think that everyone else felt the same—well maybe everyone except Minns. I have never understood Minns completely.

What Minns said was, "It was the right thing to do." I've thought about that a lot too. Maybe it was just an expression of the morality that I felt. Maybe it was a calculation that the right time to strike was when Kali had started the extraction. We had met virtually no opposition when we invaded his ship. Was it his confidence in the outcome once he'd started? Would we have fought a pitched battle that we couldn't win if we'd not waited? I don't know, and Minns would never say.

Minns went on. "I led the first boarding party. We met essentially no opposition."

He was interrupted again by the question, "How is that possible?"

Minns replied, "He was absolutely convinced that the process couldn't be stopped—at least not by a boarding party once it had started. We only saw Kali himself and one other crew member although we traversed a good bit of the ship on foot.

"We reached the Bridge and found Kali waiting for us. He was supremely confident that his plan couldn't be stopped. The first boarding party was just Mrs. Brahms and I. Once we understood how difficult it would be to stop Kali, we added Wendt and Ms. Weasley to the party."

One of the PAK asked, "Why was it difficult to stop him? Couldn't you have transported a bomb onto the ship and detonated it?"

Minns went on. "If we'd had more time, that might have worked. The only weapons we had on our ship were missiles. We'd tried two to start with. They hadn't worked. Besides that we only had an hour or so to do something. It would have been nearly miraculous to have unshipped one of the missiles and transported it to a likely spot in the ship and detonate it with the time we had."

The same PAK asked, "So, how did you stop Kali and where is he and where's Ahab?"

Minns went on, "Wendt suggested moving the ship out of the area where the debris of the collision was located. That would turn off the extraction process, and we could deal with Kali. The problem was that he'd deactivated his FTL drive by putting all of his Z-126 supply into the extractor. As soon as it had collected the critical mass, he'd initiate the Big Crunch."

One of the PAK started to ask a question but understood the reference before completing the question.

Minns went on. "Wendt's winning idea was to use the sub-light drive to slow the revolution of Kali's ship and have it spiral into the black hole. We started that process."

A PAK asked, "Did you have to kill Kali to do that?"

Minns said, "No. I had disabled him. He gave us some clues how to use his ship's autopilot. Still that would not have worked quickly enough. The final blow was delivered by Ahab. He must have understood what was happening on Kali's ship. He rammed it and accelerated the process of killing the kinetic energy of Kali's ship. It slipped through the event horizon before he'd collected enough Z-126 to end the universe."

The main PAK said, "Then Ahab went down with Kali?" It was more a statement than question, but Minns agreed. The PAK then said, "I think that covers the important points. We can deduce the rest. If any important questions arise, we'll be in touch.

One of the PAK said, "Now, the last point is what do we do with the ship that you stole."

I leaped up at that. "Stole! You sent it to us to use. We've just pulled everyone's bacon out of the fire. You owe us in a big way."

The PAK thought a moment and said, "I suppose that there's some justice in that. We'll consider it seriously."

Suddenly, Ginny was standing beside me. She said, "Just think about the fact that we've defeated Kali—with some help from Ahab. Do you really want to take us on?"

I took her arm and said, "Give the man some time to think." That pretty much broke up the meeting.

After we'd left the video conference, Minns said, "They'll think their way through it. Don't worry too much."

I wasn't as confident as he was, but I decided that he was probably right. As a matter of fact, the PAK got in touch shortly thereafter. They offered that we could fly "our" ship back to Earth. They'd come by later and return their ship to the PAK home world. That night in bed, I commented to Ginny. "They want to make sure that they get their property back. Of course, it wouldn't be that bad to have an escort. Who knows what trouble we might get into on the way across half the galaxy."

She kissed me and said, "Shut up. You'll need a guard yourself if you don't satisfy me starting right now." I did.

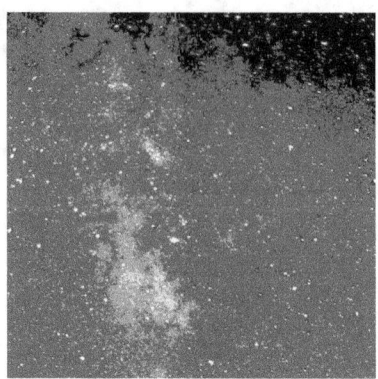

The Return

The first couple of days after the debrief we were so exhausted that we just set the ship flying and relied completely on the autopilot. We didn't even set a watch – except for Minns. We ate, slept, napped, and stared off into the confined space of the ship.

Then we got back to our normal routine. We had regular watches. We ate. We slept. We even played games to pass the months until we would arrive at Earth.

One day Ginny and I were standing watch together, occasionally watching the tactical monitor—just to make sure that we didn't fly into a sun—unnecessary, but what were you going to do besides working crosswords and talking? At one point, Ginny asked me about my previous lovers.

I answered, "OK. I'll talk about them if: one you reciprocate and two you understand that everything I tell you is public knowledge—nothing more."

She shrugged a "yes."

"All right. I'll list them in order of decreasing amount of time we were lovers. First, of course, was Minerva. You already know everything I could say about her.

"Second is you. I think you know way more about you than I ever will."

She stared at me incredulously and said, "What?"

"Well, isn't it obvious."

"No, it's not obvious. I know everything there is to know about me, but I don't know everything to know about your relationship with me—how you saw me."

I chuckled, "I saw you as a very smart, attractive, self-willed . . ."

She interrupted me there. "I am not self-willed. Go ahead."

"Well, you took me completely by surprise when you seduced me. I had no idea that you were interested."

She scoffed. "What planet were you living on? Why would I always try to be around when you and that Haley were off doing her maid of honor stuff? And didn't you notice how I couldn't keep my eyes off you?"

"Well, remember that I was married at the time, and my job was sort of keeping an eye on Haley."

She snorted, "Your job!"

"Anyway, once I got the idea that you were interested, the world became wonderful again."

"Alright. Enough of me for now. Go on."

I took her hand and said, "Of course, after you dumped me, Jaimie showed up. I guess she's number three. She sort of caught me on the rebound, and she had a lot of inside information on me that let her know the right buttons to push."

Ginny snorted, "Buttons to push, indeed. It was other things she was pushing."

"Now, now. Let's stick with public knowledge. Anyway. We've pretty much reached the end of serious relationships."

Ginny just shook her head and said, "Keep going."

"OK. Number four was someone you've never heard of. She was sort of a summer fling. Actually she was more of a July fling. It was the summer after my first year at Hogwarts. I'd gone back to the States to visit my family. On the flight over I met a student who was spending the summer at an institute in New Mexico. After the end of the institute we got together, and we kind of had a week together touring Ohio."

Ginny laughed. "What in the world is Ohio? It's not a vacation destination that I've ever heard of."

I shrugged, "It's one of the states of The States. My family lives there. And it's not that bad a travel destination. We sort of circumnavigated the state."

Ginny was still giggling. "What are the big attractions of Ohio?"

"Well, there's the Ohio river, which is longer than any river in England. It has one of the great cities of the US on it, Cincinnati." Ginny rolled her eyes, and I went on. "Then there's Lake Erie. It's one of the five Great Lakes. It's in the top fifteen lakes of the world. It has Cleveland on it."

"OK. So, I know how you broke up with the others. How did it happen with her? The summer ended?"

"Actually, it was accidental. Minerva met me at Heathrow and disapparated me off before I could do anything with . . ."

Ginny interrupted me. "You don't think that was any more accidental than when I met you at Heathrow when you returned with Haley?"

"I suppose not."

"So what did you do with Haley?"

"Oh, I had a long weekend with her in Cleveland."

Ginny shook her head and said, "You didn't even do a tour of Ohio?"

"Oh, give me a break. Cleveland has all sorts of interesting things."

"Like what?"

I said, "Lake Erie."

"Oh, yes, the fifteenth largest lake in the world."

I tried to draw my self up with dignity. "There's the Rock and Roll Hall of Fame."

That got Ginny's attention. She asked, "So, they have the Weird Sisters?"

I shook my head, "no."

"Then at least Celestina Warbeck?"

"Oh, you're just being mean."

She smiled and said, "You know that I'm just joking."

"Sure."

She smiled. "I suppose that's it, right? What could be smaller than these? One-nighters?" She hesitated—I guess waiting for my denial. It never came.

She scoffed. "I'd never have figured you for a one-night man. How many?"

"Two."

"Only two? I thought men who did one-nighters prided themselves on multiple conquests. Isn't that what you call them?"

"I don't. Both of them were absolutely unique—one in a million cases."

She released a sigh of relief. Then a strange thought occurred to her. "One in a million, eh. I suppose they were goblins." I didn't deny it. Her eyes widened in disbelief. "No. really? Goblins?"

I sighed, too. "Really only one. Like I said it was a one in a million case."

She laughed. "I suppose she was the daughter of the CEO of Gringotts." I didn't say anything. She exclaimed, "It was, wasn't it. How in the world did you ever end up in bed with the heir to the Gringotts fortune? I guess I can't blame you too much." Then she added, "But really? A goblin?"

I said, "It's more reasonable than you might think. I do business with Gringotts."

She scoffed. "Everyone who has a vault there does business with Gringotts. Why, I got a Gringotts Mastercard just this year." She paused. "You didn't have anything to do with that did you?" My silence continued. "You did! Didn't you?" Then she reached into her ever-present purse, rummaged around, and found the little rectangle of plastic.

I asked, "You brought it with you?"

She repeated the Gringotts motto, "Don't travel without it." Her mouth opened wide, and she stared at me. "You didn't come up with that little jingle, did you?"

"Well, it wasn't really original. Another organization used something like it."

She seemed to be reeling a bit at the idea that I was working with Gringotts on at least one big project. "OK. OK. I get it that you've done a lot of business with Gringotts, but did you have to sleep with the daughter for that?"

I said, "No. It's not as simple as that. You know that goblins value business acumen more than anything else."

"Yeh."

"Well, they find that sexually attractive too."

Ginny said, "Oh, give me a break. Are you telling me that this goblin gal went for you because you were good at business?"

"More than that. She was an absolute pest. I do some business nearly every month that requires personal meetings. I couldn't avoid running into Javeen no matter how hard I tried."

Ginny scoffed again. "And the dad was perfectly OK with that?"

"Oh, he encouraged her."

She shook her head in disbelief. "Well, I suppose you must be pretty rich then."

I nodded. She asked, "Just how rich?"

I took out my Kindle and opened a notepad. I keyed in a number. I said, "The last time I looked, this was about the amount in my vault." I handed her the Kindle.

She stared and said, "That has seven digits. You're lying." She used a tone of voice that I'd rarely heard from her.

I replied, "Everyone lies about emotions. I don't lie about facts. That number is the minimum that my balance was the last time that I looked."

Her mood changed. She said, "I hate you! Why did you have to show me that? I can't trust myself anymore. When I think of what I could do with that much money, it makes me gag."

I massaged her wrist. "I'm not worried about you. I know your family. I know you. You won't do anything differently from what you'd do if you hadn't seen that number."

She mumbled, "I'm not so sure." She went on, "OK. I get why she wanted to sleep with you. Why did you let her?"

"Oh, it was self-defense. I worked a deal with her. She was crazy. Half of the appeal of the deal to her was that it was a business deal with me. The deal was that I would sleep with her—no reservations—and she wouldn't bother me again."

Ginny nodded and seemed deep in thought. Then she said, "I suppose it was a decent deal for you. She doesn't pester you again, and all you have to do is endure a night with her."

"Oh, it wasn't that bad. As a matter of fact, it was actually pretty decent."

Ginny scoffed. "Then she imperioused you."

"No she didn't. We talked about it. And, well, yes—with my permission."

Again, Ginny rolled her eyes. "How could you even talk about her imperiousing you? Why would she think you might agree?"

"That wasn't it at all. She just said that she was so good that she wouldn't need to imperious me to get me into bed with her."

That made Ginny laugh. "Well you have to admire her confidence. So, how was she?"

That made me laugh. "You know that I don't kiss and tell."

"All right. All right. So who was the last lone nighter?" She interrupted me before I could speak. "No. Let me guess. I think I know. Was it the Minister of Magic, Pamela?"

"No. It wasn't . . ."

"No hints. What about Aurora?"

"No."

"Then, surely it wasn't Dursley's Pamela?"

"No."

She went through a fairly long list of possible and impossible witches. "I know! It's that cute receptionist at the Ministry. She's always flirting with you."

"No."

She said, "OK. I'll take a hint."

"It's not a witch."

She exclaimed, "It's never a giant?"

"Don't be silly."

She nodded. "So, it's a Muggle. It obviously wasn't Haley. I don't know many Muggles. Who was it."

"Well, her name was Jennifer. I dated her for a couple months when I started at Hogwarts. I never slept with her when we dated."

Ginny shook her head. "Then when did you have a one night stand with her?"

I took a deep breath. "It happened when Minerva and I were in New York."

Ginny asked, "When were you two in New York? I know you were there while I was at Hogwarts one summer. Is that when it happened?"

I sighed. Here we were just about to hit the tricky part. "You probably didn't hear about it because you didn't have a need to know. There was a little—and I emphasize that adjective—intelligence operation that was a joint effort of the US intelligence community, British intelligence, and the Ministry of Magic."

She looked to be about to object. I interjected, "No. Not the Auror Office. I know, I know. You should have been and you'd probably have heard about it if the Auror Office had been involved. Probably only gossip around the pumpkin juice cooler. However, you didn't have a need to know, so you didn't." I laughed. "You know, you do know about it now. Minns was the subject of that intelligence operation. It went south and not much came of it—until now.

"Anyway, we fell on our face. After it was over, everybody went straight home except for Minerva and me. We took a cruise on an inland waterway, the Tennessee river. When it was over we went to New York to arrange port key passage back to England."

This time Ginny's interruption worked, she was that incensed. "You mean to tell me that your 'one-night stand' was while you were married to Minerva?" You don't have to guess when Ginny's mad.

I held up a hand in defense. "Just hear me out. I told you it was one in a million event. One in a billion would probably be more accurate. Here's what happened:

"Minerva and I were staying in a hotel in New York for one night. She has a friend from the States when she was a student at Hogwarts who lives in New York. Minerva's friend was married to an Auror who was off on business. They were going to have a girl's night out. That was fine with me. I tried looking at TV in our room and gave it up. Then I went down to the hotel restaurant, bought a copy of the New York Times, scanned the front pages and set section A aside. I then pulled the crossword out. Crosswords go easier with Dewars. I had a glass, a pencil, and the crossword.

"Then, someone asked me if she could read the front section of the paper. I started to say that she could have it. I looked up, and we both recognized each other. She was Jennifer Waters. I hadn't seen her for a good dozen years. When I'd last seen her, we'd been dating. She'd broken up with me. We started off talking about what had happened with us. I invited her to sit and bought her a drink."

I hesitated to think. Recreating the mood of that evening would be hard but I had to do it. I went on. "Twelve years is a long time. We both had a lot of catching up to do. Jennifer had gone into first the merchant marine and then got a position as purser of a cruise ship. Of course, I had a complicated history myself. We spent quite a lot of time and Dewars getting caught up. Like me, this was her last night in New York.

"When we were up to the present, Jennifer pointed out that after we'd been going out for over a month, she expected that I'd spend the night. I'd refused her in a conspicuous way before one of her friends. She figured that I owed her a night."

Ginny said, "Why did you figure she was right?"

"Well, don't forget that I'd had a certain amount of whiskey in me. Also, I really did feel guilty about not sleeping with her that night long ago."

"Why didn't you?"

I sighed. "I'd never made love to anyone before. I didn't expect the offer, and frankly, I was afraid."

Ginny scoffed, "Come on, you'd never taken a woman to bed before then. How old were you?"

"I was twenty-six."

She looked at me with wide-eyed wonder. I said, "It's true."

She said, "OK. Wow!" After a pause, "Still . . . How do I know that won't happen to me? Is there another woman hiding in the weeds who will show up at an odd moment demanding a one-nighter?"

I answered quickly. "There is only one other woman whom I've ever dated. Her name was Stephanie George. She lived in the rooming house where I lived before I came to Hogwarts. She was an art student while I lived there. I had a class A crush on her while I lived there. She was stunning. She had long, silky blonde hair that fell below her hips. She was smart and a determined artist.

"She never gave me the time of day."

Ginny asked, "So, if she showed up that crush wouldn't reappear as though by magic?"

For once I could actually smile and answer that question directly. "Well, it's kind of a funny thing. Something like that actually did happen."

Ginny bared her teeth, "Oh?"

"Yes. It was during the summer holiday of my second year at Hogwarts. The previous summer I'd spent in the States. This summer I decided to stay in London. I looked first to my old rooming house to find a place to stay. My old room was let, but the landlord had re-modeled the attic into a room. It was available. I rented it.

"To my great surprise, Stephanie was still living there. It was the last thing I expected. I was sure that she'd have graduated and moved on, but there she was at breakfast my first morning there. It was a shock for both of us. Once she recovered from the shock, she started throwing herself at me."

Ginny said, "The way you describe her, Stephanie sounds a lot like Jaimie."

I thought about it and realized there were some superficial similarities. I said, "She does sort of, doesn't she?"

"Is that maybe why you find her appealing?"

I left that question alone and went back to my story. "I had a series of what I might call accidental dates."

Ginny laughed. "Accidental dates? What in the world would those be? Did you pass her table in a restaurant and trip and fall into a chair?"

I grumbled, "You're not making this easy."

Her eyes lit up, and she said, "Keep going."

"Well, I didn't have any interest in a relationship with her, but our positions had been reversed from a couple of years before. I didn't want her to go through the same agony that I had. So, I decided that I'd take her out to dinner and let her down as easily as I could.

"That was technically a date, but I looked at it more like a business meeting. I had some business to conduct, and I was going to conduct it in a congenial setting—not over the kitchen table. She was delighted that I had asked her out so quickly. That cued me into the fact that it would be either a long dinner or a very short one.

"We went to a nice quiet Italian restaurant. She was excited, bubbly, and full of talk. It was hard to break in to get her to order. Finally, the food arrived. You'd think that she'd have to slow down talking once we started eating. Right?"

Ginny said, "I bet she didn't."

"Right. Somehow she didn't seem to need to breath. She managed to talk through mouthfuls. I didn't have a chance to say anything. I thought, 'OK. We'll have dessert and surely she'll slow down then.'"

Ginny said, "She didn't. What happened?"

"Right. She suggested going to see a movie. I accepted the idea. I thought, 'I can talk to her after the movie. We'll go get a cup of tea. We'll talk, really talk—not just drink from a fire hose of talk.

"So, we went to the movie. It was a good movie. I didn't see a lot of it. She had a hand on my thigh. Then she had a tongue in my mouth and no-

337

body was doing any talking. The movie ended, and she wanted to go straight home. It was late, and I thought that we could talk there. Of course, there wasn't that much talking. By then I was getting close to desperate. Sure, sex with her would probably have been great, but it wasn't going anywhere, and I was mostly just trying to give her a soft landing on airstrip break-up. Funny, eh? Breaking up before you were ever a couple."

Ginny asked, "OK. So the point of this story is?"

"Obvious, right? If I were ever going to do a one-night stand with Stephanie, it would have been fifteen years ago in that rooming house in London—not now, not later."

"Hmmm. You sure?"

I said calmly, "Yes."

That was the conversation. We sat for a long time quietly. Then our watch ended. When we went to bed that night, we just held each other.

□

The next day on our joint shift, I asked the question that had been percolating for a while and which was about to boil over. "Ginny, what happens after we get home?"

She growled a little and said, "I don't want to face that question."

I nodded. "I don't want to either, but we'll either answer it before we arrive or it will answer itself after we do. Personally, I'd prefer to do the answering."

She gripped my hand and squeezed until I thought she'd fracture a bone. She said, "If we answer it now, it may be the end of, well, everything we value right now. Will you take that chance?"

That ended our conversation for the rest of that double shift. That night we did make love.

We never raised that question again. Nor did we count days. We knew the exact date that we would enter the Earth's atmosphere. We never named it, we never calculated days. None of the others—Minns, the BG, or Aurora—hinted that there would be an end of this flight.

338

There's No Place Like Home

The day before we reached Earth, Minns came into the Bridge at the beginning of our double watch. At the time, we didn't realize it was the day before. He broke the news to us. "Tonight's the last night before we reach Earth."

Both Ginny and I gulped in unison. You'd have thought that we were channeling her twin brothers. I found her arm looped through mine. I said, "Thanks."

Minns then surprised me by saying, "I'll take your watches and mine."

I started to object. However, Ginny said, "Oh, thank you so much."

"It's nothing. In the army, a fifteen hour watch would not be usual but it wasn't peculiar either. It's my pleasure. The two of you might want . . ." He didn't finish his sentence. He didn't have to.

I said, "You go ahead. I'll catch you up shortly." She frowned but left for the ship's galley.

I turned to Minns and said, "There's one thing that's been bothering me for quite some time. I hope you can clear it up for me."

"Maybe I can. Go ahead."

"Here's the thing. I don't understand why you insisted on Ginny coming on this mission? The obvious choice would be Jaimie. She's a witch. She's smart. She's talented. We work together well. Was it because you knew that Ginny and I had been together earlier?"

He flashed a brief smile. "First, it was not because of any relationship between either you and Ginny or you and Jaimie. Ginny was the best candidate.

"Second, she has all the qualities we needed. She is brilliant. She is hard working. She is brave. I'm not saying that Jaimie isn't, but Ginny is the tops in that criteria. She is determined. She would not give up on a mission just because it looked impossible. Jaimie just isn't as good at any of those as Ginny is."

It was my turn to frown. "Then, why not just say that up front when the team was chosen?"

Minns shook his head. "Why don't you tell me why I didn't do that?"

I thought for a minute or two and then I said, "Well, I suppose that if you'd said that at the beginning, I'd have fought you up until the start of the mission and maybe even beyond. That would not have been good."

He nodded, "That's part of it, but it's not all. By not saying anything, I led you to believe that it was an unknown factor that even I couldn't explain rationally. That short-circuited any objections that you might have had."

I scoffed. "You don't trust me much, do you?"

Minns nodded slowly. "I trust you exactly as you deserve to be trusted. I trust you to be dedicated to the mission, to give yourself fully to it, to sacrifice what has to be sacrificed for it.

"However, I don't trust you where you don't deserve to be trusted. I didn't trust you to be willing to leave your lover behind."

I thought about that for a long time and finally said, "Good judgment. I hope Ginny is patient."

He smiled. "I think you'll find that she is despite the disappointment that she gave you last year."

I nodded. Then I left to join Ginny in the ship's galley. Ginny said, "Let's fix PBJ sandwiches. They're fast and nutritious."

I laughed. "Sure. We'll need our strength."

We were still eating our sandwiches when we entered our cabin. Ginny grabbed me and said, "Two things. One: Don't eat in bed. Two: Don't talk. We have better purposes for our mouths." As usual, she was right.

However, we did use our mouths for something else. We did talk. Ginny said, "This is our last night together."

My countenance fell. "Then you've decided."

"No, I have not!" She said defiantly. "I'm just scared that one of us will decide one way, and the other will decide the other way."

I didn't press her—other than when we were spooning. Late in the night, we were both hungry. We went out to the galley and had a ham sandwich each. We fed each other and generally were able to forget the tragedy that was staring us in our faces. The rest of the night we alternately napped and made love. The experience was bizarre. It seemed to go on forever but also seemed to fly by.

□

The next day, we prepared for the end of the journey. We cleaned up the ship. We packed. That brought a question to my mind that I raised at breakfast. "We're all humans on this bus. What happens with the ship?"

The BG said, "Well, we have something of a quandary. I'd be inclined to turn the ship over to the British military or NATO or even the US military except for a few issues:

"One, there are still some very powerful weapons on-board. Of course, we don't have to give away the access codes to them, but there are some pretty smart cookies over at MI6 and the US DOD. I wouldn't be sure that they'd not hack in and unlock them."

Ginny said, "We could destroy them, couldn't we?"

Aurora said, "We'd probably have to shoot them at something. Of course, I suppose we could target the moon or the sun. Set at minimum yield they'd not make much of an impact—especially on the sun."

I said, "Well, let's not forget that this ship is strictly speaking not our property, and the PAK said that they'd drop by to pick it up."

Aurora exclaimed, "A reward for saving the universe ought to be a bit bigger than this ship!"

I said, "Look. I think we're owed a big fat reward, but one could look at what we've done and think, 'Gee, that was also a self-serving act. After all, they're part of the universe as well.'"

Ginny put her hand over mine and said, "There's very little self-serving about you. I should know."

Minns had the last word, as he often had. "Now that we're in the standard FTL communication lanes, I've contacted the PAK. They are sending a ship with a crew for this ship. It should arrive in a few days after we arrive on Earth. I volunteer to stay on board in deep Earth orbit until they do arrive."

Ginny spoke up then. "I volunteer Wendt and me to baby-sit the ship until the PAK arrive." I was surprised but didn't object for a second.

Minns chuckled. "Well, I would be happy to set foot on terra firma a little sooner. That's why I didn't join the Navy or Air Force. I like having solid ground under my feet. I have no objection."

Aurora smiled. "I see where this is going."

Ginny couldn't keep a smile off her lips. She just said, "Don't you dare!"

Aurora just smiled as well.

The next day Minns contacted the USS Ohio. It was in dock at its home port. After some negotiation with the captain of the Ohio and then with Her Majesty's Navy, it was decided that a British Trafalgar class submarine would rendezvous with our ship and accept Minns and the Brahmses on board to be delivered to the nearest Scottish coastline. Also, if feasible, the Ohio would rendezvous with Ginny and me as before—provided of course, that the Ohio could reach the North Atlantic by the time that the PAK dropped us off.

Then the BG entered programs to get us to the agreed-upon location in the North Atlantic where we would rendezvous with the Trafalgar sub that would pick them up and to get us back up to the deep orbit where we'd wait for the PAK. I asked the BG just where we would wait for the PAK.

The BG said, "We're going to send you up to the L2 Lagrange point of the Earth/moon system. It has several advantages over other locations.

"One is that it's always easy to find it. Everywhere else, the position relative to either the Earth or the moon is constantly changing. Another is that the Lagrange points are pretty stable. You don't have to work to keep your ship there. It happens pretty automatically. The L2 Lagrange point isn't super about that but for a short period of time, it's OK. Another advantage is that you can't see the L2 point from the earth. You're safer there from nosy Earth neighbors."

Ginny nodded and said, "It also gives us a view of the far side of the moon all the time." She leaned over and whispered in my ear, "Romantic."

The BG said, "The Trafalgar's captain has said that he can reach the rendezvous tomorrow an hour after local sunrise. We'll meet him there."

□
□□

The next day we saw the great blue marble rapidly expand in our screen. You could hardly see the continents except for North Africa. The clouds covered almost everything else. We must have been at least a half hour coming down through the cloud cover, but it seemed like minutes. We broke through the cloud cover, and there below us was the long thin line of the Trafalgar.

The BG took over from the autopilot. It was only half human-controlled though. A reticle showed on the monitor at the command seat. It was centered on the sub. The autopilot took the spaceship where the reticle was centered. We quickly approached the sub and came to rest about a meter above the sub's deck. Once it was clear that the ship was resting in place, the BG lowered the ramp. He, Aurora, and Minns walked down to the deck. There were a ship's officer and a couple of enlisted men with assault rifles. The ship's officer checked them against photos. I walked down with the BG, just to make sure all went well.

I shook hands with Minns and the BG. Aurora hugged me and said, "Take good care of Ginny." They entered the sub via a hatch in the sail. I re-entered our ship. Ginny was waiting on the Bridge in the command seat. I took the weapons officer seat next to her. She raised the ramp and engaged the auto-pilot program to take us up to L2. The flight took us fairly close to the moon. We saw the meteor-shattered surface close up. As we passed the moon we had a look back at the Earth.

I commented, "That's the last that we'll see of the Earth for a while."

Ginny took my hand. "You know, we are the loneliest couple of people there have ever been."

"How do you figure?"

"Even when we were tens of thousands of light years from Earth, there were other people around. When Minerva died, there were still a couple of other people with you. The nearest human to us is more than what?"

I squeezed her hand and said, "More than a quarter of a million miles away." I smiled. "But, you know, I don't feel that lonely."

⊡⊡

The next couple of days were in many ways similar to spaceflight with the rest of the old crew. There were significant differences, though. We didn't have to be quite so circumspect with our public displays of affection. At one point, Ginny and I were on the Bridge talking as we often had before. She caressed my leg as she said, "You know we could stay here indefinitely."

I nodded. "We have food, water, air indefinitely."

"Sure. There's no disease up here. The food is healthy. We can exercise. We could live forever? Well, for a very long time together."

"Yes, all we have to do is talk the PAK into letting us have the ship. As we've said, it's a small price to pay for our gigantic favor for them."

I chuckled, and she sighed. Then I took a deep breath. We really had to discuss the dragon in the room. So, I kicked it off. "We've been holding off on this discussion for quite a while. It's time."

Ginny was subdued. "Do we have to? We've surely still got weeks and weeks? Days and days?"

"Probably."

343

"Which."

"Days and days."

She nodded. "OK. You go."

A long pause ensued. Then I said, "We both know that when we land on real land there will be someone waiting for you. He's going to want to know when. He probably won't say anything more than that—just 'when'."

"You know, I don't have an answer for that."

That sounded positive. I said, "You don't have to have an answer to that for me—ever."

She had a crooked smile on her face. "Maybe I want to answer that."

"Well, if you were going to answer that, what would it be?"

She moved her hand up to my side. "It could be the fifth of never."

I took a deep breath. "I never thought you might be open to something more permanent than comfort in a horrible situation. Would you give me a date—for you and me."

"Yes."

"Wow. When we get back, will you invite me to your Mum and Dad's? Soon?"

There was a wide, happy smile on her face. "Sure."

That night, in bed, Ginny said, "You know what?"

"No, what?"

"It's just like a honeymoon."

"Sure is."

Then a sad idea occurred to me. "Do you realize that I'm at least sixteen years older than you?"

She shrugged. "So?"

"Well, when you're in your prime—say fifty—I'll be in my upper sixties. You'll have to take care of a doddering old fool for the best years of your life."

She actually laughed at that. "Look. In the first place, you're not sixteen years older than I am."

"Sure I am. When you entered Hogwarts at the ripe old age of twelve, I'd been teaching there for two years. I was twenty-six when I started at Hogwarts!"

Her smile didn't falter. "I've thought this out a lot more carefully than you have. Listen. You're actually at least four years younger than you think you are. You forget that when the bitch, Jaimie was using your body, you're were restored to the age that you had been when she took over by Dursley's polyjuice potion."

I screwed up my face and said, "Whaaat? It restored my genetic makeup but did nothing much for the rest of my body."

She just clucked her tongue and said, "Silly man. Age is mostly genetic. Your age is genetically programmed and kept track of by your genes. Every time you restored your genetic makeup, you turned back the clock on your body."

"Hmmmm. So then you figure that I'm actually a dozen years older than you?"

She gave a positive nod of her head and said, "At most."

I went on. "Then, if you're right, I'll age slower than you will. Currently, the deal that I have with Jaimie is that we will alternate—three years alive and three years gone. So that makes me age half as fast as you."

Ginny nodded and added, "I've been thinking about that too. I think you should re-negotiate the deal."

I was firm. "I'm not reneging on my promise."

Ginny could be pretty firm, too. "I'm not bloody asking you to renege. I'm just saying, 'Change the exact terms a little.' It makes more sense for both of you to make it a year on and a year off. Everybody gets the same amount of time and you don't have to have that depressing three year gap."

"Hmmm. I think you've got a point."

She hurried on. So viewed that way, in twenty-four years when I'm a pre-prime fifty, you'll also be fifty. Another twenty-four years when I'm a spry seventy-four, you'll be a slightly post-prime sixty-two."

I broke in. "Yeh, and in another twenty-four years when you're a doddering ninety-six, I'll be a spry seventy-four."

"See. It all evens out in the end."

I said, "Somehow, I think there's something screwy there, but when are things not screwy when you're dealing with witches."

The rest of our time at L2 was just like a honeymoon. We tried to remember every exotic meal that we'd ever had and re-created them in the auto-galley. We watched the stars. One day, we did a little excursion down to the moon. It was a little harrowing. I had to save the current program that Brahms had programmed into the auto-pilot to take us back to Earth—just in case. Then I flew us down to the Aitkin Basin near the South Pole. We put on our spacesuits and walked on the moon. We probably reached the limits of the spacesuits, but they held up, kept us not too cold and not too warm, and let us walk around. We sat on a rock and looked up at the stars.

When we were back in the ship, Ginny said, "This is the most romantic trip that I can imagine. You know what we ought to do?"

I was way ahead of her. "Let's make love in one-sixth gravity."

She was way ahead of me. She already had clothes off and had her legs wrapped around my body. It was hard, of course. Getting in a good pose was hard too.

That night, we did make love on the moon. I was sure that we were the first to do that. The next day we decided that we'd probably pushed the limits of what we ought to do with the ship. So, we returned to L2. It was easier than I expected to get us back there. The old autopilot programs were still around. I entered the latest—just taking us to L2. It got us there. When we were in bed that night, Ginny said, "What do you think? Did I sort of forget to use protection last night?"

"I think you are a hard ass that just might have done." That sort of set her off. We had another great night.

Those last couple of days were heaven in the heavens. Then we got a message from the PAK. "Prepare to turn the ship over to an expedition coming to take it home."

The honeymoon was over. The next day a ship arrived. It docked with us. Two PAK wearing spacesuits came through the lock and took possession of the Bridge. We asked for one last night before they took us to Earth. Their answer was that they'd already contacted the Ohio, which would take another day to reach the rendezvous point. We used that day well.

Who Goes There?

The day was a sad one. It wasn't that we didn't want to return to Earth. It was just that somehow we both had the feeling of grief, of something irrevocably lost. It wasn't unfamiliar. I'd felt that way at the end of every vacation that I'd ever had—whether it was at the beginning of third grade or returning from a trip to the States.

This one positively scared me. What would happen to Ginny and me. It was easy sitting on the far side of the moon where you couldn't even see the Earth and imagining this wonderful life you could have together. It was very much another thing watching the Earth expanding with every passing second. We were flying straight at a swirling mass of clouds over the North Sea that didn't look welcoming.

The seas were choppy and even the experienced hand of the PAK pilot couldn't keep our ship perfectly aligned with the Ohio. It's deck pitched and rolled. When the ramp was lowered, the deck of the Ohio clanged against it loudly. The wind was blowing sheets of water across the deck. At least there were two crew members and an officer whom I thought I recognized as Wainwright, the XO.

I held Ginny's arm as we walked down the ramp. At the bottom, a crew member wrapped each of us in a life vest. Ginny's crewman helped her through the hatch to the interior of the sail. I shook Wainwright's proffered hand and walked into the interior. As soon as the hatch was dogged, the PA announced, "Prepare for dive." Shortly after that we were tipping down at a small angle. Ginny grasped my arm and asked, "Are we sinking?"

"Yes, but it's good. Once we get a little ways down, we won't feel the storm going on above." She nodded.

Wainwright led us to Officer Country. I knew where we were going. When we arrived, Wainwright took us to the Officer's Mess and filled us in

347

on what was happening. "We could get to the coast of Scotland in a day, but we couldn't get you ashore with this gale blowing. It may take a day or two more to get you to the beach. You'll each have to bunk in with an officer."

I asked, "Could we bunk together?"

Wainwright's mouth opened and closed soundlessly. "Well, I'll have to re-arrange cabin assignments. I'll see what I can do." He left us. I suppose he was consulting with the captain. It took him a couple of hours to return. We made ourselves mugs of tea in the microwave.

Ginny commented, "You know I couldn't ever get a decent cup of pumpkin juice in that damn ship. I suppose there wouldn't be one here?"

I shook my head. Before we'd finished the tea, the XO had returned. "I've finagled a cabin for you two. The second officer has agreed to bunk in my cabin and has given you his. I think that you'd have a hard time sharing a bunk—they're all compact here." We both smiled in answer.

Wainwright led us to the cabin. Once we'd tossed our stuff in, there was precious little room, but we were grateful. Wainwright said, "This is different from other cruises you've taken. We're confident that you're not a danger to us, so there are no guards. If you would like a tour of the ship, I'd be glad to oblige, Ms. Weasley."

She thanked him and he said that after the evening meal, he'd take us around. In the mean time, we were free to visit the Head, the Officer's Mess, or our cabin. The tour was the only interesting thing that happened while we were on the ship.

Wainwright made it interesting. We got to look through an open bulkhead at the nuclear reactor. He commented, "That is as close as you will get to the power that drives the sun." We went to the missile room. He stood by one of the tubes and said, "We could go a long way toward ending life on Earth with what's in these. It would be good-bye to the Louvre, the Eiffel Tower, Big Ben, the Lincoln memorial, Congress, and a whole lot of other places."

Ginny squeezed my arm and whispered in my ear, "Could we visit those places in the States?"

I answered, "If I have any say about it, yes."

We saw the crew's mess and got a quick look in the Bridge. Then it was over and we were back to the Officer's Mess and boredom for the rest of the cruise. Of course, we could have cut a little time off the cruise by disapparating when we were a couple of hundred miles from the shore, but we really interested in shortening the time.

We received the word that we would land on the beach about sunrise the next day. We spent our last night on the sub spooning—about the only thing we could do in the confined quarters despite our ardent wish to do more.

We dragged our belongings up to the deck and were helped on-board a rubber boat. As we were clambering down the sides of the sub, Ginny asked me, "Is it true what George said about your fall in the water the first time you did this?"

"Your brother was exaggerating. It wasn't the first time, and I maintain that it was either George or Fred that caused that little mis-step."

Ginny just said, "Um-hum."

We sailed slowly from the ship to the shore. There was someone standing on the beach waiting for us, but it was still pretty dark out. I couldn't tell who it was. I was pretty sure that it must be Potter. It seemed ironic to me that in the end it was Potter whom I feared the most of all the wizards that I'd known. He alone had the power to take the joy of my life away from me.

I was determined that it wouldn't happen—not this day, anyway. As we neared the shore, I wondered if it were actually Potter standing there.

□

The wind kicked up just before we reached the shore, and I leaned forward in the rubber boat to avoid the worst of the rocking and swaying. I swayed and couldn't get a good look at the person waiting for us. I swung over the side of the boat, landed in the water, got my feet wet, and righted myself.

Then, I found a wet kiss planted on my mouth. Then it was in my mouth. I would have applied more analysis except that the tongue had hardly found a place in my mouth and her hands around my waist when we disapparated somewhere.

The first thing I saw after my nausea lessened was a lady pulling platinum blonde hair away from her face with one hand while holding me with the other hand and kissing me again. This time, I recognized the kiss. There was no doubt about it. It was the full open mouth kiss of Stephanie the art student. There was the long platinum blonde hair too. There was just one problem. Stephanie was definitely not a witch. I have to admit that Stephanie could arrest your attention with her kiss, but even she had to come up for air at some point. When she did, I finally got a good look at my surroundings, including her.

She had to be Stephanie. She had the same long platinum blonde hair, the same height, the same mannerisms, and by God, the same kiss. How could she not be? Well, Stephanie was never a witch. Stephanie didn't know about Hogwarts, which was where we were. Where we were was pretty darn cold. That was the first thing I said, "Why is it so cold?"

She smiled. "Well, you've been away for a long time. Don't you know that it's winter. As a matter of fact it's Christmas Holiday here at Hogwarts." She was right. It was darn cold. There wasn't any snow, but that wasn't really unusual for Hogwarts at Christmas.

I had been adding things up. It didn't seem reasonable. I decided that I needed to take hold of the situation and quickly. I reached in my pocket for my purse. I opened it in my pocket one-handed. I fished around for my Glock. Then an idea occurred to me. I said, "Let's go into Hogwarts. I want another wizard or witch around. We'll go find Slughorn." I'd taken her hand and was dragging her along.

She said, "Slughorn's not there."

I had an awful premonition. I asked, "Nothing happened to him?"

She laughed, "No. He's taking the Christmas Holiday to have a reunion of the old Slug Club. I think they're doing it in Bath."

I insisted in going in to check. We went up to Slughorn's office. Even Sally was gone. We ran into someone whom I recognized as a seventh year who said, "She's off with her husband somewhere for the Holiday."

"Right. Let's go down to Filch's office. He's got to be here."

She said, "Well, believe it or not, Filch and Ms. Pinz are taking a holiday in London."

I almost swore, "Give me a break! What about Dursley?"

"He and his Pamela are in the Azores for . . ."

I chimed in, "For the Holidays."

"Right."

Then I had an inspiration. "Now, I KNOW that Hagrid is still here."

She shook her head. "He and Madame Maxime are taking a little holiday in Paris."

"So no one's here?"

"Just us and the House Elves."

I thought about that and came to a decision. "I've got to find another wizard. Let's go to Hoggsmeade."

She said, "Fine. We'll take the floo."

I said emphatically, "NO floo. We'll walk. It's not that far."

"OK. But, get your coat. It is winter, isn't it."

I nodded. She wanted to go up with me, but I insisted that she stay in the main hall. I breezed into my office and found a coat in my apartment closet. I hurried downstairs and found whoever she was.

It was a cold walk. We walked together, and I found her arm occasionally bumping against mine. We got to the Broomsticks. I half expected it to be closed. However, it was open. We entered. It was as quiet as the proverbial grave. There were a couple of gaffers nursing beers at the bar. Madame Ross-Muerte came to us and asked what she could do for us.

I said, "Breakfast. Can we have a table in the corner?"

She waved her hands around, indicating the array of empty tables, "Choose whichever you want." I picked one in the corner. We sat and ordered tea and orange juice. She came back quickly with it. I certainly knew the menu here. I was ready to order. I looked the question at Stephanie. I decided that I didn't have another name for her, so I'd just call her the only name I knew—Stephanie.

She said, "I'll have oatmeal and dry toast."

I thought, "Good guess." I ordered two eggs sunny-side up and toast with jam. Then I asked, "Madame Ross-Muerte, can you tell if someone has used polyjuice potion?"

She frowned at me. "I would think that of all people you would know all about that. The only way is to test their knowledge that only you and the Doppelganger should know."

"Right." Ross-Muerte left and I turned to Stephanie. I said, "OK. How about telling me about yourself. You are the spitting image of a woman I knew long ago, Stephanie. If you are Stephanie, convince me of it."

Stephanie said, "Oh, where to begin. Back at the rooming house where your room was opposite mine. I've told you that I had an awful crush on you when we both lived there. How about when you came back, and I was close to graduation? I could just have eaten you alive then." She continued her recital of facts, ending with The kiss. "You know my kiss, don't you. Has any other woman kissed you like that?"

I said, "Very convincing. Still . . ."

By this time our food had arrived and we were well into the meal. She said, "You're right. I'm not Stephanie."

"Then who are you?"

She had a coy look on her face as she said, "Stay the night with me and I'll tell you."

I thought a moment and said, "Let's take a walk and I'll decide." I paid for our meal. We went out and took a walk toward the lake hand-in-hand. We didn't talk. The walk was slow and thoughtful on my part if none other. Finally I asked Stephanie, "The only way that you'll tell me about yourself is if we sleep together?"

She smiled, "Yup."

□□

The walk took most of the day with a break for a late lunch. When we ordered, I asked Ross-Muerte, "Have you got a room for us tonight?"

She smiled, "For 'us'?"

I simply said, "Yes." and she said, "Yes."

We went shopping in the town. Well, really it was window-shopping. We returned to the Broomsticks and went up to our room. In the privacy of our room I asked, "OK. Who are you really?"

She shook her head haughtily. "Not until you pay up."

We kissed. It wasn't Stephanie's kiss. Hours later, I sat up in bed and looked at her. Her long platinum hair spread out over her body. It was silky, thick, luxurious. I said, "You couldn't be Jaimie."

She laughed bright peals of laughter and said, "It took you long enough."

I said, "Well, I don't understand this at all. Why didn't you track down Stephanie and steal a little hair from her to make polyjuice potion to impersonate her?"

She still smiled. "That's so easy I wonder that you didn't think of it yourself. My goal was to win you back from Ginny."

I persisted. "How could you know that I needed winning back from anyone?"

She clucked her tone and said, "You and she were alone together for months and months. She was your lover before I was. She's smart, funny, beautiful. How could you not fall in love with her again?"

I growled and said, "Hmmmmmm. Still, why not use polyjuice potion."

She shook her head sadly, "I didn't want you for a night or week of nights. I wanted you forever. polyjuice potion eventually fails you. Someone or something reveals your true identity. Then where would I be?

"No. I had access to most of your memories. I could search them to find what characteristics of a woman excite your *libido*, make your ticker turn over, inflame your senses.

"I found them and applied them to me. The result seems a lot like Stephanie. She would have long, smooth, silky platinum blonde hair. She would be lithe. She would use little makeup—almost invisible. She would have that patented Stephanie kiss. That's what I became."

I asked, "OK. But surely you would get tired of being someone you aren't. You'd revert to your normal self, and that would be the end."

She smiled again. "There you are wrong. My normal self isn't that much different from Stephanie herself. I don't use lots of makeup. I have long silky hair just not platinum blonde. I don't normally kiss like Stephanie, but with the practice I've had, I think I actually have come to enjoy it."

Then we spooned for a while. When I woke up, Jaimie was in the WC working on a shower. I rubbed the sleep out of my eyes and changed places with her when she was finished. We kissed as we exchanged places. I had the shower going when a loud tapping sounded out in the office part of our apartment. Jaimie shouted, "It's just an owl. I've got it."

I didn't think about it at that moment, but later when I was out of the shower, she started talking. "The owl was a note from the Minister of Magic. You're cordially invited . . ."

I interrupted. "How are you reading me an owl directed to me? I should be the first to see it."

She clucked her tongue. "Now, you know better than that. That poor bird didn't know what to do. I'm you, you know, sort of. You're with me as well. Don't be hard on it. It was really confused."

"Anyway, you're invited to a meeting."

I interrupted again. "Can you at least let me read it myself."

She scoffed and handed the message over. It was an invitation to a debriefing session the next day at the Ministry in the Minister's Conference Room. Of course, the owl was hanging around for an answer. I quickly scrawled, "I'll be there at 9 AM as requested. Thanks for the offer of lift from Ms. Weasley. I'll accept." I folded it and quickly tied it to the owl's leg. I'd gotten a lot better than I had been at tying those notes on. Jaimie tried to get a look at the note, but I blocked her and gave the owl a toss out the window. I then said, "In case you're wondering, I accepted the offer of a lift to the meeting."

She almost snarled but turned it into a scoff. "You've got a better offer. Your lover could give you a ride." I had to work hard to keep from laughing. The irony was that my lover was giving me a ride. Jaimie/Stephanie had over whelmed me the day before. I saw a chance to buy back my youth and the first love of my life.

That left me the rest of the day to work on lesson plans. We really had to work hard to figure out how to split up the seven levels of classes between the two of us. We had a friendly argument about who got fourth years and up. Both of us wanted them. I traded fourth and sixth years for fifth and seventh. Lesson planning was miserable, trying to take over the classes that Jaimie had planned.

We took a late working lunch down in the kitchen with the house elves. I talked Kretur into joining us for a few bites to eat. He was very hesitant but Jaimie made the difference. She said, "Kretur. I've always enjoyed your food. You should have the chance to see how much we enjoy it. Join us and see it first hand?"

Kretur was flummoxed at first. Then he said, "Is yourself really wants Kretur to join her for lunch?"

I chimed in. "Of course. Believe me, I know her better than anyone else. She does."

His eyes swivelled back and forth, down and up again. Finally he said, "I is agreeing to have a glass of pumpkin juice with yourself."

I let him pull up his own chair and glass of pumpkin juice. I lifted my cup of tea and said, "Here's to you and all the house elves." He didn't know what to do, but when Jaimie lifted her cup as well, he got the idea. We clinked glass and cup. That almost resulted in pumpkin juice over everyone because Kretur wasn't expecting it, and he pushed too hard on our cups. Anyway, we all got a little laugh out of it—even Kretur.

Kretur drank his pumpkin juice as we started lunch. He was still uncomfortable sitting with a witch and a Muggle, but even made a little small talk and then left. Almost as soon as he had gone, Jaimie sidled a little closer to me and lowered her voice. "As soon as we're done with this lesson planning, I think we can still get a fun late night in, don't you?"

I took a deep breath. This was going to be hard. Of course, Jaimie picked up on it immediately. "No fun tonight."

"Nope."

"Would you like to explain?"

"This is the way it is. Tomorrow is not an ordinary meeting. It is a debrief of one of the most . . . "

"Yes?"

I thought. What could I say? Nothing really. "Well, I really can't talk about it. It's very secret."

"Oh, come on. It's me, Jaimie! What's the difference. Nobody's going to know."

I frowned. "Look. The first thing that they're going to ask me is who else knows about this. I can't say that you do."

"Then don't."

"Look. They might figure it out."

She stared into my eyes. "It's a witch you're talking to. I can handle that."

I grimaced. "This is not the bad old days when wizards were obliviating Muggles right and left. We're not going back to that!"

She shrugged. "OK. No obliviation. I don't have to know what happened. So, why can't we just fool around a little?" She reached under the table and stroked the inside of my thigh."

354

I shook my head back and forth. "I have to practice what I'm going to say. It's a long story, and I have to get it right. If I don't, I'll have to go back again and again till they're satisfied—maybe days and days. Just let me work this my way."

"OK. You can work in the office. I'll just be fooling around in the bed . . . room." She winked.

"That's exactly why I can't do it in the office. I'm going to go somewhere that I'll be alone."

She squeezed my thigh. "Where is that?"

"Never you mind."

"Oh, come on. I won't be a nuisance." Somehow it didn't sound like whining or wheedling. She had that kind of knowledge of me. She knew just how far she could push without sounding whiny. That was her danger for me. It was the little things that made her hard to ignore. Heck, it was hard not to stare at her constantly.

I tried to sound exasperated, but it was just so very hard to do that I almost gave up. However, I did manage to put a frown on my face. "Look this is just making things harder on both of us."

She interrupted me. "That's good though."

I couldn't help laughing. "You know what I mean. I've got a job to do, and I bloody well need to do it well. I've got to have peace and quiet and the opportunity to think of something other than your lithe body."

"You can do more than think about it, you know."

That was it! If I didn't leave then, I never would. I walked out the door with the parting admonition, "Just get a good night's sleep. I may have to pull an all-nighter." This time Jaimie did whine, but I was careful to try to make sure that she didn't follow me.

I decided that the best place to go in the castle was the astronomy tower. Before being married, Aurora had lived in an apartment off of the platform at the top. Now, she was rarely there. She wasn't this night. I spent the night pacing while I examined the last months for all the significant events, people, and place. That was occasionally interrupted by gazing out at the intensely silent sky punctuated by the stars' exclamations of beauty.

I spent the entire night up there. Eventually, I'd done all I could, but I was afraid to return to my bed. Who knew what I would reveal through pillow talk? I would be totally beat, but there were worse things. I went down to the kitchens to find something to eat. With almost everyone gone, the house elves weren't doing regular meals. There were just a few elves pottering around. Kretur was there and wanted to fix me something.

I said, "I just want to fry myself an egg."

He opened his mouth to say something, and then just shrugged. I asked him, "Can I fix something for you?"

He actually laughed. "It being a crazy week. Why not? Doing an extra egg. Sunny side up?"

"That was what I was planning." I fried the egg. It was something that you don't forget how to do. Kretur toasted some bread and brought out orange marmalade. We had breakfast together in the kitchen.

We ate mostly in silence, but Kretur asked me a question as we neared the end of breakfast. "What is yourself going to do? Is yourself staying?"

I sighed, "If there's one thing I've learned living here, it's that there is no predicting the future. If I leave, it won't be voluntary. I think."

I went up to my office. I arrived and found Jaimie sleeping on the sofa. She rose sleepily and said, "You really meant it when you said that you were going to do an all-nighter!" She gave me a hug and a kiss on the cheek. I struggled into the WC where I washed up. Then I went to the apartment to change into fresh clothes. I must have been moving pretty slowly. When I got out into the office, Ginny was already there. Jaimie was sitting at the desk, and Ginny was standing beside the hearth. Stony silence reigned.

The tableau lasted through five long breaths. Then Ginny said, "It's time to go." I walked to her. Jaimie got up and started to approach us. Meanwhile, Ginny took my hand, pulled me into the hearth and said clearly, "The Ministry of Magic." We walked out into the Ministry.

The receptionist said, "Come over here, Professor, so that I can give you your temporary ID." She apparently had it printed already. She attached the ID to my breast. She patted it twice and said with a big smile, "There you are, professor."

We walked off. Ginny smirked and said, "Well, there you are professor."

I grimaced. "That's not funny. Let's take the stairs. We're running a little late." Ginny nodded and we entered the emergency exit. When we reached the Minister office level, we entered.

The receptionist said, "Oh, good. Everyone is in the Conference Room already." She stood and led us down the hall. It was ironic. We probably knew the way as well as she did. We entered. The Conference Room table was utterly full to overflowing. There were sixteen of us. Many I recognized. They were grouped by country. From the US were Philip Ballard representing science I suppose, the captain of the Ohio, someone whom I didn't recognize but turned out to be from the US embassy, and of course, me.

I was also in the group who had traveled to space. The others were, of course, the Brahmses, Ginny (who sat next to the Wizarding group and next to me), and there was an empty spot for Minns. I wasn't the least surprised that he wasn't there.

Next there was the wizarding group, consisting of Ginny, the Head of the Auror Ministry, and Pamela Moertl, the Minister of Magic. I was surprised to see Professor Slughorn there. I guessed that he represented the nearest thing to a scientific representative from the wizards. The Personal Assistant to the Minister of Magic, Joyce Poynter , was there as well.

Finally, there were the English Muggles. They consisted of General Parker (now with two stars), a physicist of some note from a University, someone from the Foreign Office, and the First Assistant to the Home Office Minister.

What is the Gage Hotel Like in the Winter

The meeting started properly with a quick introduction by the Minister of Magic. "Our purpose is to debrief the team that went to assist the PAK. We hope that everyone will agree to listen to the Who, What, Where, Why, and How of this mission without too much interruption. Since Professor Wendt is rather good at summarizing things, I will ask him to give us the dragon's eye view."

I was interrupted immediately by the Muggle Home Office Assistant who asked, "There's an empty chair. It's supposed to be for a Phillip Minns. Why isn't he here?"

So, suddenly I was telling the story. "I think I can quickly answer your question as part of the beginning of this narrative, so please just allow me to."

I could see that the Home Office Assistant was going to be grumpy, so I decided to treat him with deference. He nodded assent. "The story begins with Phillip Minns. To understand what happened, you have to remember Minns' background."

The troublesome Home Office Assistant immediately made his grumpiness apparent. "Who the bloody hell is this Minns?"

I couldn't help the next thing I said even though I knew it was going to cause more trouble. "Minns features prominently in the report, '*A Report on the Appearance of Superluminal Flying Objects*.' Have you read it?"

Grumpy said, "No one said that it was a pre-read for this meeting."

I looked over to Pamela (aka Minister of Magic) and asked, "Do you have a copy here?"

She said, "I can provide you with one." She turned to Joyce and said, "Would you please go find a copy?"

I said, "I can give you all a quick overview about Minns. I would recommend that anyone who hasn't read it to read it during lunch. We should take a long lunch hour to allow that." Pamela agreed. Then I went on. "Minns was part of a team of four geniuses who constructed an interstellar space ship a couple of years ago."

All of the military people in the room jumped up in unison apparently channeling the Weasley twins. They all exclaimed something like, "We have faster than light interstellar spaceships!"

It looked like this was going to be a day of disappointments for people. I had to admit, "No. We don't. They constructed the ship, and it was flown away never to be seen again."

The Ohio captain said, "You don't just get together with three of your best friends and build a space-ship—even if you're Elon Musk. They must have been supported—perhaps clandestinely—by a government. That government must have the ship."

"Well, these were not being supported by a government—unless you count ISIS. Believe me, ISIS was not doing it voluntarily. Anyway, they stole a half billion quid from ISIS, hired a few subcontractors to help them, and sent the ship off with a few youths." Half of the people in the room were ready to object, but I got in ahead of them. "Look, these guys were geniuses who could do things that you can't imagine.

"Now I told you that story so that I could tell you this one. Minns walked into Hogwarts one day with a strange story."

The grump asked, "You witches keep yourselves to yourselves. This Minns must have been a wizard, right?"

I turned to Ginny and asked, "Wizard?"

She said, "Bloody hell, no."

I went on. "Anyway, Minns told us that the PAK had a problem that they needed help with. He could help. He asked us to get in touch with the PAK and offer his help."

Parker had been looking up and to the left. He said, "How could he get in touch with them. There was only one interstellar radio device. We controlled it. The only theory that we had was that they somehow deduced that someone on Earth could help them."

The BG said, "I hacked into the control system of the interstellar radio and inserted a message for the PAK. The message came from Minns. Somehow he knew that the PAK needed help."

I went on. "The PAK sent a ship for Minns and whomever he wanted to take with him."

Ginny said, "As some of you know, Minns specified who would go with him. The four of us were those people."

I went on. "We arrived at the PAK home world. It was devastated.

Someone had killed somewhere between five and ten percent of the PAK population in one terrible strike."

Pamela asked, "Why?"

I continued. "The people who attacked the PAK were led by . . ."

I was interrupted by the grump. "Wait! One question. I thought the PAK were these supermen who were both geniuses and physical titans. Someone wiped their asses for them?"

The BG said, "Yup."

Pamela insisted, "What was the motivation?"

I said, "The attackers were led by a psychopath who believed that he was an avatar of Kali."

The grump said, "I know a bit about India and the Hindu gods. Kali was a destroyer. Somehow I could imagine such a person going on a killing spree, but how could he mount such an attack without lots of help?"

I answered, "Well. He had a much bigger goal than just killing a lot of people. The Hindu tradition is that the universe is recreated once every 28,000 years. Each recreation has a different god as the sponsor. The next change was due any time now and Kali was to be the new sponsor."

The Ohio captain asked, "Destroying the PAK planet is small potatoes compared with destroying the universe. Why did this Kali waste his time on the PAK?"

Aurora said, "The way that he was going to recreate the universe was to force it through the Big Crunch."

The grump asked, "I've never heard of the Big Crunch. What is that? And what does it have to do with the PAK?"

Aurora went on. "The Big Crunch is the opposite of the Big Bang. It is the collapse of the universe to a point. The Big Bang was caused by the Inflation Field. Every field is intermediated by a particle. In this case, it's the inflaton. Every particle has an anti-particle. In this case, the anti-inflaton. That particle causes space to contract explosively . . . er, whatever. Kali was going to generate a huge flux of anti-inflatons that would cause the Big Crunch.

"Kali's problem was that the only known source of anti-inflatons is high energy interactions involving very high atomic number elements. There was only one known way to create those high atomic number elements. It is very inefficient.

"The PAK are the ultimate theoretical physicists. Kali wanted an efficient way of creating high-Z nuclei. He forced them to reveal how to do that."

Ballard summed up, "So, Kali wanted to destroy the universe. He was going to use anti-inflatons to do it. He didn't know how to create them in quantity. So, he forced the PAK to tell them how to do it. Do you know the answer?"

Aurora said, "Yes, we do. Collisions between neutron stars and other neutron stars or black holes create the long-lived Z-126 elements in large amounts. So, all he had to do was find a collision sight that was not older than a few million years and was fairly close."

The BG said, "He then went to the premier observational astronomers to help him find a collision site."

The grump smiled for once. "So, that's what happened."

I added, "At least so far."

Pamela said, "You may not realize it, but it's already half noon. Since we're taking a long break, we should start now and get together at 1:30 PM. Objections?"

There were none.

I said to Ginny outside the Conference Room, "Let's get away to some-place where we won't run into any of these people."

She agreed, "The Broomsticks?"

"Sure."

□

The Broomsticks was as quiet as the tomb. We took a spot near the blazing fire in the hearth. We were both familiar enough with the menu that we ordered drink and meal at once.

When the waitress had disappeared, Ginny said, "OK. What's going on between you and that bitch, Jaimie?"

I said, "She is brilliant. She did a few changes to her appearance—long hair always worn down rather than up, less makeup, platinum blonde hair rather than rich, deep brown. She changed her behavior slightly—a different style of kissing, more aggressive physical style. Most important, she knew from the inside what my 'tells' are. She knows when I'm excited and when I'm bored. She knows what little motions, words, hints turn me on."

Ginny took my hand in hers and said, "So, she was a witch but she didn't use witchcraft to ensnare you."

"Yes, she used her inside information of me."

We sat silently for a while. Our drinks arrived and then our food. We ate silently for a while. Then a tear dropped down Ginny's left cheek. She said, "There's only one possible solution."

I thought I knew where she was going with this, but I wanted her to say it rather than just assuming it. "Go ahead."

"We have to run away. When I say, 'away', I don't mean to London or

361

the Continent. I mean far away—at least across an ocean. Another thing. We should leave soon—today—maybe even right now. Do you really need to go back to Hogwarts to get anything you really need?"

I started to object. Then I thought about it carefully. I said, "Well, you know, maybe I don't really need anything from my office. I have my purse that contains my passport, my credit card, my Glock, a fair number of galleons and pounds. Of course, there are a few other odds and ends, but I could get on quite nicely with what I've got with me now."

"You see! We could leave today—just after the meeting."

"Yes." I thought about that.

Meanwhile, Ginny asked, "Where would we go?"

I thought out loud as I often do when I'm doing my deepest thinking. "Well, we'd not want to go to the usual places that I go. Eventually, Jaimie will find us if she really wants to, but we don't want to make it easy for her. It should be hard." I then ticked off places—none of which would be good. "There's Washington, DC. There's Ohio. There's San Francisco. None of those would be good."

Ginny asked, "Well, then, where would be good?"

I thought for a while and talked through my thoughts. "The States are vast with many remote places. We don't want just remote, though. We want someplace that we can live in fair comfort but not so comfortable that it be-comes or is a popular place to stay." That thought of needing a comfortable hotel made me think of two places. One was wonderful but in a popular area. The other was remote. Both were in Texas. One was the Menger in San Antonio—too popular by far. The other was in Southwest Texas near one of the most remote National parks. It was a park where only real devo-tees of living with nature went. That decided me. "It's the Gage Hotel."

Ginny laughed, "Never heard of it."

"That's the idea. It's a very comfortable hotel with a decent restaurant, but the tiny town it's in has nothing else to recommend it. There's a Na-tional Park only thirty or forty miles away—that's practically next door in west Texas. It's far away from major highways."

Ginny stared hard at me. "You're sure about this. I'm ready to go to the Transportation Office to buy a port key right now."

It took only a moment's thought for me to say, "No. We'll not go di-rectly there. We'll go to a large Texas city where we can buy clothes and other necessaries."

Ginny added, "And near a branch of Gringotts."

"Right." I then said, "We really need to get to the local Gringotts branch so I can get some cash. Maybe you should as well."

She scoffed. "You know it."

So, I slapped a bunch of galleons down and waved at Tom as we passed the bar on the way to the hearth. I said, "I left plenty of cash. Take the extra and give all the staff a good tip."

Tom smiled his almost toothless smile and thanked us on behalf of everyone. We went to an Atrium hearth rather than the Minister of Magic's hearth. The ever-friendly receptionist smiled and asked me to come over so that she could check my temporary ID badge. She looked at it and patted it down happily and sent us on our way. Our way took us to the Ministry branch of Gringotts. As we entered, the bouncer . . . er greeter at the door actually greeted us. "Welcome, Professor Wendt. It's always good to see you in our establishment. What can I help you with?"

I said, "I need to take some cash out of my virtual vault. Both galleons and pounds. I'm afraid it will be a good bit."

"Oh, no worries. We're always happy to help such a depositor as you, sir." He then led us behind the counter and said, "How much? If it were going to be a lot, I don't want others to know that we bend the rules a bit when it comes to withdrawals from virtual vaults."

Ginny raised her eyebrows but said nothing.

The goblin looked both ways to make sure that no one was paying us any special attention. Then he asked, "How much?"

I said, "Twenty thousand pounds and ten thousand galleons."

The goblin looked like he'd swallowed his tongue. He seemed to be gagging but he managed to say. "The galleons should be no problem but we rarely get much demand for pounds at this branch. I might be able to satisfy your request. I'll go see right away." He did.

While he was gone, Ginny asked, "They were awfully deferential to you. Are you a vice-president?" My face must have betrayed something because she said, "You are, aren't you?"

"No, I am not!"

"Well, then you're something. What is it?"

"Oh, I am a consultant from time to time."

She scoffed. "Like you were a consultant on this battle to save the universe?"

"Maybe."

As we were talking the goblin returned with two stacks of bills banded together. He said, "I've got your galleons. I've got a stack of one hundred galleon notes banded together. Unfortunately, we didn't have enough pounds. I've bound together one hundred one hundred pound notes and ninety one hundred pound notes. As a little apology, we're providing you with ten hundred dollar bills. I hope that satisfies."

I said, "That's very appreciated. Now, I think Ms. Weasley would probably like to withdraw some money as well."

She nodded. "I'd like a thousand galleons in smaller bills please and maybe a five hundred dollars in fifty dollar bills." While he was happily trotting off, I opened my purse and stuffed the wads of cash in.

When he returned, he practically begged us to provide some other task he could do for us. One occurred to me. "Gringotts has branches overseas. Could you tell me where the nearest full service branch to Dallas, Texas is?"

He smiled. Well, for a goblin it was a smile. "Yes, every branch has a parchment scroll with a complete list of branch locations." He ran off to get it.

Ginny slapped my back. "I've never seen a Gringotts employee ever render service with a smile. You must really have done some top-flight consulting for them."

I looked down to the floor and tried to look modest. I don't think Ginny was buying it. The goblin returned with a massive scroll. He was examining it as he came. "Let's see, where is Texas?"

"In the United States."

The goblin mumbled, "It would be at the end of the alphabet." He rolled through it for a while. Then he just flung one end so that it rolled across the floor. We walked to the end. He started rolling it up, mumbling, "Zanzabar, Yemen . . . Ah! Here we are, the United States. Wyoming, Washington . . . Texas . . . Texarkana, Midland . . . AH, Dallas. Oh."

Ginny asked, "What?"

"Oh, it just says, see Plano, Texas. I'll have to unroll a little." He did. Then he said, "There's a major branch office in Plano, Texas at the intersection of Legacy Road and the Dallas North Tollway, whatever that is."

I said, "The Dallas North Tollway is just a big highway. Thanks. We can be on our way now."

We left Gringotts. Ginny took my hand and said, "I'll show you the fire escape entrance to the Travel Office." She led me to a fire escape that I'd never seen before. We only had to go up one level. I recognized the hall we were in. I'd been there before. I was leading the way then. Ginny asked, "Have you been here before?"

"Yeh. A long time ago with Minerva."

We reached the entrance, and then Ginny took over again. She picked up a form and started filling it in. She commented, "I can fill in most of this, but when I'm done, I'll have you fill in the blanks that I don't know." She was pretty quick. When she finished, she handed the form to me. There were a few blanks, such as, "Do you have a UK passport? Any passport?" Another was, "Do you need assistance with local maps?"

There were questions that made me laugh. Ginny asked what was so funny. I said, "Are we taking any Fantastic Creatures or banned creatures with us? Do they really expect anyone to answer that 'yes'? And here they ask, 'Are you taking any weapons?' Now, really, how could it make a difference? Everyone is taking a wand. You don't get a much more dangerous weapon than that."

She sort of shrugged and said, "Well, every government form has silly questions, right? Are you going to register that Glock of yours?"

I had to admit that she was right and added, "What Glock?" I filled in the remaining blanks and handed it to Ginny.

We went to the counter and stood in line behind someone who wanted to travel to the Transylvania woods to go on a Dragon-watching tour. When we came up, the bureaucrat scanned the document with little interest until he came to one question. He asked, "It says that you only want a one-way port key. Are you not sure when you're returning and will get one when you're ready to return?"

Ginny answered, "No. We are planning on staying forever."

He said, "Well, I hope the missus will like the Wild West, Mr. Wendt."

She opened her mouth, perhaps to correct the impression but then said nothing. He said, "Very well. You've requested an old sock as a port key. That shouldn't be a problem. We'll have it ready for you sometime tomorrow."

Ginny quickly asked, "You can't get it before the close of business today?"

"I'm afraid not. We have a backlog that we need to fill first."

Ginny retorted, "Not even for an Auror?" She flipped the lapel of her robe to reveal the Auror shield.

"Oh, I didn't know whom I was with. Of course, we can manage it for you. It should be ready in two hours."

As we left the office, I commented, "You have your own set of perks, don't you?"

She scoffed. "Not for long. As soon as we get that port key and get away, I'm sending my resignation owl to the bureau."

We went up the stairs again to the Minister's office. We were waved in by the receptionist. When we arrived in the Conference Room, we were again the last even though there were still at least ten minutes until we were scheduled to resume the meeting. Pam said, "Let's get going since everyone is here." The Foreign Secretary was reading the report that we'd suggested. He laid it down and just nodded his head toward me.

Pam said, "Well, Professor Wendt, please continue your narrative."

I did. "To review, the alien who called himself Kali was determined to destroy the universe, hoping it would be remade in his image. We were at the home world of the PAK.

"I think that Minns thought that we could handle the problem more effectively than the PAK who were dealing with world-wide disaster."

The BG immediately spoke up. "I don't know what Minns's motivation was and I think it's silly to think we can guess it. In point of fact, the PAK were essential to our saving the universe." There was a shocked silence that filled the room with something like dread. This was the first time that anyone had actually said out loud that the universe was on the brink of the end.

The grumpy Assistant to the Foreign Minister opened his mouth without saying anything. Then he blustered a bit and said, "You're just exaggerating."

Aurora looked at him as though he'd just escaped from crackerbox palace. "We were there. Believe me, we were at the brink."

Everyone looked at Ginny who sneered. "I can't believe that you'd doubt Aurora but would believe me." When everyone kept staring, she exclaimed, "Yes! We had almost bought the farm—everyone, everywhere, for all time."

They then looked at me, as though I could change reality by magic. I said, "Look. Something that I didn't mention yet, we might as well take up right now.

"We 'stole' the ship that carried us to the PAK world. They were under attack at the time, and it was possible to sneak off while Kali's fleet was occupied with the PAK. Anyway, we followed them to an astronomical observatory to end all observatories. I won't go into the atrocity that we witnessed there. They coerced the astronomers to find a star system where there was a neutron star collision about to happen.

"We followed Kali's main ship from there. Along the way, he slowed down just enough to detonate a super-giant star in a supernova explosion that was probably never matched in the history of the universe. That explosion will probably kill off a number of nearby civilizations. That was just small potatoes to him. I think that he did it as a small scale test of the general principle of using anti-inflatons to trigger the Big Crunch."

The BG interrupted again to say, "I think it was just to throw off any pursuit."

I went on. "Whatever. We caught up with him at the collision site shortly before it happened. We tried various things to prevent his collection of Z-126 atoms. We finally had to board the ship. We didn't have to fight our way to the Bridge. It seemed very strange. I think that they weren't defending the ship because Kali was convinced that he'd won already, that

366

his plan was inevitable. So, it didn't matter if he died defending the ship or in the universal conflagration that he thought was about to happen."

Pamela asked, "So, how did you defeat him?"

"I came up with the idea of plunging Kali's ship through the event horizon of the black hole that had just collided with the neutron star. Minns somehow figured out how to use the ship's controls to spiral it through the event horizon. It was good plan if I do say so myself. However, it wouldn't happen fast enough for it to work."

At this point, the BG picked up the story. "A PAK fleet had been following both Kali and us. One of the ships had taken a short cut to the collision site. It arrived in time for its captain to drive his ship into Kali's. That collision forced Kali's ship through the event horizon before it had collected enough Z-126 to destroy the universe."

At this point there was a Babel of questions. Pamela quieted everyone down and sorted out the order of people asking questions. She appointed herself first. She asked, "What's all this about event horizons. What can that possibly mean?"

Aurora said, "There's a type of star called a black hole. It's called a black hole because its gravity is so strong that no light or anything at all that falls into it can get out. The 'event horizon' is the point of no return. Once you cross it you're lost."

Pamela pointed at the captain of the Ohio. "OK. So, why didn't this super weapon destroy the universe. Surely, it could keep collecting Z-126 after it crossed the event horizon?"

Aurora answered. "To be honest with you, I don't know whether inflatons can cross an event horizon, but, I think there's no reason to ponder that. The amount of Z-126 to cross the event horizon was probably too small to use. Besides that, the ship was probably torn apart by tidal forces before it could have finished anyway."

Ballard was next. "The captain of that PAK ship must have been crazy. Why wouldn't he try other things before crashing into Kali's ship?"

I said, "I think you're right. I think he was crazy. His family had died in Kali's attack on the PAK world. He wanted personal revenge more than he wanted to save the universe The last words we heard from him just before his ship rammed Kali's was, 'From Hell's heart I stab at thee.'"

The Assistant to the Minister of the Interior asked, "Why are we hearing all these references to Earth history and myth?"

Aurora said, "I think that's not so strange. The PAK had a language translator. The way those things work—at least here on Earth—is that a huge collection of language samples and translations from the literature of the languages involved are put in a database. Among those language sam-

367

ples there were surely many Earth legends, myths, history, and so forth. The translator software chose names and references that English speakers would understand."

The Assistant to the Foreign Minister asked a question that I suppose was meant to demonstrate his new knowledge of Minns. "How is it that Minns didn't recruit some of his friends for this project. You know. People like Reynaldo, Connover, and so on?"

The BG answered that. "I don't know. My bet is that he thought he wouldn't need any help."

The Grump kept at him. "Come on. This Kali laid low the PAK. Minns didn't really think he could single-handedly defeat him. . . Did he?"

The BG said, "You read about how we couldn't make any headway against Minns despite having the full force of the States behind us. Who am I to think that Minns was wrong."

The grump was grumpy to the end, mumbling something incoherent. Pamela took control. "I think we're done here. All of the people who are available from this mission are under my authority. They will all write complete reports of this incident and return them to Ms. Poynter by next week. We will collate and distribute them to you all once the editing process is complete. This meeting is adjourned now." She said that final word with such finality that no one objected. That made Ginny and me happy. We swiftly rose as one and started for the exit.

Unfortunately, the Minister of Magic was not done with us. She said, "The four of you." The Brahmses, Ginny, and I tried to pretend that we didn't think that she meant us. However, Pamela made her intent pellucidly clear. "Yes, you lot who were in space. I want to see you in my office—now."

Apparently, we were not done. She led the way out of the Conference Room toward her office.

□□

Even though her office had a conference table that would comfortably seat five, guest chairs were set up around her desk, which would comfortably seat maybe three. We were squeezed in together with her sitting behind the desk. Her personal assistant was nowhere to be seen. No beverage was offered. It was not exactly a welcoming atmosphere.

When we'd all sat, she stared from one to the other of us as though she were trying to decide what to say. She finally did begin. "I suppose you all think that you submit your little reports and you're done, right?"

We all looked from one to the other and the BG said, "I'll bet we're not."

"You'd win that bet. Do you realize that almost every other year some terrible thing happens that makes Tom Riddle look like a shy schoolboy. Then we have a series of meetings with the usual cast of suspects including you four. I have to beat the bushes to find you lot and my hair turns grayer every time. Well, I'm done with that. You all have to be on call 24x7. We'll get paging galleons for all of you that will light up and ring wherever you are."

Ginny looked over to me and then said, "Well, I wasn't going to announce this until tomorrow but Wendt and I . . ."

Pamela broke in. "I don't care who's in love with whom or who's been sleeping with whom. You both are on duty and available even when you're in bed—together or not."

She then turned to the Brahmses, who had been hunkering down. I suppose they were cultivating the Zen art of disappearance. No matter, Pamels said, "You lot. The same goes for you two. I know who's been sleeping with whom. It doesn't matter, you're in it as well."

She looked around the room as though there might be someone else whom she could hook in for 24x7 coverage. Then she said, "Dismissed. Watch for the owl with your special coin." We all got up and trudged out of the office.

Aurora asked if we wanted to go drinking with her and her hubby. Ginny and I happily declined the offer with thanks. They trudged down the hall in front of us. We almost skipped down the hall hand in hand. We reached the Reception Area. The BG opened the door for Aurora and stayed in the door to let someone else in.

The Doppelganger

The next person to enter the Reception Area was Jaimie. She confidently walked up to me, linked an arm with mine, and clasp our hands together. I realized two things: that our fingers were intertwined and that I was gazing into her eyes. She gave her head a little toss and her sparkling, shimmering, silky hair flowed over our linked arms. My heart raced with the thrill. She brought our lips together in a kiss that caused me to wrap my free arm about her and draw her near.

She said, "I have a wonderful idea for tonight." If it had been bivouacking on the Amazon, I'd have wanted to do it. We drifted over to the floo connection and through it to the Cauldron. I was so spell-bound that I didn't even notice the transition through the floo network. By this time, my ecstasy was so complete that my eyes were closed, and I barely heard Jaimie request a room.

We glided up the stairs to our room. Jaimie opened it. We entered. My arms were around her and her robe disappeared as though by magic. She drew me onto the bed. Her fair, flowing hair enveloped me and set my senses spinning as though I were a victim of vertigo. Her mouth covered mine. Her tongue slipped between my lips and I tried to say something, but I realized that there was nothing in the world left to talk about.

The End

About the Author

 William Wilkin lived in a small Southern Ohio town until he began his college career. He has a Bachelor's degree in Physics from The Ohio State University and a Master's degree in Physics from The University of Chicago. He has a career in corporate Information Technology and currently lives in Nashville, TN.

He enjoys music, both "serious" and "classic Rock". He reads classic Detective fiction and Science Fiction & Fantasy as well as trying to stay current in Physics.

He began writing seriously about 2005. He has a blog, in-mid-world, where he writes about Science Fiction & Fantasy and re-motely related topics.

www.ingramcontent.com/pod-product-compliance
Lightning Source LLC
Chambersburg PA
CBHW072112250626
47159CB00007B/2418